TANGLED DECADENCE

EGOROV BRATVA
BOOK 2

NICOLE FOX

Copyright © 2024 by Nicole Fox

All rights reserved.

No part of this book may be reproduced in any form or by any electronic or mechanical means, including information storage and retrieval systems, without written permission from the author, except for the use of brief quotations in a book review.

❀ Created with Vellum

ALSO BY NICOLE FOX

Zakrevsky Bratva
Requiem of Sin
Sonata of Lies
Rhapsody of Pain

Bugrov Bratva
Midnight Purgatory
Midnight Sanctuary

Oryolov Bratva
Cruel Paradise
Cruel Promise

Pushkin Bratva
Cognac Villain
Cognac Vixen

Viktorov Bratva
Whiskey Poison
Whiskey Pain

Orlov Bratva
Champagne Venom
Champagne Wrath

Uvarov Bratva

Sapphire Scars
Sapphire Tears

Vlasov Bratva
Arrogant Monster
Arrogant Mistake

Zhukova Bratva
Tarnished Tyrant
Tarnished Queen

Stepanov Bratva
Satin Sinner
Satin Princess

Makarova Bratva
Shattered Altar
Shattered Cradle

Solovev Bratva
Ravaged Crown
Ravaged Throne

Vorobev Bratva
Velvet Devil
Velvet Angel

Romanoff Bratva
Immaculate Deception
Immaculate Corruption

Kovalyov Bratva

Gilded Cage

Gilded Tears

Jaded Soul

Jaded Devil

Ripped Veil

Ripped Lace

Mazzeo Mafia Duet

Liar's Lullaby (Book 1)

Sinner's Lullaby (Book 2)

Bratva Crime Syndicate

*Can be read in any order!

Lies He Told Me

Scars He Gave Me

Sins He Taught Me

Belluci Mafia Trilogy

Corrupted Angel (Book 1)

Corrupted Queen (Book 2)

Corrupted Empire (Book 3)

De Maggio Mafia Duet

Devil in a Suit (Book 1)

Devil at the Altar (Book 2)

Kornilov Bratva Duet

Married to the Don (Book 1)

Til Death Do Us Part (Book 2)

Heirs to the Bratva Empire

Can be read in any order!

Kostya

Maksim

Andrei

Princes of Ravenlake Academy (Bully Romance)

Can be read as standalones!

Cruel Prep

Cruel Academy

Cruel Elite

Tsezar Bratva

Nightfall (Book 1)

Daybreak (Book 2)

Russian Crime Brotherhood

Can be read in any order!

Owned by the Mob Boss

Unprotected with the Mob Boss

Knocked Up by the Mob Boss

Sold to the Mob Boss

Stolen by the Mob Boss

Trapped with the Mob Boss

Volkov Bratva

Broken Vows (Book 1)

Broken Hope (Book 2)
Broken Sins *(standalone)*

Other Standalones

Vin: A Mafia Romance

Box Sets

Bratva Mob Bosses (Russian Crime Brotherhood Books 1-6)

Tsezar Bratva (Tsezar Bratva Duet Books 1-2)

Heirs to the Bratva Empire

The Mafia Dons Collection

The Don's Corruption

MAILING LIST

Sign up to my mailing list!
New subscribers receive a FREE steamy bad boy romance novel.

Click the link below to join.
https://sendfox.com/nicolefox

TANGLED DECADENCE
BOOK 2 OF THE EGOROV BRATVA DUET

"You didn't really think you'd get a happily-ever-after, did you?"

Cian is terrifying me.

The Irish killer stole me on my wedding day.

And now, he's revealing secrets that threaten to burn everything—and everyone—I love to ashes.

I need to get back to Dmitri.

He's the only one who can keep our unborn child safe.

But escaping Cian is just the beginning...

Because Dmitri has secrets of his own.

Starting with the unseen houseguest upstairs...

And ending with the hideous truth about what really happened to my sister.

TANGLED DECADENCE is Book 2 of the Egorov Bratva duet. Dmitri and Wren's story begins in Book 1, TANGLED INNOCENCE.

1

WREN

The first time Rose miscarried, she wasn't even trying to get pregnant.

She and Jared had been together only a few months. They were still in the getting-to-know-each-other phase, which is why she didn't even tell Jared she was pregnant when she peed on that stick and it turned positive right away.

"What the hell do I do now, Wren?" she asked me, as though *I'd* have the answers.

"Yeet the baby into the woods and let it be raised by wolves?" I joked. I used humor as a coping mechanism a lot back then. It was easier to pretend to laugh than it was to actually face anything that was happening to either of us.

But she didn't laugh. Truth be told, neither did I. The joke faded away and silence rushed in to take its place. Both of us sat staring at the blank walls, as if the future was playing out there on a projector screen.

"You have to tell him, Rosie," I'd nudged her gently.

Her eyes drifted to mine, but it didn't feel like she was even looking at me. More like *through* me. *Beyond* me. "*He's on a camping trip this weekend with his friends. I'll tell him when he gets back.*"

She never did, though.

She didn't have to.

She woke up the next morning, and the problem had taken care of itself.

Six years later, she and Jared started trying to get pregnant intentionally. Twelve months of that felt like divine punishment, she always told me. *If I'd told him about the first one, maybe it wouldn't have...* She could never quite bring herself to finish that sentence.

I didn't believe in divine punishment. Still don't. But I do believe in cruel ironies.

Life, in my experience, is full of them. And blaming yourself never helps solve a damn thing. That's exactly what I told Rose the first time she voiced her punishment-from-above theory. It's what I told Mom every time she tried to blame herself for why Dad left us.

And yet here I am, sitting in a barren little room with a door I can't unlock, dressed in my captor's clothes because they're the only things available to me, blaming *myself* for getting kidnapped.

Again.

Cruel ironies. They arrive at their cruelest and most ironic just when you've convinced yourself that they don't exist in the first place.

And who knows? Maybe they don't. Do I believe in them because they're true? Or are they true because I believe in them?

Better question: am I losing my goddamn mind?

I'll admit: there are moments in this room—plenty of them—when my own thoughts don't make sense to me. Like I've found myself on a train headed somewhere I've never heard of, taking a path I've never seen, and there's no way in hell to get off.

And in the spirit of cruel ironies, there is in fact a literal train track running just past the tiny box window of this house-or-whatever-it-is. Two weeks or so in here and I have yet to hear a single train go by, but something about a rail leading from nowhere to nowhere makes me inexplicably sad.

Two weeks. My God. It's so easy to let each second slip by numbly, but they're stacking up higher and higher.

Two weeks. Fourteen days.

Fourteen whole days of sitting up here. Sleeping. Eating. Obsessing. Repeating. Sleeping. Eating. Obsessing. Repeating. Sleeping. Eating. Obsessing. Re—

I bounce off the bed when I hear the latch unlock from the outside.

Cian is coming.

The fact that I'm actually excited to see him is an indicator of just how desperate I've become. Cian's the only one who actually talks to me like a person. The two other men who visit me with clothes and food just stare blankly at me when I speak. They ignore me when I ask questions. They retreat and lock the door again whenever I start pleading.

"Hello, Wren."

I sink to a perch on the edge of the mattress with a hand placed protectively over my stomach. "Cian."

His gaze flickers down to my abdomen and he winces, then tears his eyes away. "You haven't eaten," he observes, gesturing with his head to the tray on the desk that I've started scratching symbols into to pass the time.

"I wasn't hungry."

He's lost weight. Lots of it, it seems—an improbable amount for only two weeks of time. His shirts droop loosely from his shoulders like he's nothing but a coat hanger with legs. Even his voice sounds hollow and emaciated.

"Do you need anything?"

I arch an eyebrow. "Is that a trick question?"

He sighs. "Like vitamins or something. I can get them to you if you tell me what you need."

"What I need is to visit my doctor. I need to have a check-up. I've been having some cramping and—"

"I can't take you out of here, Wren."

"I have preeclampsia!" I lie in a sudden manic fit of inspiration. "This is a high-risk pregnancy. I need my doctor's support if I'm going to deliver this baby safely."

He eyes me somberly, not blinking even once. I wish he'd say something, but he doesn't.

My voice drops to a low quiver. "Please, Cian. I know you. You're not a monster. Just take me to see my doctor. You can stay with me the entire time. I'll behave."

"Somehow, I doubt that."

To my surprise, he uses the wall as a crutch and lowers himself down to a seat on the floor. He winces and mutters under his breath as he moves, like every little action pains him. I note the scab under his eye where I clawed him after he told me Bee was dead. Most of the mark has faded, but there is still some light purple bruising. It's nice, strangely enough, to have a visual reminder that I can still do damage if I choose.

I'm not helpless; I'm not powerless.

There's a strange scent coming off him. Stale, bitter. Hell, maybe that's just what desperation smells like. I would know, wouldn't I?

Although, what exactly he has to be desperate about, I have no freaking clue. He's the one with all the cards up his sleeve. But he acts as though he's just as much of a prisoner as I am.

"Didn't anyone ever tell you that you don't get to play the victim when you have all the power?" I snap suddenly, unable to bear the wheezing pressure of the silent room.

His eyes float up to mine and he stays quiet for a little while longer. Then he snorts through his nose without cracking a smile. "Nobody has any power, Wren. None of us do."

I frown. His eyes aren't quite *right,* in a way I can't explain. It's not that he's drunk or high or delirious—at least, I don't think so. Lost in his own sadness, perhaps. I bet I don't look so different.

But this isn't like any of the conversations we've had before. So, sensing an opportunity, I inch down to the carpet and sit across from him with my back against the bedpost. It goes against every instinct to get close to my prison warden, but I make myself go anyway.

Just see what happens next, suggests the voice in my head. *Find out what's changed.*

Cian watches me warily, though he doesn't retreat. I drop my head to ease the tension and toy with the ragged edges of the carpet.

"Do you remember the night you and Jared went away on that fishing weekend?" I ask suddenly. He stares at me blankly. "You told us you caught a bunch of fish, but they smelled so bad on the way back that you dumped them on the side of the road."

His eyes widen. Then he sighs. "It wasn't a fishing trip, Wren." I wrinkle my nose as his breath catches up to me.

Amendment to my earlier observation: he's *definitely* drunk.

"It wasn't?"

He shakes his head. "We were gambling. He lost ten grand playing craps and he was deadset on staying. *We gotta stay, man. Gotta keep going. Rose needs this.* He swore he'd make it back."

My nose wrinkles up. "Jared wasn't a gambler."

"How do you think we met?" he asks with a pitying look in my direction. "How do you think they paid for IVF, Wren? Doctors aren't cheap. Jared managed a bar and Rose was a paralegal. You think they just had a money tree in their backyard?"

I pull my legs up and rest my chin on my knees, if only to keep my lip from wobbling out of control. "So you knew he was desperate and you decided to point him in the direction of your thug brother."

His lips pinch together in the beginnings of a sneer. "Believe it or not, I actually advised Jared *not* to go to my brother. You called him a thug…" His gaze flickers to the window behind me. "… but you're wrong. He was much, much worse. My brother was a monster."

"Didn't you work for him?"

"It was expected of me."

"So you did what he said? Without question?"

"*'Even in death…'*"

"What?"

"Nothing," he mumbles quickly, picking at his cuticles. That's when I realize how bloody they are. Torn stumps of nails, barely clinging on. Apparently, these past two weeks haven't been easy on him, either.

"Why am I here, Cian?" I ask bluntly. "It's obvious that you don't know what the hell to do with me. So why keep me?"

He drags his face up from his hands to look at me again. At this angle, the moonlight slotting through the window fills the hollow of one cheek, leaving the other one shrouded dark. His nose looks brutally sharp, his eyes like the faintest pinpricks of light at the far end of tunnels that keep going and going and going.

"Because the powers that be won't let me release you so easily," he sighs at last. He shakes his head as though he's trying to get rid of the voices in there. "My brother made a deal with the devil. And the devil is ready to collect."

"Your brother is dead. Shouldn't that release you from whatever deal he made?"

He laughs dryly. "It doesn't work like that in the underworld. I'm held to Cathal's promises. I have to pay for his sins."

Against all odds, I find myself feeling sorry for the sad man sitting opposite me. He used to laugh loudly. He used to smile easily. He told stupid jokes that made Jared laugh and Rose roll her eyes.

I can't recognize a thing about him anymore. He's barely human.

"That's not fair."

"Since when has life ever been fair?" He reaches into his pants pocket and pulls out a thin silver flask with his initials etched onto the surface. "The only thing you can do is survive." Then he tosses back the contents of the flask. As he closes it back up, he throws me a sympathetic glance. "I'd offer you some, but I don't want to be accused of damaging the heir."

I flinch. *Heir.* God, how I loathe that title, that word. It puts so much pressure on this tiny, innocent little being who has no concept of the weight of expectations that his existence has manifested.

"My son is not an 'heir,'" I hiss. "He's a *baby*. And he sure as hell didn't ask for any of this."

"None of us did," he whispers. His breath rattles out of his throat like a dead man's cough. "I am sorry about everything, Wren. Especially Bee."

I bury my face in my hands. It's going to be very hard to keep my cool if he insists on talking about her. "That's two sisters you've taken from me now," I murmur, dropping my hands. "Two."

"It was never meant to happen. She was never meant to die. What happened at the wedding…" He trails off and his gaze falls into his lap once more.

"What?" I demand. "Can't find excuses for your choices anymore, Cian?"

His head bobs on his neck like daisies in the wind. "I was taken off-guard. The men had different orders than the ones I'd given them."

"Ah," I croon mockingly. "'The powers that be had spoken,' is that right? It's not *your* fault, though, is it? Nothing that's happened has been *your* fault?"

His eyes glom onto me. That eerie hue of blue might be scary if I didn't feel so much pity for him. He's like a corpse that the Grim Reaper forgot to collect. "I was never meant to be don. I was the second son. I was raised to follow orders."

"So that's what you're still doing?"

Anger ripples across his eyes. It's the first real sign of life he's shown. He rises to his feet and pulls out a phone, a small, shitty hunk of black plastic riddled with scratches and scars. He flips it open, aims it in my direction, and shoots a photo of me before I even realize what he's doing.

"What was that for?"

"I just want Dmitri to know that you're okay. That you're safe."

"To know—*what?* Why?"

"Because if my woman and child were taken by the enemy, I'd want to know that they were being treated well at the very least."

He turns towards the door and I feel that familiar sense of panic rise to my throat. "Wait!" I exclaim, struggling to my feet. "Cian, please—wait."

He pauses reluctantly, though he won't turn around. "I can't let you go, Wren," he says before I can even plead my case. "I wish I could. I take no pleasure in keeping you here, especially in your condition. But my hands are tied."

"They don't need to be," I insist. "You are the don now. You can decide not to do business with the devil. You can tell him to go fuck himself!"

"And risk him coming after me and my men? Their families?" he suggests brusquely. "No, I won't be the kind of leader who fucks over his own people."

"You fucked over Jared," I hurl at his back. "Or doesn't he count?"

Cian winces. It's amazing how a man well over six feet tall can seem so small and frail. "Jared made his choices. Rose made hers. Don't hang their mistakes around my neck. Lord knows I have enough of my own as it is."

My heart is racing as he walks out the door and pulls it shut. What did he mean by *"Rose made hers"*? Did he mean that she knew about Elena? Or is he just talking about the gambling?

I rush the door and pound my hands against the pockmarked surface. "Cian! Wait, come back!" I hear the lock thud into place, but I keep pounding. "Cian, please! Come back!"

"I'll get you some medicine for the preeclampsia," he croaks from the other side. "That's all I can do at the moment."

I keep screaming, even as I hear his heavy footsteps walking away and fading into nothingness. When I'm sure he's not coming back, I twist around and, with my back to the door, plummet to the floor. Tears stream down my cheeks as I struggle to grapple with my new reality—the reality of where I am now and the reality of who Rose and Jared really were.

I feel like I've lost them twice over now.

But even in the midst of all this turmoil, there's one tiny little sliver of light. A tiny little flare of hope that burns every time my son flutters around inside me—

Reminding me that, even in the darkest of moments, I'm not alone.

2

DMITRI

Incoming Call from: **Locksmith.**

It's not a call I can afford to miss. So despite the fact that I'm standing amidst the burning ruins of an Irish safehouse, I answer.

The voice is heavily altered, crackling with strange synthesizers and pitched inhumanly low. "I've been hacking into the Irish's security systems for days now and still nothing. Even the safehouses have been emptied out."

"No shit," I growl. "I'm standing in what's left of one now. There were only five fuckers manning the place."

My resident hacker lets out a disgruntled hiss. "The entire Irish mafia can't have just disappeared into thin air. They've got to be somewhere."

"Somewhere offline," I agree grimly. "Somewhere with no cameras, no security systems, no surveillance."

"Which means no chance for me to trace them."

"Keep searching. O'Gadhra has a few businesses still up and running. Monitor everyone who goes in and out. They may be hiding in plain sight." I exit the house through a crumbling back entrance. The fire we set won't reach here for another few minutes, but the heat is already overpowering. Sweat slides down my back, practically boiling the second it beads up on my skin. "Did you try tracking the numbers I gave you?"

"The pictures are being transmitted from burner phones. Each is deactivated immediately after sending. They're all dead ends."

"Fucking Cian," I spit as I hold out a palm and let one flake of ash settle there. "He's goading me."

"Perhaps," Locksmith suggests. "Or maybe he's trying to reassure you. Turn down the temperature. Float the idea of a truce."

Grinding my teeth together, I throw a nod over to my nearby soldiers to clear out. There are five Irishmen bound and gagged in there; this burning house will serve as their funeral pyre.

"Fuck a truce!" I roar. "He shot to hell any chance of a peace treaty the moment he decided to crash the wedding."

"Speaking of the wed—"

"Don't," I snarl. Locksmith falls silent instantly. "Don't you dare say her name. She's dead. Buried. Gone. That's not changing any time soon, so what's the point in talking about her?"

The silence lingers uncomfortably. "I understand."

"Keep digging. Keep searching. If anything comes up, call me immediately. Day or night, it doesn't matter—I'll pick up."

I hang up and storm down the road to where my SUV is parked. Aleksandr is leaning against the hood, his face lit up by the orange flames beginning to engulf the house. He gets in when I approach and turns on the ignition. In the distance, I can hear the first faint sounds of an oncoming fire truck.

"Nothing?"

I scowl. "He can't hide from me forever."

"He's banking on the fallout between you and Vittorio to keep him safe a little while longer," Aleksandr deduces shrewdly. "It's what I would do."

"He knew," I hiss. "He *knew*. He knew Bee wasn't pregnant. He was trying to expose us."

The fire truck breezes past us at the top of the hill. Aleksandr executes a U-turn and drives calmly down the road, away from the Irish rathole behind us. The rest of my men spread out in anonymous, mismatched vehicles of their own, vanishing into the night like we were never even here.

"The day of the—the event..." Aleks ventures, carefully avoiding any mention of the word "wedding," which has become forbidden terminology in the two weeks since it happened. "... Vittorio was pissed that Bee was taking so long. He stormed into her bridal suite while she was in the bathroom. I caught him in there trying to intimidate Wren. She was convinced that he wasn't buying her surrogacy story."

"What did he say to her?"

Aleksandr's hands tighten on the steering wheel. "I don't know, brother," he says gently. "She didn't take me through the whole conversation. We were seconds from walking down the aisle ourselves. There wasn't time."

When he pulls one palm off the wheel, I notice he's left sweat marks on the leather. You wouldn't know it from looking at him—not the way you'd know it from one glance at the rage that burns on my face all hours of the day now—but he is suffering, too.

I can't fault him. I was hard on him the first week after Wren was taken. All I could see—all I *cared* to see—was that I'd left her in his care and he'd lost her to Cian.

Planning Bee's funeral at the same time didn't help. It was two full days of the worst case of déjà vu. Bee's coffin, light as it was, felt as though it contained two bodies.

Ping.

I glance down at my lockscreen, freezing when I see that it's yet another unknown number. Aleksandr knows the drill, too, because he glances sideways at me. "Him again?"

I open the picture Cian's sent me. This makes the fourth in fourteen days. Except this one's different from the three that preceded it.

For one, Wren's not asleep. Her back's not to the camera. She's on a carpet on the floor with her legs pulled up to her chest and her arms wrapped around them. If I didn't know better, I wouldn't be able to tell she's pregnant; her face certainly doesn't give her away. Her cheeks are too hollow, skin too pale and sallow, eyes too huge in their sockets.

I do the math in my head before I can stop myself from wandering down that road yet again. She could go into labor at any minute.

The thought that I might not be there with her is bad enough.

The thought of her having our baby while she's in the custody of Cian fucking O'Gadhra makes my blood burn.

I keep staring at the picture, trying to find some kind of clue in her face, in her surroundings, in the weave of the damn carpet she's sitting on. But the room is utterly generic. It could be any house in Chicago.

Curling my hand into a fist, I pound it against the dashboard. "She needs medical care. She needs to see a real doctor. She needs… more than that *mudak* is giving her."

"What about Locksmith?" Aleksandr asks urgently. "Surely there's something—"

"There's nothing. As far as Locksmith is concerned, Cian is a ghost."

"Sounds like he doesn't want a war."

"It's a little too late for that."

Aleksandr's sigh sets me off. "What?" I demand, whirling in my seat to face him. "If you've got something to say, then fucking say it."

Aleksandr's jaw clenches. "We have Vittorio to worry about, too, brother," he reminds me warily. "I understand you need to find Wren, but I don't want you to be so consumed with getting her back that you forget to watch your own borders."

It's not that I'm underestimating Vittorio; I just can't allow my focus to be split. Not when my son's life hangs in the balance. Not when *Wren's* life hangs in the balance.

I've lost too much already. And if there's one thing that this whole ordeal has given me, it's *clarity.*

Well, clarity in part.

I can't say for sure what Wren means to me or what she is to me. All I know is that I cannot bear to lose her.

"Vittorio has never forgiven a slight, Dmitri," Aleksandr reminds me. "And you made a fool of him in front of the entire underworld. He's not going to forget that easily."

"Nor do I expect him to. I want him replaying that day over and over again in his head. Then I'll have the excuse to do to him what he did to Bee all those years."

Aleks's eyes bulge in alarm, But I don't ask for his opinion. I don't care about anyone's opinion on this subject.

I made my decision the moment that first handful of dirt covered the lid of Bee's coffin. The cycle of trauma didn't end with her death.

But it's going to end with Vittorio's.

3

WREN

I became an expert eavesdropper when I was five.

For a full month, I was convinced that I had singlehandedly discovered the magic power of a glass held up against a door. The key tool in any eavesdropper's arsenal. And I, Wren Bethany Turner, at the ripe old age of five, had made this most spectacular invention all on my own.

But God, how I wish I hadn't.

That's how I knew that Mom and Dad fought at night after Rose and I were in bed. It's how I knew that Dad hated Grandpa, even though he gave the best hugs. It's how I knew that Mom didn't like the way Dad looked at my friend Casey's mom at the nativity play or that Dad worried about the fact that we ate out too much, Mom worried about the fact that we didn't go to church enough, and they both worried about money.

I was too young to know what most of that meant, but there was still a kernel of guilt attached to my eavesdropping.

Mysterious as the topics may have been, I knew I wasn't supposed to be doing what I was doing.

But knowing stuff seemed more important than respecting my parents' privacy. My five-year-old self had no concept of privacy anyway. And when I did get old enough to know better, taking care of Mom and Rose seemed more important than letting them keep their secrets, too.

I have that same sense of responsibility now as I press my empty water glass up to the door and strain my ears. Except it's not Mom or Rose I'm trying to protect; it's the squirming baby in my belly.

Every day, he kicks a little more, a little harder. Sometimes, I feel as though he's trying to tell me something. Baby Morse Code, saying, *Get us outta here, Mama. I don't want to be born in captivity.*

Captivity is for zoo animals. Not for babies. Not for *my* baby.

I can hear Cian prowling outside—ready to walk into my room and partake in another half-drunk conversation, maybe? Or take another candid photograph without my consent? I have no clue; I just have this hope that, if we can talk a little more, maybe I can convince him to give in to his conscience.

I lurch back when I hear his footsteps grow closer—but then I hear the telltale buzz of a vibrating phone.

"What?" he barks. "Yes... yes... *In ainm Dé,* man... Listen, I've done everything you asked for, even after that shit you pulled at the wedding... I know... Yes, I understand but—" He breaks off and retreats a few steps.

My brain is going haywire. His puppet master was at the wedding? "Done everything you asked for"—what could that mean? I commit every kernel of information to memory, even if it doesn't add up right now.

"Listen to me…" I'm hoping for a name, but whether by chance or intention, he doesn't let one slip. "She's almost nine months pregnant. This isn't fucking right… Yes, I remember… Fine then."

His voice softens as he retreats again. I moan in frustration and let the glass fall from my hand and roll across the floor.

It's been a week since Cian last came in. I've spent that time thinking through every iteration of possibilities I can wrap my head around, but the only one that's seemed viable is what I'm about to do. If it fails, I don't know what'll happen next.

I just know I can't let my child be born into a cage.

I pick up the dropped glass, slip into the bathroom, and shut the door. Then I wrap the glass in a towel and put pressure on it until I feel it crack under my weight. Seconds later, I hear him enter my room. When I unwrap the towel, I have a handful of glass shards. One gleams in the fluorescent light, jagged as a knife.

Perfect.

"Wren?" I hear Cian call from just outside the bathroom door.

I ignore him and pull up my skirt. I can't cut myself anywhere obvious; he'll see through the ploy immediately. So I lift my leg and prop it up on the counter, which is quite a feat considering I'm the size of a beluga right now. I pluck up the shard of broken glass between two and hold it to the soft flesh of my upper, inner thigh.

At the last second, I pause. *Oh, God... am I really going to do this?*

My hand is shaking. The thought of cutting into myself feels so wrong. But I'm running out of options.

It's this or nothing.

"Wren? You alright in there?"

Biting down hard on my tongue, I slash the shard of glass over my skin. At first, I feel nothing. Then comes the sharp, stinging, gnawing pain. It's weird how much that pain makes me want to laugh. I dump the offending shard of glass in the wastebasket, along with the whole towel, glass shards and all, and pull my skirt back down.

"*Wren?*"

I open the door and limp out. The nerves have left a sheen of sweat coating my face. All the better to help sell this little charade.

"I'm... not doing so good..."

He blinks in confusion. He looks paler and skinnier than ever. "What do you mean? What's going on?"

"I told you I had a serious medical condition," I gasp, keeling over with my elbows pressed to my knees. I can feel the blood trickle down my inner thigh. I hope to God I haven't overdone it and given myself a serious injury. If that wound needs stitches, I'm screwed.

"What about the pills? The—the—the damn blood pressure pills. I sent you them. You're supposed to—"

He *had* sent the pills—and I'd promptly flushed them down the toilet. "Of course I've been taking them!" I protest. "But clearly, they're not working. Which is why I wanted you to take me to see my doctor. She's the only one who can treat my—*ahh*—"

"Fuck!" He lunges in my direction, though he freezes just short of actually touching me and drops his arm. "Wren…"

Biting down on my lip, I shake my head. "Something's not right… Something's really…" I put my hand under my skirt, careful to get as much blood on my fingers as I can manage before pulling it out again. "Oh, *God*…"

"Fuck." Cian's eyes bulge. "Fuck. Fuck. Fuck!"

I look at him desperately. "I have to see a doctor, Cian. My doctor. This isn't normal… ahh, it hurts…"

"As ucht Dé," he hisses as his eyes narrow with anxiety. "Okay, why don't you lie down and—"

"Lie down?" I snap. "Lie *down?!* I might be losing my baby and you want me to lie down and do what: wait for him to die?"

He's sweating now far worse than I am, rivulets of gray perspiration dripping down his temples. "I'll—fuck, I'll get you a—a doctor, goddammit!"

I cry out wordlessly. My clever ploy is slowly starting to feel like a car without wheels. If he gets some random doctor in here, they're going to discover that I'm bleeding out of a manufactured cut in my thigh and then the jig will be up.

"I need Liza. Only she'll know what to do." I grab his arm with my bloody hand, leaving smears of red on his skin. "Please, Cian. I'm begging you. You're better than this."

He looks aimless, helpless, hopeless. His eyes keep roaming around the room like there are instructions written on the walls if he just squints hard enough.

"I wanted to be," he croaks softly.

"I've lost so much already. I can't handle losing my baby, too." The panic is building higher and higher. If he simply refuses to take me to Liza, then I'm out of ideas. "And you can't afford to have this baby die on your watch." That gets his attention. "Dmitri will burn down the whole of Chicago if it means finding and destroying you."

His lips are chalk-white now. He licks them again and again. "It might not matter either way. He's going to go apeshit on me regardless."

"Not if I plead your case."

His eyes snap to mine. "Why would you do that?"

"If you take me to Dr. Liza right now, I will vouch for you," I promise him. "I will tell Dmitri that you did whatever you could to help me, to save this baby. He'll listen to me, Cian."

I have no idea if that's true or not, but I don't need it to be true; I just need Cian to believe it can be.

He closes his eyes for a moment and swears through his teeth again in Gaelic. "Fuck." His eyelids pop back open. "Alright. Alright, fuck. I'll take you to see your damn doctor. But I'm staying with you the entire time, is that understood?"

He eyes me suspiciously. I swallow hard, trying not to let my relief ruin my performance. "Hurry please." I wince. "I feel… strange…"

A low, anguished hiss escapes Cian's lips as he wraps an arm around my shoulders. "Put your weight on me. Let me know if you're feeling faint."

He's surprisingly gentle as he leads me through the house. Fresh blood trickles down my leg with the motion. But I embrace the pain; I welcome it.

When it comes to my son, I'll do whatever it takes.

I'll cut myself a thousand times over if I have to.

4

WREN

He helps me into the backseat of his truck, going so far as to prop up a pillow underneath my head. Pillow or no pillow, though, I'm thirty-two weeks pregnant—"comfort" is a thing of the distant past.

Cian gets into the driver's seat and rolls down his window. "Follow us," he orders someone I can't see. "Stay outside the hospital the entire time. If you see any funny business, alert me immediately and move in. We're going to make this a fast visit."

As he starts up the engine, I meet his eyes through the rearview mirror. "That's optimistic of you."

"You'll be fine."

"Wishful thinking?"

"You've been stressed," he dismisses. "That can't have helped your preeclampsia. I'm sure once your doctor gives you the right medication, you'll be fine."

"And back in captivity, huh?"

He glares at me. "Don't make me regret this, Wren."

I hold up a hand. "Sorry, sorry. I'm just... scared." It's not even a lie; I *am* scared. Not specifically for my baby's life necessarily, but for the situation surrounding his birth.

My baby can't be born in a cage.

I rest my head against the pillow and stare up at the truck's shiny ceiling. It feels good to be out of that room. At least things move and change here. In the room, the walls stood stony and still all the time and my mind was starting to invent hallucinations to cast into the blank spaces. This, as small of a change as it is, is better.

Weird, the things you appreciate when you get to experience a little freedom.

"Cian, can I ask you something?"

"I'd rather you didn't."

"Come on. Distract me."

He sighs. "You can ask the question. I can't promise I'll answer."

"It's about Rose."

He frowns. "Why ask me about your sister? You knew her better than anyone else."

"Yeah, I thought I did, too. Turns out, there was a lot about her that I didn't know. She hid a lot from me."

"I wouldn't take it personally," he advises cautiously. His hands grip and regrip the steering wheel and his free leg pistons up and down.

"How can I not?"

"Because I don't think she kept things from you because she didn't trust you. She did it to protect you."

"Because she knew who you and your brother were, didn't she?" My voice trembles and suddenly, I regret starting this conversation at all. Do I really want confirmation that Rose wasn't the innocent soul that I always thought she was? Maybe believing in her innate goodness is just self-preservation at this point.

Sometimes, the lies we tell ourselves are the only things keeping us whole.

"Yes," Cian answers before I can tell him not to. My stomach plummets. "She knew."

That hurts, but if I stopped asking questions now, I bet I could still hold on to my untainted memory of her. I could purge that little tidbit and go back to loving Rose the way I always have.

But, biting my lip, I feel a tear slip down the side of my cheek. Denial has never really been my strong suit. It took months for Rose to realize that Dad wasn't coming back. It took Mom years.

But me? It took me only minutes to figure that out.

"So she was aware that Jared was a gambler?"

Cian sighs wearily. "I don't think she knew at first. But after Jared's first big win, he told her how he got the money. I don't think either one of them thought it would become a years' long obsession. And when things got hard, he became so sure it was their way out. *'It's not an addiction, Cian—it's salvation.'*" He shudders like the memory pains him.

I shudder, too. Jared's face flashes through my head. Lopsided grin, one dimple, cute and roguish and funny as all hell when he chose to be. He was suffering, too, though, wasn't he? Rose was in the bathtub with bloody water swirling around her, yes, but Jared's pain was all inside.

I breathe slowly and make myself look at the ceiling again until the tide of grief ebbs away. "How big a hole did they dig themselves into?"

He winces as though he's been expecting the question. "Big enough that my brother got involved."

"D-did… um… did Rose know about Elena?"

His eyes slide to mine in the mirror, equal parts cold and sad. "That deal was between Jared and Cathal, Wren. Not even I knew about it until Jared had already taken Elena."

I freeze. If I don't sit up now I'm definitely going to throw up. "Jared took Elena?"

"Wren, maybe this is not the right time to—"

"Cian."

He sighs again, but he doesn't make me keep arguing with him. "He had no choice, Wren. He owed Cathal millions by then. He'd been on a steady losing streak for a year. It was either write off the debt by doing whatever Cathal asked. Or watch Rose die in place of Elena."

Before I can even process all that, the car starts to slow down.

"We're here."

I wipe the tears from my eyes and wait until Cian has parked. He helps me out of the car and I sleep-walk through the hospital with his arm looped around my waist for support. He speaks to the nurses and, soon enough, we're shown into an examination room with fluorescent lights so bright they hurt my eyes.

"Dr. Liza will be with you shortly, Mr. and Mrs. Beckhoff," a nurse in bright pink scrubs says before leaving and closing the door behind her.

I laugh bitterly and let my eyes flutter closed as my head lolls back on the crinkling exam table paper. "Congrats on your wedding, Mr. Beckhoff."

Cian snorts in response. "Well, I wasn't about to offer up our real names now, was I? If your doctor decides to tip Dmitri off, at least we'll have a head start."

"Guess you thought of everything. Criminal mastermind."

When I peek at him, he's got the hint of a smile in one corner of his mouth. It's heartbreaking to see, actually. So much sadness in that face with just one little spot of joy.

"You know, I always liked you, Wren."

"Just not enough to stand up to whoever it is who's pulling your strings."

That's all it takes. The smile wilts away. "No one's pulling anything," he says. "I made a decision."

"To be someone's bitch?"

His eyes narrow. "To protect my people."

"At the expense of other people?"

"If that's what it takes, yes."

I can almost admire that—or I would, if me and my baby didn't happen to fall into the latter category.

I sigh. "For what it's worth, I liked you, too."

The door opens and Dr. Liza walks in with a cheery smile on her face. "Mr. Beckhoff, I presume," she greets, giving Cian a friendly nod. Then she turns to me. "Mrs.—" The smile freezes on her face. "Wren?"

Cian steps behind her, close enough for the move to be threatening. "Her name is Mrs. Alison Beckhoff. Is that clear, Doctor?"

The shock melts off Liza's face in seconds, replaced once again with her professional smile. "Crystal." She swallows and the cords of her neck stand out with tension. "Welcome, Mrs. Beckhoff. I see you're quite far along."

"It's preeclampsia," I offer her. "I'm bleeding… Something's not right with the baby."

Liza doesn't bat an eyelid. "Let's take a look, shall we?"

As I pull my legs up, Cian sidles closer. I clamp my knees together again and glare. "Do you mind?"

"I'm not leaving the room," he growls.

"Fine. But stand over there."

Rolling his eyes, he moves towards my shoulders. Only then do I raise my legs and part them. I'm pretty sure Liza instantly spies the cut at my thigh, but her expression never falters. "Okay," she says in an authoritative voice. "We have some breakthrough bleeding."

"Is that a bad thing?"

"It's not bad or good," she demurs. "We just need to normalize your blood pressure and get you back on the right medication. Let me just go and get your chart—"

She turns towards the door but Cian blocks her immediately. "I'm afraid I can't let you leave this room, ma'am."

Liza doesn't waver. "I need her chart to prescribe—"

"Then call in a nurse."

She sighs. "I'll send a message."

"No. You'll call in. I want to hear what you're asking for."

My heart is thudding hard. Cian is blocking us at every turn and I can see my window of opportunity closing slowly. Which means, if I'm going to drop a hint about my location, it's going to have to be here and now, in full sight of my watchdog.

Once the nurse arrives with my file, Liza makes a show of looking through it. I'm desperately hoping Cian can't read a medical chart, because if he does, he'll be able to see that there's no sign of preeclampsia anywhere on it.

"Okay, let me just give you a mild dose of hydralazine. That'll reduce your blood pressure and you'll start to feel better after that."

She moves to the table and busies herself with bottles and needles. I have no clue what she's injecting into me, but I trust Dr. Liza. She's capable and smart. Now, if I can only drop a hint without Cian getting wind of it…

"This is going to sting a little, Wren—"

"Alison," Cian hisses.

"Right. Alison." Liza looks me right in the eye. "Don't concentrate on the stinging. Think about something pleasant. A pleasant childhood memory, maybe. Tell me about it."

I swallow and nod. "Right. Pleasant. Yeah. My, uh… my dad used to have this old convertible when I was younger. He'd take us on Sunday rides. I loved driving around in it."

"Yeah?"

I nod. "It felt so freeing, riding around in the backseat with the top down and the wind in my face." I chance a glance at Cian, who's looking down at this phone. Good—if he's not concentrating, this is going to be a whole lot easier.

"It used to be my favorite way of getting around… until I took the train."

"The train, huh?" Liza nods as if she understands.

"Yup. We used to ride the Red Line to see our grandmother every other weekend."

"Must have been fun."

"It was fun. Until the train stopped coming." I flare my eyes, hoping she picks up on that. "A track without a train doesn't make sense, don't you think? So we had to switch to the Blue—"

"Are you done with that?" Cian spits suddenly, looking up from his phone.

"Um, just another sec—"

"No, we're done," Cian barks. "Tape some gauze down and let's go, *Alison*."

Shit. Liza's forced to release me and the moment the IV's not connected anymore, Cian grabs my arm and yanks me off the table.

"Cian! What the—"

"Silent," he snarls so fiercely that my jaw snaps shut. He pulls me through the hospital and I trip along after him, panic rising to my throat like vomit. When we get to his car, he shoves me inside roughly and rushes to the driver's seat.

The moment the doors are locked, he starts reversing out of his parking space. "Do you think I'm a fucking idiot?" he barks. "'A track without a train'? Did you really think I wouldn't get that?"

I cringe against the venom in his voice. I've fucked up royally. Now, not only have I screwed up any chance I have of being rescued, but I've also gone and pissed off my captor. I'm not so sure the semi-humane treatment I've received these past few weeks is going to continue after this.

With only one hand on the wheel, he rips out of the hospital parking lot and dials in someone. "Change of plan. We're not coming back to the safehouse. Meet me at the backup location. Take the remaining men with you."

No. No. No!

"Cian—"

"Do you even realize what you've done?" he roars, pulling us onto the road. "I've been the only one keeping him from killing you! Now, I'm not sure it'll be—"

"Cian!" I scream, seeing the truck coming at us from the side. "Watch ou—"

My body constricts around my belly as the massive beast of a vehicle slams right into us. The scream lodges in my throat as the world explodes. I feel the crush of wind and pressure and glass and fear.

And then it feels like I'm falling.

5

DMITRI

FIFTEEN MINUTES EARLIER

I've spent the last few weeks sleeping in the studio.

I use the term "sleeping" loosely. A couple dozen hours in a couple dozen days doesn't do much to make a man feel well-rested. Every time I wake up, I'm caught between two different realities.

There are days when I wake up expecting to find Elena sleeping beside me. And then there are the days I wake up searching for Wren. It's fucked-up. So is my head, churning between the past and the present, reminding me constantly of all my failures, of all the women in my life I've let down.

It started with my mother, a woman I haven't thought about in years. But I've been thinking a lot about her lately. Probably because she kicks off the list of female relationships that have fallen to pieces in my hands.

I don't remember many details about her. I have no pictures to look back on, no visuals to hold onto. But I do remember that she had dark hair like Aleksandr and me. Sharp features made her look older than she was. She had a cleft in her chin and eyes that disappeared when she smiled.

I remember that she used to take Aleksandr on piggyback rides around the garden and when she tucked us into bed, she'd make up stories about a woman who fell in love with the moon.

My paternal grandmother used to call her "fanciful." Otets preferred to say she was batshit crazy. I grew up with this notion that she was simply unpinnable, dancing as she wished back and forth across the line between sanity and madness.

The clearest memory I have: one night, she slipped into my room and woke me up. It was the last time I ever saw her. But I didn't know that when I blinked my eyes open to find her face hovering above mine.

"Come with me, Dimi. We can run away together."

"Where are we going?"

She smiled and her eyes disappeared. *"Anywhere you want. To the moon."*

"I don't wanna go to the moon," I mumbled, hiding my face beneath my blankets. *"I wanna sleep."*

I can still hear her last words to me, filled with disappointment, stained with unshed tears. *"Please, my sweet boy. Come with me. Please."*

I said no again. I was seven; I didn't know what she was asking me, and in truth, I don't think she fully did, either.

She sighed and kissed my forehead and when she pulled away, she left behind her tears. I wiped them off, turned over, and went back to sleep.

"Dmitri?" The door squeaks open and Aleksandr sneaks in. Judging from the dark circles around his eyes, I'm not the only one who hasn't been sleeping.

"I'm awake." I sit up against the hideous green couch that Wren decided she loved and gesture him over. "Any news?"

Even in the dark, I can see him shake his head. "Nothing so far. Just spoke to Locksmith. Nothing new there, either."

"What about Liza?"

Aleksandr sighs as he drops onto the armchair, legs cast askew. "If Cian has to take Wren to a doctor, it's not going to be Liza." He cracks his knuckles, yawns, and squints at me. "Did you manage to get some sleep?"

I glance at the clock. It says twelve, but I couldn't honestly say if it's noon or midnight, not with the curtains drawn as tight as they are. Who cares in the end, anyway? Night, day—it doesn't fucking matter anymore.

"No."

He starts to say something, but a buzzing sound interrupts him. I look down at my phone, startled to see an unexpected name on the screen. My eyelids twitch with anticipation as I hold the phone up to my ear.

"Liza?"

"They just left," she gasps. "They just fucking left."

I'm on my feet in an instant. "Where?"

"I'm at the hospital. I don't know where they're going," she says, tripping over her words. "She tried to tell me where he's keeping her, but I think he got suspicious. He might be moving her, Dmitri. He might be—"

"It's okay. I've got this. You did good calling me."

I hang up while she's still talking and dial in Pavel's number. "Pavel, where are you?"

"Uh, outside St. Joseph's, where you told me to—"

"Wren and Cian are exiting the building as we speak. I need you to get eyes on them. Do whatever it takes to get Wren back unhurt. I'm coming."

∼

The car roars all around me, but it's not enough. Not fast enough by a longshot, though I have the gas pedal pressed to the floor and people scream and swerve out of the way as I rip through the city.

The hospital looms ahead. Aleksandr is saying something in the passenger seat, but I can't even hear him over the crackling bellow of the engine.

"Dmitri, look out—!"

I leap the car onto the sidewalk. The curb tears against the undercarriage and thus millions of dollars' worth of Ferrari's finest mechanisms get shredded to pieces, but I couldn't give a fuck less.

Wren needs me.

So I'm coming—by any means necessary.

We reach a horde of people sprinting in the opposite direction, which can mean only one thing: Pavel must be close. I throw the car into park and leap out, gun in hand, just as gunshots wail through the air.

Civilians go streaming past me. I run upstream, round the corner, and find Pavel crouched behind the open door of his truck as he ducks out of range of the half a dozen Irish soldiers unloading at him.

All I grunt is, "Where?"

He points, I follow his finger, and then I'm off and running again, Irish bullets be damned. They zip past my ears like hornets as I zig and zag from one hiding spot to the next.

I'm distantly aware of more of my men answering the call that Aleksandr put out as we sped to the hospital, but most of my attention is focused on the car mangled a dozen yards away from where Pavel is stationed.

It's smashed all to hell on one side, broken glass everywhere, metal frame crunched and bent—and through the shattered window, I see a familiar shock of soft brown hair.

"Wren!" I roar.

I rip the ruined door off its hinges and hurl it aside.

She's curled up in a ball on the floor of the back seat, trembling like a leaf. Her arms are peppered with fresh scrapes, but otherwise, she looks unhurt. She scrambles backward at the sound of my voice, too terrified to realize what's happening.

"Wren," I try again. "It's me. I'm here."

That seems to get through to her. "D-Dmitri...?"

"It's me, *moya devushka*. I'm here."

A sob escapes her lips. She looks exhausted and relieved at the same time. "Thank God," she sobs. "Thank God."

I reach for her and she moves easily into my arms. Breathing hard, I lift her out of the car and carry her to one of my men's vehicles.

"If any of the Irish are still alive," I hiss to Aleksandr, "kill them."

Then I get into the backseat of one of the Wranglers and order Pavel to drive us out. Her belly is big. Big enough that keeping her in the crook of my arms is difficult.

But I refuse to let her go.

Now that she's finally back where she belongs, I'm never letting her out of my sight.

6

WREN

He doesn't stop touching me.

His arms are already wrapped around me, but it's like he needs to check to make sure I'm really here with him. He keeps stroking my back, my shoulders, my face. He tucks a lock of hair back behind my ear. Every time the vehicle jerks or brakes, he holds me just a little bit tighter.

Strangely, I find that I don't mind. After weeks of uncertainty and insecurity, he feels safe and comfortable and wholly certain.

So does our destination.

I never expected arriving at the penthouse to feel like coming home, but that's what it is. I see the illuminated sign for The Muse at Haven Crest and I can finally breathe again.

"How are you feeling?" he asks as we ride up the elevator, his arm looped around my waist.

"I, um... I'm not quite sure," I admit. "It hurts all over."

He nods grimly. "I've already contacted Liza. She's on her way over as we speak."

I just sigh and burrow into his embrace.

We stop at my apartment, not his—which I assume is for my comfort, not his. I'm sure if Dmitri had it his way, he'd chain me to his bed and never let me leave. But I've had enough of cages for a lifetime, and I think he can sense that.

Still, it feels vaguely wrong to come in here. The apartment is still half-empty and it feels aloof, sterile. I find myself longing for the life and warmth of the penthouse upstairs. I want the room to smell like him, because every time he pulls even an inch away from me, the air starts to feel toxic and foul. It's *Dmitri's* scent I want to breathe in, not the tang of generic lavender cleaning product.

Quashing those thoughts, I allow him to lead me into the bedroom. But when he tries to pull me towards the mattress, I resist, turning instead towards the window seat.

"You need to lie down, Wren."

"I've spent the last three weeks lying down. I want to look out a proper window. I want to see the city."

I hike my dress up and try to hoist myself onto the window seat. That proves hard to do with my belly and the oozing scab of my cut, but Dmitri helps me up despite the disapproval on his face.

Then his eyes fall to my legs. "Is that blood? Fuck. I should have taken you straight to a hos—"

"Dmitri," I interrupt softly, placing my hand on his arm. "It's okay. It's not what you think. I cut myself."

He freezes. "You... cut yourself?"

I chew on the inside of my cheek. "It was the only way I could convince Cian to take me to see Dr. Liza. I cut my inner thigh and pretended as though my preeclampsia was acting up and Liza was the only one who could help me."

"You don't have preeclampsia."

I shrug. "He didn't know that."

He releases a soft whistle and the first hint of a smile I've seen since the car crash twitches in the corner of his mouth. "You're a marvel." Then the smile disappears. "But I still need to get you cleaned."

I grimace and hook my hand in the crook of his elbow to drag him down onto the window seat with me. "I can't get up right now, Dmitri. Actually, no—I just don't want to get up."

He considers that for a moment, then he nods. "Okay. We can just sit here for a while. Can I get you anything while we wait for Liza?"

"I'm okay. He fed me well, actually. I always had enough to eat and drink."

The ripple of anger that flushes across Dmitri's face is unmistakable and terrifying. His entire body constricts; even his knuckles go white. "If he treated you well, it was for his benefit, not yours."

"I'm not so sure."

"Do you need a reminder of what happened?" Dmitri's eyes flash fiercely. "He fucking abducted you, Wren."

"So did you."

I cringe internally. Okay, so that probably wasn't the best thing to say under the circumstances. I honestly didn't mean it to come across as a reprimand; I'm just trying to make a point.

But Dmitri is long past listening.

"I was trying to protect you. From men like him," Dmitri snaps. "You're carrying my son!"

"I know! I know. I didn't—"

"Cian is a bottom feeder. I made the mistake of assuming he was harmless, compared to his brother, but I can see now that I was wrong—"

"Dmitri—"

He pounces off the window seat and starts pacing furiously around the room. "Three weeks. Three fucking weeks! He kept you for *three fucking weeks* and sent me goading pictures to rub my failure in my face."

"Your failure…?"

"I failed to keep you safe. I failed to keep you secure. Just like I did with—"

He breaks off, but I don't need him to finish the sentence to know who he's talking about. Elena's unspoken name hangs between us heavily. My skin prickles with unease, the weight of my newfound knowledge pressing down on my shoulders like a boulder.

"Fuck," he mutters. "Fuck!"

Now that my anger at him has faded, I can feel the guilt surging beneath it. He told me the truth. He tried to explain and I'd brushed aside his pain in favor of my own.

Before I can get to the apology, the door opens and Dr. Liza bursts in. "Wren!" she exclaims. "Are you alright?"

"Sore," I confess. "And tired—"

"The cut on your thigh," she says urgently. "I'm sorry I couldn't take care of it when you came in; I just didn't want him to get suspicious."

I wince at my own stupidity. "I already screwed up on that one. It was stupid to think he wouldn't figure out my clue."

"What clue?" Dmitri asks.

"I was being held in a little house that faced an abandoned railroad track. In all the time I was there, I didn't see one train go by."

"Shit," Dmitri hisses as his face pales. "I know exactly where that is."

"I wasn't very subtle."

"Hey." Liza moves to my shoulder. "You did what you could with what you had. Now, let me examine you, make sure everything's okay with the baby."

Dmitri doesn't move, not even when Liza lifts up my skirt and examines my cut. He stares down at it so hard that I get self-conscious. He sees me fidgeting and fixes me with a hard glare. "Don't even bother to ask, Wren. I'm not going anywhere."

Liza must have as much prior experience with that tone as I do, because she doesn't even try to ask him for space. She just straightens up and starts fishing in her bag. "You went deep, but at least you don't need stitches. I'll clean the wound first. Once that's done, I recommend a hot bath."

The doctor takes her time, but Dmitri stands there, patient and motionless, for the entire process, like he's carved from stone. The moment Liza's done and satisfied with her handiwork, she pats my knee. "You did good, Wren. You're stronger than you look."

I smile. "Yeah?"

"Hell yeah. You did good, mama."

She starts to help me get off the window seat, but Dmitri beats her to the punch. He wraps an arm around my waist and hoists me onto my feet. "I'll take it from here, Liza. I expect you to be on call for the next few weeks."

"Of course." She scoops up her things and disappears through the door, leaving us alone.

As soon as she's gone, Dmitri starts to haul me toward the bathroom. I push myself off him and take a few wobbly steps backward. "I can bathe myself, Dmitri. I'm pregnant, not invalid."

"You might need help getting in and out of the tub."

I frown. "You calling me fat?"

He almost smiles before he kills it. "Can we skip the part where you object to everything I say and just humor me here?"

Sighing, I crumple forward and nod. "You're lucky I'm tired."

As it turns out, I do need help getting into the tub. But it's not until I'm forced to undress that I realize what I've just agreed to. "Um... can you not look at me?"

"Why?"

I peek down at my swollen belly and try to control the blush on my cheeks. "Because… I'll be naked."

"I've seen you naked before."

"That was different. And I wasn't quite as pregnant back then."

Something ripples across his eyes. "For God's sake, Wren, don't be ridiculous."

"Just don't look, okay? I'm asking you."

He sighs and turns his head away pointedly while still offering me his hands. I pull off my clothes quickly, take his hands and keep my eyes on his face to make sure he's not looking as I lower myself down into the tub. Once I'm submerged, I pull my feet up and wrap my arms around them so that my belly disappears altogether.

"Can I look now?"

"If you must."

He turns around and lowers himself down on the edge of the tub. Then he picks up a bright green loofah, dunks it in the lukewarm water and starts stroking it down my back. I can't even bring myself to protest; it feels so damn good.

Despite my best efforts, my gaze slides to Dmitri's face. God, I've missed it. I just can't bring myself to say that to him. We left things so… unfinished. We were in the middle of a standoff that seemed to have no resolution.

And now?

Everything feels different.

"Is it true?" I ask softly. "Is she really dead?"

I refused to believe Cian when he first broke the news to me. Even as I held onto denial, though, I spent the first few days in a fog, losing time to tears and grief. A part of me clung onto the hope that maybe Cian didn't have all the information. Maybe he was just playing games with me.

Part of me still hopes that.

Dmitri's eyes betray nothing. His perfect façade never cracks, but he stiffens imperceptibly. "Yes. Bee is dead."

"God…" I whisper, looking down at the ripples of water skating around my body. "I was hoping—" I break off with a half-choked sob and cover my face with my hands. "What happened?"

Dmitri sighs. "We don't have to talk about this now."

"I want to know."

"Wren—"

"Please, Dmitri. She was my friend, too."

He hesitates, his jaw softening ever so slightly. "She took a bullet right underneath her heart. She went into cardiac arrest before we could get her to a doctor. It was quick and painless for her."

I close my eyes so the tears don't spill over. "Cian told me you had a funeral for her?"

"It was a small affair. Just the Bratva." His voice wavers and wobbles, but it doesn't crack.

I peek out of one eye. "What about her family? Why weren't they there?"

"Because the bullet didn't just take Bee out. It also outed her pregnancy… or lack thereof."

I gasp. "Oh my God. So Vittorio knows that she was faking it?"

"He knows everything," Dmitri says with a grimace. He stares off into space for a moment. "At least in death, she's safe from that bastard."

I don't know what to say. Neither does he, apparently. He just keeps running the loofah over my pink skin. I expected to see his unhinged wrath at Bee's death, but to my surprise, there's none of that. He almost seems… detached? Like he can't quite believe she's gone, either.

That's the thing about people like Bee. How can death claim someone who's larger than life? Impossible. There's just no way.

"You can't blame yourself for her death, Dmitri. You know that, right?"

He holds my gaze for only a moment before it dances away again. "I was her best friend, Wren. I'm the *pakhan* of the Egorov Bratva. This is all happening because of who I am. It's most definitely my fucking fault."

"Dmitri." I place my hand on his arm and the loofah drops. My self-consciousness dissipates underneath a much-needed injection of perspective. What does it matter that I'm big and bloated right now? At least I have blood in my veins and air in my lungs.

I'm alive.

"I'm so sorry," I whisper.

Those silver eyes flicker with regret. "These last three weeks have been hell," he croaks. "The thought of losing you and the baby… It was a living nightmare. I can't risk your lives again. So from now on, no more work, no more unnecessary outings. Until things are resolved with the Italians and the Irish, you're staying right here with me."

It must be the grief. Or the exhaustion. Or just the mental trauma of the last several weeks. But what he's saying…

It sounds pretty damn good.

7

DMITRI

The first time I met Beatrice Zanetti, she was ten years old.

Otets had commanded that I come along to the Italian don's mansion to "get the lay of the land." I wasn't sure what my presence would accomplish, but it wasn't the kind of invitation I could decline. So I put on my suit like he told me to do, and I went like he insisted.

I was forced to exchange pleasantries with Don Vittorio, who at the time had only a sprinkling of gray through his dark hair, and then I was relegated to the gardens while the men got down to business.

I found her sitting by the pool. She was fully dressed with her skirt hiked up to her knees and her feet dunked into the water.

"You the Russian prince?" she asked with a defiant jerk of the chin.

I nodded. *"You the Italian princess?"*

She gave me a nod. *"Wanna sit with me?"*

"What are you doing?"

"I was thinking it'd be kinda cool to have gills. Then I could live in the sea. There's a whole lot more sea than there is land."

Great, I remember thinking. *This chick's nuts.*

"My papa says I'm probably going to marry you one day," she added.

I'd laughed right in her face. *"That's never going to happen."*

She didn't even pretend to look insulted. She just tilted her head to the side and regarded me from a different angle. *"Why not?"*

"Because I don't plan on marrying. Ever."

She smiled. *"Me neither. But don't tell my dad. He gets mad when I want things that are different than what he wants for me."*

"Fathers are like that."

"Yours, too, huh?"

"Big time."

We were quiet for a while. Eventually, I slipped off my shoes and socks, rolled up my slacks, and put my feet in the water next to hers. Her skin was so olive and tan compared to mine.

"I'm gonna be the next don, you know," she told me confidently. *"Papa says girls don't inherit, but I'm going to prove him wrong. I'm going to be better than any son he could have ever had."* She glanced up at me suddenly with a seriousness I would come to know so well. *"Would you form an alliance with me?"*

I thought about it. *"Yeah. If you don't end up being crazy."*

She laughed and offered me her hand. We shook on it and that was that.

I'd discovered sooner rather than later that Bee was, in fact, crazy. But it was one of her best qualities. She was unapologetically herself and, as far as I was concerned, the people who couldn't see that were short-sighted and stupid.

Her father most of all.

I throw the pictures that Aleksandr just handed me onto the desk. They're grainy, but Cian's and Vittorio's faces are indisputable. "When was this meeting?"

"Three hours ago," my brother answers, sweating from the forehead. "It was quick. They came separately, left separately, with backup."

"So they don't trust each other."

Aleks snorts. "Who in their right minds would trust Vittorio? That shady piece of shit has 'backstabber' written all over his wrinkly ass face."

"I should have killed him when I had the chance."

He straightens in his seat. "Was that ever really an option?"

"It was more than an option; it was the plan. We were going to wait a year or so after the wedding. Make sure all the t's were crossed and the i's were dotted. Give myself some legitimacy within the mafia before ending the old fuck once and for all."

"'We,' huh? So Bee was in on it?"

I laugh at the memory of her eyes brightening in the dark of my living room. "Who do you think came up with the idea?"

Aleks shakes his head and whistles low. "Killing your own father... That's cold."

"You've seen the scars on her back. Do you really expect love or loyalty to survive through all that?"

"Hey, hey," he protests quickly, throwing up his hands, "I wasn't judging. I'm just... processing. How detailed was this plan of yours?"

Sighing, I slump back in my chair. "That was the sticking point."

Aleksandr leans in, clearly intrigued. "Do tell."

"Bee insisted that she would be the one to do it. I felt that we needed to go clean and simple. His death needed to look like an accident if I wanted to keep my staying power within the Zanetti ranks. Lord knows Dante, Alberto, and Valentino would have started sniffing around for any sign of funny business." I exhale wearily. "But Bee... She wanted to be able to look him in the eye before he died. She wanted him to know that she was doing it. And that he had only himself to blame." I scowl and snap back to reality, glancing back down at the pictures on my desk. "But that was then. Things have changed. This is going to make it a lot more complicated."

"They outnumber us now," Aleksandr points out quietly.

"Fuck numbers. We will win because we have to. I'm not bringing my son into an uncertain world."

"I hear you, brother, but let's be real: our world is always going to be uncertain. It's part of the package. You will always be a target because of who you are and your family will always be targets because of who they are to you."

He's right, as much as I hate it. The irony is that, even when I think I'm in control, I'm not. That changed the moment I decided other people were important to me. First, Elena; then Bee; now, Wren.

"I'm going to go check on her."

I start to get to my feet but Aleksandr blocks me. "What's going on there? Have you sorted shit out with Wren?"

"How is that any of your business, *brat*?"

He shrugs nonchalantly and gets to his feet along with me. "Bee's not here to bust your balls and be your voice of reason. So it falls on me."

"Sit down and leave me alone," I growl irritably.

Shockingly, he doesn't. Instead, he puts both hands on my shoulders. "She may not have been born into a Bratva, but she sure as hell handled herself like she was. The girl is smart; she thinks on her feet, she fights for herself, and she doesn't let a shootout force her into bed for a week."

I flinch. Elena once spent a week in her room after being shot at by one of Cathal's thugs. She was scared to step foot out of the apartment. She jumped at loud noises and saw monsters around every corner. It took a lot of coaxing to get her to leave her room, and even longer to convince her to leave the apartment.

"Low blow."

He winces uncomfortably. "I regretted it the moment it came out of my mouth. Forgive me."

I brush past him and drift slowly towards Wren's room. I left her sleeping in her bed twelve hours ago and when I walk in, she's still out, her breathing peaceful and soft. I stand there and watch her for a long time.

Her belly is huge, pushing up the sheets in a gentle swell that makes my heart thud. My child is in there. My future.

Our future.

Aleks may have regretted the memory he brought up, but he was right: Elena had been totally unprepared for my lifestyle. But there's a chance that Wren might have the steel required to survive in this world.

Bee noticed that in her.

So did my brother.

Maybe it's time I started noticing, too.

8

DMITRI

She sleeps for almost twenty-four hours straight.

Liza had warned me that that might happen. A combination of mental trauma and physical exhaustion forces the body to just cease operations and reboot. To pass the time, I end up prepping a big meal: *pelmeni, pierogi* and a hot *shchi* that reminds me of cold winters in Russia when my grandmother was still alive.

Wren finally peers around the corner just after eight, looking fresh-faced and well-rested. Her hair spills down her shoulders, smelling of oranges, and she happens to be wearing one of the t-shirts I'd put into her closet this morning while she slept.

I might like the sight of her in my t-shirt a little *too* much.

"Welcome to the waking world."

She smiles nervously. "I feel like I slept for days."

"Just one."

Her eyes pop. "I slept for a whole *day?*" she balks. "Seriously?"

"You needed the rest. And now, you probably need food."

She sniffs the air and swallows audibly. "It smells amazing in here. Did you make all this yourself?"

"You already know I can cook."

"Not like *this*," she argues, gesturing to the mountain of soft, juicy *pelmeni* on the kitchen island. "There's cooking and then there's *cooking.* Are those dumplings?"

Before I can even answer, she crosses the room and perches herself on a stool, swoops on a *pelmen,* and takes a bite.

The moan that follows is worth every ounce of effort I poured into them.

"How'd you learn all these recipes?" she asks around a mouthful of food.

"My grandmother taught me." I pull open the drawer under the cutlery cabinet and take out her old recipe notebook, the pages yellowed and crackling. "She left this for me in her will."

Wren takes the notebook gingerly and leafs through the pages, murmuring softly as she goes. She gets through half the book before she glances up at me. "Were you close?"

I shrug. "In a way. Cooking was her preferred method of conversation. She was a woman of few words. If her nose wasn't buried in a recipe book, it was buried in a Bible."

"I can relate to that," she says with a bitter laugh. "My mom was the same way. She joined a prayer group after Dad left and after that it was all about Jesus, all the time."

"That must have been lonely."

She bobs her head left and right. "Yes and no. I had Rose." She flinches almost immediately after saying Rose's name. "Sorry," she mutters. "I didn't mean to invite the elephant into the room."

It's amazing to me that *she's* the one apologizing. "It's okay."

"No, it's not. You lost someone, too. I kinda... pushed that aside because I was so focused on the people *I* lost."

She tries to pick up her expression unsuccessfully. I prod the plate of *pelmeni* back towards her. "Eat *pelmeni* now. We'll worry about the elephants later."

That gets a smile out of her and she meekly resumes eating. I can't help but watch her chew, taken by the way those plump lips dance and shift. It's weird, the things that are turning me on.

The fact that I can see the swell of her belly underneath my t-shirt.

How her body shivers every time she pops another *pelmen* into her mouth.

The tiny sigh after each swallow, like she's sad the flavor is gone.

All those weeks of worry wilt away—until she looks up and realizes that I'm staring at her. That unleashes a storm of blushing. Clearing her throat, she licks some gravy off her lips. "I'm making a lot of noise, aren't I?"

"High praise. I'm flattered."

She flushes an even deeper shade of scarlet and reaches for her glass of water. "Aren't you eating?"

Since I can't spend the entire time staring at her, I heap some food onto my plate, though I have no appetite for any of it.

"I noticed the room next to mine is fully furnished," she remarks as I idly chew.

"I'll be sleeping in there for the time being. Consider me your security." I leave out the part about how I've been sleeping there the whole time she was taken prisoner.

"You really don't have to do that."

"I have to protect my son." Her face falls and so I hurry to add, "I have to protect you, too."

That stops her frown in its tracks. "Overcompensating much?" she jokes. She gnaws on her bottom lip like she wants to say something else but she's not sure if she should. In the end, she eats another bite of food and the moment passes.

"How's your leg?"

She looks puzzled. "Hm?"

"You cut yourself," I remind her dryly.

"Oh. Right. It looks good. I removed the bandage a little while ago to let it breathe. It's healing, I think."

I find myself on my feet and rounding the island to get to her. "Let me see."

"Uh, that's really not necessary. It's—" She gasps as I take her leg and hoist it up on the stool without bothering to ask for permission. She freezes as I tuck it on my lap and push up the hem of the shorts she's wearing.

She's right: the cut is looking better. But I pretend as though it needs closer inspection. I let my fingers trail over the bruised skin around the wound. Every little touch makes her shiver.

"You'll live." I keep my hands on her thigh as I look up, catching her eyes with my own. Her lips are parted softly. It would be so damn easy to lean in and kiss her. But there are still so many unspoken conversations left between us. Little potholes in the road from my mouth to hers, each as dangerous and bottomless as the last.

Too dangerous to cross right now, I think.

My cock doesn't agree. But then, he rarely agrees with the rational part of my brain when it comes to Wren.

"Dmitri…"

"Yes?"

"I know things between us were pretty messed up before I was… you know…" She bites the inside of her cheek and glances away, looking a little lost. "I guess I just wanted to say that I don't want that to continue."

I'm surprised. It's not absolution, but it's far closer to it than I ever would have expected. This wasn't spilled milk or some little faux pas. I literally killed her sister and brother in law. *Intentionally.* Premeditated and everything.

No one is *that* forgiving.

She swallows and drags her eyes to mine. "But, um, the thing is… we have to think about this baby." Her hand flutters up and down her belly. "If we're gonna do this together, we're gonna need to coparent. And that means at the very least, we need to try to be friends."

Friends. I fucking loathe that word. It's gravel on my tongue, coarse and sharp and filthy.

Wren must see the distaste on my face, because she flinches. "I'm not saying it's gonna happen overnight. But we owe it to our son to try." She takes a deep, steadying breath. "We owe it to Bee, too. She would have wanted us to get along."

She wanted more for us. But instead of saying as much, I just nod. "We're getting along now."

Wren just frowns. "I've been back for barely twenty-eight hours and I've been sleeping for twenty-four of them. Besides, we haven't actually talked about anything. Properly."

"And talking is important to you?"

"I've tried sweeping things under the rug before. Didn't really work out." I cock my head to the side curiously and she blushes and looks towards the *pierogi*. "William wasn't too big on the whole 'communication' thing. I mean, he talked a lot; there just wasn't very much room for *me* to speak."

I scowl. "Sounds like a prize."

She shrugs. "Most rich, powerful men have a hard time realizing that other people's opinions matter as much as their own."

"Ouch. Point taken."

She smiles guiltily. "That's just been my experience. That's all I'm saying."

"Present company included?"

"What do *you* think?" she asks, fixing me with a scowl to match mine.

I snort. "Fine. I'll do my best to *communicate* with you."

"That includes listening, you know." She hesitates, then adds, "It also requires compromise."

I lean in close so there's no mistaking what I'm about to say. "When it comes to your safety, I'm afraid I'm not compromising on that. Nor will I apologize for it. Especially now that we have *two* enemies to deal with."

Her forehead scrunches up tight with worry. "Are you really gonna take on both the Italians and the Irish?"

"Yes," I snarl. "And I'm going to win."

"Cian and whoever he's working with will—"

I stiffen at the mention of that bastard's name and Wren falls silent. I still haven't worked out my frustration over the kidnapping. After a good night's sleep, I may need to rail on a punching bag with the fucker's face glued to it.

"There's no 'whoever.' Cian is the don. He's the one who calls the shots. He's the one who will pay the price."

She shakes her head adamantly. "That's not exactly true. Apparently, his brother made a deal with the devil and—"

"Enough. We don't need to discuss this now."

"Don't you want to know what happened to me in captivity?" Wren asks with a puzzled double-take.

"Not if it means humanizing that bastard."

Her eyebrows hit the ceiling of her forehead. "You literally *just* promised you would listen."

Just goes to show: no good deed goes unpunished. "And I will. But first, I need you to rest, recover, *eat*. Liza mentioned that your pressure was too high for her liking. You need to keep stress levels to a minimum—which means staying away from subjects that cause it to spike. We'll talk about everything when the time is right, but that time is not now. For now, I need you to take care of yourself and the baby."

She nods reluctantly. "Alright."

Then I pull out her cell phone and pass it to her. "Syrah's been texting you all week. I had to impersonate you a few times to assure her that everything was alright. She's pretty damn suspicious, though. A phone call might help calm her down."

Wren looks down at the phone with a mournful sigh. "I have no idea what to say to her."

"As far as she knows, you've been sick the last few weeks and the doctor has confined you to bed rest. Because of your low immunity, you couldn't be exposed to too many people, which is the reason I gave her for why she couldn't visit you."

"And what about phone conversations?"

"You were always sleeping or too tired to talk."

"No wonder she's suspicious. I'm *never* too tired to talk to her."

I clear my throat pointedly. "She's under the impression that —and this is a direct quote—your *'hot boss is controlling and he should know that you like control IN the bedroom, not outside it.'*" I allow myself a tiny smirk at Wren's shocked face as her jaw flops open. "She had a lot of interesting things to say about me, actually."

"And I am not commenting on any of them!" she blurts. "Those were private messages meant for me!"

"Understood. I wouldn't even dream of asking you to clarify all those fantasies you've apparently been having about me."

"*Shh!*" she hisses, looking around the room like someone embarrassing might be eavesdropping. "I'm reading here… oh, *God!*"

I chuckle quietly and help myself to more food. For the first time in weeks, I finally have an appetite.

9

WREN

"Why can't I come see you?" Syrah demands.

"The doctor is worried about infections. She doesn't want to expose me to anything unnecessarily. The last trimester has had a few… complications."

Of the mob life variety, to be specific. But Syrah doesn't need to know that.

She does huff out an impatient breath. "Fine. I don't like it, but fine. You know, for a second there, I honestly thought you'd been, like, taken hostage by the hot boss and his hot wife."

My reply sticks in my throat. I probably should tell Syrah about Bee, but I can't bring myself to go there. If I say the words out loud, they'll be true, and if they're true, then God only knows how long that pain is going to last.

It sounds dumb and dumb is exactly what it is, but that's how my brain is working these days. Logic is a thing of the past.

"I'm not a hostage; don't worry. Everything is fine."

I can practically hear Syrah's suspicion through the phone. "You'd tell me if anything was up, right?"

"Of course!" I cringe at the way my voice goes up a handful of octaves into a barely believable pipsqueak. "It's just that I'm not gonna be much fun, anyway. I'm basically confined to a bed all the time with nothing but TikTok and books for company."

"What about B—"

"Ah, shoot, Syrah, I'm really sorry, but I've gotta go. Baby's pushing down on my bladder."

"Okay, call me later?"

"Okaysurebye!"

I hang up as fast as I can and drop the phone like it just stung me. I'm gonna have to explain my life to Sy one day; I can only hope that, when I do, she forgives me for keeping her out of it.

Sighing, I swing my legs off the bed and heave myself to my feet. I fell asleep way too late last night after several hours of mindless scrolling, but I got in a few good hours of snoring anyway. My body is still catching up on all the rest I didn't get while I was trapped with Cian.

After a long shower, I end up in my new closet rifling through the clothes. Most of them don't fit anymore and the ones that do all belong to Dmitri. I grab one of his t-shirts and press it to my nose. It still smells like him, all manly and smoky.

"Dammit," I mutter to myself as I drop it in self-directed disgust.

What the hell am I doing, sniffing his t-shirts like a lunatic? The thought of him catching me like this is mortifying. But without much else in the way of options, I pull on the shirt and a pair of his boxers and slink out of the room.

"Dmitri?" I call down the hallway.

He emerges from his room almost immediately, brows furrowed. "Everything okay?"

"The only clothes that fit me are yours."

He skims over what I'm wearing. "And that's a problem for you because…?"

"Because I want to wear *my* clothes."

"Why?"

Why? Because every time I smell your scent, my brain turns to pudding and my vagina feels like it's about to jump off the nearest bridge. Because every time I think about this same fabric brushing your bare skin, I get jealous of it and want to throw IT *off the nearest bridge. Because you drive me insane whether you're near me or not.*

Because I'm crazy.

Because you make me that way.

Because I'm falling in love with you.

What I settle on saying in the end is, "Because I can't keep wearing your clothes all the time."

He blinks slowly. "Are they not comfortable?"

"That's not the point."

"Then for fuck's sake, Wren, what is the point?" he snaps in exasperation.

"The point is that I'm not yours to *control*!" I cry out. "I'm not yours to command and I'm not yours to dress. I have to have a say in my own life, starting with what I wear."

His eyebrows arrow together and his nostrils flare. "Very well. I'll handle it." He turns towards his room as though he's already bored with this conversation. "Was there anything else?"

I move a little closer to the door and peek inside. It looks like a very comfortable setup in there. Almost *too* comfortable. "What do you mean, 'You'll handle it'?"

"I'll have a couple of the boutiques bring their maternity lines over here and you can pick whatever you want."

My jaw drops. "Seriously?"

"You have a need. I'm meeting it."

"It's completely unnecessary. I can just go upstairs to my old room and see what I can find up there. Half my clothes are still there anyway."

"I'll have Aleks bring them down."

"It won't kill me to take the elevator upstairs."

He doesn't even bother to look at me when he replies. "You're not leaving this apartment, Wren. As I said, if you want something from upstairs, all you have to do is ask for it."

Is it just me or is he being *super* shady about the upstairs apartment? Is there another reason he's down here with me?

On second thought: whatever. I have to pick my battles and fighting over who gets to physically retrieve my wardrobe is not the hill I want to die on.

He nods in satisfaction when I don't answer. "I have work to do, so I'll be leaving soon. But Aleksandr will be here with you while I'm gone."

I tilt my head to the side. "How is he?"

"He's had worse bullet wounds. This one didn't even crack the top five."

"My God," I breathe. It's amazing how cavalier he can be about something as serious as a gunshot wound. *Is this how my son's going to talk in twenty years? Will he be comparing gunshot wounds with his father and uncle and chuckling about 'the one that almost killed him'?* I shudder at the thought.

And then I shudder again when Dmitri's warm fingers stroke the curve of my jaw. "I'm sorry," he says, which are two words I wasn't aware he knew to string together. "I keep forgetting that you're not used to all of this."

"Can you really get used to casual violence?" I whisper hoarsely.

"It's not a matter of getting used to it, Wren. You just accept what it is."

"Did Elena?" The question flies out of my mouth before I can think twice about it. I rush to add, "I'm sorry. You don't have to answer that."

He surprises me by sighing. "I thought she had." He runs a hand through his hair, leaving it sticking up in forlorn spikes. "I honestly believed that she was ready for life as my wife. But as it turned out, she had no idea what she was signing up for. And she was right to be scared."

It's on my tongue: the apology I should have given him already. At the very least, an explanation. *I know what happened to Elena and I'm so fucking sorry.*

"Dmitri—"

He clears his throat pointedly. "Call if you need anything." He retreats into his room. The door swings closed.

I stare at it, wishing I could be there for him the way Bee had been. But it's a naïve thought. I'm not Bee. Nor can I be.

So I head off towards the kitchen as loneliness settles in the pit of my stomach. "Get used to it," I tell myself softly. "This might be the rest of your life."

~

Aleks arrives just after Laura Hanover leaves with her team from the Benne Boutique. I'm pretty sure I disappointed the crap out of her.

I ended up with only a handful of things, a few practical pieces that I plan on re-wearing a lot. She kept pushing expensive silk dresses and white linen pants in my face and I kept telling her that I wasn't planning on going out much after the baby was born. Hell, I can barely go out *before* the baby is born. What's the point in nice things if they'll just wither and die in the darkness of my closet?

I'm full swing into the pity party when Aleks walks into the living room with a box of doughnuts in his hand. I rush over to him and throw my arms around him. "I'm so glad you're okay!"

"Me?" he balks, setting down the doughnuts the moment I release him. "You're the one who was kidnapped."

"Sure, but I get kidnapped all the time. At this rate, I'm used to it."

He snorts. "Don't let my brother hear you make that joke."

"My humor is lost on him." I give him a thorough onceover, satisfied that he looks mostly good. There is a small scar where he was shot, but all things considered, I was expecting a lot worse. "Glad you didn't lose the arm."

"It was touch-and-go there for a while," he jokes. Then the smile drops off his face. "Speaking of glad, I'm glad Dmitri assigned me here today, actually. I've been wanting to apologize to you."

I blink at him. "Apologize? For what?"

Now, *he* looks confused. "For God's sake, Wren, you were under my custody and I let you get captured! I've spent the last three weeks wracked with guilt."

"Aleks, don't be ridiculous. That wasn't your fault."

"It was. I should have stayed with you no matter what."

"I'm the one who should be apologizing to you. If I hadn't run away, you wouldn't have been shot in the first place. My only excuse is that I wanted to make sure Bee was…" I stumble on my own tears. "*Shit.*" I drop heavily onto the couch and wipe them away. "I still can't fucking believe she's gone."

Aleks stands awkwardly to the side, gazing out at the city's skyline. "Yeah."

"Will you sit with me?" I pat the cushion next to me and he joins me, albeit somewhat reluctantly.

"What was her funeral like?" I glance towards the doorway even though I know that Dmitri's not in the apartment. "I would have asked Dmitri, but he seems keen on avoiding any real conversation about Bee."

Aleks fixes me with an expression that seems to read, *And you thought I'd feel differently?* "It was a simple service."

I can't help but scowl at him. "Gee, thanks for the details. You really paint a vivid picture."

He half-sighs, half-laughs. "Sorry. It's not the easiest thing for me to talk about, either."

"No, yeah, of course not. I'm the one who should be sorry." I feel like an idiot for assuming that, just because Bee and Aleksandr weren't as close as she was with Dmitri, he'd be willing to talk to me.

I'm about to apologize when I hear a strange thumping sound coming from right above us. I jolt, looking up at the ceiling. "What was that?"

"Uh… probably Dmitri?"

"He said he was going to be at work all day."

Aleksandr shrugs. "He probably just came home early."

I decide it doesn't matter. I don't need to know his exact whereabouts all the time; I just *want* to, which in and of itself is troubling. So I try instead to push him out of my head altogether. "You wanna watch a movie with me?"

"As long as it's got lots of blood and gore."

I cringe. "Ew. No blood. No gore. Something with banter and meet-cutes and slow-motion dancing in a field of daisies, preferably."

"You're a mean negotiator, Wren," Aleks grumbles, but he sinks back into his seat and gestures toward the TV. "Go on. Roll the footage. Torture me."

Soon enough, *Notting Hill* plays across the screen. Julia Roberts asks Hugh Grant if she can stay for a while, and he tells her, *"You can stay forever."*

I don't know whether to shudder or to smile. Reality feels a bit too much like a movie these days. Mine has blood and gore aplenty.

Will it have a happy ending, too?

10

DMITRI

"I've got news and it's not good."

Gnashing my teeth together, I make room for Aleksandr at the dining room table, shoving my files away with an irritated grunt. That's the thing about running legitimate businesses: they don't give a fuck that your world is going up in flames in the shadows.

Aleks sits down adjacent to me and deposits his phone on the table. "I have a recording that I think you should listen to."

Judging by the look on his face, "not good" might've been an understatement. "Who is it?" I venture cautiously.

"A couple of Italian *mudaks* walked into the club I was at last night. You were curious about Vittorio's payback plan? Well, I think I've uncovered it: death by reputation."

The teeth-gnashing intensifies. "How fucking predictable."

Aleksandr's nostrils flare in silent warning. "As far as plans go, it's a good one, brother. He's trying to undermine you.

He's trying to—" He breaks off and opens his phone. "You know what? Just listen to this shit."

He presses play and the recording starts. Clinking glasses, cross-talk, the shuffling of feet and clothes and chairs dragged across floors.

"... heard the Italian princess is dead'?" The first voice is nasally with a grating edge that makes me think of someone thin and spindly.

"You heard right. Got her head blown off at her own damn wedding." The second talker is deeper and dumber than his friend.

Then a third voice chimes in, my least favorite yet. *"Nah, I heard she was poisoned. Dropped to the floor during her vows with blood pouring out of every hole in her body."*

"Does it matter how she died? The point is, she's dead as a damn rat, man. Vittorio Zanetti's daughter is dead and her Russian fuck of an almost-husband couldn't save her."

"Maybe he didn't want to."

"There's that," concedes the nasally bastard.

"There's nothing but the facts! He failed to save her. The Irish pulled the wool over his eyes. It's not the first time they've done it, either. You've heard about his first wife, right? Some white trash fuckin' nobody? She was killed, too. Cathal O'Gadhra gave the order himself."

"Well, Cathal died for it."

"Maybe, but not before he struck the winning blow. Apparently, all you have to do to incapacitate the Russian king is kill one of his queens."

Laughter ripples through the throng of men and my stomach twists with fury. There must be at least six of them, sitting around and swapping rumors like a bunch of old fishwives.

"Cian O'Gadhra is a dead man walking."

"Oh, I wouldn't be too sure."

"You kiddin' me? He killed the Zanetti princess. Vittorio's old, but he's still a mean bastard. He'll want payback."

"The old don blames no one but Egorov for what happened to his girl. There's talk..." Whoever's speaking hushes and I can hear more rustling as they all lean in to hear him. His voice, when it emerges again, is a barely audible croak. *"There's talk that, apparently, he was fucking some two-bit whore on the side. Knocked her up and was planning on forcing the Zanetti broad to play the mother. And here's the kicker: someone's been sayin' to me that the whore in question was bangin' the Italian princess, too. Playin' 'em both—you believe that shit?!"*

The cluster breaks up with grunts of derision, laughter, murmured thoughtfulness. One man in particular is unconvinced. *"Fat fuckin' chance of that, stronzo. No child of Vittorio Zanetti could ever be gay."*

"Ha!" A hand slaps the table. *"You must be on the good shit to believe that Beatrice Zanetti didn't bat clean-up for the other team, brother."*

More indistinct cross-talk as they all start laughing and cracking vicious jokes at Bee's expense back and forth. My teeth go tighter and tighter, my knuckles whiter and whiter where they're gripping the edge of my desk.

When it settles down again, one of the more thoughtful idiots speaks up first. *"Surely, this means that Zanetti will go after Egorov's slut, right? I certainly would if he pulled that shit on my daughter."*

"Not so fast. Apparently, Cian O'Gadhra already beat Vittorio to the punch."

That puts them all silent for a moment. Then someone asks, *"What does that mean? She's dead?"*

"Dead, abducted, tortured, raped—you name it, it either happened already or it's gonna happen any goddamn second."

"Shiiiiit," one proclaims. *"I can't imagine Dmitri Egorov would take that lying down."*

"The bastard loses wives like fuckin' coins in the couch cushions, man. He couldn't do a thing about it if he tried."

I've had enough. I'm this close to smashing Aleksandr's phone into dust on the table. He seems to sense the same thing because he retrieves it and turns off the recording. "I just thought you should know…"

I try to unlock my jaw, which is an effort unto itself. "Double security around Wren. Make sure she—"

"Brother," Aleksandr interjects gently, "don't you think that's the problem?" I frown and he continues hastily before my temper gets away from me. "Hiding her away only fuels the rumors that she was taken. And clearly, *someone* is fueling them plenty without our help. Wren needs to be seen. She needs to be seen as being under your protection, specifically. You need to grab hold of the narrative and twist it to your advantage. There are dozens of conversations like this happening every night around the city, man. We need to take control of them."

He's not wrong, not by a long shot. But his advice goes against my natural instincts. For the first time, I find myself thinking, *What do I care what they say about me?*

But this is about more than just me. This is about the Egorov Bratva, too. And neither my Bratva nor the man who leads it can be seen as weak.

Too much hangs in the balance.

"Have I mentioned that I hate it when you're right?" I sigh at last.

"Frequently. Every time I'm right, in fact."

I meet his eyes miserably. "I despise exposing her."

Aleksandr nods in sympathy. "I get it, dude, I really do. But this serves a dual purpose. Reclaim the story *and* give Wren some room to breathe. She's not some caged bird you can keep locked away. It's a nice place you've got here, but at the end of the day, it's still four walls and a roof."

It's a subtle reminder that Wren is not Elena. Elena craved the cage, so long as I was in there with her.

Wren, on the other hand, wants *out*. Wren wants blue skies and room to stretch her wings.

I can't blame her for that, no matter how much I hate it.

"I'll think about next steps where Wren is concerned," I assure him. "As for the narrative, you're right: we need to put some fresh details out there. Get in touch with Locksmith: we'll need some tech expertise to get the story we want circulating right where we want it."

Aleksandr arches a brow, intrigued. "Which story is that?"

"The one where Beatrice Zanetti died unexpectedly days before her wedding. Make sure the circumstances around her death are vague. I want people guessing."

He rises to his feet. "I'll get right on it."

On his way out, he almost runs into Wren in the doorway. She stifles a shriek and comes to a standstill. "Hope I'm not interrupting anything."

"Nope, we just finished. He's all yours. I doubt you like to share, anyway."

She blushes as he sashays away, whistling some irritatingly jaunty song. When we're alone, she slides over after stopping along the way to pour herself a glass of orange juice. I suspect it's mostly to have something to do with her hands.

"You didn't show up for breakfast this morning," she says. It's more of a statement than a question, like she won't allow herself to actually ask it outright.

"I was working."

I curse myself for my gruff tone, but fucking hell, I don't know how else to be around Wren. She's not a woman I have a blueprint for and it makes me stiff… in more ways than one.

"Dmitri, um… we really need to talk."

I lean back in my seat. "Then talk."

"It's about Cian. I know you hate his guts—"

Despite having had every intention of staying calm, my anger gets the better of me. "*You* should hate his guts. The motherfucker took you, hurt Bee, and destroyed a plan that was years in the making."

She frowns and tilts her head to one side. "What plan?"

"It doesn't matter now."

She sighs and places a hand on her belly. "Well, then I'll stick to what does matter. He treated me well during my captivity. I had a clean, comfortable room, and food, and—"

"So I'm supposed to let him off the hook because he fed you a fucking charcuterie board and replenished the toilet paper?" I scoff. "Not a fucking chance."

The more I push her, the more determined the set of her jaw becomes. "I'm not saying anything like that and you know it. I'm just telling you my honest experience." Her throat bobs as she swallows. "And I'd be lying if I said he treated me badly. In fact, he acted as though he didn't want me there at all. He *told* me so."

"And you believed him?" My tone drips with condescension. I can't stomach that, after all this, she's still pleading his case. Going to bat for a man who wanted her dead and was just too cowardly to pull the trigger.

"Considering he was drunk off his ass at the time... yes, I believed him."

That makes me pause. "What do you mean, 'He was drunk'?"

"He mostly just avoided me. And when he did come into my room, the visits were always short. I mean, he was polite, but curt. Definitely not chatty." My fingers curl automatically as I imagine what it would feel like to wrap my hands around his thick throat and squeeze until he stopped moving. "But one day, he walked in reeking of booze and sat down on the floor with me. He seemed... down." Wren's eyes cloud as she remembers. "It felt kinda like he was battling with a guilty conscience. He told me point blank that he didn't want to keep me there, that he felt bad about taking me at all. He also said he was taken off-guard at the wedding. He gave me the impression that the shootout happened without his permission."

She looks utterly convinced, but I can't trust anything she's telling me. Just because he was convincing doesn't mean he was telling her the truth. For all she knows, he was putting on a performance in the hopes she would buy it.

Well, mission fucking accomplished in that regard. *Well played, O'Gadhra.*

"He was lying to you, Wren."

"That's what you keep saying. But why? What would he gain from that?"

"For one, he's a manipulative bastard and he probably enjoyed the game. For another, he was probably hedging his bets. Trying to cover himself just in case I managed to get you back."

Her hair flops over her forehead as she shakes her head. "I don't think that's what he was doing. Things aren't always as black and white as you make them out to be, Dmitri." She scowls at me through the curtain of her bangs, eyes bright and fierce. "Most people aren't purely good or purely evil. Most of us are just flawed fuck-ups who are trying to do our best. You. Me. Cian, too."

"You don't know Cian—"

"I know him a heck of a lot more than you do. Have you ever actually talked to him? Ever had a meal with him? Ever—"

I jolt to my feet and seethe, "If you thought I was interested in breaking bread with the man who helped kill my wife, you thought very fucking wrong indeed."

She flinches back, her expression clouding. The stubborn set of her jaw doesn't change, though. "Except he wasn't responsible for Elena's death, was he? It was Cathal who was behind it. You told me so yourself."

"He was complicit, if nothing else. That's all I care about."

"*Complicit*," she repeats quietly. "So you're holding him accountable for his brother's sins."

I lean in so that we're nose to nose. "You bet your ass I'm holding him accountable."

She holds my gaze, not shying, not flinching. "And there's no room for forgiveness?"

"Fuck no!"

"Then why should *I* forgive you for killing my sister?" she cries.

Well… *fuck*.

I feel like a fool. Played so easily. How had I not seen where this was heading?

She doesn't lean away from me. Her breath is cool and citrus fresh and her eyes burn with the strength of her convictions.

I used to consider Bee my biggest challenge in life. Her personality was as big, as bold, every bit as stubborn and fierce as mine. But compared to Wren, Bee was child's play.

And the thing is, I could walk away from Bee.

Wren is different. That baby in her belly means I *can't* walk away. And that look in her eye makes sure I *won't*.

"I don't expect you to forgive me," I say gruffly. It's a piss-poor answer and she knows it.

And even still, her voice is gentle when she replies, "You haven't even asked."

The air is thick and boiling. If I look too deeply into those eyes, I might just end up doing something stupid. Like professing feelings that I'm not even sure I believe in.

"And I'm not about to," I spit instead as I tear myself away and charge for the door, just to put some distance between us.

But even when the door slams shut and my eyes follow suit, all I can see is the look on her face.

All I have to do is ask.

So why won't I?

11

DMITRI

Wren spends the first ten minutes of the drive with her head craned back, staring out the moonroof. After she's had her fill of the tinted sky, her neck swivels from side to side like an oscillating fan. And when even that goes still, her eyes dart around as though she's never seen the outside world before.

"Are you okay?" I'm not used to silences when they come from her.

"Sometimes, I feel... barely human."

My eyebrows pinch together. "What do you mean? Are you in pain?"

Her lips crack open a quarter-inch and ironic laughter bursts through her lips. I watch her mouth as she laughs—her lips are dry, chapped to all hell despite layer after layer of Vaseline and gloss. She can try to hide it all she wants, but I can still see the after-effects of her capture splayed across her body in a million subtle ways. Her skin is pale, her arms and legs ashy; she fidgets far more than she used to.

I plan on making him pay for all of it.

"Pain?" she echoes. "Pain is the one thing that constantly *reminds* you of your humanness."

I sigh. "Are we getting philosophical now? Because I'm not sure I have the energy."

She falls silent again.

And again, I feel like a top-shelf asshole. "Wren…"

She doesn't turn back to me, though I notice her flinch at the sound of her name. "I need to be able to talk to you, Dmitri," she sighs before I can figure out a way to apologize without actually apologizing. "I need to be able to tell you what I'm thinking and what I feel without worrying that it's going to turn into a fight."

I heave a sigh of my own. "You'll get no fight from me today."

"Today, sure," she whispers. "And what about tomorrow?"

I wish I were confident enough in myself to give her some reassurance. But the honest truth? I've never had to curb myself before. I've never had to compromise or listen or consider another person's thoughts or feelings. Elena never expected it of me. She never seemed to expect anything of me other than my mere presence—and even that was more of a gift than an expectation.

Bee's words filter into my consciousness. *How can any healthy relationship be so one-sided?* It's not a mirror I want to look into right now.

"I'm not in the habit of making promises for tomorrow."

She lets her forehead loll against the window. "Elena must have been a saint."

I swallow the jab on the tip of my tongue. I just promised not to fight her today and I intend to keep that promise, selfish though it might be. The cameras are waiting for us where we're going and I need to put on a show for the world.

"We'll be there soon. Stay close to me at all times."

"Are you going to tell me why we're *really* doing this?" she asks, her breath fogging the glass.

"I've heard Lamaze can be very beneficial to new parents."

She snorts. More fog. Little puffs on the window, physical proof of how little she trusts me. "That's a great line. Now, how about the truth?"

"How about you just trust me?"

"Sorry, I'm not in the habit of blind trust. You want me to trust you? You're gonna have to tell me what you're playing at."

We round the corner and the Lamaze studio comes into view. I park in front, get out of the car first, and walk around to Wren's door. Already, I can spy two photographers with their cameras poised at the ready, but I pretend I don't see them. It's not until the moment Wren steps out onto the pavement that the flashes start to go off.

"What the…?" She gapes over at the small throng of photographers that are starting to amass. Then those huge eyes land on me, wide with alarm. "Dmitri…"

It feels good hearing her say my name in that way—like she's looking to me to fix something. Looking to me for protection.

"Don't worry," I assure her. "Just ignore them."

The shock on her face dissolves into suspicion. I throw an arm around her waist and steer her towards the tinted glass door. Just before we disappear underneath the frame, she looks back over her shoulder. There's a chaos of flashes and then I close the door.

As soon as we're inside, Wren whips around in the subtly perfumed corridor and glares up at me. "Explain yourself."

I arch an eyebrow. "What do you mean?"

"You're all about anonymity. If those photographers were out there, it's because you *want* them to be. Am I right?"

It's moments like these that I get why my father valued empty-headed women. The smart ones notice too much. And they ask too many questions when they do.

"You're… not wrong."

"This whole time, I've been your dirty little secret—and now, you want me exposed?"

My fists clench at my side. "Not *exposed*; I want you shielded," I growl. "Right now, everyone thinks that you're Cian's captive—"

"—which I was—"

"—and I need to make sure they know that you're safe and under my protection."

"You just don't want your enemies to think you can't protect me."

I see movement through the second set of glass doors that lead deeper into the studio. "This is a conversation for another time, Wren."

"I'm just a pawn in your game, aren't I?" I almost wish she said it angrily, but instead, the words wilt and die on their way past her lips.

Not anger, but sadness.

Not rage, but resignation.

"This isn't just about you and me, Wren—"

"Of course not! This is about your precious freaking Bratva. This is about your *reputation*. That's what's most important to you. Everyone else is either a pawn or an obstacle, and you move us around however you please."

She doesn't give me a chance to respond before she pivots hard on her heel and storms into the Lamaze studio with her back arched straight.

The class, predictably, is a nightmare. It's amusing that I thought it could be anything different. The instructor coaches us and a small handful of other expectant parents through poses, breathing, trust exercises.

But even when Wren is nestled between my legs, her back flush to my stomach, I can feel her radiating the exact opposite of trust. It's fear, doubt, uncertainty beaded up in every drop of sweat wicked from her to me.

My dick doesn't know about any of that, obviously. It just feels her near me and it *wants*. Truth be told, it's not the only part of me that wants Wren closer and closer and closer still.

There's another part—a real human would call it a "heart," though I'm not sure I even have one of those—is begging for the exact same thing.

Let her close.

Keep her close.

Safe, not caged.

Protected, not imprisoned.

But those are such delicate lines. I've spent my whole life stepping right over those as I please. She's determined to make me mind my footsteps.

How can I, though? It's my world in my arms right here. Wren and my child inside of her… every fucking thing that matters is encased in the circle of my touch. I want so badly to lock them there forever.

But I'm learning more and more every day that, when it comes to Wren…

What I want is rarely what's best.

12

WREN

"Is it *true*?"

I recognize that voice. It's Syrah's *I-can't-believe-you-kept-this-from-me* voice. It's her *I-thought-we-were-friends* voice. Except that, for the first time in our friendship, it's directed at me.

"Sy—"

"Is it true, Wren?" she interrupts. "Is Bee really dead? Or is that just tabloid bullshit to distract from the fact that you're apparently fucking her fiancé?"

My heartbeat is so loud that I can barely hear her. I'm lodged between two horrible truths—my only real friend knows I've been lying to her, and Bee is in fact dead.

"I... I can explain."

"Famous last words, huh?" The words are clipped at first, but then her voice softens. "Okay, fuck, fine. I suppose I should let you explain."

"Bee's dead." I cringe as soon as I say it—two little words shouldn't hurt so bad.

Syrah sucks in a breath. "I was sure that was a lie," she murmurs. I try to launch into a legitimate explanation, but instead, I get caught up in a sob. On the other side of the call, I hear Syrah's breathing ratchet up a couple of notches. "Shit, Wren, I'm so sorry. I know you two were close."

"W-we… were…"

"But, like, *how*?" she gasps. "She was so close to her wedding day. She was so happy, so full of life. I just… I can't believe it."

"Yeah." I sniffle. "That makes two of us."

There's a poised moment of silence. "This is a lot more complicated than I realize, isn't it?"

I barely resist snorting. *Everything* is complicated. "I'm so sorry, Sy. I can't tell you everything. I wish I could, I just… can't."

"Tell me this: are you in danger?"

I shake my head, even though she obviously can't see. "I'm safe. Dmitri's protecting me."

"So it's true. Like, the rumors, I mean. About him being involved with shady people."

Ah, how to explain to your best friend that Dmitri is the literal *king* of the shady people? "I trust him. That's all you need to know right now."

I can almost see her: an arched eyebrow, probably chewing her bottom lip to ribbons. "And… what's going on between the two of you?"

Rip off the Band-Aid, Wren. Only way to do it. "Okay, so, I'm gonna tell you something, but you have to promise not to freak out."

"Oh, my—you're a regular soap star right now, girl."

Miserable laughter bubbles through my nose. "Trust me; I'm aware. What I'm about to tell you will definitely cement that title."

"Go on then. Let's hear it."

"There was a mix-up at the fertility clinic. When they inseminated me, it wasn't with Rose and Jared's sample."

A long pause follows. I just wait for her brain to process. "Uh, so what you're saying is, you're *not* carrying Rose and Jared's baby?"

"No. The baby's mine."

"And the father?"

"I'll give you one guess."

She's gonna get it in three, two, one... "Fuuuck!"

I smile tiredly. "Bingo."

"Fuuuck me!"

"Actually, I was the one who was fucked," I mumble with another crazed-sounding laugh.

"Forgive me for continuing to pry, but do you by chance happen to mean that literally?"

I cringe yet again because it's true. I have only myself to blame for getting cornered into the second half of the story before we've even finished wading through the first. "Well..."

"Oh my God, so the tabloids have it right?" Syrah shrieks. "You *are* with Dmitri?"

"Tabloids?" I gawk into the phone. "What are you—" I break off to do some too-little, too-late processing of my own: those photographers at Lamaze the other day weren't just there for decoration. They served some purpose in the game that Dmitri is playing. "Is that how you found out about Bee?"

"It's a mess out there," Syrah rushes to explain. "Everyone's saying different things. Some say that Beatrice Zanetti called off the wedding and fled the country to escape her 'arranged marriage' with Dmitri. Others are claiming that she got killed in some sort of family dispute. There's even one that says Dmitri killed her himself in a fit of rage. Is…" She takes a breath to steady herself. "Is any of that true?"

"Beatrice *is* dead," I croak. "And technically, her marriage to Dmitri was arranged." When Sy starts to balk again, I jump in to add, "I know it's weird. But Bee agreed to the marriage. She and Dmitri are…" I swallow hard. "They were best friends. It was meant to be a marriage of convenience."

"But *why*?"

"Because her father expected them to marry. Because then Dmitri and Bee would have inherited her family's fortune and influence. But mostly, because Dmitri would have let Bee live her truth, which her father would never have allowed."

"What does that mean, 'live her truth'? What truth?"

I look around my room, wondering if the walls have ears. I'm not sure I should be telling Syrah so much. But weirdly, it helps to share the fragmented, convoluted story gushing around in my head. Even if it's not the whole story. "She was gay, Sy."

Her breath whistles softly. "I had a feeling."

"Really?"

"I mean, I didn't think too hard about it, if I'm being honest. She was engaged to a man, ya know, and a smoking hot one at that. So it was just a feeling. I didn't really question it."

"Yeah, neither did I."

"Until...?"

"Until I walked in on her one night doing the dirty with some girl she met at a club."

"*Damn*. This just gets juicier and juicier."

"You can't repeat any of this to anyone else, okay?" I press adamantly. "Promise me."

"Consider me Pandora. I'm putting the secret in my box and locking it tight."

"Pandora let all the deadliest sins *out* of the box."

"Oh, shit, I knew I had that wrong. Scratch that. I'm not Pandora and there's no box. I'll keep my mouth shut. I promise. One last question, though."

I sigh and slump back. "You might as well."

She chuckles softly. "How are *you* doing?"

I have to take a breath before I can even think of answering that one. "I have no idea," I admit. "It's been a surreal few weeks. I really miss her."

"So just to be clear... it wasn't bed rest you were on these past few weeks?"

So complicated. I've told so many lies and half-truths that I barely remember what's real and what's not anymore. "Partly, but not wholly." I whimper miserably. "I promise you that, one day, I'll explain the whole story."

"I can be patient when I have to be."

"Love you, Sy."

"Love you, Wen-Wen."

Laughing, my nose scrunches automatically with distaste. "You know I hate that nickname."

"It never fails to make you laugh, though. And if you ask me, laughs are in short supply these days. Take 'em where you can get 'em."

She's right about that. We move onto lighter topics and I laugh until the moment I hang up. But once I do, it takes only a few moments for that sense of ease to leave my chest. I miss Syrah, but I can't really spend time with her. I miss Rose and Bee, but I will never again be able to spend any time with them ever again.

There is one person I *could* spend time with. Problem is—I shouldn't.

But Syrah's given me a new reason to seek him out. So I step out into the hallway and stand poised between our shared wall, wondering if he's on the other side of his door or if he's spending the day at the office.

Egorov Industries seems like another lifetime ago to me now. A different Wren. A Wren with a flat stomach and an untainted view of the sister she idolized.

I shove aside the melancholy and head down the hall and make a right when I hear the click of a door being pulled open.

I turn left to see Aleksandr appear. "Hey, is your brother there?"

"Oh, is he ever. The sourpuss is ensconced behind his desk like the Lord of the Pompous Assholes that he is." Aleks throws a mischievous smile into the room and holds the door open for me. "He's all yours."

"Thanks."

In my head, I add silently, *If that were true, none of this would be happening.*

13

WREN

I'm walking through the door when I hear a loud thud from the upstairs penthouse. Aleks's cough feels almost like it was intentionally timed to try to cover up the sound.

I stop short in the threshold of the door. "What was that?"

The answer comes from Dmitri, who rises smoothly and beckons me into his office. "I'm having some renovations done on the penthouse. Just the construction workers fucking up my instructions."

His explanation is plausible enough—so why is it that Aleks looks away as though there's something to hide? I try not to give in to suspicion. I have enough to deal with without adding additional mysteries to my plate.

The door clicks shut behind me and I step into Dmitri's office. "How are you feeling?" he asks in an emotionless rumble.

I square my jaw. "Confused. Frustrated. Blindsided."

"So physically fine then?"

"Why on earth would you arrange for those tabloid hacks to photograph us at the Lamaze class? What purpose did that serve?"

He fixes me with a mildly curious gaze. "Did you come across one of their stories?"

"I don't read that trash. But Syrah does."

"Ah."

"That's all you have to say? 'Ah'?"

He steeples his fingers together and sits back in his chair, jaw clenched every bit as tight as mine. "I need to keep them guessing, Wren. If my enemies are confused, it makes it harder for them to come to me. At *us*."

Frowning, I venture forward. His desk is still between us and that gives me some security. Probably of the false variety. "Your enemies... You're referring to Cian? Or Vittorio?"

"Both. Others. All of them."

I realize I'm angry at the same time that I realize that Dmitri's not the one I'm angry at. "Vittorio really didn't come to her funeral?"

Dmitri's teeth mash together. "It was better he didn't. The fucker didn't love Bee, didn't mourn Bee. He didn't deserve to be at her funeral."

My head droops like a dying flower. "*I* should have been there."

My eyes stay downcast toward the carpet, but I can feel Dmitri get up and walk towards me. His presence, as always, engulfs me without him having to lift a finger. Even now, like always, I'm still not sure whether I want to lose myself in it or run screaming from it.

"She wouldn't have wanted you crying over her body, Wren. She would have wanted us to get drunk and swap stupid stories about her."

The smile breaks through my unshed tears. "Then I would have cried just to spite her."

His fingers graze across my cheek, so damn gently, and yet he leaves a trail of heat behind. "Why don't you sit down?"

I want to—but I also don't want to move out from underneath his touch. It feels good, this dangerous proximity. Except when I lift my eyes, his face is blurry for a second.

"Wren?"

He grabs me as I tumble forward. I try to straighten up but that only causes me to trip harder. "S-sorry," I say quickly. "I don't know what happened…"

"Sit down," he orders firmly. "Are you feeling light-headed?"

"A little…"

I feel like an idiot as he leads me to a chair and sits me down like I'm a child. All of a sudden, I'm intensely aware of my massive stomach, my bloated calves, my sallow skin and puffy eyes.

"Sorry," I say again and again. "I'm sorry."

"Why do you keep apologizing? You're pregnant and stressed. I can't believe you've lasted as long as you have. Stay here—I'm going to get you something to drink."

Before I can thank him, he's off towards the bathroom. Only then do I realize that he's sat me down behind his desk. In his intimidating, brown leather swivel chair. I drag my gaze up and find myself staring at the burning bright light coming off his open computer screen. When I realize what's on the display, my jaw drops.

Are those *cribs*?

I blink, but it doesn't go away. I am in fact staring at a browser featuring row after row of baby crib options. I can't help but lean in and peer closer. Some of the options have been favorited.

I jump in place and damn near scream when I hear a pointed *"ahem."* I can't exactly pretend I haven't been nosing through his computer so I don't even try.

"You were crib-shopping." It's halfway between a tease and an accusation.

"Considering our son will need one soon, yes, I was." His face twists into a scowl. "What is so funny about that?"

I shrug, trying to fight a smile. "I guess—" I glance back towards the screen. "—I just expected something more... menacing to be on the screen of the most notorious Bratva don in the city." I shrug. *"How-to-lose-an-enemy-in-ten-days* kinda stuff, ya know? *Ways to dissolve body parts in acid.* That kind of thing."

His lips twitch, the closest he'll get to laughing. "Sorry to disappoint."

"On the contrary, I'm not disappointed at all." I take the water he's offering from his hands. "I think it's nice that you care about this stuff."

"This is our son we're talking about."

Ugh.

Swoon.

I clear my throat before I say, do, or reveal something incredibly stupid. "So, er, uh, what else have you been looking up?"

He drags up another chair beside me. Close enough that our hands bump against one another when he sits down. I wonder if he's hard right now, like he was at the Lamaze class. The class was over an hour long and by the end of it, I had a blossoming bruise on my right hip from where his erection was digging into me.

As far as problems go, it's not a bad one to have—unless that erection belongs to the man who killed your sister. I'm annoying myself with how repetitive I am, but it's only because I need the constant reminder on a loop in the back of my head to keep myself from getting carried away.

It'd be too easy to succumb to the tide of feelings and fantasies. These walls can only keep Dmitri-induced mania out for so long.

And the clock on that is ticking.

"You can see for yourself," Dmitri replies, pulling up another page.

"Oh my God… You have a Pinterest?!" I gawk before bursting into laughter.

He fixes me with an annoyed glance. "What's so funny about that?"

"Big, bad Dmitri Egorov has a Pinterest page that's filled with strollers and diaper dispensers and soothers with little soft toy animals hanging off the ends. I'm speechless."

"Those soothers came highly recommended," he says with a stony expression. "The bloggers love them."

"You read the blogs, too? Stop. I can only take so much."

"I like to be prepared."

Again, his lips twitch, so close to a smile. Mine do the same before I turn away to hide it. "Do I get a say in any of this?"

"Of course. Veto anything you like."

I do a double take. "Really?"

"You are his mother." His voice is gentle now, stripped of the icy crackle it had earlier. "Whenever you're ready, we can go through this board and finish the nursery together."

"I…" I swallow hard and try again. "Yeah. I'd like that."

Then I make the extremely stupid mistake of looking right at him. Those deep gray eyes hold hues of blue and hazel under the soft warm lights. I can hear the loyal sister in me yelling, *Mayday, mayday! Look away, you horny bitch!*

But another part of me is pushing me toward a fresh start. Toward the possibility of a happy future. My vagina is inclined to agree.

"Wren." Dmitri's eyes are locked on me as intensely as mine are on him. All it would take is for one of us to lean in and that'd be that. Game over. Lights out. "I have something important to tell you."

I gulp. "Okay…?"

His face looks as murderous as I've ever seen it as he leans ninety-nine percent of the way into kissing me and says, "If you tell anyone about my Pinterest page… I'll kill you."

Both of us burst out laughing at the same time. We laugh until our cheeks hurt, until our sides burn, until the good kinds of tears pour down our faces—well, my face, not his.

Dmitri and I are not meant to be—I know that. Our pasts conspired against us long before we'd even met. There's no hope for a happy ending here. Maybe our son is the only happy ending we can ever hope to have.

But maybe, just maybe…

That'll be enough.

14

WREN

I haven't been able to go into the nursery yet.

I'm not sure why. Maybe it's the pressure of impending motherhood. Maybe it's the dozens of little decisions I'm going to have to make with my unreachable, unknowable baby daddy. Maybe it's the initials-carved swing that feels like a looking glass into my past.

So instead, I lie in bed, half-asleep, trying to remember things that I'd clearly missed when Rose and Jared were alive. It's odd, the moments that your memory pulls up when you force it to remember. Hard to decipher what's real and what's just a scrap of a dream.

My eyes flicker open, just long enough to see that I'm in my bedroom with the blinds drawn. Light is creeping into the room from behind the curtains but it's the silver glow of moonlight. Subtle and non-invasive. Which means sleep has abandoned me halfway through the night once again.

I sigh and let my head loll back on the pillow.

I remember that Rose's last miscarriage was a bad one. I remember that in particular because it was the first time that Jared seemed to take the loss as badly as Rose. He stopped eating. He stopped smiling. There were nights he didn't come home.

I went over to Rose's place, a few days after she told me she'd miscarried again. She wasn't expecting me and I had the feeling when she opened the door that she was disappointed to see me.

"Everything okay?"

Anger flickered across her eyes. *"I just lost another child. So, no. Not great."*

I flinched back. *"Shit, Rose. That's obviously not what I meant."*

She sighed heavily. *"I'm sorry. I'm being a bitch."*

"You're allowed. Be as bitchy as you want. I can take it." The fact that she still hadn't let me into the apartment made my hands itch. I felt awkward and out of place, fidgeting on her doorstep.

"I just thought you were Jared," she explained.

"He's not home yet?"

She looked away from me and gestured me into the apartment. *"He might have to cover extra shifts for Gavin. Probably won't get home 'til late."* She sounded nervous, uncertain. I just figured it was because she didn't want to be alone.

"I can spend the night with you," I offered.

She'd never turned me down so quickly or so bluntly. *"No thanks. I'd rather be alone."*

It was an odd reaction. Even in our darkest moments, even in our saddest, neither one of us ever chose to be alone when we could be with each other. But that could be explained, right? I justified her brusqueness as extreme grief. I'd been hoping, even then, that she'd finally decided to give up. To let it go, because the price was obviously too damn high.

She was losing parts of herself. Every miscarriage robbed her of something.

I worried that, one day, she'd have no more parts left to give.

"Are you sure you want to be alone right now?"

My eyes flicker open as the rest of the memory hacks its way into my subconsciousness. I can see Rose standing in front of my bed, her jaw made of granite and her expression made of steel as she snapped at me, *"Yes, I want to be alone. I just said I wanted to be alone. Jesus Christ, Wren— we can't be joined at the hip our entire lives. I'm married. I have my own family. It's time you found yours and let me live my life in peace!"*

There's nothing like a long-repressed, traumatic memory to wake you up at night. Personally, I'd have preferred a bucket of ice-cold water.

I blink a couple of times and run my hands over my face, just to make sure I'm really awake. As sleep starts to fade, the memory becomes clearer, undeniable.

Yes, it really happened.

Yes, Rose had really said that to me.

And yes, it really fucking hurt.

"Call me if you need anything." That's all I said before I left her that night.

I cried as I walked back to my apartment, which happened to be only a stone's throw away. For the first time ever, I felt embarrassed by that. *Can't be joined at the hip our entire lives.*

"God," I whisper into my palms. It hurts like it just happened.

I never understood why she said what she'd said to me that night. Especially because she called two days later and asked me out to lunch. She sounded like her old self when she told me she missed me and she'd been craving sushi and that she was buying.

Except the lunch never happened.

Because the next time I saw Rose, she was lying on a metal tray like a slab of meat with a sterile blue cloth covering the length of her body. I was told I couldn't actually see her—the body was unrecognizable, anyway.

That was what the graying, middle-aged cop said as he explained what had happened. *"Fire, you know. Car went boom."* He was nice, sympathetic; he took his time when he broke the news to me. I guess I was just distracted by the fact that he looked a little like my dad. Or at least, what my dad looked like fifteen years ago.

Thud.

Bang.

I drop my hands from my face as I jerk in place and raise my eyes to the ceiling. There's no chance that Dmitri's construction crew are still up there working. What would be the point of getting them to work through the night?

Thud. Bang.

Dust falls from the rafters, shaken loose by either ghosts or contractors punching in some extreme overtime.

"Ghosts," I whisper decisively to myself. "The lack of sleep is getting to you."

I force myself out of bed, my mind still throwing up possibilities like darts at a dartboard. Maybe Dmitri has a woman up there. Maybe he met someone while I was in captivity. Maybe he moved her in there and he just didn't want to tell me yet.

Every suggestion makes my stomach churn harder.

I shuffle to the door in the corner. It's supposed to connect straight to the nursery. I've never used it before—but then, I've never needed to. Right now feels like as good a time as any. Witching hours are good for doing things you'd never do in the light of day.

The door is huge and bulky, but it barely makes a sound when I shove it open. That was probably Dmitri's doing. I can see him standing over some hapless construction worker, supervising application of oil to the joints.

I don't want it to make a fucking sound, he'd snarl. *If it wakes up my family even once, I'll know who to blame.*

Speaking of Dmitri…

To my surprise, he's here. He's standing at the opposite corner of the nursery with his back to me, wearing black briefs that cling to his sculpted ass and nothing else. The moonlight makes his skin glow silver.

It takes a moment for my eyes to adjust, but when they do, I see that he's painting. It's the color we chose yesterday from a catalog. Azure blue for the back wall, because I wanted my baby to be surrounded by nature's colors. He'd told me that he'd get a team in to paint the wall as soon as he could.

Except there's no team. There's just him. A father painting his son's nursery in the dead of the night.

Did my father ever do anything like that for his daughters? Had he painted murals on our walls? Built us rocking chairs? Did he give a fraction as much of a damn about our births as Dmitri does about our son's?

The simple answer is no. No, he had not. He hadn't even wanted to be in the delivery room with our mother when she gave birth to us. I vaguely remember Mom telling our neighbors about it in that jokey-serious way you share unhappy stories so you don't make other people feel uncomfortable about them.

The flip side of that coin was my ex. William spared no expense where his children were concerned. He used to tell me that he had a special coordinator when he was designing his children's nurseries. He'd spent fifty grand on each one without batting an eye.

But money meant nothing to him. Add a zero, take one away—who gives a shit? He gave it freely because it wasn't a symbol of anything at all.

Which is why, seeing Dmitri standing there, his bicep rippling as he pulls the roller brush down horizontally, makes my eyes damp with tears. He could be paying someone else to do this for him. But he's here, doing it himself. Because he wants to create something beautiful for our child.

That, to me, is a *real* father.

The kind that doesn't need perfect as long as it's personal.

Yes, he is capable of terrible things. But he is capable of beautiful things, too.

This baby in my belly for one.

Stroke after stroke after careful, thoughtful stroke of azure blue paint, for another.

I retreat backwards through the doorway and shut the door as softly as I can. I creep back to my bed, nestle under the covers, and try to find a comfortable position. But after several minutes, it's painfully clear that I'm not going to be comfortable until I get rid of some of this pent-up energy rattling around in my head.

And in other parts of my body that shall remain nameless.

Biting my tongue, I push up the slip I'm wearing and slide my fingers into my panties. I'm wet already. Only the slightest touch forces a moan from my lips.

I bite the inside of my cheek. He's right next door. I can't afford to put on a show, especially considering *he's* the star of it.

So taking extra pains to be as silent as possible, I keep touching myself. Because apparently, I'm done trying to deny my attraction to him. I'm done pretending that the fact that he murdered my sister has destroyed my feelings for him.

I'm pretty sure I'll regret this tomorrow, but for right now, I close my eyes and think about those beautiful granite muscles applying *different* kinds of stroke, after stroke, after stroke.

He'd have to fuck me from behind, though; I'm too big to be taken any other way. The moment I think about being on all fours in front of him, more desire pools between my thighs. I sigh deeply, clinging onto that feeling as I rub my fingers over my clit.

Pleasure crowds out the last vestiges of guilt. All the soreness and fatigue that clings to my bones evaporates into thin air. It's nice to know that, underneath all the pain I've endured these past few months, I'm still me.

As I increase pressure on my clit, rubbing harder in fast circles, I imagine Dmitri lying over me, his cock taking the place of my fingers. His hard chest pressed against mine. Those perfect eyes fixed on me like they can see every thought that sears through my mind.

It builds all at once and I'm not prepared for the force of pleasure that swells up inside me. Which is why I cry out.

Loudly.

Way, way too loudly.

I clamp down on my tongue immediately after, but I know without having to look that it's too late. I pull my hand out of my soaking panties and twist to the side, hiding my face against a pillow. My breathing is heavy and my skin is coated with sweat. I count the seconds… but everything is quiet.

Quiet.

Quiet.

And then…

I feel warm air on the side of my face. His breath smells of whisky. "Wren," he whispers softly.

Despite my best intentions, I turn and meet his gaze. He's closer than I expected. I freeze in place, wondering if I'll have to admit what I'd just done. I'm in no fit state to think up lies. If he asks, the truth is gonna spill out of me.

Yes, I was masturbating to fantasies of you.

No, I don't regret it.

But my God, how I wish I did.

"Was it a bad dream?"

Ah, sweet relief. He's given me an out and I reach for it clumsily. I nod a few too many times before biting down on my tongue again.

"Are you okay?"

I nod again, wishing he would touch me. Hoping that he'll kiss me. Somehow, it feels like less of a betrayal if *he* makes the first move. If he does it, I'm just helpless to do anything but go along with it, right?

We all know that's a lie. But that's okay. It's a pretty one. A comforting one. And pretty comforts are what I need most of all right now.

"You have no idea what you do to me," he whispers.

The thud of my heartbeat almost drowns out the words. But I feel them take root inside me. They resonate deeply. And two desperate, eager little words keep throbbing on the tip of my tongue like a pulse.

Kiss me...

For a moment, I think he hears it.

I think he'll do it.

Then he blinks, breaking the spellbinding eye contact. The heat of his breath disappears. His gaze rips away from mine. He slips back to the nursery and I don't even have the closure of hearing the door click shut.

"Dmitri," I murmur to myself, "you have no idea what you do to me, either…"

15

WREN

"Well, Wren, I couldn't be happier. Everything looks great."

Dr. Liza scribbles something onto her clipboard and turns back to her monitor. She's whistling a jaunty tune, pleased as punch with all the results of today's checkup.

I, on the other hand, barely manage to muster up a nod.

Ever since the midnight not-quite-encounter with Dmitri in the nursery, I've been a hazy mess of memories and fantasies. Carrying on a normal conversation takes everything I've got in me.

"Wren, you okay?"

Dmitri leaves his position by the window and strides over to the examination table I've been splayed across for the entirety of the appointment. I try to sit up a little, but instead, I just slide helplessly down on the table like a beached whale.

"Fine," I reply, but it comes out all croaky.

"Are you sure?" His eyebrows are hitting the roof of his forehead. "You seem like you're… far away."

As Dr. Liza excuses herself and steps out of the room, I swallow hard, trying to articulate what I'm feeling. I find myself producing weird, garbled sounds, not words.

"Hey, hey," Dmitri croons. "It's okay. I know. This is overwhelming."

"I'm sorry," I blurt. "I don't know why I'm being such a spaz. I've had almost ten months to prepare for this."

"You were preparing to have a baby that you would hand over to your sister and brother-in-law." It amazes me how he can bring them up so casually. "You were prepared to be an aunt, not a mother."

Panic. That's what I'm feeling. I shake my head again and again. "I'm not ready. I'm not ready. I'm—"

"Of course you are."

I let out a harsh, unflattering laugh. "You're not really that confident."

"I am." Again, he leaves no room for insincerity. "You're the most capable woman I've ever met, Wren Turner. I have no doubt that you'll make an exceptional mother."

I squirm in place. "That's a lot of pressure."

"And you're not alone, you know. You have me."

I know he doesn't mean that in a romantic way, but it certainly sounds like it. Or maybe I'm just hearing what I want to hear. "You have your own life."

"My life will revolve around my son. My family. My only purpose is to *protect* the two of you."

I'm vulnerable right now and it's making me careless. *What about when you meet someone else? What then?* The question is on the tip of my tongue before I pull it back. Worst case, I sound jealous. Best case, I sound needy, clingy, desperate.

Neither one is a good look.

But then, I haven't been rocking the best looks lately. Nervous as I am about having this baby, I'm also very, very ready to not be pregnant anymore. I'm ready to do away with my massive stomach and midnight bladder cramps and spine pain at all hours like I'm being sniped from a distance.

"So…" Dr. Liza walks back into the room with a fresh container of vitamins for me. "Shall we talk about the delivery?"

"What about it?"

She winks and gives my knee a friendly little pat. "I thought we could discuss options. The baby could come any day now and we should have a plan in place."

"Um… push the baby out?"

Laughing pleasantly, she takes a seat on her stool and crosses her legs. "Some women opt for C-sections in advance. But personally, I don't recommend going that route unless there's a medical reason for one. You're young and healthy; I see no reason why you shouldn't have a natural labor—if that's what you want, of course."

"I want to go the natural route. It's what Rose and I always discussed." I cringe instantly and somehow, my eyes find Dmitri's.

"Is it what *you* want?" he asks.

I think about that for a moment. "I... want to have this baby naturally. But... I'm worried about doing it without an epidural."

"Then you don't have to," Dr. Liza assures me. "I can—"

"It's just—" My eyes dart between her and Dmitri. "—Rose wanted me to have the baby drug-free."

I'm expecting some anger from Dmitri. But he doesn't give anything away as he steps a little closer to me. "Wren, when you discussed those things with Rose, you were having *her* baby. But this is *your* baby, *your* labor, *your* delivery plan. You get to choose."

I don't know why, but that's stressing me out. "What do you think I should do?"

"Whatever you're comfortable with."

My eyes narrow. "Not helpful."

His fingers brush against my arm. "You're nervous about having the baby without any drugs?"

"Well, yeah, I'm no superwoman."

He opens his mouth, then snaps it shut at the last moment. "Dr. Liza can arrange an epidural for you if you want one. If you want to go all natural, then you can do that, too. I just don't want you to choose that route because you think you have to."

"I don't want to feel pain," I whisper in a small voice.

His jaw clenches. "Good. I don't like seeing you in pain."

His fingers twitch towards me, but he doesn't actually touch me. It feels as though he's been trying desperately to keep me at arm's length since I came back. The disappointing part is how successful he's been.

But I have his words from last night to fuel me whenever I find myself searching for reassurance. *You have no idea what you do to me.* My masochistic side is desperately hoping I hadn't dreamed that part.

"Pain's a part of life."

His eyes brighten dangerously. It makes me afraid I've said something to piss him off. Then he leans in, close enough that I can see the flecks of gold in his gray eyes. "Not if I have anything to say about it."

I've never felt this before. This sense of security, of safety. Ironic, considering how much pain I've endured purely because I fell into Dmitri's world. But it's not really about how much he's capable of protecting me—it's about the fact that he *wants* to.

No one has ever wanted that responsibility before.

Until him.

16

DMITRI

"Your *vors* are here."

Aleks's voice has an anxious edge to it. Or maybe I'm projecting because I'd rather be at home with Wren than handling business at Egorov Industries. "All of them?"

He nods. "All of them. Including Gennady and Ira."

Scowling, I leave my papers on the desk and get to my feet. "I'm shocked that *mudak* hasn't jumped ship yet."

"The underworld doesn't take kindly to traitors."

"No, but it certainly makes use of them."

He pulls his eyebrows together. "I think you're getting paranoid, man."

"'Paranoid'? We have two fucking mafias on our backs and you're calling me *paranoid*?"

Sighing, he scrubs his face clean. "It's one thing to be suspicious of your enemies. It's a totally different story to be suspicious of your friends."

"They're not my friends; they're my fucking *employees*," I retort. "And they're talking entirely too loudly for my liking."

His frown returns as he goes still. "What does that mean?"

"Locksmith," I say shortly; our hacker's name is all the explanation required. "Apparently, some of my men have been disgruntled with the action—or lack thereof—in the last few weeks. Money's been moved from accounts. It seems not all my men think I'm going to win this war."

"You haven't exactly kept them in the loop," Aleks suggests.

My fists clench. "I don't have to tell them a goddamn thing if I don't want to. I'm the *pakhan*; they swore allegiance to follow without question."

He holds up his hands in self-defense. "I'm just keeping you informed. That's my job."

I sweep past him and out of my office. My new assistant is a sour-faced, bottle-dyed redhead in her mid-forties. She came highly recommended and, so far, she's proven to be halfway competent. She's also smart enough not to say a word as I storm past.

But that doesn't change the fact that she's not Wren.

I check my phone as I step into the elevator and hit the special access button that will take us to the bowels of Egorov Industries. My screen is empty. No calls or messages from Wren all day. She was sleeping this morning when I left, so I sent her a text message letting her know I'd be at work, to call if she needed anything. Her answering text had been short and succinct.

Thanks but I'll be fine.

I'll be fine. It's annoying how much that bothers me. The fact that she doesn't really need me. It makes me wonder if part of my attraction to Elena was fueled by this weird god complex. It served my ego to have Elena look at me as though I was the center of her universe.

Wren doesn't look at me as though I'm the center of anything.

More often than not, she looks at me as though I'm a nightmare monster she wishes she could run from.

The elevator doors spit me out into the dark basement. The corridors are lit up with recessed light fixtures that do little to ward away the oppressive darkness. It looks like exactly what it is: a playground for death and pain. I hate to play into sinister stereotypes, but if this part of the building is ever discovered, it needs to look like an abandoned plan for a parking lot.

I find my men in the furthest reaches of the basement. When I walk up, the ones who are sitting rise quickly to their feet.

"Gentlemen," I greet.

It's returned by a chorus of greetings, but that doesn't mean I don't notice the ones that mumble along, eyes wavering skittishly from side to side.

Fucking Gennady.

He stands lost in the center of the group, as per usual. That's by design: he's not a man who likes to stand out. *Observe and listen without ever catching anyone's attention* is how he operates. His looks work for him in that regard—boring and forgettable. There is a place in my world for men with that kind of skill set.

Right now, though, I'm having a hard time remembering why I need Gennady at all.

"*Pakhan* Egorov," Pasha says with a smile. "It's been a while since we had a meeting."

"Some would say too long," Gennady adds. His smile is fixed. It looks like he's screwed it on.

"You included, Gennady?"

His smile grows wider and much less natural. "I've been trying to talk to you for over a week now. I was always told you were too busy."

"Because I *was* busy. Do you assume that what you had to say was more important than what I had to do?"

The atmosphere has shifted dangerously. The smiles have dropped by half and all the men have tensed. Gennady seems to realize this, too, because the coward in him starts to take over. "I-I didn't mean to offend, Dmitr—"

"You will address me as *Pakhan* Egorov," I growl. "Especially since it seems you need to be reminded of who I am."

Gennady's mouth snaps shut. His beady eyes lower to the ground, but only for a second. I can understand his conundrum—were I in his place, I wouldn't want to piss off the top dog. But I also wouldn't want to look weak in front of my brothers.

"Forgive me, sir." The words come out jagged and reluctant, like each one costs him dearly. "I simply wanted to convey that there are rumors circulating—dangerous ones."

"If you hear rumors, shut them down."

"We don't know ourselves what's true and what's not. We've been in the field trying to do damage control while you've been locked away with your new toy."

He didn't mean to say so much. His nostrils flare with panic the moment the silence settles. The men closest to him inch away, sensing what's coming next.

Apparently, so does Aleks, because he takes a step to my right. "Brother…"

"Wren Turner is no toy," I say politely. "She holds the future of this Bratva."

Gennady glowers at me. It seems I've succeeded in making him think that there won't be consequences for his loose tongue and lack of respect. "You said that once about the Italian princess. Now, she's six feet under and you expect us to believe that some nobody slut is the future of—"

I swear I meant to keep him talking a little longer. I meant to make it clear that my judgment would only ever come after careful thought and deliberation. Anger is not always the trigger. But the way he talks about Wren…

I'm not willing to just stand there and listen to him run her down to my face.

There are consequences for badmouthing my woman.

I pull the gun out so fast that Gennady doesn't even register the weapon until I pull the trigger. He's still talking when the gunshot rings out with a thundering report…

And then he drops dead, his sentence left forever unfinished.

I hear Aleks's muttered "Fuck" as I start scanning the faces of my men. Some look shell-shocked; others simply resigned. A few look like they've gotten an early birthday present. I stare down all of them. "Does anyone else have reservations about my leadership?"

"No, sir," several of them chime in at once.

The few who stay silent just nod warily, chancing glances down at Gennady's body. I understand my brother's trepidation. It's never good news when a *pakhan* culls one of his own. *Vors* are meant to be protected by the inner circle. If the king starts turning on his own court, then how can loyalty be expected?

But I'm not about to let fear stop me from protecting my family. The time has passed for careful action.

"Answers come to those who are patient," I declare. "And above all else, *loyal*." I let the word sit for a moment. "Beatrice Zanetti was never pregnant with my heir. It was Wren all along. Anyone who says a word against her is a dead man walking. Is that understood?"

All my *vors* slam their closed fists against their chests—a sign of obedience and fealty. It's an Old World gesture, brewed in blood, which is why it carries the weight it does.

"Can I count on you?" I ask them collectively.

They keep pounding their chests until they've created a chorus that reverberates off the walls of Egorov Industries' basement. I make sure my gaze sears through every single one of my men. I want them to know I'm in control.

That I'm watching.

I can't afford to close my eyes now.

17

DMITRI

I can hear Aleks shuffling around behind me as my *vors* file out of the room. All that's left of Gennady is a deep red stain on the cement floors. That's going to need a special clean-up crew before the floors are spotless again.

One thing about running a Bratva in the basement—the housekeeping never ends.

Ignoring my brother, I pick up my phone and call Locksmith. "Been a while since I got a call from you," the hacker's voice chirps in computer-modulated tones. "I was worried you'd forgotten about me."

Grinding my teeth together, I remind myself that Locksmith has an important role to play. Keeping them happy is tops on my priority list. "How could I, when you make so much fucking noise all the time?"

All I hear for a moment is faint, staticky chuckling. "I'm guessing you're not calling to ask about my workout regimen, so what can I do for you, oh blessed liege?"

"I need some target sourcing so I can interrupt the Irish cash flow. New ventures, something vulnerable and ripe."

"Getting antsy, are we?"

"It's time to cut them off at the legs. I'm not fucking around anymore."

"You really want to antagonize Cian at this stage? When the Italians are—"

"I made you my hacker," I interrupt coldly. "Not my *vor*. If I want lessons on strategy, I'll ask for it. Until then, do the job I hired you to do."

The inevitable snort comes, impatient and annoyed. "Very well. I will do your bidding like the lap dog I so clearly am to you. I'll have the info to you within the hour. Two, tops."

Rolling my eyes, I hang up and turn to find that Aleks is still pacing. Right over the spot where Gennady had his brains blown out.

When he hears me end the call, he meets my gaze and stops pacing. "Do you really think that was a good move? Slaughtering one of your own in front of everyone?"

"Do you really consider that a smart question to ask?" I lob back.

"I'm just saying—"

"He was a stone's throw from moving against me. I saw a problem and I took care of it." I stare down my brother until he looks away. "And I don't need anyone's permission to do it."

"No, not *permission*," Aleks acquiesces. "But what about *advice*? Your *vors* exist to temper your worst impulses and give you counsel. Do you think any of them are going to be willing to speak up now if you insist on killing the ones that do?"

"Don't be stupid," I spit. "He wasn't advising me; he was questioning me. There's a difference."

He sighs and wilts. "I know, I know. Fuck, I *know*. Gennady needed to be dealt with, but—"

"When did you become such a scared old woman?"

He bares his teeth at me. "Alienating your inner circle will end your reign sooner than you'd like, Dmitri."

"My reign is only just beginning, little brother. You think I'm worried about any one of those men? They're loyal—and the ones that aren't will die the same way that Gennady did. Consider today a lesson."

The fire goes out of Aleks eyes. His shoulders sink and he nods. "I get it. Message received. You don't need anything from me where the Bratva is concerned. But are you at least willing to take advice from your brother about a personal matter?"

I frown. I'm already wary. "Depends on what it is."

"When are you going to tell her everything?"

"'Everything'?" I almost want to laugh in his face. "Why the fuck does she even need to know everything. She's involved in none of it."

"Except that she was kidnapped by one of your mortal enemies and it's guaran-fucking-teed that they still have their sights set on her."

"They're not getting anywhere near her."

"That's what you said before. And then…"

He doesn't dare to finish that sentence, but he doesn't need to. Anger flickers in my gut like lit coals. "She's nine months pregnant, brother," I snap. "She doesn't need the stress."

"You really think learning the truth would stress her out?" he asks evenly. "In my opinion, I think it would go a long way in helping—"

"I'm playing the long game here. The fewer people who know the truth, the better. I don't want Wren compromised with information she's not capable of handling."

That, to my surprise, draws a laugh out of him. "That woman is capable of handling a fuck ton more than you give her credit for."

He's not wrong. But the idea of sharing my plans with her… my *secrets*… makes me shiver with discomfort. "I'm not in the habit of sharing sensitive Bratva information with outsiders. My own *vors* don't know the truth. You really think I should tell Wren?"

"Yes, and you know exactly why." He takes a deep, steadying breath. "Bee would want her to know. If she were here right now—"

"Except she's *not*, is she?" I snarl. "And even if she was, it wouldn't change a fucking thing. I make the rules, brother. I decide who knows what and when. Right now, Wren needs to focus on delivering that baby and nothing else. Is that understood?"

The vein in Aleks's forehead throbs. "Yes, sir."

"Good man. Go tie up Gennady's loose ends. I want everything clean before we hit the Irish."

I turn my back on him and stride back out into the shadows of the building's underbelly. I'm walking out into the sunlight again when my phone registers an incoming notification.

WREN: *Image*

I open it to find a picture of Wren's naked belly. *"Blyat',"* I mutter, coming to a stop when I realize why she sent it. If I zoom in, I can almost see the indent of a tiny little foot. It's fucking amazing.

Another message comes in while I'm still staring at the picture.

WREN: *he's been kicking all day and im exhausted. *crying-laughing emoji**

WREN: *And hungry.*

Without thinking twice about it, I return her text.

DMITRI: *Dinner it is. La Luna in thirty minutes. I'll have Pavel pick you up.*

WREN: *Can't say no to that :)*

I'm getting in my car when my phone pings again. I'm expecting another text from Wren, but it's Locksmith instead.

LOCKSMITH: *the Black Serpent. u r welcome. coordinates incoming.*

Grinding my teeth with satisfaction, I pull out my phone and text two of my most trusted *vors* with the information. I drive fast so that I can take care of this before I need to leave for La Luna.

When I pull up on the street next to The Black Serpent, a dingy bar near Wrigleyville, Pasha and Delph are already waiting out front.

Both approach my window. "How do you want it done?" Delph asks.

"As obviously as possible," I answer immediately. "I want the motherfuckers to know exactly who did it."

"Got it, boss. We'll take care of it."

I wave them off with a satisfied nod and then I start the drive to La Luna. I've scarcely put half a mile between myself and the boys before I hear the explosion. The orange rust of fire splinters into the sky and I catch the smoke spirals surging in my rear view mirror.

Death can be beautiful when it wants to be.

~

I'm a few minutes early to the restaurant. I pick the best table and wait for Wren, conscious of the curious stares cast in my direction. Pretty sure there's a few surreptitious photos taken of me, too.

Good—let them take their pictures. Let them gossip among themselves. Let word reach Vittorio and Cian if it has to.

I want the whole fucking world to know that Wren is *mine*.

She appears moments later, wrapped in a silk green dress that doesn't even bother to hide her baby bump. I can see that she's taken pains to try, though. I don't understand why she's quite so self-conscious. I've never seen a pregnant woman more radiant than she is.

I rise and pull out her chair for her. She slips into it nervously, her eyes darting around the restaurant. "This place is amazing."

I look around absentmindedly, noticing the aura for the first time. The tablecloths are striped in bold black and white lines. The chandeliers are bronze antiques and fresh white gardenias gleam in the centerpiece of every table.

"It tastes even better than it looks," I assure her as I take my seat.

"Yeah, I know."

Raising my eyebrows, I look at her questioningly. "You've been here before?"

She shrugs as though she'd rather not talk about it. "Um, yeah… William used to bring me here once in a while. They have a private room in the back. I used to think he was just being thoughtful and romantic. It was a while before I figured out that he just didn't want to be seen in public with me."

I tuck my hands under the table so she can't see that they're balled into fists.

"Sorry," she mumbles, her cheeks going from subtle pink to dark mauve. "I shouldn't have brought him up. I keep going down dark roads lately."

My first instinct is to agree with that sentiment. I don't even want to be reminded that she had a life before me. That she had other men in her life before me.

Ironic, given that I'm not sure what the fuck we are to each other right now. Reluctant co-parents, yes.

Beyond that…? Hell if I know.

"He was a part of your past," I manage to say, graciously enough.

Her smile is tentative and shy. "I used to pride myself on not being a cliché. And somehow, I ended up being the girl with daddy issues."

"Do you have any contact with your father?"

Her eyes bug out in alarm at the mere suggestion. "No. Nor do I want to." The answer slides off her tongue easily, but it comes too fast for me to trust. She seems to realize the same thing because she blushes and sighs. "I mean, the truth is... I pretend like I don't give a damn about him—but every once in a while, I do check up on him."

Her eyes flit from side to side like she's scared to let them settle on me. "Wren," I say softly, putting my hand over hers. She freezes, a startled exhale escaping her lips. "Go on. You can tell me things."

"Can I?" she asks shakily, hiding her self-consciousness behind a laugh. "That's news."

"Look at me."

"I'd rather not."

"Why?"

"Because whenever I look into your eyes, I end up saying and doing stuff I shouldn't." She cringes. "Like *that*, for example."

I suppress a weirdly proud grin. "Fine. Let's return to safer subjects then. What would *you* like to talk about?"

Her smile turns grateful. "The nursery," she rushes to fill in. "It looks beautiful, Dmitri. I can't believe you did all that yourself."

I shrug. "It wasn't all that much work."

"And the carved toy cabinet by the window… It must have cost a fortune."

"Not really. It was an old cupboard that I had restored before I started carving."

She stops short, her eyes going wide with disbelief. "I'm sorry—are you saying *you* did those carvings?"

I nod. "I like to tinker around with carpentry from time to time. It's cathartic."

She gapes at me, her mouth hanging open for a second. I have the urge to lean in and claim her lips, and it takes all my willpower to stay seated with my hands at my side.

"You're amazing," she breathes.

I chuckle. "Didn't realize you had a fetish for carpentry."

"I have a fetish for men who use their hands." The moment she says it, she flushes again. "Um, what I meant was… Oh, *God*. See? This is what I mean. I start babbling like an idiot."

"You're no idiot," I assure her softly.

"Agree to disagree." She removes her hands from her face and takes a deep breath. "Thanks for inviting me out for dinner. I was tired of sitting in the apartment all day long."

"It was my pleasure."

"But can I ask you a question?"

"Yes?"

"Is it my imagination or are people staring?"

I follow her gaze to the table adjacent to us. The older couple turn away pointedly and I have to resist the urge to roll my eyes. I turn back to Wren with an unconcerned expression. Of course they're staring—but despite what my brother thinks, she doesn't need to know everything.

I have a faint inkling that this might all come back to bite me in the ass sooner rather than later. But for right now, I'm determined to keep her shielded from all of it.

"Of course people are staring," I tell her smoothly. "Look at you. How can they not?"

18

DMITRI

"Wren?"

There's no sign of her when I walk into her room. Then I notice that the bathroom door is ajar and there's a low moan radiating through the gap.

I shove my way in to find her keeled over the tub, wincing in pain.

"Wren, fucking hell! Are you okay? Is the baby coming?"

She straightens up when she hears me, but she keeps one hand plastered on her lower back. "No, no, nothing like that." Her forehead is beaded with sweat. "Apparently, I've made too comfortable of a home for him in here." Her voice has a scolding tone but she runs a hand over her belly affectionately. "It's just the random spurts of back pain from lugging around this gigantic stomach." Pointing at the water, she explains, "I was just gonna soak for a while. Water's the only thing that makes me feel light anymore."

I reach for her robe. "Let me help you."

She backs away from me as though I've pulled out a knife. Her eyes flicker down to my extended hand. "That's okay. I don't need help."

"You just almost cracked your spine in half from trying things on your own. I'd say help is exactly what you need."

She scrunches up her nose and scowls in my direction. "I'm not getting undressed in front of you again, Dmitri."

"Why not?"

She blanches. "Because I look *hideous,* okay? And I don't want you to see me like that. And I know you helped me into the tub not long ago, but I was freshly rescued and experiencing some PTSD and I didn't care as much then. But now… now, I'm gonna have to ask you to leave before I take off this robe."

I raise my eyebrows. "Did you just say you think you look hideous?"

She clutches the robe tighter around her body. "Well—"

I step forward and corner her against the edge of the bathtub, leaving her no room to flee. "You are fucking breathtaking, Wren. How can you not see that?"

She cringes and looks everywhere but at me. "The last thing I need is some false flattery, Dmitri. Don't blow smoke up my ass. I'm not in the mood."

I'm actually pissed off. So much so that I grab her by the hips and swing her around towards the mirror. I keep my hands on her shoulders and force her to face her reflection. "Look at yourself," I command. "I don't see 'hideous' at all. All I see is a strong, capable, beautiful woman who's unnecessarily hard on herself."

Wren's eyes flicker from me to her own reflection. Then her gaze falls to her stomach. "My stomach—"

"Is a testament to your strength. After everything you went through these past few months—" I wrap my arms around her and lace my hands on her stomach, just above hers. "—you kept this baby safe. I couldn't have picked a better woman to carry my child."

She stays quiet. Her breath is the only sound, the soft rise and fall of her chest the only motion. At last, she murmurs, "You don't mean that."

"I mean every fucking word."

She peels herself away from me and turns around so that we're face to face. "A better woman to carry your child would be a woman you're actually in love with."

Is she testing me? Is she expecting something from me? I have no idea. All I know is that she's looking to me for answers I don't have.

"I don't think in hypotheticals. *You* are the mother of my child. And I'm happy that you are."

She blinks and a tiny tear appears at the corner of her right eye. She brushes it away. "Fine. Maybe I do need some help to get in the tub."

I reach forward before she changes her mind and pull delicately at the tie-up holding the robe together. It comes apart easily, revealing her perfect naked body underneath. Instinctively, she tries to fold in on herself, but I put my hands on her shoulders again and shake my head.

"Wear your pregnancy proudly, Wren. You've earned it."

Her fingers keep fidgeting, but she keeps them by her sides and lets me pull the robe from her. Her body has changed a lot since the first time I saw her naked. Her flat stomach is a distant memory and her breasts are far bigger than I remember.

But I stand by my words: she is fucking perfect.

And the fact that she doesn't seem to know that just pisses me off.

I force my eyes back up and take hold of her elbow as I coax her to the edge of the tub. It does a strange thing to my chest when she lets her weight lean on me, when she trusts me to support her.

Once she's submerged in water and bubbles, she sighs. "This feels amazing."

Her eyes flutter shut and I take the opportunity to admire her—her sharp collarbones, the graceful arch of her neck, the way her lips part as she relaxes into the water. I could sit here and stare at her all day. I could lose hours in admiration to her, if I'd only give myself that kind of freedom.

Except I'm not at liberty to give that kind of freedom in the first place. "I'll leave you to your bath."

Her eyes fly open. "You're leaving?" She sounds almost disappointed.

"I figured you wanted some peace and quiet."

She bites on her bottom lip. "Yeah, I did..." My eyebrows arch and she blushes. "But now, I want you to stay."

What a miracle those little words are. Only a few weeks ago, I was certain she wanted me dead in retribution for her sister. Now, here she is, naked and vulnerable...

And she wants me to stay.

I start stripping off my clothes and her eyes go wide. Pretty sure she didn't mean she wanted me to get in the tub with her, but I'm going to pretend that I've misunderstood. If she wants me to stay out of her bath, she'll have to say so.

She doesn't.

Once I'm naked, I slip into the opposite side of the tub. Her eyes stay glued to my erection until it disappears under the bubbles.

"Did you need any more proof that you're not hideous?" I tease.

She blushes and looks away from me. "It doesn't take much for a man to get hard," she mumbles.

"I'm not like other men."

She pretends to be fascinated by the bubbles just to avoid looking at me. "That's what all men say."

"If you're uncomfortable—"

"I'm not." Her eyes move hesitantly to mine. "I *should* be. That's the problem."

She still wants me. After everything she knows, after everything she's seen… she still fucking wants me.

"You shouldn't feel guilty."

"But I do," she whispers in a mournful croak. "I should want to be as far away from you as possible. I should hate you."

"But you don't?"

She glares at me accusingly. "You know I don't."

"Then what do you want?" With every second that ticks by, I move a little closer, determined to bridge the gap between us.

"I don't know. That's the other problem."

I shake my head. "I think you do. I think you knew what you wanted the other night when you found me in the nursery."

She swallows. "You didn't say anything."

"Because *you* didn't. I figured you didn't want to be seen. But then I heard you cry out in the next room…"

She flushes and I know that my initial suspicion is dead on. Excitement pools in my chest as I run my hands against her calves. She looks transfixed, as though she can't take her eyes off me.

"It was a… a bad dream…"

"Was it really?"

Her eyes flutter hypnotically. "Y-yes. Just a dream."

"You were sweating. Your breathing was heavy. And when you opened your eyes, you looked wide awake."

"Some dreams can do that to you," she insists.

I run my hands up and down her thighs, getting closer and closer to her center. I wish the scent of citrus and lavender weren't so overpowering—I want to be able to smell *her*. The scent of her dripping pussy, the saltiness of pleasure as it evaporates off her body.

"Okay then. What were you dreaming about?"

"Dmitri…"

"Tell me, *moya devushka*."

Her chin falls to her chest, like speaking to the water instead of to me makes it easier to voice the words. "I was dreaming about you."

"What was I doing in the dream?"

"Y-you were... touching me."

My fingers graze her pussy and I press down gently, enough to make her twitch with the first of many tremors to come. "Like this?"

"Yes."

"Was I kissing you?"

Her eyes brighten. Her reflection on the surface is a rippling thing of beauty. "On my neck first." She sounds eager now. Impatient. "Then my lips."

My fingers dig into her hip and I pull her into my lap. She gasps as my cock slides against her slit without pushing inside. I kiss her neck softly, teasing her with feather-light touches that mirror what my fingers are doing between her legs.

"D-Dmitri..." she moans.

"You never have to resort to dreams or fantasies when you're with me, *moya devushka*. Just come to me. Tell me what you need and I'll give you everything you want and more." It's a reckless promise, but I'm as intoxicated by the moment as she is. "What else do you want from me?"

She moans, low and soft and slow. It sets my skin on fire. I grab her hard and pull her closer.

"This is exactly where I want you," I growl, making sure my cock is placed perfectly against her pussy. "This is where you belong."

She writhes against my hardness, her soapy breasts shivering with every movement. "No… I can't belong here."

"Does it feel wrong?" I challenge.

She seems to be at a loss for words. Or maybe my cock is just a little too distracting. Either way, she runs a hand over my chest.

"Just kiss me," she begs. "Make it feel right."

Say no more.

I kiss her furiously, with all the pent-up emotion that's been building inside me from the moment she was taken. Her breathy little gasps unleash the animal in me and I have to hold back to keep from fucking her the way I want to. At least her belly is a constant reminder that I must be careful.

But I don't hold back with the kisses, and she doesn't seem to mind. She gives as good as she gets. Her tongue duels mine for control until we're both just heaving masses of nerve endings. When we finally break apart, my cock is pushing into her slit, desperate to be swallowed up by her warmth.

"Is this what you dreamed about, baby?" I growl in her ear.

She shudders. "More… please…"

I ease myself inside her and she whimpers, the most delicious sound I've ever heard. But that first thrust does something to her. Unlocks something. Erases some pain, some hesitation, some fear.

"*Mmm…*" she groans. "Yes, yes, *yes…*"

As I bury myself to the hilt, every trace of her self-consciousness disappears. At the flip of a switch, she's riding me wildly, her hands on my chest, her half-wet hair flipping around her head, water sloshing up and over the sides of the tub.

It'd be so easy to let go already. But, impossible as it feels, I grit my teeth, grab her ass, and dig in my heels. This woman deserves more than three fucking minutes.

Fuck—considering the blue balls I've had to tote around this past week, *I* deserve more than three minutes.

Wren's eyes flutter backwards and pain pinches against my chest as she digs her nails into my skin. She doesn't notice or care, though—she just keeps bouncing devotedly on my cock, trying to choke the orgasm out of me like the tantalizing little siren she is.

"Take me like a good girl," I snarl in her ear. "Ride me like you deserve it. Fall apart for me. Give me every fucking bit of you."

When she finally cries out that she's coming, I let loose the reins on my own orgasm. Hot cum fills up her tight pussy and every muscle in me roars with the release.

Slowly, Wren stills.

Slowly, the water stills.

Slowly, the room and the heat and our hearts ease back to something resembling normal.

But not everything is completely at ease. With Wren nestled against my chest, barely breathing, I feel a sudden, tiny thump.

"Was that a kick?"

Wren peels her head off my shoulder with some effort, a sleepy smile on her face. "I'm so used to it now that I barely notice. Yeah, that's our little guy."

Our little guy. I like the way that sounds. "He's strong."

"He is," she says fondly. "Ah, there he is again."

I can feel him, pushing insistently at his mama's belly, probably wondering what the hell is going on that's got his mother's heartbeat racing. I palm her belly and feel him respond right away.

"That's our son," I whisper. "That's our little boy."

We stay in the water until our skin turns pruney. Then I help Wren out of the tub. I make her stand still while I towel her off, dabbing every inch of her skin until she's dry and glistening.

I'm so lost in admiring the beautiful new curves of her body that I barely notice the wall that's starting to come up around her. But by the time I straighten up and meet her eyes, I can sense that something has shifted.

She doesn't return my gaze; she looks away pointedly and slips out of the bathroom. I follow behind her quietly, waiting for her to break the silence.

"I'm gonna skip dinner tonight," she says abruptly. "I'm not hungry."

"You need to eat, Wren. The baby—"

"Then send in a tray," she says curtly. "I don't want to go out."

"You don't have to. We can eat in the kitchen—"

She whips around towards me, her eyes bright with passion. "This is not *normal*, Dmitri," she cries. "What just happened in there—" She gestures towards the bathroom. "—that shouldn't have happened at all. I can't believe… I can't believe I allowed it."

"Wren, listen—"

"I want to be alone, Dmitri. *Please.*" Her voice is firm, borderline pleading. Any kind of conversation will only serve to dredge up the past and, since I don't have the energy for that, I nod and leave her to wrestle with her demons alone.

It was good sex. It was a pure moment.

But even that can't fix everything.

19

WREN

The worst part about having hot bathtub sex with your baby daddy and former boss who also happens to be your sister's murderer?

You can't exactly talk that shit out with your friends.

Or in my case, friend—singular. I've purposefully avoided talking about Dmitri during my last three phone calls with Syrah. She always tries to go there, but I bat away every question smoothly.

(At least, I think I'm being smooth. I have no idea if it translates.)

The point is, Syrah's let me get away with it. I can tell she's worried about me, but she doesn't want to stress me out, either. I desperately want to talk to her, but what would I even say? That in a moment of weakness, I succumbed to the walking aphrodisiac that is Dmitri Egorov? That I let him soap me up and give me one of the best orgasms of my life? That I spent the next four days trying to avoid him unsuccessfully?

How would that conversation go exactly?

ME: *Yeah, I was just so damn horny. Pregnancy hormones, iykyk.*

SYRAH: *Totally understandable. Get it, girl.*

ME: *No! Absolutely not! I shouldn't have let my guard down!*

SYRAH: *Why the hell not? He got you pregnant—he can get you off, too.*

ME: *Sure, sure. But what about the fact that he killed Rose and Jared in cold blood?*

SYRAH: *WHAT THE FUCK?!*

ME: *Yeah, sorry. I should have mentioned that little detail earlier.*

SYRAH: *He killed Rose and Jared and you actually fucked him in your bathtub?*

ME: *Exactly. I'm a horrible person.*

SYRAH: *You were supposed to be the sensible one between us. Why would you do such a thing, Wren?*

ME: *I don't know. He just... he does something to me.*

SYRAH: *Is he threatening you? Manipulating you? Controlling you?*

Me: Worse. He's being nice to me. Ever since the bathtub sex, he cooks almost all my meals. He had a massage therapist visit me yesterday for a two-hour session. He got the library and the theater room stocked with all my favorite books, movies, and snacks. He's had my entire wardrobe replaced with branded maternity wear. He's even building our son's nursery from scratch. And the swing, Syrah! He found the childhood swing that Rose and I scratched our initials into and he installed it in the nursery!

SYRAH: *If he hadn't killed your sister, I would swoon!*

ME: *But he* **did** *kill my sister.*

SYRAH: *Didn't stop you from fucking him in the tub.*

ME: *I hate myself.*

SYRAH: *You should. I would, too.*

I snap out of my masochistic little dream sequence and resist the urge to slap myself across the face. Syrah would never say that last part. At least not out loud.

She might think it, though.

I unfold my legs and get off the living room sofa. Not even Chicago's skyline can distract me from the internal conflict that's been raging inside me since Dmitri walked out of my bedroom that day. The day I'd compromised my morals and let him…

I fall into that moment—the way his hands caressed my calves as they snaked higher and higher up my legs… The way he looked at me—not like some ugly pregnant cow, but like a desirable and attractive woman. And the way he kissed me…

My pussy throbs hungrily at the memory.

No! Shut it down! I cannot afford to go there, not even in my head. Crossing that line once was bad enough. But fantasizing about it in my free time? That's a new level of low. And yet, I find myself falling into it so easily.

The fact that Dmitri has been a freaking *dream* since the bathtub incident—and *yes*, it qualifies as an "incident"—is certainly not helping. I swear to God, it's like he's vowed to make this as hard for me as possible.

Starting with how he hasn't once brought up what happened between us. He's always unfailingly polite and extremely thoughtful and he acts as though there was no line breached, no boundaries compromised.

We eat dinner together, which of course he prepares from scratch by himself. And then he says goodnight and waves me off to my room. I didn't expect him to take the whole *respecting-my-wishes* thing quite so seriously.

Half the time, I'm not sure if I'm grateful or disappointed.

Then there was last night. I was sitting on the sofa in the living room with a book on my lap. It was only slightly chilly, but nothing I couldn't handle. Except for the next thing I knew, I'd had a cashmere blanket thrown over me.

"You've got goosebumps," Dmitri answered in reply to my questioning gaze.

Since I can never concentrate on anything else when he's around, I put down my book and started rubbing my ankles absentmindedly.

"Is that swelling?" he asked immediately.

I tried—too late, clearly—to hide my fat sausage feet underneath the blanket, but he'd just pulled them back out and stared at them.

"It's normal to swell at this stage of my pregnancy," I told him self-consciously, trying to wriggle my way out of his grip. "Dr. Liza said it should go down in a day or two. I just need to rub them a li—" I didn't even finish my sentence before he started kneading the soles of my feet gently. "You really don't have to do that…"

He ignored me and just kept going.

Half an hour later, my feet felt great. My vagina? Not so much. Apparently, she was jealous of all the attention my feet were getting.

Which is why, immediately after he finished, I jumped off the sofa and high-tailed it to my room.

I paced until my traitorous lady bits stopped throbbing and the after-effects of his foot rub had worn off. Then I got into bed and spent a good hour resisting the urge to masturbate before falling into an exhausted sleep that inevitably gave way to a never-ending series of wet dreams that make me shudder even to think about.

All in all, it's been a rough few days. It's a bloody cage match between guilt and desire and there are moments when I honestly don't know which one will win out.

I'm rooting for guilt, if only to keep me from doing something stupid—like falling hard for the man responsible for the biggest hole in my heart. But there are times when reality manages to burn through all that wishful thinking. When I'm faced with the glaring truth that I started falling a long time ago.

And there's no wind strong enough to blow me back up to the top of *that* hill.

If only I could talk to Syrah. And I mean *really* talk to Syrah.

But I can't. Because she would never understand. This is not the kind of situation anyone can understand unless they've been through it themselves. And I'm pretty sure there's no support group for Women Who've Been Kidnapped And Accidentally Impregnated By Their Hot Boss Turned Bratva *Pakhan* Turned Personal Villain Who Robbed You Of Your Best Friend-Slash-Sister.

Really rolls off the tongue, doesn't it? *WWBKAAIBTHBTBPTPVWRYOYBF-S-S Anonymous.*

Membership includes: me, myself and I.

A buzzing sound draws my attention towards my vibrating phone on the coffee table. It's Syrah. *Speak of the devil.* I'm not really in the right headspace for a long conversation, but I'm too lonely right now to pass up the call, either.

"Hey, Sy."

She dispenses with the pleasantries. "How's your Saturday looking?"

"Um, lazy. I'm too tired and swollen to do much of anything other than sit on the couch and snack."

"How about I get some more snacks and join you?"

Cringing, I grab my blanket and pull it tighter around me. The cashmere is a deep aquamarine blue, velvety soft, and it has the added benefit of smelling like Dmitri. I wonder if that was intentional on his part. A mental psych-out, perhaps? A way to get in my head and soften me up from the inside?

"Wren?"

Concentrate, you obsessive psychopath! "Sorry, hon, I've been exhausted all day. I'm afraid I won't be fun company. I'll probably fall asleep during this conversation."

"Well, you certainly sound relaxed."

I'm glad someone thinks so. I feel like I just swallowed a live wire. "I'm getting there. We'll catch up soon, though. I promise."

"No worries. Just as long as you're comfortable and well taken care of."

I don't even have to lie about this one. "I am. He makes sure I have everything I need. All I have to do is mention something in passing and it's in front of me the next day."

She lets loose an excited giggle. "How much have you tested that theory? Because you could really milk that, if you were so inclined. He's like a genie with abs."

Laughing, I lie back against the sofa and try unsuccessfully to find a spot that makes me feel less pregnant. "He'd rise to the challenge. Trust me."

"Sounds like you fell ass-backwards into the best-case scenario."

If she only knew. "Yeah. Something like that."

"I'm guessing everything is going smoothly there?" she asks tentatively. I make the mistake of hesitating and she pounces on it right away. "What is it? Is he being a jerk?"

"No, no, no," I rush to correct her. "It's more the... opposite problem."

"He's being too *nice?*" She snorts. "If you're actually complaining about that, I might have to come over there just so that I can whack you over the back of the head."

How to explain without actually explaining? "He's being, like, really wonderful lately. I'm talking *extra* nice, *extra* thoughtful, extra—"

"Extra dreamy," Syrah drawls, cutting me off. "I get it. Woe is you. I'm struggling to see the problem here."

"Sometimes, I feel like we don't *talk*," I stammer. "Like we can't... We, um, don't have real conversations. It feels like he's holding things back. I know I definitely am. I just don't want all the other stuff—the massages and gifts and home-cooked meals—to distract from the fact that we're having a baby together and we don't really know where we stand with one another."

I let out a low breath while Syrah's tongue clicks softly. "Hon, I am still failing to see the problem. You want to have a real conversation with the man? Then do it. Sit him down and *talk* to him. You're having his baby; it's justified. What's he gonna do? Run from you?"

"If he does, I certainly won't be able to chase after him."

Syrah laughs for a moment before she gets serious again. "My point is, have you really even tried to talk to him?"

I sigh. "I guess not."

"Then try. I say try *now*."

I cringe at the very thought of even attempting this conversation. "I wouldn't even know where to start."

"Start simple," Syrah says confidently. "He's been taking care of you, right?"

"Yes," I reply cautiously, unsure where she's going with this.

"Well, then, how about you return the favor? Cook him a meal for a change," she suggests. "Surprise him with that pesto pasta you used to make for me on *Bridgerton* nights. I could bathe in that shit. Start with something light, warm him up, and then pivot into what you really want to talk about."

I nod slowly. "That's a good plan."

"Duh, of course it is. I came up with it."

A tired chuckle escapes my lips. "Thanks, Sy. I don't know what I'd do without you."

"Probably just complain about all your champagne problems."

Laughing, I let that one slide off my back. I can't expect her to understand when I haven't told her even half of the real story. Hell, I may never tell her the whole story. She doesn't need to know how and why Rose died; I'm happy to carry that burden on my own.

But it does make me miss Bee all the more. She was the one person I didn't have to hide a damn thing from.

Although, to be fair, I'm pretty sure she would have given me the same advice that Syrah just had. *Stop being a wimp and talk to the man.*

"Okay, Wren," I tell myself softly. "You've got yourself a game plan. Now, it's time to act on it."

20

WREN

No one dresses up for pesto pasta at home.

And yet here I am, trying to pick out a slimming dress that will make me feel both comfortable and pretty. Not that feeling pretty should be a priority tonight. But still, I find myself swapping out dress after dress because none of them are perfect.

In the end, I opt for a shimmery, periwinkle blue wraparound that stops *juuust* short of being too much. I leave my walk-in confidently…

Then stride back in two minutes later and snatch up some lip gloss like it's the secret weapon I need to make this night a success.

My second walk-out sticks. I make it all the way to the kitchen, where my pesto pasta sits patiently on the stove, waiting for a last minute heat-up before serving.

It's almost seven and the city is losing light slowly. Dmitri texted earlier to let me know that he was going to be home by 7:15. That's another one of the thoughtful gestures he started recently—letting me know when he was leaving the apartment and what time he would return.

Strangely considerate of him.

I haven't eaten anything since lunch, but I'm not hungry. All my hunger has been overtaken by nerves and the vague hope that something positive will come out of this dinner.

If not, I'm gonna smack Syrah over the head with something heavy.

Thump. Thump.

I spring away from the stove and lunge towards the door so that I can peek around the corner towards the elevator. But there's no sign of him yet. It's only then that I realize the thumping sound I'm hearing is coming from upstairs.

Weird.

Dmitri's been steadfast about his whole "noisy renovation team" explanation, but for some reason, I find it strange. The upstairs penthouse was nothing if not pristine and the idea of trying to improve on it seems almost laughable.

I'm being ridiculous—I know that. It's probably the combination of nerves and the drudgery of waiting, but I find myself inching towards the elevator, wondering if maybe a quick trip up-deck is justified? I mean... weird though it sounds, I kinda *miss* the upstairs penthouse. And if I'm caught, I figure I'll just blame it on the hormones.

Fuck it. A quick walk won't hurt. As far as I'm aware, curiosity has never killed any cats.

I punch in the passcode for the upstairs penthouse, but almost immediately, the light flashes red. ***Access denied.***

Incorrect passcode.

Can that be right? I try again and I'm met with the same message blazing across the thin horizontal screen. Shrugging, I turn away from the elevator. I shouldn't really be surprised; Dmitri has always been a real stickler for security. He probably changes the codes quarterly.

Ping!

I whirl around as the elevator doors slide open and Dmitri strides through in his linen navy blue suit and white, open-collared shirt.

My first thought is, *God, does he look handsome.* My second thought is, *A little chest hair and you go ga-ga. Embarrassing.*

"Hi."

He looks surprised to see me standing at the entrance. Then his gaze slides down my body appreciatively and his eyebrows arch. "You look gorgeous."

It's annoying how fast I blush. "Thanks," I murmur. "Hope you're hungry." I twist around and make for the kitchen, thankful to turn my back on him until I can get my cheeks to stop burning.

By the time I'm facing him again, I feel moderately in control of my face. He takes off his jacket and folds it neatly over the back of one of the bar stools. "Smells great."

I'm pretty sure he's just being polite, because I can't smell anything myself. "Let me just get the pasta on the fire again. Warm it up a little."

My hands are shaking as I stir the pot. The pasta's dried up, so I add some milk, cream, and salt to bring it back to life. At this rate, I have no idea if it will even be edible. I'm too distracted, too self-conscious to be in the right state of mind for cooking.

"Do you need some help?" he asks from my left shoulder.

I flinch so hard I knock right into him.

He twists me around, his hand firm on my waist as he steadies me. "You okay, *moya devushka*?"

"Fine," I mutter. "Just… um… dinner will be ready soon. You can sit down."

He backs off with a frown and I manage to get the pasta into a large bowl without any further clumsy mishaps. But by the time it's on the table between us, I'm wondering how I managed to let Syrah convince me this was a good idea. I've gotten needlessly dolled up for what I'm sure is going to be a subpar pasta dish and an uncomfortable, unproductive conversation with a man who has an unnatural hold over my common sense.

"Um—bon appetit." *Why the hell did you have to attempt a French accent?* "God," I cringe, "no wonder the French hate me. I hate me, too."

He chuckles. "No one could hate you." Then he quiets for a moment, his face going serious. "Thanks for cooking tonight. You didn't have to."

"I wanted to," I insist. "You've been doing all the cooking and I wanted to do something for you."

"Well, I appreciate it. It's been a while since someone cooked for me who wasn't paid to."

I feel my resolve waning instantly. Would it be so bad to just sit together and have a pleasant dinner and not talk at all?

Would it be so bad to indulge in a few innocent domestic fantasies, as long as I don't act on them?

He takes a bite of my pasta and moans in appreciation. "Delicious." Then he smiles at me and I realize that there's no way I won't act on my fantasies—the raunchy ones and the domestic ones alike—if he continues to smile at me like that.

I drop my gaze. "You don't have to butter me up. I can take honest criticism."

"I'm saying it because it's true. Simple and delicious."

"I, uh, made dessert too. Again, nothing fancy. Just an old recipe my mother taught me."

His eyes slide to the little vase of flowers I set up earlier when I was getting the table ready. "If I'd known this was a date, I'd have showered first."

"I like the smell of your sweat."

His eyes snap to mine and that's when I realize *I just said that out loud!* "I, um… That wasn't supposed to come out… um, that is… That's not what I meant to say."

He just stares at me with that intoxicating gray gaze and a slight smirk. "What *did* you mean to say?"

"That this is not a date."

"My mistake," he rumbles with faint amusement. "The lip gloss and the cleavage-baring dress threw me."

Instant regret, hot and heavy. What possessed me to choose this dress of all dresses? Sweatpants and oversized t-shirts—*that* has been my uniform at home and I should have freaking stuck to it. How the hell am I going to segue into a serious conversation now?

I feel dumb. Blindingly obvious, like a little kid playing hide-and-seek without realizing his feet are sticking out from beneath the curtains.

"I just wanted to feel good about myself," I manage to mumble, somewhat belatedly. "Fake it 'til you make it, right?"

He drops his fork. "I understand that you're very pregnant and probably deeply uncomfortable all the time. But trust me, Wren: no woman is more beautiful than you are right now."

I'm glad I'm sitting down, because if I'd been standing, he definitely would have noticed my legs buckle. "*No* woman?" I echo. "Surely there's at least one out there."

Dmitri is unfazed. "It's the truth as I see it."

I'm not gonna lie: it's exactly what I need to hear. But it's also the *last* thing I need to hear. All these compliments are battering down the walls I've built, and in the face of those crystal gray eyes, I realize just how weak those walls were to begin with.

"Why are you being so nice to me?" I blurt out because I'm honestly tired of the circus in my own head.

He blinks slowly, not answering at first. "I'm treating you the way you deserve to be treated. I'll admit I wasn't always a gentleman in the past—but I intend to be now."

"Why?"

"Do I need an ulterior motive?"

I shrug. "You tell me."

"You don't trust me, do you?" He clears his throat and sighs. "I can't exactly blame you for that. I haven't done anything, especially lately, to earn your trust. But rest assured, I'm being nice because I care about you, Wren. You're the mother of my child."

It's a good speech—but is it a romantic one? Or is it simply a peacemaking tactic? Is he trying to pave the way towards a cohesive and functional co-parenting relationship or are there undertones to his words that mean something more?

I probably should ask, but I'm too damn scared to. Which is why, instead of asking what I really want to—*Where the hell do we go from here?*—I end up squeaking in a high-pitched, nasally voice, "I've got to check on dessert."

Considering dessert is a no-bake cheesecake, it doesn't really require much mollycoddling. But I need to concentrate on something that's not Dmitri for just a minute or two.

So I poke and prod and clank around to distract myself. By the time I go back to my seat, I feel a little more at ease, a little more in control of the situation.

"How was work?" I ask.

He nods. "Fine. We might have a new client who wants us to spearhead the design of his new business space."

I perk up eagerly. "An interior project. Those are my favorite kind."

"You always had such extensive notes on those clients."

"Because they were interesting. I used to wish I could be on the design team for one of those projects. Truthfully, that was my goal."

"You mean to say you didn't want to be my assistant forever?"

Smirking, I stab more pasta with my fork. "Shockingly, no. I had slightly higher aspirations."

"But you just stayed because you loved your boss so much."

I laugh and stick my tongue out at him. "I just had bigger dreams for myself, you know? I didn't want to always take notes for the boss; I wanted to *be* the boss."

He eyes me thoughtfully. "There's still time."

I roll my eyes. "Sure. Between breastfeeding and the two separate mafias who are after you—and, by association, me—I'll have loads of opportunities to work on getting my career off the ground." Sighing, I push around the remaining pasta on my plate. "Somehow, I don't see that happening."

"Are you really writing yourself off so soon?"

"I'm not writing myself off," I snap. "I'm just being realistic."

"You were willing to be the surrogate for your sister, Wren. You seem to have a habit of making the improbable possible."

"Since when did you become my cheerleader?"

His big shoulders roll. "Just calling it like I see it."

I shake my head. "Well, stop it. It's unnerving."

He laughs and cleans his plate with the fork. "Let me take care of the dishes while you get dessert. It's only fair that I do the clean-up."

Giving him a shy nod, I make my way to the fridge and pull out the cheesecake. It smells like lemon and gingerbread and it looks almost identical to the one Mom used to make for Rose and me on Sundays.

Shoving aside the weird feeling of melancholy that stirs up in me, I cut up two slices and deposit them onto clean plates, very aware that he's watching me closely from the sink.

It's been an entire dinner and I haven't brought up one single talking point yet. Syrah made it sound so simple on the phone. But now that we're up to dessert, it feels like my window of opportunity is closing slowly.

I turn with both plates in my hands. "I... um... I wanted to cook dinner for you today so we could talk."

He lifts an eyebrow. "Ah-ha. So *you're* the one with the ulterior motive."

I flush. "No, that's not—"

"I was only joking, Wren," he chides gently. "If you need to talk to me about something, then by all means, go right ahead."

I chew on my bottom lip a little longer, trying to muster up the courage. It's far too late to turn back now.

"Is it about what happened the other night?" he tries.

I wasn't planning on bringing up the bathtub sex at all. But now that he has, it feels like the soapy elephant in the room. "Well... not exactly. But as long as we're on the topic—"

"We don't need to be ashamed about that."

I stare at him incredulously. "Maybe *you* don't, but I do."

"Wren—"

"No," I interrupt, turning and walking away to put some distance between him and me. "That was a mistake. I let things go too far." There's a little voice in the back of my head that's telling me that this is not how I meant for this conversation to go. I was going to be calm, in control, unflappable. And yet here I am, stuttering over my own words or letting them run away from me altogether. "I was vulnerable and you were there and it… it just happened. It can't ever happen again!"

I'm not even sure I really want that, but now, I've gone and said it. *Take a deep breath, you hysterical fool. Just a deep breath.*

I don't listen to my own advice, though. I just keep plowing ahead blindly.

"We are going to have this baby and that means we have to try and get along for his sake. But that's where it ends. We can't blur the lines anymore. No more bathtub shenanigans —" *Ugh, that's the worst word choice of all time.* "We're co-parents and that is all."

Dmitri gives no sign of what he's thinking. His expression is everything I wanted to be tonight—cool and confident. I feel even more unhinged in comparison.

"Wren," he rasps, sending a shiver down my spine, "since we're here tonight to open the lines of communication, let me be clear: we are more than co-parents. And I think you know that already."

I let out the breath I've been holding in. He's never been quite that honest before. It gives me the courage to be honest in return.

"If that's true," I croak softly, "then tell me why you did it. Why did you kill my sister?"

21

DMITRI

My first instinct is indignation.

I'm not used to being questioned. I'm not used to justifying my reasons. And here she is, demanding both. Asking for something that she has no right to.

Except…

She *does* have the right to ask. She has the right to know. And I need to put aside my *pakhan* crown and be a man for a change.

I need to be the man *she* needs, more specifically.

Not controlling or possessive. Not even protective. No—she needs a man who can see things from *her* perspective long enough to sympathize.

Maybe even to…

Fuck, I can't believe I'm saying this…

To apologize?

I don't know how to do such a thing, but fucking hell, I'm willing to try. Seeing Wren's beautiful green eyes fill with tears, knowing that I'm responsible for them—that sticks under my skin like a shard of glass. Everything I've done to try to make it better clearly hasn't worked.

Rose's death is an open, festering wound that requires lancing. Maybe this conversation is the hot edge that will do the job.

"You know why I killed her," I start softly.

She nods. "Yes. You've told me the story, but I need to hear it again. I need you to walk me through it."

"That will only hurt you, Wren."

Her hands tremble as she runs them down her face. If it's an attempt to calm herself, it doesn't do a damn bit of good, because she only starts trembling more.

"I'm hurting anyway," she confesses. "I might as well know everything. And I want you to start from the beginning."

"The beginning?"

Her jaw tightens. "You were right: this didn't start with Rose's death. It started with Elena's."

Fuck.

Something hot and prickly flashes over my body. "Are you sure?"

There's a tremor over her lips before she replies with a meek, "Yes."

I take a deep breath. "Let's go to the living room. I'd prefer if you were sitting down for this."

She pales but doesn't argue when I lead her into the living room. I sit down first so that she can decide how close or far she wants to be from me. She eyes the sofa I'm sitting on. There's an armchair to my immediate right and another one on my far left. She surprises me by choosing the empty side of the couch. Close enough that I can touch her; far enough that I have to lean forward to do it.

It's more than I expected. Probably more than I deserve.

I decide to give her one last warning. "Sometimes, ignorance really is bliss, Wren."

"I know that. But I've lived with ignorance for long enough. I want to understand why you did what you did. It's the only way I can… we can…"

She leaves the sentence unfinished, but I understand exactly what she means. It's the only way the two of us have any hope of being more than co-parents.

So, despite my reservations, I launch into it from the start.

I repeat things she already knows. How Cathal had it out for me. How he picked the perfect scapegoat to use against me.

She listens unflinchingly, right up until I mention Elena's name.

"Elena hated leaving the apartment," I explain. "She was borderline agoraphobic. She had weekly appointments with a therapist, but Dr. Seraphine usually made house calls. The idea was that, when Elena started to make progress, she would start going to Dr. Seraphine instead of the other way around."

Wren leans in. "Can I ask something? Why didn't Elena like to leave the house?"

I pause and weigh the question. "She called herself an introvert. But the truth is, I think she was just scared. She was raised in the foster system and it abused her. Once she found a safe place with me, she just didn't want to leave it." I pause for another second, recognizing some old regret from another lifetime. "The irony was…"

"Your world isn't a safe one," Wren finishes for me.

I nod. "Exactly. The therapy sessions started after Elena was targeted driving home from a spa day with Bee. She was shot at several times and one bullet managed to pierce her arm. It was a flesh wound, nothing serious, but the experience shook her to the core. After that, she refused to leave the penthouse under any circumstances. I gave her time, but when it became clear she was getting worse, not better, I had to bring in reinforcements."

"Did the doctor help?"

"Four months of intense therapy and Elena finally decided to leave the apartment to meet Dr. Seraphine in her office. The first session went well, so Elena agreed to go the next week, too. I thought it was… I thought it was the beginning of a new chapter."

My jaw clenches painfully. I feel a weird sense of pressure build inside me. What the fuck *is* that?

Oh, right.

Regret.

"Dmitri…" Wren's voice is soft and gentle.

Why does it sound like *she's* the one trying to comfort *me*? That's backwards. That's just fucking *wrong*.

I glance at her and Elena's face folds into Wren's. Will that always be the case? Will I always see Elena in the shadows between memories?

"I should have driven her there, back, everywhere. I should've never let her out of my sight." My voice sounds curt and gravelly to my own ears. God only knows how broken it sounds to Wren. "I fucking should have *been* with her. But… there was an attack on one of the Egorov safehouses. Cathal's men. Some even claimed that Cathal was among them. I didn't even think about it; I left Elena in the hands of two men who are both dead now and I went to deal with the situation—without knowing it was a fucking red herring."

She inches closer. "Dmitri…" Once again, that's all she says—but somehow, it pushes me through.

"It sounds naïve to say so now, but I was confident she was protected by virtue of being my wife. There's no way Cathal would move on her and risk igniting a war between us. But he was smart about it. He made sure I saw him that day. He made sure that all his most important lieutenants were present, too. He made it hard for me to suspect that he might have orchestrated Elena's abduction."

"But you did suspect him?"

"Yes, of course. He wasn't as slick as he thought he was. The man who took Elena was clumsy. Far too clumsy to be a part of any organized crime ring. And Cathal's men all had alibis. But in the end, all I had to do was pick at a few threads before the whole thing started unraveling…"

My memories start to get away from me. It's been a while since I relived the whole thing in such detail. But I remember it all, clear as day—walking into Dr. Seraphine's office to find it turned upside down. The therapist's body was found later. Her throat had been slit and then she was dumped into the Chicago River like garbage.

"I found Elena's body four days later after scouring the entire city. In the same neighborhood as her last foster home. There were cigarette burns all over her body. Whiplashes across her back that had flayed her skin wide open. Red streaks around her neck indicated she had been choked, but her autopsy revealed that she didn't die through asphyxiation. Her body was pumped full of drugs. Enough to take down a fucking bull. She'd died maybe an hour before I found her..."

I stare off into the Chicago skyline as I trail off, momentarily forgetting that I have an audience. It's only when I hear a little sniffle that I remember that Wren's with me. I turn to her to find her cheeks soaked in tears, her body shaking with sobs that she's trying her best to hold in.

"Fuck, Wren... I'm sorry—"

It's weird how easily those words flow out of me. I thought apologies would come hard.

They're nothing compared to my desire to wipe her tears away.

She shakes her head vehemently. "Don't apologize to me. Not for that. Jesus, Dmitri, *I'm* the one who's sorry."

Instinctively, I reach for her. I don't gather her up in my arms like I want to, though—I just put my hand on her arm. She does the same, her fingers falling against my bicep, loose and curled. We're linked now, in the form of a clumsy infinity sign. Each one of us beginning where the other ends.

"I would have lost my mind," she whispers.

"I can't say I didn't. I thought murdering Cathal would help quiet the beast inside me. But it turned out that wasn't enough…"

I expect her to pull away from me. But all she does is tighten her grip and dig her nails into my skin. "You wanted to take out the man who was responsible for taking her life."

"It took me some time to tease out his identity. Cian did a good job of trying to shield Jared, but in the end, I found—" *Them*, I mean to say. *Them*. But I can't bring myself to say it to her face, so instead, I go with, "Him."

Wren shakes her head. "I can't believe that Jared would be capable of that. Cigarette burns, whip lashes… He wasn't a violent man, Dmitri." She looks at me earnestly as though she thinks that'll make me believe it, too. "He was… he was *good*."

My voice cracks like ice. "He was not the man you thought he was."

She flinches back and this time, she does remove her hand from mine. She wraps her arms around her body. "Okay, you may be right about that." She sighs deeply. "But Rose?"

"Rose was an innocent who got caught in the crosshairs of a game she wasn't fully aware was being played." I meet Wren's eyes. "I regret what happened that night, you know. If I could go back in time and spare her, I would. If only for your sake."

Another lone tear slips down her face. "They told me it was a car accident."

"It was a car *chase*," I correct. "I had my men corner them at a predetermined intersection. I had a gun aimed at them. Jared saw it, panicked, and the car skidded. They crashed into a lamppost. When I pulled Rose out of the car, she was unconscious."

Wren's jaw goes slack. "W-was she already dead?"

Fuck, how I wish she was now. "No. She wasn't."

Wren sobs loudly, but she clamps a hand over her mouth as though she's ashamed of the sound. "S-so... you did it?" she presses. "You killed her?"

"If it's any consolation, she was still unconscious when I pulled the trigger."

I expect that weak comfort to be met with anger. Fury, even. But instead, she blinks furiously, unleashing more tears. "S-so she d-didn't feel any pain?"

"No. There was no pain in the end."

Her breathing comes in ragged spurts and her cheeks and her chest are blotchy with spots. For a moment, I worry that I've told her too much. That I've been too honest. The woman is nine months pregnant and I've chosen *this* moment to tell her in excruciating detail how I killed her sister.

Then again, *she* was the one who chose this moment.

I just decided not to fight it anymore.

"My God," Wren rasps, dropping her face into her palms and sobbing into them.

I want to comfort her, but I don't know if she wants me to touch her. All I can do now is be honest. "I'm sorry, Wren. I'm truly sorry for taking away someone you loved so dearly. If I could take it back, I would. In a heartbeat. I'd do anything if it meant you didn't have to suffer like this." I'm not sure she's even listening to me, but I keep talking anyway. "I was a monster who was out for blood. It wasn't enough to kill him; I wanted to hurt him the way he had hurt me. An eye for an eye—that's how I saw it. But I should never have set my sights on her. She was innocent in all this and I should have left her out of it."

"*God*," she breathes desperately. "Stop. Just stop."

I fall silent as her breaths come in heavier and heavier. I wait patiently, bracing for the moment she tells me to fuck off and leave her alone. There's a blinding hollowness in my chest that's starting to grow.

If she wants nothing to do with me… I'll just have to accept that. But it won't change anything, not really. I'm not letting her or my son out of my sight. If she decides to hate me, she'll have to learn to live with that hate.

She'll have to learn to live with *me*.

When she finally wipes away her tears, her eyes are red and swollen. She looks like she's been crying for hours. I hate myself for what I've done to her.

"You have every right to despise me, Wren. I would understand if you did."

She flinches at the sound of my voice. Another sob bursts through her lips. "That's just it," she exclaims. "I *don't* hate you."

Then, to my utter amazement, she crawls right into my lap.

The hollowness in my gut dissipates instantly. I start to feel something. Happiness? Relief? Who the fuck knows? They don't make names for this. They don't make neat little stories with happy endings. Everything here is torn up and fucked up and skewed wrong from the start.

I just know that *this* part of it feels right.

Wrapping my arms around her, I pull her as close as I can while she buries her face in my shoulder. I rock her back and forth until her breathing drifts back to normal.

Then she pulls her head back and looks at me, her fingers grazing up and down my jaw. The strokes are soft, tender. "If I didn't know the whole story, it would be so easy to hate you," she says softly, like she's talking to herself. "But now, I *do* know the whole story. Yes, you took something precious from me. But he took something precious from you first. And you had the power to strike back." Another tear falls. I can feel the weight of each one. "Who's to say I wouldn't have done the same thing in your place?"

"You wouldn't have," I say confidently. "You're far too good. Far too pure."

She frowns. "No one is that good or that pure. You're not a saint, Dmitri. And neither am I." She closes her eyes for a moment. "But despite that, I'll be honest: I don't know where I fit into your world."

"At my side," I whisper to her immediately. "Always."

Her eyes flutter open. "It's a beautiful thought…"

"But you're not sure?"

"How can I be?"

It's a fair question. I nod and she leans her head back down against my chest. Whatever this is between us, it doesn't feel resolved yet. But it doesn't feel quite so *un*resolved either. I suppose you could say it's a start.

Nothing more.

Nothing less.

22

WREN

I slink down the corridor in the direction of Dmitri's voice.

He sounds pissed, but not in a *heads-are-gonna-fly, top-secret-Bratva-business* kinda way. More like in a *we-need-to-cinch-this-contract-or-lose-to-a-competitor* kinda way. Very corporate. Weirdly, I find myself drawn to the call as much as to his voice.

It's not that I'm bored, necessarily. It's more that I miss the liveliness of the workplace.

I miss seeing the same faces every day and swapping stories in the lunchroom. I miss rushing to meet deadlines and worrying about missing notes during important board meetings. I miss the hustle and bustle of the grind.

I miss waking up each day and having a purpose.

Other than the purpose of growing a human being, of course.

The door to his office room is conspicuously open. I feel like that's a new change, too. A literal open-door policy that's meant to be reassuring to me, I think. Maybe it signifies the shift that's taken place ever since our conversation two nights ago.

Not that anything major has happened since then. But a sense of calm has settled between us. It's easier to be together. Easier to compartmentalize the past from the present.

Which is why there's no guilt or discomfort attached to me actively seeking him out, for no particular reason other than I want to see him; I want to be near him.

And yeah, I may be just a little bit bored.

He's growling at someone on the phone, his back angled towards the door as he glares at the skyline sprawled out at his feet. "For fuck's sake, this is the third mockup you've shown the client. If she's not happy, then you're doing your fucking job wrong, Mitchell."

"Mitchell from the design team?"

Dmitri's gaze lobs over to me and he nods. He doesn't seem annoyed to have me in his space, though. In fact, he waves me over and keeps talking. "Yes, I'm looking at the mockup right now. Have you talked to her?"

I can hear the frantic babble of a panicked explanation from the other end. I'd feel sorry for the man on the receiving end of Dmitri Egorov's anger if it were anyone else but Jackson Mitchell. As it stands, the guy's a condescending prick with hands that start wandering inappropriately every year at the company Christmas party. So no, he gets no sympathy from me.

"... And you think you've accomplished that, have you?" Dmitri asks tersely. "Well, if that were the case we wouldn't need to do a *fourth* round of revisions, would we?" He scowls and listens for three more seconds before he interrupts again. "I'm not interested in excuses, man. I want solutions. If you have to do a fifth mockup, I'm taking you off this project."

With that mic drop moment, he hangs up. "Incompetent idiots," he mumbles. Then he turns to me, his gaze softening considerably. "Sorry about that."

It's still strange to me, this new version of Dmitri. The polite, thoughtful, caring version. The one who says "sorry" and means it. It's strange, unsettling… and very, very sexy.

"Don't worry about it," I squeak. "What's wrong?"

"Just a new project for a big client and it's not getting off the ground. We might lose her at this rate."

"Her?"

"Madison Montgomery."

My eyes fly open. Everyone and their mother knows Madison Montgomery. Fashionista, heiress, absurdly gorgeous it-girl with a brand new line of designer bridal wear that's already got every American female between the ages of sixteen and sixty frothing at the mouth.

"You're joking," I say. "Really?"

Dmitri nods. "She wants to open a bridal boutique here in Chicago. She loved the space we got her so much that she wanted us to design the interior, too. Except Mitchell keeps fucking it up."

I roll my eyes. "Yeah, of course he does. Mitchell has no vision. He's a copycat artist. The man doesn't have an original thought in his head."

"And you're telling me this only now?"

I smirk and slide in behind him, draping myself over his shoulders. "You never asked."

"Did I have to?"

"Duh. You were the boss. I was the lowly assistant. And you didn't exactly encourage free-flowing dialogue between the two of us."

He chuckles and encircles my wrist with his fingers. "Fair point. Now, tell me how to—*mmm*, whatever the fuck you're doing to my shoulders, don't stop."

I increase pressure and he sighs again. It gives me a fierce sense of pleasure to be able to do something for him. It scratches some primal itch to preen and primp and just *touch* him in ways he'd never let anyone else close enough to do.

"What did you want me to tell you?"

"Can't remember."

I swat him lightly on the back of the head. "Try harder."

He laughs as he closes his eyes and sags back in his seat. It's so strange to see all the tension erased from his face. To hear a soft moan of satisfaction as his lips part and that ever-present furrow in his brows vanishes.

Without opening his eyes, he gestures towards the stack of mockups on his table. "Tell me why Mitchell is so fucking useless."

Suppressing a smile, I continue with my shoulder massage. "For starters, he gets his best ideas from Delia and Connor. They have far less experience but much better design sense. Mitchell's good with spaces and property deals, but he sucks when it comes to turning those spaces into something special." I bear down on a rigid knot of tension in Dmitri's neck. "Also, he's too egotistical to take into account what the client wants. He ends up making it all about *him.* Thirdly, he lacks charisma. Fourthly and most importantly, he's a creep."

"A creep?" Dmitri repeats, swiveling around to face me and cracking one eyelid open.

"He has this way of undressing you with his eyes," I admit. "He's done it to me countless times—and *no,*" I say quickly when his eyes go wide with possessive anger, "he never touched me or asked me out or anything like that. But he does makes comments that can easily qualify as sexual harassment."

"Why is this the first time I'm hearing about this?"

"Because you didn't care," I say bluntly. "Nor would you have if *I* had been the one to tell you."

He grinds his teeth together, then exhales wearily. "Fair."

I wave a hand in his face and turn to the mockups on his desk. "The designs aren't horrible," I acknowledge. "But there's room for improvement."

"Then improve them."

I cringe at once. Any idiot could've seen that that was the next logical stepping stone—I guess I just never really thought that Dmitri Egorov would ask for my opinion.

"I don't have any real experience," I stammer stupidly.

"Try anyway."

And just like that, I'm sweating under my arms. And down my back. And on my forehead. And in other places that shall remain nameless.

"Okay," I whisper, reaching for the mockup prints. At first glance, I can pick out half a dozen details that I would change. But I start with the biggest adjustments first. "First off, he hasn't utilized the space well. This is meant to be a luxury bridal boutique. It has to be different from all the other stores hawking dresses." I take the second mockup and place it right in front of Dmitri. "This arrangement is decent, but he's closed off each space. Why not open it up, have one room flow into the other? Why not create the illusion of more room? Airy, bright, free-flowing?"

I glance eagerly at his expression, waiting for some sort of reaction, some sign of approval. But apart from a slight "Hmm," he doesn't give away a thing.

"And here," I say, pointing to the crenelated arch along the back wall that overlooks a courtyard garden, "He's made it so jagged and masculine. Let the garden talk to customers, you know? Let the light in. Give these women beautiful white spaces like canvases for them to project their fantasies onto."

Dmitri purses his lips. "All good suggestions."

Is he just humoring me? He has to be. I'm way out of my depth here.

All the girlboss Instagram accounts are screaming at me in my head to stand up for myself, to not apologize for taking up space—but I just can't do it. A lifetime of conditioning tells me to hedge. To back down. To shrink.

"Like I said, I'm no expert, but I have an eye for spaces. And I know enough about Madison Montgomery to know that she'll appreciate a design that's out of the norm."

Not bad, girl. Not bad at all.

"Okay."

I have no idea what that means. I'm weighing whether or not to ask him when Dmitri moves first. He picks up his phone again and starts dialing in a number. Then he transfers the call to the speaker and sets it back down on the table.

"Yes, Mr. Egorov?"

I suck my breath in. *Is that Jackson Mitchell again?*

Dmitri doesn't so much as give me a warning glance. "Mitchell, I'm bringing in a new designer to help you with the Montgomery project."

He's not—He can't—He wouldn't... My eyeballs feel as though they're about to jump out of my sockets.

Apparently, I'm not the only one who's blindsided, because Mitchell starts hemming and hawing. "M-Mr. Egorov, I respect your judgment but—"

"They say anything that follows a 'but' cancels out everything that was said before," Dmitri interrupts smoothly. "If you trust my judgment, then there's no room for buts. And if you don't, then you can get the fuck out of my office building."

I'm mouthing, *What the hell are you doing?!*

Dmitri just ignores me. "She's young and inexperienced, but she's wildly talented and her vision will help get this next mockup approved. So I'm assigning her to your team as project manager. Do what she tells you to do."

This time, I do more than just gesture theatrically in the air. I reach down and put the call on mute, cutting off Mitchell's indignant stuttering.

"What are you *doing?*" I cry out.

He lifts his eyebrows calmly. "I would have thought it was obvious."

"I wasn't giving you a sales pitch. I was just trying to help!"

"And you have. But unless you want Mitchell taking the credit for your ideas, I'd suggest you jump on this train and stop worrying about stepping on people's toes."

That last point pierces through my sense of panic. Is that what I'm worried about? No. Well, yes *and* no. I really don't want to piss Jackson Mitchell off by undermining him.

But I'm also worried about failing. It's so much more painful to fall on your ass when you desperately want to stay on your feet. The much easier option is just to accept your place on the floor.

I chew on my bottom lip. "Everyone's gonna assume I got the job because we're fucking."

I didn't mean for it to come out quite that vulgar, but it did anyway, and now, Dmitri's cocked eyebrow and slight smirk have me blushing through my nerves. But I stand by my point. That *is* what people will think, like it or not.

"Let them believe what they want," Dmitri says dismissively. "I'm hiring you because I think you can do this. End of story."

I eye his phone, conscious of the fact that Mitchell is still on the line, probably chomping at the bit to undo this catastrophe. "He's gonna hate me."

Dmitri shrugs. "That's his problem, not yours. If he mistreats you in any way, all you have to do is let me know."

I roll my eyes. "Right. 'Cause tattling to the boss is gonna make me *real* popular."

"You shouldn't care about being popular," he growls. "You shouldn't care about being liked. You're too fucking special to care about shit like that, Wren. Do the job and do it properly and you will earn their respect."

That hits home.

I find myself nodding. "Okay."

With a satisfied smirk, he takes the call off hold. "Mitchell?"

"I'm still here, sir. You were saying—"

"I was saying that Ms. Turner will be coming on board as project manager. And if anyone has a problem with that... well, my door's always open."

And so is your window, I think wryly.

"Uh... um... I see," Mitchell stutters. "I have no problem with it, sir. It's just that... *I'm* the manager for the Montgomery project."

"And I'm sure you and Ms. Turner will work together flawlessly."

"Ah, um, yes... of course."

On that shell-shocked note, Dmitri says goodbye and hangs up. I let out a whistling breath and run a hand through my hair. "The poor man." I stare at him while I shake my head. "I can't believe you just did that."

"I didn't do anything. *You* did." He gestures to the mockup plans cast around his desk. "Everything you said made sense. I need a competent person on my team and you're currently unemployed. It's a win-win."

He has a point there. Having a job, a *real* job, will go a long way in making me feel like more than just a useless broodmare.

"I just want to make one thing clear," he says. I hold my breath, waiting for the other shoe to drop. "You don't have to work if you don't want to. If you'd rather be a stay-at-home mother, that's fine with me. I just want you to have the choice."

Wow. That's not the shoe I expected to be dropped.

Suddenly, I'm battling the very real urge to kiss him. And I'm not talking about a demure *thank-you-for-believing-in-me* kiss either. I'm talking full-on, tongue in mouth, *I-wanna-rip-your-clothes-off* kind of kiss.

And since I'm dangerously close to losing that battle, I just thank him awkwardly and get the hell out of his space.

23

WREN

Project Manager. Never in human history have two boring-ass words sounded so exciting.

Projects? Lame.

Managers? Gag.

But me, a project manager?!

I feel like a motherfuckin' rockstar.

I keep see-sawing between extreme excitement and extreme nerves, neither of which help me sleep any better. So I end up in my newest happy place: the nursery.

Dmitri's working late, so I'm on my own tonight. His absence is bothering me more than I would have thought.

Somehow, subtle as can be, he's managed to work his way back into my heart. I sit down on the swing that he gifted me, the first gesture in the new paradigm shift between us, and I marvel at how inevitable it all feels between us.

Maybe fighting it was just stubborn pride on my part. Because the truth is, how could I not consider the possibility of giving my son a real family? How could I not give my baby two parents who love each other... maybe?

I mean, the love part is a certainty on my side. I've scraped and clawed to deny it, but I've lost that battle fair and square.

With Dmitri, of course, nothing is quite so clear.

I grip the ivy-circled rope and swing gently back and forth while I admire everything that Dmitri has created here. Two of the walls are painted, one in blue and the other in a soft, jungly green. The remaining wall has been papered over with a forest watercolor print. Through the thin trees, I see running water, fat squirrels, the outline of deer drinking from the stream.

At first, I thought it would clash with the view on the opposite side of the room, but I've changed my mind. Now, I think it works together—the idea of forest quiet in combination with big city hustle and bustle. Makes you feel like you can have both things at the same time.

Not that that's a metaphor or anything.

The furniture is mostly handmade. Carvings along the arms of the rocking chair, little frolicking rabbits chasing each other up the backrest and down the posts. Woven carpets are thick and lush underfoot.

I go wandering around, touching this, stroking that, mostly because that's what makes it all feel real. When I can see the things my baby will love, when I can feel them and smell them, I start to believe that all this is actually happening.

I pause at the clothes chest. It's eerily similar to the one Rose and I picked out together on one of our many trips through the city's baby boutiques. An old steamer trunk, huge and thick, lined with brass. I run a finger along the edge of the lock, then push the lid up.

A scent rises to greet me. Something uniquely baby-ish. Lavender and powder and a third thing that doesn't quite have a name.

I hold my breath as I reach down and pluck the top garment off the stack. It's neatly folded, but as I bring it up to my nose, it falls loose and releases more of that scent.

I bury my face in it. Out of absolutely freaking nowhere, tears spring to my eyes. *How many times did Rose do this, I wonder?* Stand in the middle of an empty nursery and dream of a future she wanted so badly?

"Something wrong?"

"Ahh!" I whirl around to find Dmitri leaning against the far wall. "I didn't even hear you come in."

"That's because you were a little preoccupied with sniffing that romper like an addict."

Snorting, I roll my eyes and put the romper away. The lid goes closed and a puff of air whooshes out, almost like it's sighing at me in disappointment. "It just smells a little... off, somehow. Rose's clothes smelled different."

"And... that's a bad thing?"

I shrug. "It's not good or bad. I just... I don't know. I don't know how to explain it, really."

He pushes himself off the wall and saunters toward me. The closer he gets, the more his smell joins the mix. Icy and minty and musky and *fierce*. "What did you do with those clothes?"

"They're in a storage unit a few blocks from my old apartment," I admit. "I couldn't bear to throw them out or give them away." I turn and walk away from him for reasons I don't fully understand. His smell added on top of the baby clothes' is too much, I think. I busy myself fussing with trinkets on the floating shelves. "It feels so unfair. That I should get to experience all this and she didn't."

"You feel guilty," he observes. It's not a question.

"I feel a lot of things." Just then, I hear a slight thud from the upstairs penthouse. "My Lord, when are they gonna finish up there?"

"Soon, hopefully. It's taking longer than I expected."

"What exactly are you changing?"

"You'll see soon enough."

I'm glad to hear that. There are moments when my mind runs away from me and I start thinking up all sorts of conspiracy theories. I've even started dreaming in conspiracy theories. Just the other night, I fell asleep to the thudding upstairs and woke up sweating a few hours later after a particularly vivid dream that involved walking into the upstairs penthouse and finding Rose locked up in one of the rooms, thrashing chains against the floor again and again.

I shake my head to dispel the stupid thoughts. It's just construction sounds. Normal sounds. Rose isn't up there.

Rose isn't anywhere, really.

I walk over to Dmitri and touch his chest for a moment. "I'm finally tired," I confess in a low whisper. "I think I'll go to bed."

He bends down and presses the faintest of kisses to the top of my head. "Sweet dreams, Wren." I start to leave, but he snares my wrist and makes me look at him. "Everything will be okay."

I didn't even know I needed to hear that. I lean my head against his shoulder for one more moment and close my eyes.

I decide to believe him.

24

DMITRI

Aleks flies into my office so hard that the door slams into the wall and sends a spray of dust cascading through the air.

I start to growl, "The fuck is wrong with—" Then I notice his face.

Pale. Sweaty. Furious.

I jump to my feet. "What happened?"

"That *motherfucker* happened," he spits. "They attacked us in retaliation for that shithole you torched."

I can't say I'm surprised. Retaliation is to be expected when you deal in power games. "Where'd they hit?"

"The cement factory in McKinley Park. It was fucking savagery, man. Like goddamn animals. We lost thirteen men."

No wonder he looks so unhinged. "Who?"

"Artem. Denis. Daniil. The whole crew."

I wince. My brother loves with his whole heart, and I know damn well that every single one of those losses will haunt him to the end of his days. "We're gonna get them back for this, *brat*," I tell him confidently. "We will avenge their deaths."

He sags into the nearest armchair. All the rage that brought him storming in here is gone now, replaced with a hollow sort of misery. "Daniil was gonna propose to his woman next week. He had the proposal all planned out. He…" He trails off, lost in his own grief for a moment. Then he raises his eyes to me and I see the embers of revenge still burning in there. "We need to fucking *act*, Dmitri."

"And we will, I assure you. But we need to be careful."

"*Now*, you want to play it safe? After you went all commando on that stupid fucking bar?"

"No, I want to play it *smart*," I retort, planting my fists on my desk. "I want to systematically wipe them out until there's no trace they were ever here in the first place. Just because we're not killing everyone we see yet doesn't mean we aren't at war, Aleks." That seems to mollify him, at least a little bit. I meet his eye. "I swear to you, the Irish will pay for this."

Aleks freezes. "Brother, it wasn't the Irish who attacked us." My blood starts to boil before he even finishes his sentence. "It was the Italians."

My breath catches in my chest. "Vittorio," I croak.

He nods. "He's trying to send us a message. Trying to say that they're stronger than we are. And right now, he'd be right. If we went up against the Irish, we'd win easily. If we went up against the Italians, we'd win easily. But both? Together?"

His scowl dissipates. Now, he just looks worried.

But fuck his pessimism. I've never met long odds that didn't just motivate me to be better, stronger, faster, more ruthless.

Let Vittorio align himself with whoever he wants; it won't make a bit of difference.

In the end, all my enemies will burn.

~

"To Artem!"

A chorus of cheers fills the night. The fire that burns between us throws dancing shadows onto the walls as the men of the Egorov Bratva raise their vodka glasses in tribute to our fallen comrades.

"To Denis!"

Another round of howling and stomping. The clink of glasses forms a melody that chimes just beneath the cacophony of noise.

"To Daniil!"

This time, the cries are led by Aleks, who rises shakily to his feet and roars louder than all the rest, stomping his foot into the ground. He's well past drunk at this point, but I'm not about to rein him in. This is the way death is meant to be grieved—with alcohol and cheers and stories about those who've passed.

Bratva men don't go quietly into the night.

I stand removed from all the ceremony, stone-cold sober and watchful of every man in the room. I'm certain of their loyalty. Every person here has been vetted and cleared and proven a thousand times over.

These soldiers are the ones who will deliver me my victory. I just need to figure out *how.*

Because the truth is, no matter how confidently I reassured Aleks, he was right: we are outnumbered. Which means that being smart isn't just one of many choices; it's my *only* choice.

Pavel walks over and offers me a glass of vodka. I accept it, just as I'd accepted every other glass I've been handed. But I don't drink it. I just let it sit. I smell it.

I won't drink until we win. Until every threat to my family and empire has been extinguished.

"… Okay, okay, settle down, men. I have a story about Daniil," Aleks calls out as he sits on the table and nearly tips over one of the half-empty bottles of vodka. "Fuck," he mutters absentmindedly, "where was I? Oh, right. Daniil—"

"Daniil!" the men cry, all piss-drunk and bloodthirsty.

"It was his first day in the field…"

With the men's attention focused on my brother, I put down the glass and slip out of the building. No one notices and I doubt they will anytime soon.

It's almost two in the morning; Wren will probably be anxious about where I am. I'm hoping she'll be sleeping when I get to the penthouse—but not only is her bed empty, the light is on in the nursery.

I sneak inside and find her seated on the carpet, surrounded by a pile of new baby clothes.

Well, to say the clothes are "new" is debatable. They're certainly unused, though. And obviously homemade. From what I can tell, Rose wasn't the best knitter. But she liked color and there's heart and warmth in all the things she'd made for her unborn children. I see her love in every stitch.

I sink down onto the carpet next to Wren and run the back of my hand against her face. She sighs deeply and falls back against my chest, allowing me to see the dry tear tracks carved down her cheeks. I expected this when I arranged the delivery from her storage unit, but that doesn't stop my chest from spasming with a feeling dangerously close to sorrow.

As I keep stroking her cheek, her eyes flutter open. Her eyebrows pinch together like she's struggling to recognize me. "D-Dmitri…"

"Come on. Let me get you to bed."

She shakes her head vehemently and sits upright. "Where were you?"

"I had business to take care of. I'm sorry I couldn't be here sooner to help you with all this," I say, gesturing to the clothes at our feet.

She picks up one of the tiny sweaters closest to her. It's made of white and yellow stripes and there's a little honey bee stitched into the front pocket. "I can't believe you brought me Rose's trunk."

"It's what you wanted, wasn't it?"

She nods. "It was. But…"

"But?"

Her expression crumples, like she wants to cry more but she won't give in to the impulse. "I guess I wasn't sure if you wanted our son to be dressed in the clothes my dead sister made for her babies who were never born." She cringes at the harshness of her own words.

"I just want you to be happy."

A fresh tear slips down the side of her face. I guess she had more to shed after all. "You get a say in this, too, you know."

"If I objected, I would tell you, Wren."

She shudders. "You don't think it's a little... morbid?"

"I think it's love. Love can take many different forms."

She lets out a relieved half-laugh, half-sigh. "They're not fancy or expensive—" she says, holding up a little red onesie and taking a big whiff of it. "... But they smell like her."

"Then let's fold them up and add them to his wardrobe, shall we?" I get to my feet and offer her my hands. She slips them into mine and I pull her up. As she rises, though, she stumbles forward and nearly bumps her chin against my chest. I catch her, wrapping her up in my embrace.

Wren lingers there for a moment, her cheek nestled against the base of my throat. "Thank you for... for everything," she whispers.

I touch her cheek with the backs of my knuckles. She does that laughing sigh again. *That's love, too,* I think to myself. *Just another form of it.*

With a sigh of my own, I disentangle myself and Wren and I get to work silently. She folds clothes and I stack them up in the steamer trunk, one impossibly small outfit at a time. Compared to the outfits already in there, these are shabby and ill-formed.

But they're *loved*. Made with the stuff. Filled with the stuff. Every last fiber straight-up drenched with the stuff.

So, ill-formed or not, they belong on top.

After a while, Wren starts to talk. She tells me little stories about Rose picking out yarn colors or cooing over one miniscule baby sock. She remembers her sister, one anecdote at a time. I just listen and smile and I don't stop myself from not-so-accidentally grazing her hand as she passes me one item after the next.

That's love, I think yet again. *Just another form of it.*

25

WREN

Something's up.

I may be in happy nesting mode, but that doesn't mean I'm oblivious. Dmitri's getting a heck of a lot more calls recently. In the old days, he used to flick them away in favor of giving me his full attention when we were together, but lately, he's been answering every single one. And he always sounds annoyed. In some cases, downright angry.

Whenever I ask him about what's going on, he acts as though they're just standard business calls and nothing is out of the ordinary. But since he's speaking Russian, it's pretty clear to me that one, they're not ordinary business calls, and two, he's intentionally keeping me in the dark.

But I've decided not to let it bother me too much—because the truth is, I kinda like this nesting stage. And I *love* having a job. A real job. Not the *Personal Management Team* bullshit that Dmitri once tried to palm off on me.

Of course, Jackson Asshole Mitchell has been curt and cold with me from our very first call. But as long as he doesn't get rude, I can put up with a little professional saltiness. I did kinda hijack his project; not to mention, I stole his job title to boot. A little sass is justified.

"*Another* one? Fucking hell, this is getting out of hand!"

I whirl around on my revolving chair and inch closer to the door. That's definitely Aleks talking, because Dmitri left only a half an hour ago with an advance apology for missing dinner tonight.

"I'll make it up to you tomorrow," he'd promised. "With interest."

Then he kissed me on the forehead and headed off—but not before I noticed the frown lines taking up permanent residence on his forehead.

I push open the door and peer around it. Aleks has his back to me. His spine is rigid with tension and he keeps gesturing wildly in the air. He's a lot more theatrical than Dmitri is. I wonder if that's a second child thing.

"… I don't give a fuck, man. Stick to the plan or you'll have to answer to my brother!" Aleks cuts the line and growls with frustration.

I clear my throat softly.

Aleksandr spins around like I just cocked a gun at him, though. He barely relaxes even when he realizes it's me. "Wren. What are you doing on this side of the penthouse?"

I hold the door open for him as he walks over to me. "Your brother presented me with my very own office space yesterday."

Aleks glances at the sleek oak desk, the modern light fixtures, and the colorful carpet on the floor. "He set this up fast."

"Have you heard? I'm on the payroll now."

"Right, right. Co-manager on the Montgomery project. Congrats."

"Come into my office, Aleks," I say in a cheesy Wall Street guru voice. "Take a seat."

"Why do I feel like you have an ulterior motive?" he asks cautiously.

I give him a wide, innocent smile. "I was just gonna have some powdered doughnuts and tea. I thought you might like some?"

"How can I say no to that?" he concedes with a sigh.

I show him to a seat in the dual armchairs and wait until he has a mouth full of powdered doughnut before I spring my question on him. "So… what's going on?"

"Dang it," he grumbles, sending a spray of sugar everywhere. "I knew there was a catch."

"There's something going on, Aleks, and I want to know what it is."

He swallows hard. The gulp is painfully audible in the quiet room. "Nothing's going on."

Narrowing my eyes at him, I grab the edge of the doughnut tray and drag it out of his reach. "Do you think I'm a dummy?"

He sighs with a long, mournful glance at the now-distant doughnuts. "Listen, Wren, you should probably talk to Dmitri about—"

"He doesn't want me to worry."

"And you think *I* do?"

"You're a reasonable man."

"That implies my brother is not."

"Correct. He isn't. And, as it turns out, neither am I." I grab the nearby trash can and hold it at the edge of the coffee table with the doughnut tray tipped up just enough that the first few crumbs start to tumble down. "You want another doughnut or no?"

"Wait!" He hisses. "You play a dirty game, Turner."

"Please?"

"Oh, fuck it, you're a grown woman." He grimaces and falls back in his chair as I set the doughnut tray back levelly on the table. "Things with the Irish and the Italians are escalating. They hit a couple of our businesses. A safehouse, too."

"Just... all of a sudden?"

Aleks hesitates. "Uh. Well..." He looks pained, like he wishes he'd never agreed to this conversation in the first place.

"Well, what?" I demand. "Just tell me, Aleks. I can take it, I swear."

He growls frustratedly. "Ugh, alright, alright, you little terrorist. *Technically,* Dmitri is the one who kicked off the latest round of this whole retaliation back-and-forth."

"What did he do?"

"He blew up a bar that belonged to the Irish. A pretty lucrative one at that. They were... less than pleased."

I blink in surprise. I'm no criminal mastermind, but with what I understand about this whole situation, it doesn't make a lick of sense for him to lash out so pettily. "Why on earth would he do that?"

"Why else, Wren? For you, of course. He needed to respond to your abduction. He could only really do that after you were safely back with him. But he did it to send a message: anyone fucks with you again and there'll be hell to pay."

"Except that they're retaliating now, too!" I exclaim. "And they've got a lot more men than you guys do, right?" I slump back in my seat, mirroring Aleks's posture. "I can't believe he started a war over me. I'm not—That's not…"

"He didn't start the war; he's finishing the war that Cian started." He rises to his feet and snatches up another doughnut. "Don't look so long in the face. This is life in the Bratva. And you're very much a part of it now. I'm gonna go deal with another situation. You just sit tight and focus on the new job, okay? Let us do ours."

He's almost out of the door when I lunge close and grab his wrist. "Dmitri isn't out there alone, is he?" I ask. "I mean, like, he's got backup right?"

Aleks chuckles. "It's sweet that you're worried. But I wouldn't waste time fretting over him. It's like that old saying: if you see Dmitri in a fight with a bear… go help the bear."

With that, he gently extricates his wrist and disappears down the hallway.

It's quiet and lonely when he's gone. Aleks has a way of making things sound easy, breezy, simple as could be. When I'm with him, I can believe all of that.

When he's gone, though, nothing seems nearly as sunshiny.

I take a deep breath and place my hand on my stomach. "It's okay, little one," I tell my son softly. "It's all gonna be okay."

26

WREN

I'm sitting up in bed when Dmitri walks into my room.

"You're still up," he remarks. As usual, his expression gives nothing away. There's no way you can tell he's embroiled in a full-scale, three-way mafia war by looking at him.

I swing my legs off the bed and get up with my shoulders squared. "Why did you do it?"

I don't mean for the question to come out quite so accusatory, but I don't want him to shut down the conversation before I've got a chance to get it going.

He stops short. His right eyebrow flickers up. "Do what?"

"Blow that bar up."

The left eyebrow rises to join the right. "Who told you?"

"No one. I overheard Aleks talking to someone on the phone." No point getting his brother into trouble when he's my only real source of information at the moment. "It's true, isn't it?"

To his credit, he doesn't bother to lie. He just nods. "Yes. It's true."

"Well?" I press. "You must have known that all hell would break loose? So why did you do it?

His jaw turns to rock. "Because they hurt you, Wren."

"Why does that even matter?" It's hard to get the words out when my heart is fluttering wildly in my throat like it is.

"Because, *moya devushka*, *you* matter."

"To you?" I ask softly. "Or to your empire?"

He takes a step towards me and gathers me up in his arms. "Both, of course. But mostly to me." His eyes are intense. I've never seen them like this before. The gray has turned a deep shade of blue, like the bottom of the ocean, the last place the sunlight reaches before it's snuffed out altogether. It feels like I'm down there with him, on a level only he and I can be in. "You mean everything to me."

Oh, God.

The last vestiges of my walls come tumbling down around me. I can't freaking fight this anymore. God knows I've tried, but it's failed time and time again.

I want this man.

I need this man.

I fucking *love* this man.

And if he really means what he just said... he just might feel the same way about me. Surely, *surely*, that should be enough for anyone.

So what do you do when you've reached a decision point like that? You do what I do: throw my arms around him and kiss him on the lips. Hard and desperate and filled with all the passion and need I've been trying to repress these many months. It pours out of me like hot lava and Dmitri meets my need with fire of his own.

I expected ripped clothes and bruising kisses and hard, relentless sex.

But he surprises me. He's gentle. Tender. He peels my layers off with careful fingers, piece by piece, until I'm standing naked in front of him. When I try to cover myself self-consciously, he utters an impatient growl and cups my face with his palm.

"Never hide how beautiful you are," he hisses fiercely, almost like he's scolding me.

Then, without warning, he lifts me into his arms. The gasp gets clogged in my chest. "D-Dmitri!" I yelp. "Put me down! I'm too heavy."

He doesn't so much as strain. He looks as relaxed as ever as he walks me to the bed. "Please. You're light as a feather."

It's not the smoothest lie he's ever told, but ironically, it does make me feel lighter. He lays me down on the bed and hovers over me, looking into my eyes for a second before his lips come grazing along the side of my neck.

I murmur and sigh. I'm still aware of my stomach, but it's not consuming all of my attention the way it normally does. I feel like so much more than just a pregnant woman.

For the first time in months, I feel like a *woman*.

He kisses his way down my body. My nipples have been sensitive lately and he seems to be aware of that because even when he sucks one into his mouth, he keeps the pressure light and teasing.

I moan, needy for his heat between my legs, but he takes his time. He runs his tongue over the curves of my hips, the underside of my breasts. I'm a twitching, writhing, sopping mess and he hasn't even touched me where it matters yet.

"P-please…" I whimper.

He drops a kiss at the peak of my belly and then slides down lower, disappearing behind it. It's annoying that I can't see him anymore. But a second later, the annoyance vanishes underneath a ripple of pleasure as his tongue meets my clit.

"So fucking wet," he observes with a delicious chuckle.

"For you," I whine back. "Only for you."

Forming sentences is difficult, so I'm mostly hoping that my breathy cries and moans will translate to what I'm trying to say, which is *Just fuck me already!* But there's no urgency in the way that Dmitri eats me out. He acts as though we have all the time in the world.

Grabbing fistfuls of the bedspread, my back arches as he starts lapping at my clit with his tongue. My exhale comes out of me in a never-ending "Fuuuck."

"What is it?" he croons. "Tell me what you want."

"I want *you*. Now. Fuck me," I gasp in a very unladylike voice. "For God's sake, just fuck me."

"Oh, I plan to," he says with a chuckle. "But first, I'm gonna make you work for it. Come for me like my good little slut and maybe I'll give you what you're begging for."

Well, when you phrase it like that, sir...

I end up stuffing my hand in my mouth to keep from screaming. It's half-pleasure and half-frustration. I just want to get off and I want to do it with him inside me. But I can't even reach him right now and even if I could, the thought of pulling his sinful mouth off of my dripping pussy makes me want to cry.

"Yes!" I wail as he adds two fingers to the mix and the speed of his tongue increases. "Yes, yes… fuck yes…"

It's gonna happen. It's gonna happen. It's gonna—

Before the wave crashes, the heat around my clit disappears. Suddenly, his face hangs overhead, those gray eyes fixed on mine with an intensity that sends a shiver through my chest.

"You didn't think it would be *that* easy, did you, darling?"

"You're evil," I protest. "Teasing a pregnant woman like this is criminal."

"I'm not *teasing* you," he corrects. "Not really. I'm *claiming* you, baby. I'm reminding you that you are fucking mine. All mine. This pussy is mine. Those moans are mine. That baby in there is *mine.* Have I made myself clear?"

He nudges my vagina with his cock and I nearly leap into the ceiling. "Yes! Yes, that's clear."

"Then tell me who you belong to."

My chest feels like it's expanding. It's like I can take in more oxygen. It's like I can breathe a little easier. It's like I could float away on a cloud if I wanted to.

"You," I assure him emphatically. "Only you."

He grins, pleased and evil and beautiful and so fucking perfect that I could die. Then he pushes himself inside me and I cry out, my nails digging into his shoulders.

"All yours," I moan. "Fuck yes… I'm all yours…"

I say it again and again and he demands that I keep repeating myself, until the words become as much of a blur as his thrusts into me. And when I finally come, with sweat dripping down my back and dirty promises burning on my lips, it feels like something has just been cemented between us.

That wasn't sex.

I mean, it wasn't *just* sex.

That felt like a *commitment*.

We shower together afterwards. He soaps me up and washes me off tenderly, then dries my hair and combs the tangles out before bed. By the time he pulls back the covers and helps me onto the soft mattress, I'm so exhausted that my eyelids are closing before my head even hits the pillows.

Still, I reach for him, knowing that tonight, he will sleep next to me. "This is real, isn't it?" I whisper sleepily, forcing my eyes open so that I can see his face when he answers.

His expression is, as always, unreadable. "Yes," he murmurs, so low that I almost miss it. "Very, very real."

"We're not just friends anymore? Not just co-parents?"

He shakes his head, but he doesn't give me a verbal answer. Just tugs the covers higher over me so that my chest is covered. Then his hand finds my hip in the warm darkness. "You're going to have to help me, *moya devushka*. I've never done something like this before. Show me how to be with you. I want to give you everything—but first, you need to ask for it."

I nod and he nods right back.

"Good girl."

"But you have to… try harder." *Keep your freaking eyes open, Wren. This is important!* "You have to put in the work, too." Remembering those lonely weeks before his fake wedding to Bee wakes me up a little. "After I found out the truth… you disappeared on me."

Dmitri's breath comes out in a mournful sigh. "I thought that's what you wanted."

"I wanted you to *fight* for me. When you didn't, I assumed it was because you didn't care."

His jaw tightens. "Of course I cared. I always fucking cared."

"Then tell me. Better yet, show me."

My eyes have closed again. I feel a soft fluttering kiss against my forehead. "I can do that," he promises.

"And Dmitri… no more lies, okay? If this is gonna work, you need to be honest with me."

The silence stretches on for a while. Or maybe I'm just so tired that I've lost all sense of time. Then finally, his voice reaches me.

"I'll do my best."

That night, I sleep better than I have in years.

27

DMITRI

I wake up feeling powerful.

Fuck the world. Who would dare to stop me? I could take on the Irish and the Italians single-handedly and burn their empires to the fucking ground.

There are no prizes for guessing what's gotten into me. Or rather, what I've gotten into. I glance to my side and see the source of my power. She's angelic in her sleep. Face smoothed of all worry, all self-consciousness. She looks like she did at the peak of her orgasm.

Blissful, in every sense of the word.

And fuck me, I felt the same. Her body has bloomed like a rose, all softness and curves and dewy beauty. And it's all mine for the taking.

I took as much as I could, given her condition. Even now, it's hard to resist wanting more of the same. Unable to resist, my fingers travel over her body, tickling her nipples and shimmying down her hips as she sighs and shifts in place. When she parts her thighs, I see her glistening.

I'm not the only one who's still craving seconds.

My cock jumps hungrily, but I ignore it. I don't want to wake her up. Not just yet anyway.

Part of the problem is the last kernel of doubt still remaining. It's deep—very deep—withering away in the darkness where I've kept it. But it won't die, the stubborn fuck. There's only one way to get rid of it: expose it to the light.

No more lies, okay? If this is gonna work, you're gonna have to be honest with me.

I should have come right out and told her then and there. But something held me back. Call it pride, call it stupidity, call it my inherent sense of self-sabotage… but it had kept me from telling her the truth.

It's a simple fix. All I have to do is wake her up right now and just fucking *tell* her. But as my fingers float toward her again and drag lightly through her wetness, I decide later is just as good as now.

"Dmitri…" It comes out in a low moan, laced with a smile.

"Didn't get enough last night, I see."

Her smile gets a little bigger, a little hungrier, though her eyes stay closed. "Apparently, neither did you."

She's right about that. So I take her in my arms and fuck her slowly. I bury my face in her neck when she comes and, as she moans, I can feel our son kick hard against her stomach.

"Jeez," she whispers in the aftermath, "I think you woke him up." She twists around inch by inch, wincing as she faces me.

"Ugh, I can't wait to not be pregnant anymore."

I run a palm up and down her belly. "I like you pregnant."

She scowls. "Yeah well, get ready to say goodbye to this belly, 'cause I'm not gonna be that way much longer."

Smirking, I kiss her forehead. She smells like... me. Fuck, does that feel good.

I take one more deep inhale, then shove myself out of bed with a sigh. "We have work to do," I announce. "Things to move around."

"What kind of things?" Wren asks in confusion as she props herself up on her elbows, hair deliciously mussed and eyes still furrowed with sleep.

"I'm moving in here. If you think I'm gonna spend another night without you at my side, you're delusional."

Her jaw drops open, but the flush on her cheeks tells me that she's more pleased than she cares to admit. Still, she suppresses the smile and edges herself off the bed. "If our new relationship status means that you think you can boss me around and make all the decisions without my input, you've got another thing coming, buddy."

My exhausted cock perks up immediately. "Is that right? Tell me more about what's coming."

She keeps her teeth clamped down on that smile, no matter how bad she wants to set it free. "We may be 'together—'" It's deeply annoying to me that she puts the word in air quotes. "—but that doesn't mean you get to decide everything without discussing it with me first."

I get a fraction of a second to admire her full body as she rises to her feet before she snatches the silk robe hanging off the white chaise and yanks it on. But even after she's cinched it around her waist, I can see her hard nipples poking through the thin fabric.

I saunter closer to her. "Some things aren't really up for discussion."

"*Everything* is up for discussion, mister."

"Wrong." I shake my head slowly. "For example, if I see a man looking at you, I reserve the right to beat the shit out of him. No questions asked. No discussion necessary."

Wren's still insisting on trying to look indignant, but her eyes are dancing with a familiar fire. She *likes* this side of me. The caveman side. The brute. "And would you stand for it if I said the same?"

"Oh?" I tilt my head. "Would you fight for me, *moya devushka?*"

She squares up and raises her chin high in defiance. "If I'm yours, then you're mine, Dmitri Egorov. And if some bitch thinks she can get her hands on you… well then, she's got another thing coming. Got a problem with that?"

"None whatsoever." I lightly palm her forearms, then slide down to her hips and tighten my hold on her. "Which brings me to my next point. You're living in my house, you're carrying my baby, and I plan for you to be in my bed every night for the rest of our lives, so I think it's time to be thinking about something else."

Wren frowns. "What kind of 'something else'?"

I tap the empty space on her left ring finger. "*This* kind of something else."

A little disbelieving guffaw escapes her lips and she clamps both hands over her mouth. Then she stares at me through her laced fingers with wide eyes. "That's insane," she murmurs. "*You're* insane."

"I think it's the sanest thought I've had all year."

I mean every word of that. I want this woman. And I want her forever. Not because she's beautiful. Not because she's carrying my baby. Not because I have to secure my legacy.

But because she makes me feel fucking strong.

And powerful.

And complete.

Because she makes me happy. And I haven't been happy since…

Since the motherfuckers took everything from me the first time.

It's all a neat conclusion when you look at it like that. I am going to make Wren my wife; I am going to slaughter the Irish and the Italians alike; I am going to give Elena the justice she never got.

Most of all, I am going to give myself the fresh start I've been craving.

And I will give Wren the future she deserves.

28

WREN

As it turns out, pregnancy isn't so bad when you're having constant, steamy, third trimester sex and being waited on hand and foot by a handsome Russian with a scowl that could make Lucifer jealous.

Although I haven't been on the receiving end of one of his signature scowls for a while now. Matter of fact, I've seen more smiles in the last few days than I did in my whole first year as Dmitri's P.A.

It's weird, though: the more comfortable I get with our domestic routine, the more I start to question things.

Can I trust this fragile peace?

Can I let myself be happy?

Can I believe that this thing between us will go the distance?

If it were just me, it might be easier—slightly—to jump in feet-first. But I have my son to think about. If I make the wrong choice, *he's* the one who'll suffer.

My childhood was a textbook case of unhappily married parents.

I don't want to repeat the same mistakes that they made.

Of course, it's hard to imagine that we could end up like my mother and father. Dmitri *cooks,* for God's sake. My father's idea of cooking was grabbing a beer out of the fridge after a long day of work.

(Well, he said "work." Who the hell knows what he was really doing?)

Today's the first morning that I wake up before Dmitri. I spend a good few minutes staring at his face in trademark stalker fashion. Only when I start feeling too much like a pervy little creep do I turn away and slip out of our room.

Our room. It took me a while to get used to, and now, I can't stop saying it. Can't stop thinking it, either. It strikes me that this is the first time I've ever lived with a man. I never stayed with a boyfriend long enough for it to become a live-in situation and we all know what a disaster my relationship with William was. "Relation*shit*" doesn't even begin to cover it.

But every little nook and cranny of living with Dmitri feels surprisingly natural. I love going to bed together. I'm always the little spoon. Ironic, considering just how bloated and huge I feel all the time these days.

I love waking up with him even more. He's usually wide-eyed and alert by the time I rise, if not already swooping back through the door with a tray of breakfast in hand.

It's an easy thing to let myself get spoiled.

Which is why, since this is the first time I'm actually up before him, I decide to turn the tables and bring *him* breakfast in bed. My cooking skills are painfully limited compared to the Bratva's version of Gordon Ramsay over here. No eggs Florentine or brioche French toast with raspberry-basil compote today. No, it's a simple bowl of granola mixed with yogurt and a few slices of toasted bread with scrambled eggs. I barely resist the urge to throw an Emeril-esque *"Bam!"* of parsley at the plate.

I walk into our—*our!*—bedroom to find Dmitri already awake and on his phone. "There you are," he murmurs, tucking away the phone. "I was wondering where you'd run off to."

Smiling, I set the tray down on his lap. "Surprise! I thought you could enjoy breakfast in bed for a change."

He examines the tray with interest that's a little too transparent to be real. "Looks good."

"Don't patronize me. It's granola, not gourmet."

Chuckling, he spoons some granola into his mouth and pulls an exaggerated, quasi-orgasmic face, all slack jaw and soft groans and eyes rolling back in his head. "A feast for the senses, truly."

"You realize that came from a box, right?"

"And yet it tastes sweeter than it has any right to. They do say love is the secret ingredient."

"Yeah, yeah, enough with the flattery, wiseass," I grumble, though I'm smiling as I crawl back in bed and curl up next to him.

Dmitri tilts his head to look down at me. His eyes sparkle the way they do when dirty things are about to follow.

"Fair enough. In terms of things I'd *rather* be eating, I'd say 'you' are at the top of the list." Right on cue, the silverware clacks on the tray as his morning wood joins the party, tenting up beneath the blankets.

Coffee sloshes over the rim of the mug. *Big dick problems.*

I scoot just out of reach. "There's time for that later."

"Why wait for later when you could be dripping all over my face right now?"

My cheeks flame with color. He has a habit of getting colorfully graphic when he's seducing me. Probably because it works. Every time.

Except today, I'm determined not to let him get me off-track with his hypnotic sex appeal. If I'm gonna stand my own in this relationship, I'll have to pretend for at least a few consecutive seconds like he's not the sexiest man I've ever laid eyes on.

"Because I'm trying to have a conversation with you. That's why."

He growls impatiently and sets the tray on his bedside table. "We can talk and fuck, *moya devushka*. I'm a great multitasker."

I snort. "Men rarely are."

"My performance last night would beg to differ."

"When were you multi-tasking?"

"When I was stirring the pasta on the stove *and* fucking you up against the kitchen counter."

I didn't know my face could burn this bright. "That was irresponsible on both our parts. We could have been scalded in scandalous places by burning hot pasta."

He reaches out to snag my foot and drag it into his lap. "Do you really think I would have let anything happen to you?"

"Well—"

"Nothing will hurt you as long as I'm around, Wren."

Be still, my beating heart. Gritting my teeth, I try to remember what I wanted to talk to him about in the first place. *He's distracting you again.*

"I know," I whisper softly.

"You better. But I'm happy to repeat myself as many times as it takes." He clears his throat and his smile fades into something more serious. "I want you to be happy."

I swear, I never tire of hearing him say that. "What about *you*? You should be happy, too."

"What makes you think I'm not?"

"Well…" I twist my hands together, the self-consciousness rushing through every inch of me. "You weren't exactly excited to discover I was pregnant. Which is totally understandable," I rush to assure him. "I mean, neither one of us was expecting it. And I was your assistant. And we hadn't even had *sex—*" *Jeez, I'm babbling. Stop me, please. Just freaking interrupt!* "I get that this pregnancy happened under unusual circumstances, but—" I take a deep breath. "Sorry."

"What exactly are you trying to tell me?"

The question itself is aggressive; the way he asks it is anything but. He runs a huge, smooth hand along my calf to calm me. His face is patient and open, showing no trace of the emotional barriers that once stood like freaking trauma mountains between us.

"I guess," I mumble with a gulp, "I was hoping that, somewhere along the way, you decided to be happy about this baby."

Silence. My anxiety starts to creep back up. I watch Dmitri's chest rise and fall with his breathing, too scared to look into his eyes.

And as the silence stretches on, I rush to fill it. "I mean, it's just—I know you're happy about having an heir to take over your Bratva and all. I guess I was hoping that you would be happy on a more… personal level."

More silence.

But this one doesn't last. One last breath of unease and then he's pulling all of me into his embrace and pressing my cheek to his chest. The rumble of his heartbeat soothes me, as does his hand combing through my hair again and again. I feel his voice as much as I hear it when he speaks.

"I'll be honest, Wren: this is not how I expected to enter into fatherhood." His hand stills. "But that doesn't mean this isn't exactly where I want to be."

I hate how my own voice comes out shaky and insubstantial. "Yeah?"

"It doesn't matter to me how our son came to exist. What matters is that he *exists*. He's part of both of us and that makes him special. Extra special, in fact, because he brought you to me. How many other children can make that claim?"

A teary laugh escapes my lips. "Not many."

"See? He's not even born yet and already, he's exceptional."

My bottom lip trembles and I try to bite back my tears. I can't even blame this on hormones; this is all Dmitri. "Do you mind if I ask you a personal question?"

"Go right ahead."

"It's about Elena."

His smile doesn't falter. "Consider me warned."

"Did you ever think about having children with her?" I clear my throat and add quickly. "Just FYI, there is no wrong answer. And no answer is okay, too."

He breathes quietly. "Elena was so young when we got married. I didn't have children on the brain in a serious way. I always assumed we would have them one day, but I suppose I was thinking about it like it was strictly business. Legacies and heirs, like you said."

"Oh."

"But then Elena told me she didn't want children. So we were at an impasse. I didn't push her too hard. I was immature, prideful. I thought that, if I changed my own mind, it would be easy to change hers when the time came."

"Did she say why she didn't want kids?"

Dmitri falls silent for a bit. I worry that I've pushed this conversation too far and I'm about to apologize when he speaks again. "It's funny... I'm not sure Elena was honest with me about the real reason."

I frown. "How would you know that?"

"Because Bee told me just before... the, uh, wedding. She told me that Elena wanted kids; she just didn't want to have them with *me*. Because of the world I lived in, the circles I traveled in… All I knew was what Elena told me. That she was scared to be a mother because she didn't think she could be a good one."

I sink into his side and run my fingers lazily through his chest hair. "Maybe both reasons are true?"

"Maybe. Maybe not." He sighs. "Either way, I didn't know my wife as well as I thought I did. Turns out, Bee knew her a hell of a lot better."

"Yeah, well, color me surprised."

He glances down. I can feel the heat of his frown even without looking back up at him. "What is that supposed to mean?"

I cringe. "Um, nothing." He keeps staring and I cave like papier-mâché. "It's just… you're not always the easiest person to be honest with, Dmitri. You don't really allow a lot of space for… other people."

He pokes me in the side playfully. "Are you saying I'm an egotistical control freak?"

"I'm saying… your personality is so big that sometimes it's over-powering."

"It hasn't been for you," he points out.

That actually makes me smile. "I've held my own?"

"Enough to annoy the hell out of me," he confirms. "At first." Then he shifts and I can almost feel a sense of ease trickle back and forth between us as lines of tension go slack. "But lately… lately, I've realized that I *need* someone who can push back. I need someone who'll hold me accountable. I need someone who's my equal."

I risk a glance up at him. Something ripples across his face, but it's gone before I can catch it. I'm not sure if he's having some sort of existential revelation or just coming to terms with his new reality.

Either way, when he turns his gaze on me, his features soften.

"Elena was a wonderful person. She was sweet and kind—but she was still just a girl when I met her. You, Wren… you are a *woman*. You're the woman I need by my side from this point on."

Smiling, I slip my hand into his. He doesn't have to use his words to say he loves me.

The touch of his fingertips on my face says it loud enough.

29

DMITRI

I'm stuck in downtown Chicago traffic when my phone goes off.

Aleks's name flashes across the dashboard screen. When I accept the call, I growl, "You better have good news for me."

"Hold on—I lost at rock-paper-scissors, so Locksmith gets to tell you. Lemme put you on speaker." He's obviously eating something because his words come out all crunchy and muffled. "Okay, you savage, go on. Tell him."

I hear the grate of Locksmith's modulated laughter. "Guess who wants a meeting with you?"

I know the answer before she can give it. "This is the third time Cian's asked for one. He must be getting real fucking desperate."

"Guess again. It's not Cian asking this time."

My hand tightens on the steering wheel. "Vittorio?"

"*Ding-ding-ding!* You are correct, sir!" Locksmith is giddy with enthusiasm. "Can you believe that arrogant motherfucker actually came down off his high horse long enough to request a powwow?"

"Considering we took down his third business in the last week alone, I can see why he's getting nervous. And considering we're going to blow his depot to rubble next, he ought to be."

"Speaking of the next hit," Aleks interjects, "what're we thinking timing-wise? I'll have to squeeze this one in between the two Irish properties you already have scheduled to be—and I believe I'm being technical here—torched to fucking smithereens.'"

Between the moment with Wren this morning and Vittorio's capitulation this afternoon, I'm in enough of a good mood to laugh. "We can push that," I decide. "The Irish are still scrambling from our last attack. They're not getting back on their feet anytime soon. We can focus on the Italians for now."

"They might rally faster than you think," Aleks cautions. "Their existence depends on it."

"That's by design. If they weren't desperate, they wouldn't be calling." As the traffic slows to even less of a crawl, I make a detour down an uncrowded street.

"It could also be a trap," Locksmith ventures.

"I've considered the possibility. Which is why I'm not entertaining their calls at the moment. I want them to really sweat before I deign to give them so much as a return call."

"Please," Aleks snorts. "You may not have to talk to either *mudak* with the way things are going right now. If we keep cutting off their lifeblood, they might just run away with their tails tucked between their legs."

"As nice as that sounds," I muse, "I also want to look each of them in the face before I end their lives. I owe that much to Elena. To Bee."

There's a crackle of silence on the other line. "What are you worried about?" Aleks asks at last.

"What makes you think I'm worried?"

Locksmith snorts. "Please. We all recognize your *I'm worried* voice. Kinda sounds like you have a stick up your ass. A different stick than the usual one, that is."

I roll my eyes, but they aren't wrong. "I've been thinking lately about this alliance between Vittorio and Cian. There's something fishy about it. Makes me wonder how long they've been conspiring against me."

"It can't be that long," Locksmith says. "I mean… up until the Red Wedding, Vittorio had put all his eggs in the Egorov basket."

"That's just it: I'm starting to doubt that. The man is a cunning little weasel and he's one to hedge his bets. I think that this runs deeper than any of us know."

That suggestion is met with a thoughtful silence from both Aleks and Locksmith. "Do you think he suspected you and Bee?" Aleks suggests.

"He certainly suspected *something*."

Locksmith makes a grunting sound. "It was a good plan. There's no way he would have—"

"He had a conversation with Wren before the wedding," Aleks interrupts. "I'm gonna have to agree with my brother on this one. He knew something was up, even if he didn't know what that something was exactly."

"Okay, so what are you saying?" Locksmith asks.

"He's saying that we can't underestimate Zanetti," I answer. "He may have requested a sit-down, but I doubt it has to do with requesting a truce. If he's calling me, it's because he wants to manipulate or trick me."

"I'll see what else I can dig up," Locksmith offers.

"Don't bother. If Vittorio's got a plan in place, there's not gonna be a paper trail. He's aware that I've got hackers on my team."

"He's not aware you have *me*, though," Locksmith points out. "Motherfucker tried to buy me once and I laughed in his face. He's never forgiven me for that."

"That, among other things." I sigh and readjust my grip on the steering wheel as I weave down backroads to bypass the traffic. "Let's just do our homework here. Run more recon on the Italian depot we're hitting next. I want to make sure the surveillance system is fully mapped out before we go in."

"I'm on it."

"And if there are any other developments, call me immediately."

"Wait—you're not joining us?" Aleks asks.

"Not tonight. I have to go home, check on Wren."

"How is the missus?" Locksmith asks politely.

"Very pregnant, very strong-willed, and getting more and more impatient by the second."

"It does feel like she's been pregnant forever," Aleks says sympathetically. "Who knew nine months could last so long?"

It strikes me as we say our goodbyes and hang up that, as long as nine months has felt in some ways, it's been a blink of an eye in others. Things have changed—many things.

Like this, for example. I just hung up the phone after sending my best lieutenants off on some of the most important groundwork of our lives. And instead of following up on their efforts, instead of planning and scheming and thinking and working…

I'm about to go home to my pregnant woman to do nothing much at all.

And it feels so fucking right.

~

"How much longer, Doc?" Wren asks, turning hopeful eyes on Dr. Liza. "Seriously, you have to give me some good news. I feel like the whale that swallowed Pinocchio. I just want this little puppet *out of me.*"

Dr. Liza just smiles bracingly. "It'll take as much time as it takes, Wren. But in my professional opinion, I'd say no more than two weeks. We'll have to consider inducing if we get much farther along than that."

"Two *weeks*?!" Wren gasps, veering to me with panic as though she's hoping I can solve obstetrics for her with a simple wave of my hand. "You're saying I might be pregnant for another two whole weeks?!"

"Like I said, we can always induce labor," she repeats. "But I'd advise against it until the last possible moment. The baby will come when he's good and ready to."

"Oh, great!" Wren mutters, throwing her arms up into the air. "Then I guess he's gonna camp out there for another few years." She turns to me with her eyes blazing. "No need to look for preschools or anything—I'm sure, by the time he comes out, he'll be ready to leave for college."

I hide my laugh. She's cute when she's overwhelmed.

Joining her at her side, I run my hand along her back. "Stop stressing about this. Just enjoy the quiet while you can. In a few weeks, we'll have a screaming infant in the house and you'll wish you were back to being pregnant."

"Ha!" she snorts in my face. "Please. I will never wish for that. I never want to be pregnant again! What was I *thinking*, agreeing to do this for Rose and Jared? I mean, it's *so* not worth it if you don't get to keep the baby afterwards."

I turn to Dr. Liza with an eyebrow raise. "Is there anything we can do to make her more comfortable? Maybe even encourage the baby to come a little sooner?"

"Yeah!" Wren nods eagerly. "Yeah, that!"

Dr. Liza gives Wren a gentle pat on the leg. "I'm sure you're already aware of the natural labor inducers. I always recommend nice, long walks to my patients. Acupuncture can work, too. Sex is often—"

"Sex!" Wren interrupts. "Doctor, we've been humping like rabbits for days now and nothing's happening." She looks down at her big belly with disappointment, too irritated to be embarrassed about something that would've mortified her not too long ago. "I've walked around the apartment so many times I've gotten dizzy and I've had three acupuncture appointments in the last week alone."

"So you've done your research."

She locks eyes with the doctor and says in the most solemn voice I've ever heard from her, "I'm desperate."

"I understand. The last stage of pregnancy is always the hardest. But I must say, you're doing spectacularly well, Wren." She turns to me and gives me a sly wink. "And that goes for you, too, Dad. You've done an amazing job of creating a calm, safe space for her. Her vitals are strong and her blood pressure is normal. She's healthy as a horse and in prime shape for giving birth."

"You hear that, baby boy?" Wren croons, looking down at her belly and poking it from both sides. "Everything's all set for your arrival. There is literally not one single thing you need to wait on."

I wrap my arm around Wren and pull her into my chest. "You can't really blame him," I whisper into her ear.

"Why the hell not?" she snaps.

"Speaking as a man who's been inside you, it's really fucking hard to come back out again."

The instant blush turns her pale skin into a deep shade of auburn. But it worked; she's smiling again. Which means I've done my job.

And like everything else about being with Wren...

It feels right.

30

WREN

"These are the dumbest instructions I've ever seen in my life. I banish you to the shadow realm." With an angry snort, I ball up the offending piece of paper and launch it across the living room.

I've been on my ass on the floor for almost an hour trying to get this damn bassinet together and my butt cheeks are starting to go numb. It was never supposed to be this way.

It all looked so damn simple when I first read through the instructions. Even still, at first, I was gonna wait for Dmitri to get home. But then I thought, *No!* I am a strong, independent woman who doesn't need to rely on a man for every little thing. I can set up the bassinet on my own, right? Right, ladies?!

Wrong.

Turns out: very, *very* wrong.

It doesn't look a bit like the *"safe and happy nesting place for your precious baby"* that the instruction manual promised. It looks more like a *Saw*-inspired deathtrap that ends with a visit from Social Services.

Love that for me. My baby's not even born yet and already, I'm failing at motherhood. Maybe *that's* why this baby doesn't want to come out yet: he's nervous as hell that I'll stick him in a crib that functions more like a French Revolution guillotine.

I've been telling myself that the hormones are what's wrong with me today. But repeating that to myself hasn't exactly helped make a difference. Didn't I used to be handy? I helped Jared build an entire freaking wall cabinet once. Rose didn't do jack shit—Jared and I tackled that thing like we had HGTV cameras filming every bit of our expertise.

Where did that confidence go?

And if I can't do that simple thing, then how can I expect to keep this little one safe and protected once he's out of me? I've been kidnapped twice already and that was just while he was inside me. God only knows what the future might hold. What failures might be lurking just around the bend.

The hyperventilating is kicking in. I can't breathe. Can't see straight. Can't think past the blinding panic.

Ping.

Shit! Dmitri's home already? I was supposed to be done with the bassinet by the time he arrived. Instinctively, I move in front of it to hide the mess I've made in the living room.

He stops short when he sees me there on my knees, arms outstretched, probably looking like a complete nutcase. One eyebrow drifts up his forehead. "Wren? Are you—"

"*Itriedtobuildthebassinetmyselfandit'sacompletedisaster.*" It all comes out like a single word without pauses in between.

He looks past me at the carnage in my rearview mirror. "Hm. Not sure it's supposed to be lopsided."

Old me might've laughed at that. Current me is not amused. "Gee, thanks, Captain Obvious. I had no idea."

The other eyebrow floats up to join its twin. "You okay?"

"That's a little bit of a patronizing question, don't you think?"

He sighs and leans against the doorway, folding his arms over his chest. "Rough day, huh?"

"My day's been *fine*," I spit out. "I just need to finish this and I need peace and quiet to do it."

"I can be quiet while I help."

"No!"

He stops short, already halfway to where I'm sprawled. "No?"

"I need to do this on my own." The moment I say it, I find myself thinking, *Do I? Do I really need to do this on my own? Or am I just being insane?*

But now that I've gone and said it, I feel as though I've backed myself into a corner. *Don't back down! Never show weakness! Freeeeedoooom!*

"Wren, there's no reason for you to—"

"You think I *can't* do it? Is that it?"

Dmitri's eyebrows come down. He looks annoyingly calm. "I think you can do anything you want," he says coolly. "If you want to do it on your own, then I'll back off."

Well… that was easy. "Okay. Good."

"I'm going to the kitchen. Do you need anything?"

"Just some quiet."

He gives me a small nod and disappears around the corner. I turn back to the bassinet as my face sinks. *I'm the biggest bitch alive. And also the dumbest, apparently, because my brain is mashed potatoes and I can't do this on my own right now.*

"Shit," I mutter, crawling around the floor in search of the instruction manual I yeeted a few minutes ago.

I find it and curl up in the corner and get back to work trying to figure out why Screw Q doesn't fit into Slot 14 the way it's motherfucking supposed to. The fact that the paper is wrinkled to shit doesn't make my task any easier.

When I look up at the clock, ten minutes have passed.

I bury my nose in the instructions again. Another fifteen minutes.

Back to it. When my neck screams at me to give it a damn rest already, I look up to see we've now crossed the hour mark since Dmitri got home and I am nowhere close to cracking this puzzle.

"Goddammit!" I wail.

I glance over my shoulder to see Dmitri standing on the threshold again, this time with a glass of water. He does nothing apart from hand it over to me.

"Thanks," I mutter.

He eyes my "progress" subtly. "Can I help you now?"

I open my mouth to tell him to fuck off.

Instead, I start crying.

Great. Just great. To Dmitri's credit, he does nothing except lower himself to where I'm slumped against the wall, fold me into his arms, and hold me tight. Not gonna lie, it feels miles better than it should.

But that's exactly why I wanted to fix the bassinet on my own. I don't want to have to rely on him for everything. He already does too much for me. I used to pride myself on being an independent, self-reliant woman.

And now?

I'm just *Dmitri's* woman. A *kept* woman.

First world problems, I know. But repeating that to myself doesn't seem to make them sting any less.

"I read that freaking manual so many times," I whisper hoarsely into his shoulder. "It should be simple. It *is* simple. I'm just an idiot who can't do anything anymore."

"That's not true."

"It *is* true," I insist. It's a testament to his many powers that he can even understand me at this point. I'm blubbering all over him like some pathetic, helpless, silver spoon princess who's never even had to tie her own shoelaces.

He holds the water to my lips. "Drink," he commands. Reluctantly, I do as he says. When I swallow, he looks down at me and asks, "Better?"

"No. The bassinet still looks like a dumpster fire. Actually, it would be better off if it were in an actual, literal dumpster fire."

"I can fix it."

"I know you can. That's not the point!"

He regards me with a long, questioning look. "I wasn't aware there was a point."

"Well, there is," I huff. "I was going to put together the bassinet on my own. I have to prove that I can do shit on my own."

"Who are you trying to prove this to?"

"Myself!"

He frowns. His hand dances lightly up and down my back. "You wanna tell me what's really going on, Wren?"

"Don't do that. Don't use that tone on me. I'm not a child throwing a tantrum and I'm not a problem that requires managing."

"I don't think you're either one of those things."

There's a small but mighty part of me wondering why I'm trying so hard to get a rise out of him. Am I trying to pick a fight to push him away? Am I trying to test the limits of this new "relationship" of ours? Am I trying to see how much he'll put up with before he goes all bosshole *pakhan* on me?

"Then what am I?"

"Right now? I'd say you're an exhausted pregnant woman who's tired of being exhausted and pregnant." He's... not wrong. "Now, can you please tell me why it's so important that you set up this bassinet on your own?"

Great question. If only I knew the answer. "I don't know." Despite my earlier declaration that I'm no child, I sound pretty damn childish, even to myself.

"If you don't know, then maybe I should just finish the job."

"No!" *Why the hell can't I let this go?* "I need to do it."

"Then let me be your hands. You take the lead. I'll just be your helper."

It's a great compromise, delivered like he's got years of training in conflict resolution, and still, I find myself rejecting it. "No," I insist, inching away from him. "I have to do this *all* on my own."

"No one is an island, Wren. Asking for help is not a weakness."

"And what if I have no one to ask?"

"You have *me!*" he growls. It's the first time that he's shown some sign of annoyance, though it's just a brief flash of fire before he's back to cool and implacable. "You have me, Wren, and I'm right here, asking to help."

"But when you're not around…?"

"Then fucking *call* me and I'll drop everything else and come."

Everything he's saying is reassuring. And comforting. And amazingly selfless. And yet, it's not making me feel any better. "But what if you *can't* come?" I practically shout. "What if you can't come because you're not around anymore?"

He leans back in shock. "Why wouldn't I be around?"

I jump to my feet and start pacing. "For starters? Because you're currently in a fucking *war* with two distinct mafia dons who both want you dead! Because they killed your last wife and they probably have every intention of killing your next one, too! Because you're out every day, torching buildings, blowing up businesses, and risking your life to end this war... And because I'm terrified all the time that I'm going to lose you and then I'll be alone with this baby and no goddamn idea of how to keep him safe!"

I'm shaking hard. There's sweat pooling at my back and my spine is aching from the simple act of getting up.

But at least I have some clarity now on why there are hornets in my brain.

Dmitri rises to his feet slowly. "You've been keeping all that inside you this whole time?"

I swallow, which hurts. Maybe I shouldn't have let the volume knob on my buzzing thoughts get cranked quite so high. "Um, to be fair... they weren't exactly conscious fears until right now."

"Understandable." He nods. "There's a lot going on."

"It's really annoying how patient and mature you're being right now, you know."

He smiles and extends his hand out to me. "May I approach the bench, Your Honor?"

Goddamn him for making me smile. "If you must." Then I slip my hand into his.

He pulls me up into him and kisses the top of my head. "You have every reason to be scared. They're legitimate fears."

I hiss wordlessly and recoil. *"That's* how you decide to comfort me?"

He chuckles, but his expression irons out almost instantly. "Come over here. Sit with me."

"I don't wanna sit." I'm not sure why I'm sticking with the stubborn adolescent routine, but we've come this far, so why give it up now?

But Dmitri puts his hands on my shoulders and I feel an iron strength in those fingers that wasn't there when he was just stroking my back. His eyes have changed, too. They're stormier. Darker. "I'm done making suggestions, *moya devushka*. Do as I say willingly or else I'll have to *make* you. And I assure you—I'm gonna enjoy it."

Well, fuck me sideways with a toaster. Now, I'm emotional *and* turned-on. That's just what this little basket case temper tantrum of mine needed: an injection of horniness.

Funnily enough, though, parts of my brain go quiet when he takes over. My legs jump on board with the program first. They pilot me over to the couch where he's pointing long before the rest of me agrees.

He nods with satisfaction. "Good girl."

Oof. Wet. Instantly.

Dmitri follows behind me, his scent a constant reminder of how close he is. I expect him to join me on the sofa, but instead, he crouches down in front of me. In fact, he gets down on one knee, proposal style. He takes my hand—my *ring* hand—and places it between both of his.

"Let's talk fears first." *Talk about a mood killer.* Although, to be fair, I think I led the charge on the whole mood murder mission. "You're right: I do live a dangerous life. I do deal with dangerous men. But trust me, Wren: I'm the most dangerous one of them all."

My lip trembles. "No one is invincible, Dmitri."

"You're right. And *if* something happens to me—" I draw in a sharp breath and he grips my hand a little tighter. "—and that's a big if—I have plans in place to make sure you and the baby are taken care of."

That gets my heart beating faster. "What do you mean?"

"Firstly, I want you to understand something." He puts his hand under my chin and draws my eyes to his. "I need you to look me in the eye when I say this. I need you to understand just how serious I am."

"I'm listening."

"I'm doing everything in my power to win this war quickly. And I'm going to do my damndest to stay alive while doing it. The *only* reason I would ever leave you—the *only* fucking reason in this entire world, Wren—is if I have no other choice. Do you hear me?"

Tears well up in my eyes, but I nod again, feeling like a mute, useless bobblehead. "I hear you."

"When I'm not with you, Aleks will be. When Aleks is not with you, I will be. If neither one of us can be with you, I have Pavel, Vasily, Volkov, and Maksim all assigned to put their lives on the line to keep you and our son safe. The four of them will not engage with the Italians or the Irish. Their sole responsibility is to keep the two of you safe from harm."

"But—"

He holds up his hand commandingly and I fall silent. "You can trust all of them. They will protect you with their lives. Even if I'm gone."

Goosebumps pepper my skin at the very thought. It's horrible to even imagine—but the more he talks, the more I find myself imagining it. I want him to stop; I want to pretend as though this whole conversation is unnecessary. *Just tell me I'm being silly, goddammit!*

But hell, I'm the one who asked for it, right? And if I can't take hard truths, then I don't belong by his side.

I appreciate that he's willing to tell them to me.

His grip on my hand gets tighter. "I wouldn't be telling you all this unless I thought you could handle it, Wren. And you *can* handle it. You have to. For our son."

It's like he read my thoughts.

It's also a good reminder that the stakes are high and I *need* to hear this. "Go on."

"So should anything happen, they'll take you out of here. Out of Chicago and somewhere far away, somewhere safe. Pavel has the key to the lockbox that contains everything you'll need. New identities, bank account information, passwords, access codes. There's enough money in the accounts to last three lifetimes over."

A shiver runs down my body. "Dmitri—"

"I've thought of everything, baby. I've made sure you'll want for nothing. If I don't make it, I'm gonna make damn sure that you and my son do. I told you from the start that I've got you, Wren. I've got you. I've always, always got you."

I twist our hands around so that I'm gripping *him* now. "I know," I whisper. "I know you do. But as grateful as I am that you've thought of everything, it's not what I want." He opens his mouth but I press my fingers over his lips. "I don't want a new identity or four protectors or safehouses in Paris or Timbuktu or wherever the fuck. I want *you*, Dmitri Egorov. I want us to raise this baby together. I want us to be a family.

So do whatever you have to do to win this war—because I don't want to be a single mother. I refuse to be."

His eyes blaze with fresh determination as he nods. "Well, if you refuse... I guess I have no choice but to win."

Fresh tears slip down my cheeks. I might just be falling in love with him all over again. "You promise?"

He doesn't hesitate to answer. "I swear it."

31

DMITRI

Aleks slaps his hands together and gives me a smile that makes him look like a cartoon villain. If he had a mustache, he'd be twirling it devilishly.

His face drops when he realizes I'm not partaking in the same level of enthusiasm. "Why don't you look happier?" he demands. "We just won a big victory today, man. *Another* one. That's two Irish safehouses in two days. At this rate, there'll be scrambling to find storm drains to hide in. Isn't that what you wanted?"

"Those last two safehouses were unmanned and unprotected. They were both sitting ducks."

"And you have a problem with that because…?"

"Because it smells like a trap." My fists clench like they have a mind of their own. Aleks has never been one to question things to death—but me? I take after my father that way. "It was too damn easy, *brat*. Why the fuck would he forfeit his kingdom, one brick at a time? It makes no sense. Cian's not even trying to put up a fight."

"Because he probably knows he can't win."

"Cian cares about his men. He also has Vittorio on his side." I grind my teeth hard enough to feel a twinge of pain. "Why would he admit defeat when this war has only just started?"

Aleks shrugs. "Maybe he's not really interested in fighting?"

I know Aleks is just brainstorming, just throwing shit at the wall to see what sticks... and yet this one *does* stick. It stays with me like a bad smell.

Wren had tried to make a case for Cian O'Gadhra not so long ago. She seemed to think that he wasn't really as into this war as he claimed to be.

Is that what this is?

Or is there just something I'm not seeing?

Either way, I'm more determined than ever to make sure that Wren is taken care of should this war take a turn for the worse. "Listen, I need you to do me a favor."

Aleks rolls his eyes like the drama queen he is. "I do you so many already—but okay, fine, go ahead."

I'm not in the headspace for lighthearted banter. What I'm about to say is still sitting on my chest like a fucking boulder. "If things go south..."

"South?" he interrupts. "Hold up. What the fuck are you talking about? We're winning this war, brother. We're already on top."

"For now."

His mouth drops closer to the ground. "And what's gonna change, dude?! We've got the Irish in retreat, hiding somewhere with their tails between their legs, and we've taken down four of the Italian hotspots, too. We got—"

"It doesn't *matter*," I bark. "None of it does. They don't need to take down all our businesses or safehouses to win—they just need to take *me* down. If they target me, then they make Wren and my son vulnerable."

His throat bobs with a nervous swallow. "I get that you're worried about them—I am, too—but—"

"No. No buts. There is no room for 'but.' The whole fucking world knows she's carrying my baby now. Neither Cian nor Vittorio have anything to lose. And this is war, yes—I know that as well as anyone. With war come casualties. But I will not allow those casualties to include my wife."

It's not until a slow smile spreads across my brother's face that I realize what I just said. *Wife.*

"Is that where your head's at?" he teases.

Oh, goddammit. He's never gonna let this shit go.

I get up from behind my desk and walk towards the windows, hands clasped behind my back. "I misspoke."

Aleks is on me like the irritating shadow I never asked for. "Did you now? I believe Dr. Freud had a name for that kind of 'misspeaking.'"

"Leave it alone, Aleks."

"Have you ever known me to leave anything alone ever in the history of the universe?" He doesn't wait for me to answer his question before he's nudging me with his shoulder. "Are you seriously thinking about putting a ring on it?"

I throw him a stony glare.

That's enough—Aleks grins widely. "Fuck *yeah*." He's vibrating on the soles of his feet with giddiness and an ear-to-ear smile that, against all odds, makes my own mouth twitch in that same direction.

"It's not gonna happen any time soon," I growl, wiping my face clean again. "So don't go shooting your mouth off about this to anyone else."

"Who would I tell?" he asks innocently.

"You know damn well who."

His smile turns sheepish and he makes the sign of the cross over his chest. "Scout's honor. I won't breathe a word." Then he clears his throat. "But just between us brothers…?"

Rolling my eyes, I decide to give him a little something, if only to keep him from annoying the hell out of me. "It'll have to be after this war is over. And after the baby is born. I want to give her a real wedding, the kind of wedding she deserves. I want to be able to celebrate properly after we've declared victory over those Irish and Italian fucks."

"You'll have to propose first, you know."

He's got me there, not that I haven't already considered it. I spent last night looking down at Wren while she was sleeping, imagining how I would propose to her. Fly her somewhere exotic and slide a ring on her finger with a spectacular view as our backdrop. The Eiffel Tower, perhaps? No, too stereotypical. The Pyramids, maybe? Too hot, too sandy. Maybe the Northern Lights? But I'll be damned if I wait for the literal stars to align before I make her mine.

"I plan to."

Aleks's cheeks flush another shade brighter. "Fuck, brother, this is big news!"

I simply grunt at him and turn back to the view. "Again, this isn't happening any time soon. I want it to be perfect—and if it has any chance of being perfect, I have to put this war behind us. Which brings me to the favor I was gonna ask you."

"You want me to be the best man?" He drops into a ludicrously deep bow, his nose almost grazing his knees. "It would be my *honor!*"

I can't quite hide the smile behind my eye roll. "I'm trying to have a serious conversation with you."

"Right," Aleks says, straightening up. The smile simmers down but doesn't quite go away. "Tell me. What's this favor you want, my liege?"

"I want you to make double sure that all my contingency plans are in place." His scowl sours but I keep going. "Most importantly, I need you to make sure that Wren knows exactly who to turn to if things don't go our way. She'll need someone she can trust. And by that, I mean she needs someone she *already* trusts."

"So you're not actually planning on telling her anytime soon?"

"Brother, we've been over this—"

"Yes, we have—and I've told you repeatedly that I don't agree with keeping this from her. She deserves to know. And I think you believe that, too."

"I can't tell her now," I mutter with a scowl of my own. "She freaked out last night because she couldn't put the damn crib together on her own. She's at a sensitive stage in her pregnancy. This would tip her over the edge."

"If you think she's gonna get calmer after the little one arrives, you're fucking delusional, man. This little tidbit won't add to her stress levels. In fact, I think it just might help."

My gut sinks the way it only does when he brings up a good point. "I'll have to explain why I lied to her all this time."

Aleks raises his eyebrows. "From where I'm standing, you'll have to do that either way." He must see that he's getting through to me, because he steps closer to drive his point home. "If you don't tell her and she finds out some *other* way? *Hoooo boy*, you're gonna totally fuck things up for yourself. Stop being a chickenshit little bitch and just rip off the Band-Aid. Don't let this be the self-fulfilling prophecy that you die on."

One good point after the next. I don't know who replaced my brother with fucking Socrates, but it's annoying the hell out of me. "Fine," I snap. "I'll tell her tomorrow."

But even that's not good enough for him. "What's wrong with today?"

"Because it's almost one in the morning, you dipshit. And she hasn't been sleeping well because of how big her belly has gotten recently."

"Yeah, I noticed. Your son's gonna be a large boy."

I can't help but smile. "I hope he gets the chance to be. Now, go. Get some sleep and we'll discuss strategies tomorrow." He gives me a sloppy, tired salute and makes for the door. "Oh, and Aleks?" He twists around at the door to wait for my last words. "Tell Locksmith to be at our morning meeting. No excuses."

"Aye, aye, captain. 'Twould be my pleasure."

He leaves and I turn back to the view through my office windows. I'm not sure why I'm so resistant to telling Wren the whole truth. Actually, fuck it—that's a lie. I *do* know why I'm resistant to telling her. It's because I promised her I'd be honest with her even while I was smack dab in the middle of lying to her. It doesn't exactly inspire a lot of trust, and we've already been struggling with a lack of the stuff. What if this ruins it?

Fuck.

But Aleks's argument is still simmering in my head. *Tomorrow,* I reassure myself. *Tomorrow.*

I'll tell her tomorrow when she wakes up. With that decision made, I can justify getting in bed next to her and breathing in her deliciously sweet scent, counting her soft, fluttering breaths, spooning her ripe, glorious body.

I'm already imagining it as I pace down the hall toward our room. As much as I hate it, she's past the point where I can wake her up for midnight sex whenever I want. She needs her sleep. There'll be plenty of time for that later, once my son is out of her and the war is won.

Until then, my top priority is that she gets her rest.

Through the shadows of the bedroom, I can see only her silhouette wrapped around the pregnancy pillows she spoons to sleep most nights. She stirs and groans in her sleep as I undress silently.

Could this be it? Is it go-time at last? Is my son coming?

Then she lets out a low moan and jerks upright before I've even unbuckled my pants. The garbled scream that comes out of her is almost inhuman.

"Wren!" I vault over the bed towards her. "What's wrong? Is it your water? Did it break?"

She just makes another godawful scratching sound with her throat and shakes her head frantically. I reach for the switch by her bedside and turn on the table lamp. Light pierces through the shadows and illuminates her face.

Blyat'.

"H-headache," she manages to say—but the blood streaming down her nostrils gets in her mouth and makes her sputter. *"Urgh..."*

"Hush," I whisper as coolly as I can, trying to keep her calm. "It's gonna be okay, *moya devushka*. Come with me—we're gonna get you to a hospital."

Her eyes go wide as she realizes just how much blood she's drenched in. It's turned the front of her white slip into a fucking horror show.

I try to get her to the door, but she shakes her head vehemently and pulls me towards the bathroom instead. Okay, so she wants to wash the blood out of her mouth. Fair enough.

But even after she's washed her face, her nose doesn't let up. She stuffs some tissues into each nostril and turns to me. "It's okay. I'm fine."

"You will be..." I growl, "as soon as I get you to the hospital to see Dr. Liza."

She shakes her head again. "It's just my sinuses acting up."

"*Look* at yourself, Wren. This isn't normal."

"I know, but—"

I grab her elbow and tow her in my wake. "We're going. That's final."

As I march her out, I call Liza with my free hand. Thankfully, Wren can't put up much of a fight because she's busy trying to stop her nose. The blood just keeps coming. One tissue after the next piles up at our feet in the car, soaked straight through with red.

Dr. Liza has a wheelchair ready for us when we arrive at St. Joseph's. Then Wren is wheeled into the emergency wing and I'm left standing there like a helpless fool as she disappears around the corner.

"Fuck," I mutter, pacing along the well-lit corridor. "*Fuck*."

The hospital bustles around me. Hundreds of disasters unfolding in every direction. Hundreds of people, like me, each having the worst nights of their lives.

Twenty minutes tick by, but each one feels like fucking hours. I try to be patient, but a man can only hold out for so long. When the clock hits 3:00 A.M., I cave and dial Liza.

"We're moving her to a private room," she says instead of hello. "I'll text you the number in a second."

She hangs up on me before I can ask what the fuck is going on with my wi— my woman. Thankfully, about a minute or so later, my phone pings.

LIZA: *5th floor. Room 12. Meet you there.*

LIZA: *P.S.: She's fine.*

The news ought to calm me down, but my heart is thrumming hard against my chest as I race up to the proper. I follow a nurse into the room to find Wren lying on the bed with her nose bandaged all to shit like she's broken it.

The sight of it damn near ruins me.

I was supposed to be providing a stress-free environment for my woman, my wife-to-be. I was supposed to be keeping her safe and calm.

But the baby hasn't even been born yet and I'm already accumulating strike after strike on my record.

What happens if I fail?

32

DMITRI

I pounce on Liza the moment she appears.

"What the hell happened?" I snarl. Wren is snoring softly, so I'm not worried about disturbing her. "Is she okay? Will this happen again?"

Liza glances over at Wren. "She has sinus issues that get activated every so often. I know things seemed frightening, but it's actually not as bad as it looked."

That matches what Wren told me, but it doesn't make me feel any better. "Explain," I growl. "What sinus issues?"

"It's her body's way of letting off steam, so to speak. She told me that the last time she experienced that kind of nosebleed in combination with a headache was right after she buried her sister and brother-in-law."

Fucking hell. *How did I not know that?*

"So she's stressed. Badly."

Liza, normally unflappable, looks like she'd rather be anywhere else but here. "Well, she is going to have a baby, Dmitri. Stress is a normal part of pregnancy. And doubly so, under the… the circumstances, we'll call them." She sighs and rests a reassuring hand on my forearm. "Listen, you've been doing well creating a calm, stress-free environment for her. As well as you possibly could've done. I wouldn't take this as a personal failure; it just comes with the territory. Just keep doing what you're doing."

"What I'm *doing* is obviously not enough."

Before I'm even finished talking, she's shaking her head. "You're expecting too much. Her due date is two days from now, though it looks like this little one is planning on camping out a touch longer. So of course Wren's going to be stressed; *of course* she's going to be anxious. It's not anything you're doing or not doing. You can even take her home now, if you wanted. She doesn't need to be admitted."

I glance over Liza's shoulder at Wren. The sight of her swallowed up in hospital bedsheets is so fucking wrong that I feel sick to my stomach. She's too pale and fragile under these harsh lights. I want her barefoot and pregnant and naked in my arms—not huddled up like she's on death's doorstep.

But some risks aren't worth taking.

"I want her to stay overnight. We can't be too cautious. Besides, she's sleeping soundly and that alone is worth preserving."

Liza nods. "Of course. That's not a problem."

"And I want a nurse monitoring her around the clock. Just in case."

"I'll put one of my best on her. And I'll check on her myself between my rounds."

I give the doctor a grateful nod. "Thanks, Liza. We're lucky to have you—both Wren and myself."

As she leaves, I return to Wren's bedside and take her hand. The snoring isn't natural; it's a result of the bandages over her nose. Her lips are parted and breath whistles painfully in and out of her. Even though I know she's okay, it's still gut-wrenching to see her like this.

I don't know how long we stay like that. Could be seconds, minutes, months, years. Eventually, her exhale catches and she moans. Without opening her eyes, she murmurs my name.

"Dmitri…?"

"I'm here, *devushka*." I squeeze her hand and she squeezes mine back in response. "How do you feel?"

"Like someone punched me in the nose from the inside," she says with a little smile and a cough. "How long have I been out?"

"Not long. A couple hours, I think."

"So it's still night? No wonder I'm so tired."

"Go back to sleep. We don't have to move you until the morning." I start to pick up the glass of water on her bedside table so I can offer her a drink, but before I can even get that far, her fingers wrap around my wrist.

"Don't look so worried, Dmitri. I'm okay. This has happened before."

My jaw clenches as I sag back in my chair, Wren's fingers still clasped over my forearm. "Liza told me. After the funerals."

"And a few times after my dad left," she admits with a nod. "But it's rare. So I don't expect to make this a regular thing." Sighing, she shifts around to find a new angle in the bed. Face half-pressed into the pillows, she yawns and gives me as much of a no-nonsense look as she can muster. "You don't have to stay with me the whole night."

"The fuck I don't."

"No one knows I'm here; it'll be fine."

"The only way I'm leaving is when your security detail gets here. Until then, you'll have to put up with me."

"Security detail," she repeats through another yawn. "My God. You know, when I was younger, I used to pronounce it 'secu-titty.' Isn't that stupid?" She giggles wearily for a moment before it fades into yet another sigh.

I run a hand over her forehead until her eyes close. "Sleep, Wren. I've got you. Always."

A few seconds later, the snoring starts up again. I wait to make sure she's truly out, and then I grab my phone and dial in Aleks's number. When he doesn't answer, I call Pavel instead.

"Boss?" he murmurs sleepily.

"I want you and the team over at St. Joseph's. Wren's been admitted."

"Oh, fuck," he grunts, rustling himself to full attention. "Baby's coming?"

I fucking wish. "No. There was a… complication. But she's fine now. Just get over here so that you can stay with her while I'm out. And wake Aleks up while you're at it. Kick his ass out of bed if you have to. God knows he deserves it."

~

"Yo, bro," Aleks says, rising to his feet the moment he sees me returning down the ward hallway. "Where've you been gallivanting off to?"

I glance towards Wren's room door. "Is there anyone in there with her?"

"The good doctor. She just wanted to do a routine checkup, make sure everything was okay. They took Wren's bandages off when she woke up this morning."

"And?"

"Slight swelling around her nose but otherwise, she looks fine."

I exhale with relief. "Good." I have to resist the urge to put my hand back in my pants pocket. "Did you talk to her?"

Aleks nods. "Yeah. She was in a great mood. We even played a couple of games of Uno over breakfast. I won, not that you asked. Anyway, she asked where you were a few times, but I didn't know what to tell her."

It's obvious he wants to know, too, but for a change, he doesn't pry. Not directly, at least, though my brother is about as subtle as a hammer to the head.

"I had something important I needed to take care of."

"Right-o. Well then, speaking of talking to Wren, did *you* tell her about that little secret you're keeping?"

"No," I growl shortly. "And I'm not going to, either. I was right to keep that from her for now."

"Dmitri—"

"You convinced me last night," I interrupt. "I'd made up my mind to tell her… and then I walk into our bedroom and her fucking nose explodes like goddamn Pompeii. It was a sign, Aleks. She's in too delicate a position to handle this information. Better it comes later, when the baby's been delivered safely and she's in the clear."

Aleks opens his mouth but then snaps it shut. "Are you sure this is the right decision?"

"I'm making a judgment call. You don't have to like it, but you do have to accept it."

I can't stop replaying that snapshot in my head on a loop. Flicking on the light to see Wren drenched in blood… I shudder as it goes again and again and again.

Dr. Liza walks out a moment later. "Ah, Dmitri! Wren was just asking for you."

I give her a passing nod and head into the room. Wren's sitting up with a yogurt cup in hand. Her face is free of bandages and, like Aleks mentioned, there's swelling around her nose, but it's mild.

"Hey, you," she greets. Her face lights up when she sees me. It's insanity itself how that tiny little motion, those two little words, are enough to bring me to my knees all on their own.

This woman has a hold on me.

God help me, I think I like it.

I sit on the edge of her bed so that I'm facing her. "How're you doing?"

"Still tired," she confesses. "Still pregnant. And yet still here, by the grace of God or whatever. Where were you?"

"Missed me, huh?"

She scrunches her nose up playfully. "Ew, no. I mean… maybe a little. Like, a *very*, very—

Chuckling, I press my palm to her cheek. "It's okay to miss me. You don't have to play it so cool all the time."

She sighs. Instead of jabbing back like I expected her to, she nuzzles sadly into my touch. "I just don't want to spend my whole life missing you, Dmitri," she explains. "But yes—for the record, I did miss you."

I kiss the top of her head. "You scared me last night."

"It was just a little nosebleed."

"Your clothes were soaked in blood, Wren."

She waves my worry away. "I told you and Liza both it was nothing serious. Still healthy—this is just something that happens when—"

"I know all of that. But as satisfying an explanation as it may or may not be, it doesn't change the fact that I hate watching you suffer. Even if it's as simple as a headache."

"Well, I'm fine now. Can we go home? This hospital gown is itchy as hell."

I like the way she says it. That combination of "we" and "home"—it just melts together so damn perfectly. I reach into my pocket and wrap my fingers around the weight that's burning a hole there.

"Not quite yet. I have a question I need to ask you first."

"If it's about what I want to eat when we get home, the answer is your homemade gnocchi. I've been craving it all morning. I had a dream that I was chasing a life-sized one through the woods. Couldn't catch the little bastard."

"I can arrange that. But that's not the question I was about to ask you."

"Oh," she says, turning a flattering shade of pink. "Sorry, just a little hungry."

Smiling, I pull out the box in my pocket and hold it up to her eyes. "*This* is where I was all morning. Apparently, most jewelers—" Her eyes go wide with shock as that word hits home. "—sleep in 'til like nine a.m., the lazy motherfuckers."

"J-jewelers?" she gasps, staring down at the box with new eyes. "Dmitri, what did you—what are you—is this really—*Huh?!*"

I snap the lid open and reveal the massive princess cut diamond surrounded by a cushion of bright green emeralds. "Wren Turner, I love you. I want you to spend the rest of your life with me. Will you—"

She grabs my hand and cuts me off mid-spiel. "Dmitri! Stop." I pause as she blinks at me a few times. "You've never said you love me before."

"I would have thought it was obvious."

Her bottom lip trembles and her eyes slide down to the diamond on its velvet bed. "Y-you… want to marry me?"

"More than anything."

"Why?"

This woman. Can't she see it? Can't she see this shit that's burning out of every goddamn pore in my body? Can't she see how she's the obsessive focus of every thought, every breath, every action and impulse and emotion churning through me?

Can't she see I'd die for her?

"Because I want you to carry my name, Wren. I want you to have the protection it carries. But that's just the practical side of things. You want to know the *un*practical part? That I'm addicted to you. And I'm a jealous bastard. A vengeful one. A proud one. So I want to put a rock on your finger that announces to the whole world that you are *mine.* That you always will be. That I love you. That no one alive has ever loved someone the way I love you."

She pulls in a teary breath and tries to fumble for words, but they don't come.

That's okay. For the first time in my life, I know exactly what to say to make her smile.

"I didn't do it right the first time around. Fate gave me another chance, though. I won't fuck this one up."

Wren's mouth keeps opening and closing, opening and closing. The room is eerily silent. "Though," I add, "you do eventually have to answer the question."

She gives me a little mock punch on the arm. "Okay, okay. I'm ready. Go on. Ask me." She sits up straighter on her pillows and gestures for me to continue with her hand.

"Wren—"

"I can't *believe* my nose is all swollen and gross for the proposal."

"For God's sake, Wren!"

She cringes. "Sorry, my bad." She makes a big show of zipping her lips and throwing away the key. I wait a few seconds, just to make sure that key stays lost.

When I'm satisfied I have her attention, I clear my throat. "Wren Turner," I start, keeping it simple, "will you marry me?"

Her eyes glow with fresh tears. She smiles through them and nods fervently. "Yes," she breathes as though she's been holding her answer in for ages. "Yes, of course I'll marry you."

She falls into my arms and I pull her onto my lap. We kiss so long and so passionately that for a moment, I lose all sight of where we are. It isn't until Wren breaks away breathlessly that I realize we're still in this cursed fucking hospital.

I wipe away Wren's happy tears and then slip the ring onto her finger. It's a perfect fit. If Bee were here, she would call it kismet.

"Wow," Wren breathes, staring at the ring on her finger. "It's *heavy*."

"Nothing but the best for my wife."

"*Future* wife," she clarifies. "For the moment, I'm your fiancée."

"Not for long. I want to marry you immediately."

Her jaw drops. "How soon is 'immediately'?"

"Today if we can manage it. Tomorrow at the latest."

"Dmitri! That… that's too soon! We haven't planned anything. We don't have—shit, where are the flowers? We need flowers and a flower girl! And a dress, and music, and… and a license, too! Not to mention the fact that I'm, like, a hundred months pregnant!"

"I don't care. I want you to be my wife and I'm not a patient man."

"But—"

"We can have a big, lavish ceremony later. You can have it exactly the way you want. But right now, I just want to marry you."

Her cheeks are rosy with excitement. Those green eyes are brighter than I've ever seen them. The emeralds on her ring are seething with jealousy, wishing that one day they could grow up to be that green.

"Well," she breathes at last, "how can I say no to that?"

33

WREN

"Please don't hate me." I turn my most apologetic puppy-dog eyes on Syrah the moment she walks back into the room.

"Hate the bride? Impossible. What's up?"

"I need to pee," I admit. "Again."

Syrah snorts and waves a hand in my face. "What is a maid of honor for if not to hike up the bride's skirt so she can pee? C'mere, let's git 'er done."

She grabs my hands and hauls me up to my feet. I'm already exhausted and we haven't even left for City Hall yet. I waddle over to the bathroom with Syrah clutching me like I'm the Queen of England.

Ever since my little hospital stint, everyone's been handling me with kid gloves. It's sweet and annoying at the same time.

"You were right: I got dressed too early," I lament.

Syrah grunts as she positions me in front of the toilet. "You were excited to try on the dress. No one understands that better than I do. *And* you look amazing in it."

"Laying it on a little thick, are we?"

Syrah helps me lower myself down. Then she steps back and gives me her best scowl. "Someone's not in the mood for compliments today, huh?"

"Sorry," I mumble. "I just… I can't believe I let him talk me into this."

Syrah fixes me with a glare and clears her throat pointedly. "Ah-*hem*. You're supposed to be peeing, young lady. I don't hear the sound of pee exiting your body."

I cringe. "I'm just a little—"

"Tightly wound today. I can tell. Will you just relax and pee? It's not good to hold it in."

I get my Zen on and block out all the little anxieties that have been piling up this morning. I concentrate and do my best to relax. A few seconds later…

"Ah-ha, jackpot!" Syrah cheers. "Like Niagara Falls. Love that for you."

"You're so weird."

She grins cheekily. "You really do look beautiful, you know. This is great lighting for your cheekbones. If you hold on a sec, I'll go get the photographer…"

I stick my middle finger in her face before I finish up, suppressing a moan of discomfort, and get to my feet. I'm walking past the mirror when Syrah grabs hold of me and forces me to turn to it. "Quick pause. This is important. Go on, look at yourself. Tell me what you see."

I stare at my reflection. The girl staring back at me is recognizable, sure. But there are parts of her that are alien. Like the massive stomach, the extra weight around her hips.

"Syrah—"

"No arguing," she scolds. "Tell me what you see."

"I see a tired pregnant woman who would chop off a pinky toe to not be pregnant anymore."

"Okay, fair enough. Now, what *else* do you see?"

Frowning, I squint past my own discomfort. The dress I'm wearing was chosen this morning from a silver rack of Madison Montgomery's finest. My plan was to go traditional white, but I ended up falling head over heels when I saw this romantic, shimmery, pearl silver dress in a mix of chiffon and organza. It was understated, but there was a playful depth to it. I also didn't exactly hate that it would match Dmitri's eyes.

"I see a pretty dress."

Syrah pats my arm. "Good. You're getting warmer. What else?"

She spent a good hour getting my hair and makeup done, because, and I quote, *"If you hire someone else to do it for you, I'll hate you forever and also burn your house down."* She did good, though, all violent threats aside. The makeup is subtle and understated, just like the dress, and my hair is an intricate series of tiny French braids zigzagging across one another at the back of my head. Twisted strands of hair fall on the side of my temples, framing my face.

"I see a brilliant updo and amazing makeup."

"Fuck yeah, you do!" Syrah agrees. "And what does all that add up to?"

Sighing, I nod and give into the point I know she's been driving toward. "I look pretty damn good."

"'Pretty damn good'?" Syrah sucks in an offended breath on my behalf. "You look *stunning*, Wren. And considering you're a trillion months pregnant, that's saying something."

I can't help but smile. "You always know how to make me feel better."

"I take my role as maid of honor *very* seriously," she says. "And honestly, I'm really happy that you decided to include me in your secret, clandestine elopement. Although, again, I would have burned your house down if you'd done anything else."

I don't bother telling her that I had to put my foot down on that one. Dmitri was adamantly against it.

"She's my best friend!" I argued with him last night while we were putting together our impromptu ceremony. *"I can't get married without her."*

"The whole point of this wedding is that we do it quickly and quietly."

"It's hard enough getting married without Rose and Bee here. Don't make me do it without Syrah, too."

That did the trick. His face puckered for a moment and then he sighed. *"Oh, fucking hell, fine. If it makes you happy. But she has to keep her mouth shut."*

"What are you smiling about?" Syrah asks, fixing me with a curious grin.

"Just super happy that you could be here. It wouldn't have felt right getting married without you."

"Oh, hush, you." She wraps me up in a tight embrace and squeezes until my eyes start leaking tears. I guess I must be squeezing pretty hard in my own right, because her eyes are doing the exact same thing.

We both start giggling and fumbling for tissues as we disentangle ourselves, so we can dab the tears away before our makeup gets ruined. Lord knows I don't want Sy burning my house down if her smoky eye efforts go to shit.

Even still, when she collects herself, she takes one look at me and frowns. "Let me just touch up your—"

Knock-knock-knock.

I glance at the clock on the wall. I was told my car would be ready to leave at eleven. I still have a good twenty minutes before departure.

"Lemme see who it is," Syrah says, leaving me sitting by the bed. "Don't move."

She returns a moment later with a small box between her hands. I blink at it quizzically. "Who's that from?"

"Beats me. Just saw it at the door. No one in the hallway or anything." She gives it a long whiff. "Jeez, it even smells expensive."

She offers it to me and I place it on my lap, fingers grazing along the edge of the dramatic chiffon ribbon it's wrapped in. Syrah's right: it smells amazing, like it took a bath in Chanel No. 5 on its way through the postal system.

"More jewelry," Syrah predicts, sitting down beside me. "Guaranteed."

The box is square and flat, so I'm inclined to agree with her. My money's on a necklace. I pull at the ribbon and it falls away easily. Unlatching the box, I flip the lid up and find exactly what I'd suspected—a necklace.

But not just *any* necklace. This one has a gorgeous, bespoke pendant twinkling with a rainbow's worth of colored diamonds. It's a rose with seven petals, and on the uppermost petal is a tiny diamond bee that winks at me cheekily.

A rose for Rose.

A bee for Bee.

"Oh my God," I breathe, as fresh tears overwhelm me. "Sorry, Sy. You really will have to redo my makeup."

"Yeah," she sniffles. "That makes two of us."

We turn to each other and laugh through our tears. "He really did think of everything, didn't he?" Syrah says, eyeing the pendant with fascination.

"He always does." I pull the necklace out of its case and hand it to Syrah. "Can you put it on me?"

"With pleasure."

Once it's secured around my neck, I touch it gingerly, feeling more complete than I have in a while. I squeeze Syrah's hand and swallow all the emotion threatening to bubble up inside me. "Now, I have all three of you with me today."

"Here," she says, handing me a note that I hadn't even noticed. "It came with the gift."

It's a short note written on a small, perfumed card, but I recognize Dmitri's handwriting instantly.

Moya devushka,

It is my greatest honor to marry you today. Please accept this gift as a token of my love and devotion to you. For today, for tomorrow, for all the days to come.

Yours always,
Dmitri

"Oh, for the love of God!" Syrah says from where she's reading just over my shoulder. She's not even pretending to give me privacy. "It's stupidly unfair how good he is at this shit. I'm all swoony on the inside and the note isn't even for me."

Swatting her away, I adjust my hair and check my makeup. "I have to give him a gift, too!" I blurt, suddenly panicked.

"Do you actually have something or do you have to wing it?"

I'm too busy pacing back and forth to reply. Then I come to a grinding halt and turn to Syrah. "Can you go get Dmitri?"

"I dunno if you're aware of how this whole thing works, but you're not supposed to see each other before the ceremony. It's tradition."

I glare at Syrah incredulously and gesture to myself. "For God's sake, Sy, *look* at me. We're not exactly a traditional couple."

She bursts out laughing. "Okay, fair point. What do I say to him when he asks?"

"Tell him that I need to speak to him urgently. He'll come."

Syrah nods but she hesitates. "And you have a gift in mind?"

I give her a mischievous little grin. "It's a gift only *I* can give him."

"*Ooo*, you naughty little minx. I like it." She rushes for the door but pauses at the threshold. "Just be careful not to rip that dress. It's too pretty to ruin. Even for a man as sexy as your future husband."

She disappears through the door and I stand there with her last word on my lips. *Husband.* It's too *sur*real to *be* real. And yet why do I feel as though I've been waiting my whole life for this moment? Why do I feel as though this was always meant to happen, exactly the way it's happened?

Why does it feel so damn… inevitable?

I'm fussing and primping in front of the mirror when I hear footsteps pounding down the corridor. I jump back just as Dmitri rushes into my room, panting. "Wren? What's wrong? Are you…"

The words die on his lip and I decide then and there that *that's* the best gift he's ever given me. That look. Pure awestruck.

"What do you think?" I ask, twirling in place if only to hide how hard I'm blushing.

He's scowling when I pivot back to face him. "I thought you were either dying or delivering."

I smile ironically. "I've made peace with the fact that this baby is never coming out." Then I walk up to him and take his hands. "Notice anything different about me?"

His gaze flits to the pendant. "It suits you." His eyes shine brightly, the exact same shade as my dress. "Do you like it?"

"*Like* it?" I stutter at him. "I *love* it. It's the perfect gift, Dmitri. But it made me realize something: I didn't give you your gift."

He starts to protest immediately. "You don't have to get me anything, Wren. I—"

"Of course I do. Quid pro quo and all that."

He shakes his head. "You're marrying me. That's gift enough for me."

This smooth criminal. He's really outdoing himself today. "All the same, it would make me happy to be able to give you something. So I brought you here to give you your gift."

I lead him to the chair beside the bed and make him sit down. Then I get down onto my knees as gracefully as I can manage. Despite what Syrah said, I don't mind ripping the dress for this. Dmitri is worth it.

Except, he's looking more horrified than turned-on right now. *Hurry things up, darling. Skip to the good part.*

"Wren, what are you doing?"

"I would have hoped it was obvious," I tease. "But since you need more of a clue…" I reach for his pants and start unbuckling him. Before I can get far, he grabs my hands, stopping me. "Excuse me," I complain. "I'm in the middle of gift-giving here."

He tries to suppress his smile. "Wren, you're nine months pregnant."

I have to resist the urge to roll my eyes. *Why does everyone feel the need to remind me? It's not like I've forgotten.* "Mhmm. And?"

"And I don't want you on your knees."

He says it with utmost seriousness, but something tells me he's not wholly convinced. I reach out and palm his erection through his tuxedo pants. "Your cock seems to disagree."

"He usually does," Dmitri grunts. "But you don't have to do this."

"I know that. But I *want* to." I lick my lips. "Now, are you gonna let me give you your gift or not?"

His silence is all the answer I needed.

I unbuckle him and free his length. It's slow at first. A teasing kiss here, a light squeeze there. A touch and a breath before I'm gone again. I can feel his groans as much as I can hear them, like little tremors running below the surface of the earth in advance of the earthquake that's yet to come.

Soon, though, I'm dripping wet and little teases are as torturous for me as they are for him. So I take him in both hands and massage slowly as I twist and pump, twist and pump. Those groans grow in volume and number. When he twitches, I grin.

No one else gets to see him like this. Not a single other soul alive. He's an iron-masked titan to every last person on this planet except for me.

But when I'm on my knees and he's filling my mouth like this, I get to see that mask fall and I get to know that *I* can make Dmitri Egorov fall to pieces.

That's just one more gift he gives me.

I let his head pass my lips and then I keep going. More and more and more of him, until my throat is full and his taste is thick on my tongue and my jaw is straining to open any wider. When I peek up, Dmitri's eyes are rolling back in his head and he's spluttering my name, barely able to get past the first letter.

"W... Wr... Wre..."

It's a blur of motion from there. I bob and suck and stroke. At some point, his hand touches the back of my head. I like feeling one more point of connection. His thighs pressing on either side of me as I milk him...

And then, as black mascara tears run down my cheeks and I can't jerk him any harder, he finally erupts.

It's a never-ending orgasm. He comes rope after rope into my mouth and I take it all eagerly. Salty perfection. Dmitri finally finishes my name right as it peaks.

"Wren!" Just a grunted, gasping, growling, perfect syllable.

I may be the one on my knees, but I've never felt more powerful.

Especially when I glance up and look at my future husband. He's lying limp against the chair with sweat dotting his forehead. His chest rises and falls heavily and his eyes look like he's seen heaven and found it suitable.

"Holy *fuck*," he murmurs at last, looking at me with awe. "Where did *that* come from?"

I blush, suddenly shy. "I guess I wanted to say my vows with the taste of you on my tongue."

Those gray eyes of his spark up again. "Well then, it's only fair that I have the same experience."

Before I can stop him, he's on the floor in front of me, pushing me down onto the carpeted floor. "Dmitri," I gasp as he disappears under my dress. "Dmitri... w-we don't have time..."

He answers by going down on me like the world is burning to ashes around us. He doesn't stop until I come as hard as he did, and then a few more times for good measure.

There's a moment right near the end of it when something occurs to me. A revelation I guess, if that's even a real thing.

It's just me realizing that, as far as vows go, we can't do any better than this right here. There's something beautiful and sacred and symmetrical about giving each other this kind of pleasure before we commit ourselves to one another for the rest of our lives.

It's the best kind of promise. The best kind of reassurance. The best kind of vow.

What can I say?

We were never gonna be a traditional couple.

34

WREN

"I pledge to protect you with my life, *moya ledi*."

I've been ballooned up like *James & the Giant Peach* for way too damn long now, but even that discomfort can't hold a candle to how strange it feels to stand here while Pavel—who's never looked this serious since the moment I met him—presses a fist to his chest and bows to me.

I glance helplessly to Dmitri, but he leaves me to figure it all out by myself, refusing to share the spotlight.

Gulp. My turn to say… well, hell if I know what my lines are.

But the man just pledged to risk his *life* for me. Surely that deserves a little bow? A hug, at the very least?

"Thank you, Pavel," I say, settling for stepping forward and putting my hand on his shoulder. "You have no idea how much I appreciate that."

I remove my hand and he bows down low once more. Then he moves away and another one of Dmitri's *vors* takes his place.

The whole thing repeats itself. Vows of loyalty 'til death, lives on the line, men with grim faces kneeling at my feet. My cheeks stay fire red until the procession ends and finally, thank God, our impromptu little post-wedding reception can actually begin.

"What the hell? You didn't warn me about the pledges!"

"I told you they needed to accept you as the queen of the Bratva."

"I thought you were *joking*!"

He chuckles. "You did well. Very regal."

I punch him in the arm, which only serves to make me yelp and wince. Is the man made out of steel or what? "I'm way out of my depth, Dmitri. This is not my world."

"It is now."

With that not-at-all terrifying sentiment lingering in the air, he turns and looks at Aleks, who's lingering a few yards away from us and waiting for a chance to step in.

"Since the groom isn't doing his duty," Aleks explains, "I thought I'd step in and ask the bride for a dance."

Dmitri scowls in equal proportion to Aleks's cheeky grin. "Why don't you make yourself useful and dance your way to a perimeter check instead?" he grumbles.

Slumping his shoulders forward, Aleks sighs and starts to do as he's told—but he doesn't even get a step away before I brush past Dmitri and take up his brother's elbow. "A dance sounds wonderful. And just so you know," I call back over my shoulder, "neither you nor this baby are gonna stop me from bringing the house down."

Dmitri's scowl deepens, but Aleks and I both know him well enough to know there's a surprised smile swimming somewhere below the surface of it.

"You're gonna be good for him," Aleks tells me as we reach the dance floor and he takes up a position—a very respectful position, I might add—with one hand high on my ribcage. "The medicine he never knew he needed."

Laughing, I let Aleks twirl me around a couple of times. "I think we might be good for each other. This is the first time in a long time that I've felt so wholly *happy*."

"It shows. You look beautiful, Wren. I couldn't be happier for both of you. Even the sourpuss over there."

"What did you call me?" comes a snarling voice.

I laugh for a moment before I bury it behind a scowl to match Dmitri's. "That was barely one verse of the song! If you're gonna be possessive, then—"

"I'm *always* going to be possessive, *moya devushka*," he rumbles in my ear as he cuts in to take me off of Aleks. His hands find much more risqué placement low on my waist, dirty enough to make my skin burn even through layers and layers of tulle. "Get used to a lifetime of it."

I can hear Aleks chuckling to himself as he concedes the space and walks away. Truth be told, it's hard to focus on him, though. Or our guests, or the music, or anything other than the way Dmitri draws me in tight to his embrace and consumes every sense I have.

I smell him, see him, taste him, feel him.

And his eyes never leave mine. We're miles off-beat, but he couldn't give a shit less. He doesn't give me an inch of space between my body and his as we rotate slowly to the beat of our own drum. His *vors* know to keep their distance, to let us slice haphazardly across the dancefloor. I might've been embarrassed in the old days.

Now, I know that Dmitri Egorov walks where he wants.

And I guess I do, too, as of today. Because I'm *Wren Egorov* now.

That sends a thrilling shiver down my spine.

When the song ends, Dmitri takes my hand and tows me upstairs. We don't bother saying goodbye to anyone; I'd call it an "Irish goodbye," but we're not exactly on good terms with them right now, and besides, no one does it quite as swiftly as Dmitri does, anyway.

It's funny how my heart can race and my palms can go clammy as we ride the elevator up to our suite. I've done this so many times before—knowing what's coming, this hyper-awareness of myself and Dmitri, of the things drawing us together—but it always feels like the first time.

The tension.

The held breath.

The sneaky glances in his direction, stolen whenever I think he might not be looking.

His fingers stay laced through mine as we get off and sweep into our room. It's jaw-dropping, but I barely get a millisecond to enjoy the surroundings before Dmitri is pinning me to the nearest wall with his hips.

I can't help but gasp. "Call me your wife," I demand saucily. "I want to hear you say it."

Dmitri's eyebrow arches. "Only a few hours married and you're already issuing orders? This 'queen' thing has gone straight to your head."

"It certainly has. Someone has to keep things running right around here."

He palms my throat and bends down to run the tiniest tip of his tongue in the sensitive spot behind my ear. I shiver again, with heat blossoming right alongside goosebumps, like my body can't decide whether to freeze over or burn to pieces in Dmitri's arms.

"I've got some ideas for ways we could improve the situation."

"Oh? Tell me. I'm all ears."

"I think I'll show you instead."

Then, with a savage blur of motion, Dmitri rips my dress to absolute ribbons. One second, I'm clothed head to toe in Madison Montgomery's finest lace; the next, it's fluttering like snowflakes around us and Dmitri's teeth are bared like he's a wild animal.

Part of me wants to be mad.

But that part is very, very small.

And the part of Dmitri that I'll take as a consolation prize isn't small at all.

We're on each other as soon as I'm stripped out of my gown. Mouths clashing, tongues warring, hands pawing. I'd call it "passionate," but that doesn't even come close to doing it justice.

It's fucking feral, really. Damn near unhinged. It's like I can't get close enough to him and vice versa. I'm ripping at his clothes the exact same way he ripped at mine—albeit slightly less effectively—and kissing and suckling everywhere my mouth can reach.

We stumble into the bedroom and flop on our backs. Dmitri kisses a path down my body, then tears away the flimsy scrap of my underwear.

He licks me to an instantaneous orgasm.

Fucks me to another.

Spoons me in his arms until I can breathe again, then does it all over.

And the whole time, he keeps whispering, *"My wife. My wife. My wife."*

～

I ride the blur like I'm in some kind of bliss-suffused fever dream until I snap back to reality hours later, as we're soaking in the tub. It's lazy, delirious, perfect. Rose petals float on the surface of the water and the air smells like honey blossom and gardenias.

Dmitri feeds me chocolate truffles and sips of sparkling grape juice. And if his fingers wander between my legs and get me off again—well, he's my husband, so I'd say that's permitted.

I close my eyes, but I don't fall asleep—it's more like just dozing. Why would I sleep, anyway? What would be the point? Real life is so much better than anything I could dream.

35

WREN

"Why can't I just stay home?"

Dmitri turns to regard me with raised eyebrows. "My, how quickly the honeymoon ends, eh?"

Smirking, I whack him with the new mockup prints that I've been poring over all evening. "I'm just saying, you don't really need me there, do you? This is just another stodgy dinner for your hoity-toity clientele."

"Which is *exactly* why I need you there," he retorts. "They're all a bunch of boring snobs and having you on my arm would make tonight infinitely more interesting."

"Well, I *am* oodles of fun but—" I gesture to my stomach. "—I'm also very pregnant. Not to mention that I need to go over this mockup properly before it's pitched to Madison Montgomery tomorrow."

"You've already been through it a dozen times."

"And yet count me in for number thirteen, because I'm still not satisfied. It needs to be perfect. Mrs. Montgomery demands—"

"Fuck Madison Montgomery," he interrupts. "I need my *wife* tonight."

Argh, this stubborn bastard. He knows the magic words and he's not afraid to use them. "I don't know anyone there," I complain, even though I already know I'm gonna cave any second now.

"Yes, you do. You were my secretary for a while before things changed."

"P.A.," I correct indignantly. "And that was different. I was your subordinate; I was part of the rank-and-file. And now, suddenly, I'm on your arm and wearing clothes that are more expensive than theirs are? They won't like it."

His eyes narrow dangerously. "I don't give a fuck what they like. This is not about them. I want to show you off tonight."

"Can you show me off when I don't look like a hippo that just swallowed another hippo?"

Dmitri grabs my arm and pulls me to my feet. "How about I make you a deal?" he whispers into my ear. "For every hour you're out with me tonight, I'll give you an orgasm for your troubles."

I scowl at him, even as shivers skitter down my spine. "You fight dirty."

"You haven't seen the half of it."

Chewing on my inner cheek, I glance down at my mockups. Things have gone well so far. I've even managed to earn Jackson Mitchell's respect. I mean, to the extent that he at least doesn't purse his lips *every* single time I so much as open my mouth. It's really got me motivated to see this project through.

But Dmitri's right: I can stand to stop working for one night.

And when you dangle a carrot like that in front of me...

"Oh, alright," I concede. "I'll come."

"Yes, you will indeed." He grins and presses a heart-racing kiss into the hollow of my collarbone. "Get ready. We leave soon."

I stuff all my work back into the respective colored folders and then head to our bedroom to change. Dmitri has been sending daily couriers to stock my wardrobe, so there's no shortage of options to choose from, each item more stunning than the last.

I opt for a black, shimmery dress with thin shoulder straps and a sexy leg slit. From the side, I look closer to five months pregnant than nine, which I'll take as a minor victory. I pick a pair of sexy yet sensible nude platforms, add some brief touches of makeup, and of course my favorite piece of jewelry—the rose pendant with the bee on the seventh petal—and boom, my look feels complete.

When I appear at the elevators, Dmitri lets out a low whistle. "You look good enough to eat."

I roll my eyes to hide my blush. "No need to lay it on that thick, mister. I've already agreed to come with you. Quit while you're ahead."

Chuckling, we take the elevator down hand in hand and make our way towards the hulking vehicle waiting for us outside the tower. "Pavel's driving us?"

Dmitri nods. "I was planning to, but then I had a last-minute change of heart."

"How come?"

He gives me a suggestive smile. "You'll see." On that mysterious note, he escorts me into the back seat of the car and gets in himself. "Take us to the Four Seasons, Pavel," he orders as he buckles us in. Then he pushes a button on the side and the partition wall goes up, separating us from the driver's cabin and from the world around us.

"What's going on?" I can hear my pulse, my breathing, every rustle of fabric.

Dmitri grabs me around the waist and pulls me against him. "Just showing you that I'm a man of my word." Then he sticks his tongue in my ear and slides his hand up my skirt.

I gasp when his fingers drag through my wetness. Dmitri just laughs as he pulls his hand free and licks a drop of me off his knuckle. "Like fucking honey," he growls in the raspy tone he saves exclusively for occasions like this.

I'm still a little thrown by the unexpected left turn my evening has taken. Forty minutes ago, I was neck-deep in mockups and architectural blueprints; now, suddenly, I'm dressed to the nines in the back seat of a million-dollar armored vehicle while a gorgeous man in a flawless tuxedo licks my juices from his fingers and tells me I taste like honey.

I'm gonna need a second to catch up.

"Dmitri, I—"

But no sooner do I start to speak than he clamps his palm over my mouth. I can taste myself on him and nothing has ever seemed so erotic.

"Hush," he orders. That rasp is magnified, intensified, deepened in a way I didn't know it could. And his eyes flash like black flames to match it. "Hush and *stay* hushed. I won't be interrupted again."

I nod weakly. My head lolls back against the seat as Dmitri's fingers dance up my thigh slit and find my pussy again. The first touch is electric; the second, third, and fourth are all it takes to become orgasmic.

By the time he's buried himself to the knuckle inside of me, I'm bucking my hips and moaning recklessly into his palm. If Pavel can hear—well, that no longer seems quite as mortifying as it did a moment ago.

Dmitri's mouth drags down my top and suckles over one swollen breast. Those two points of contact send me soaring into the stratosphere.

"That's my good little girl," he murmurs softly as I come on his hand. "You're so pretty when you obey. Keep listening this well and I might even paint you with my cum tonight."

He doesn't quite stop, not even after the first orgasm has faded. He keeps going, working faster on my clit until a second orgasm is imminent. Then—

"Nuh-uh-uh, *moya zhena*," he warns. "Don't get greedy now. I've been generous giving you one orgasm before you've even devoted an hour to my boring dinner. We had a deal, remember?"

This asshole.

But I won't give him the satisfaction of seeing how insane he's made me already, even if it's blindingly obvious to anyone with eyeballs. I clamp down on my lower lip to stop from whining and/or moaning until he eats me out. Instead, using my reflection, I arrange my hair back into some semblance of order and touch up my smudged lipstick.

"How do I look?"

"Like a woman who just came on her husband's hand in the back seat of a vehicle."

I'm torn between a laugh and a wail. "Why did you have to go and do that *now*? I have to look presentable!"

He chuckles. "I could fuck you raw and come on your face and you'd still be the most beautiful woman in attendance tonight. Actually, now that I think about it…"

I shove him away with a laugh. "You wouldn't dare. Stay on that side of the car, you beast."

Dmitri laughs, though he keeps his distance as requested. "You don't have the faintest idea just how many things I'd dare to do to you, Wren. But tempt me and you might find out."

God or Satan or someone with a wicked sense of humor cranked Dmitri's filthy mouth to its highest setting tonight. I can't say I mind; something about the combination of a Tom Ford tux and depraved fantasies just stokes the heat in my belly that much higher.

We might be in for a very long night, him and I.

∼

We must be among the last to arrive, because when we do, the ballroom is packed to the gills. I'm still too flustered to have put a proper meet-and-greet face on, but that doesn't stop everyone from gawking.

We're barely two steps into the hall when a glittery older couple dart up to us. "Mr. Egorov!" the male half crows. "How nice to see you at one of our events after so long."

I've seen Mr. Arnaud before. He's visited Egorov Industries enough times for me to remember the face and the name. As far as my memory serves, he's a half-French, self-made millionaire with a popular winery that he's now expanding into an empire. On his arm is his very British wife, who's wearing the kind of expression that makes me feel like she wants to roast me like a duck and serve me for dinner.

"This is Louis Arnaud," Dmitri introduces. "And his wife, Verity."

"How lovely to meet you both, Mr. and Mrs. Arnaud," I say with a small, awkward, shuffling attempt at a curtsy.

"And this—" Dmitri says with his hand on the small of my back. "—is my wife, Wren Egorov."

That makes my blush go ten shades redder. Not just because I'm still getting used to it, but also because both Louis's and Verity's eyes go wide. Everyone in eavesdropping distance does the exact same.

But to their credit, both of them recover quickly. They compose themselves and come straight in for a hug and a kiss on each cheek. "Delighted that you could join us, dear Wren." Her eyes dip down to my belly. "May I?" She doesn't wait for my answer before running a bejeweled hand over my stomach. "Exciting times! A new baby. A new marriage."

She's clearly waiting for me to give her more information, but I just smile politely. "It is a very exciting time."

"Congratulations, Dmitri," Arnaud booms, patting him on the back. "There's a lot to look forward to."

"Business included?" Dmitri segues smoothly.

Arnaud's laughter is like a loud belch. "Always. Come this way; let me show you to your table."

As it turns out, they've reserved the best seats in the house for us. At least, that's what Arnaud claims when he gestures towards the decked-out table in the center of the ballroom, right underneath the largest golden chandelier. The centerpieces are tiny, crystalline swan boats that hold arrangements of white roses and baby's breath. I have to admit, it's tasteful.

"We have some non-alcoholic champagne I can get for you," Verity offers, patting my shoulder as she straightens up and snaps her fingers. A millisecond later, a waiter shows up and bends down to listen to her rattle off orders for all of us.

"Champagne for three, sparkling grape juice for this angel here. Canapes in the meantime because I just know that Wren's darling baby is howling for food, if my own pregnancies were anything to go by. And bring plenty of everything, if you please."

The waiter bows and scurries off. Verity looks like she's ready to launch an inquisition on me, but I'm saved from that when someone comes up to her with questions and she's carted off for hostessing duties.

I take a grateful breath as I slump down in my seat. It's hard to keep my smile plastered in place, but I do my best, because it really does feel like *everyone* is watching me. Not all the smiles I'm getting are friendly, either. Some are suspicious, others openly hostile.

Of course, when I glance over at my husband, who's been roped into yet another conversation with yet another pompous-looking businessman, I can't help but understand. I've got the hottest catch in the city. Jealousy comes with the territory.

Dmitri excuses himself and comes to join me when he sees me looking. Breathing in my ear, he asks, "Doing okay?"

As soon as I can smell him, I feel more at ease. "Better now." I graze his knee with one nail idly. "Everyone is staring."

He smirks. "Good. That's the whole point. Tonight is the perfect way to introduce you as my wife." He cups my fingers in his and gives me a gentle, reassuring squeeze. "They're also staring because you look fucking gorgeous. Who wouldn't be able to keep their eyes off—"

I look up only when I realize he's left his sentence. I expect him to be staring at me, but his eyes are fixed on something over my shoulder.

"What is it? What's—"

Dmitri grabs my chin to stop me before I can turn to look. His face is suddenly winter itself, frozen over and terrifying.

"What's going on?" I croak.

He clears his throat. When his voice comes out, though, it's still a barely restrained growl. "Cian's here."

36

DMITRI

My first instinct is to pull out my gun and open fire on the insolent motherfucker.

The audacity. The fucking *balls*. To show up here knowing I would be coming... It seems like a fucking death wish to me.

Thankfully for him, I'm in the mood to be merciful. Maybe I'll even let him walk out alive.

Or maybe not. Maybe I'll—

"Dmitri." Wren's hand cups my face, all tenderness and worry. "We're in public. You can't do anything crazy here."

"Then we'd better go somewhere private." I stand and offer her my hand. "Come. We're leaving."

"We just got here! We can't let Cian chase us out of here. It'll look bad."

Fuck me, but she's right. If we leave now, it'll just look like I'm running from him. It'll look like I'm the one who's scared, when *he's* the one that should be.

I scan the crowd and cluck my tongue angrily. It annoys me that I've lost sight of him already. All I see is a crowd of tuxedos and glitter. No blond men with death marked on their foreheads.

"You're right," I concede. "But there's no need for you to stay. Stay close to me until I can get you out of here."

Wren's hand in mine spasms. "You're sending me home? What, like some naughty child?"

Now, she wants to stay? I love this woman more than anything else in the world, but fucking hell, she knows how to set me off. "You're extremely pregnant. No one would think twice about you leaving early to get some rest."

"I'm not leaving you here alone."

"I'm not alone. Aleks is here. My men are here."

"I don't care. I want to stay." I fix her with a glare, but she's utterly unmoved. "I'm not gonna run and hide every time there's a small sign of danger. If I do, there's no way I'll stand a chance in your world."

Once again, she has a point. A very good one at that. If we weren't standing in the same vicinity as the man who abducted and held her hostage for weeks, I would be hard as a rock.

"For once in your fucking life, Wren, you will do as you're told."

Her eyes narrow into thin, feral slits. "Need I remind you, I'm your *wife*. Not one of your men. I don't follow your orders like they do." She turns back to the table pointedly and picks up her glass of "champagne." "There's no point wasting a pretty dress."

I scan through the crowd again. Still no Cian, but I do catch sight of Aleks, who extends his chin and—

There.

Cian is wearing a dark gray suit and engrossed in a conversation with Louis Arnaud. But every so often, his eyes veer around the room like he's looking for someone. If the Irish bastard is here, that means without a doubt that he's brought backup. There's no way I'll be able to get near him without causing a scene.

On the upside? The same is true for him.

Neither one of us will risk blowing our covers tonight. Which means one thing: the only reason Cian's here at all is to force me to hear him out. I've been denying his requests for a meeting. Him coming here, now, like this?

It means he's desperate.

Pavel appears at my side, muttering low in my ear. "Arrived five minutes ago. Appears unarmed, but unconfirmed."

"His men?"

"We counted twelve. There may be double that number outside the ballroom."

I nod. "Make sure he keeps a wide berth. I don't want him coming anywhere near—"

"Wren!"

He's got to be fucking kidding.

I follow the sound of that infuriating accent to find Cian approaching Wren. When he sees me striding to join her, he smoothly shifts to allow me to step in between.

"Dmitri," he croons. "How nice to see you both."

He has the gall to greet us like old friends. He has the stones to so much as look at my wife after what he did to her?! I'm this close to breaking my own rules and opening fire, witnesses be damned.

What's the worst that could happen? I blow my cover? I spend a few years in a maximum security prison? It'd be worth it to see that slimy fucker's brains on the marble of the dance floor. To paint the walls red with his blood.

The only thing that stops me is the gentle pressure on my arm as Wren gets to her feet and stands by my side. That pressure reminds me of just how much I'd be losing if I went the gun-happy route.

Sure, Cian would be dead. But I'd lose years with Wren. I'd miss my son's birth.

No, nothing is worth that.

"Cian," I growl instead, refusing to return his simpering smile.

He glances at Wren. "You look beautiful. It's great to see you."

Wren increases pressure on my arm. "Cian," she says in a somber voice, "what are you doing here?"

He looks taken aback by the question. "I was invited, of course. Same as you."

I step in front of Wren, blocking her from view altogether. "If you want to keep your eyes in your skull, I suggest you take them off my wife."

Wren grabs my arm and tries to pull me back. "Dmitri! I know you're pissed, but *please*, people are watching."

"I don't give a fuck who's watching," I snap without taking my eyes off Cian.

Cian holds up his hands, but his smile falters. "Hold on a second. I come in peace. I just want to talk. That's it."

"What the fuck would you have to say to me?"

"An explanation, for starters," he answers quickly. "I want to explain what happened with Wren."

I snort in his face. "You care about explanations now, do you? Where were your words before, when you targeted Wren the first time? It's pretty damn convenient that you want to broker some sort of truce now that you know you're going to lose. Actions have consequences, Cian. These are the consequences of attacking my wife."

He grits his teeth as sweat begins to dot his forehead. "I didn't attack her. I kept her safe and comfortable while she was in my care."

"And why did she need to be in your care at all?"

His eyes teeter from side to side like a frightened child. "I'll tell you everything, okay? Just not here. There are too many eyes."

"Too many witnesses, you mean. Care to make a bet? Because I bet you my empire that I could smash your face in right now and not a single one of these motherfuckers would testify against me."

The sweat begins to drip down Cian's cheeks. "I have information that I know you need, Dmitri. Information that could help you change the course of this war—and the future of your Bratva, too."

"Which *would* be useful to me," I agree. "... *if* I trusted anything that came out of your mouth. Which I don't." I step closer to him so that we're almost nose to nose. "Next time I see your face, Cian, I will slaughter you where you stand."

Then I grab Wren and drag her away from him. She's breathing hard as we make our way through the curious crowd. The Arnauds are by the doors, staring at us with wide eyes.

"Leaving already?" Louis asks. His eyebrows pinch together with disappointment.

"Wren's tired. The last trimester has been hard on her. We just wanted to put in an appearance."

"Of course. We—"

I don't wait for the simpering hosts to continue; I just power through. He can kiss my ass another day.

Wren keeps asking me to slow down, but I don't let up until we're in the elevator with Pavel and a few others from Wren's security detail.

"For God's sake, Dmitri, was that necessary?" she demands the moment the elevator doors slide shut.

I throw her a glare that makes her clamp her mouth shut. I'm not in the mood for this anymore.

The rest of the walk is silent. Only when we're back in the car with the partition drawn up do I sigh. "You are my partner in all this, Wren. But that doesn't mean you get to question me in front of my men."

She purses her lips as those green eyes of hers glow bright. "Well, your men aren't within earshot now. So I can say this: I don't think Cian was there to hurt us."

"Wren—"

"Don't you *'Wren'* me. You didn't hear me out the first time and, for some reason, I let that slide. But not again. Cian's not the mastermind of this operation; there's someone else pulling his strings. In fact, I would go so far as to say that he's as much a victim in all this as Bee was." My eyes snap to hers and she cowers back. "Okay… maybe that wasn't the best example. What I mean is—"

I swallow my anger and try to remember that she's heavily pregnant and doesn't need the stress of Bratva politics to worry about. "I know what you mean." I take her hand and kiss it. "Don't worry; I've got this handled."

She looks at me skeptically. "Dmitri…"

"I don't want you worrying about this. Leave it to me and you just focus on delivering our son when he's ready to come out."

"You're shutting down the conversation," she accuses.

"I'm doing what's best for my family. That's the end of it. I don't want to discuss it anymore."

With that, I turn and look out the window as I begin to brood.

I'll deal with Cian in my own way…

Whether Wren likes it or not.

37

DMITRI

Even when I accept and hear his voice, I can't believe the motherfucker is calling me.

"Vittorio."

His breath stalls for a moment. "Dmitri. I didn't expect you to pick up."

"I am the one you wanted to speak to, aren't I?"

"Yes, but you've been so… unavailable recently."

"Only for people I consider a waste of my time."

"Really, now," Vittorio says with a familiar chuckle. "How could you say such a thing to a man who was going to be your father-in-law?"

"I dodged a bullet there," I snarl. "Unfortunately, the same can't be said for your *daughter*."

"I don't understand why you're so angry. I did you a favor."

If he were in front of me now, I would wrap my hands around his throat and release pressure only when his eyeballs have exploded from their sockets.

"Now," he continues, "you don't have to be married to a raging dyke. You can fuck whoever you want, whenever you want. You're welcome."

"That was always the plan, asshole."

Vittorio laughs, though it sounds more like a dying man's wheeze. "Ah, I see. You were going to marry her, pass off that whore's baby as my grandchild, steal my empire under the guise of inheritance… and then what? Kill me off after a year or two? Maybe just poison me in my sleep?"

"Oh, it was going to be a lot more painful than that."

"I appreciate the innovativeness. I bet my daughter came up with it all on her own?"

"Your daughter was fucking brilliant," I spit. "She was smart, funny, capable, and ruthless—but only when she needed to be. She was everything you are not. She would have been twice the don that you are."

"She was a fucking *woman*." His friendly, wheedling tone slips for a moment—but only a moment before he pulls it right back in place. "She couldn't have led men."

"Just goes to show you didn't know a fucking thing about her."

"I'll give her this much: she didn't make a sound when I lashed her. There were men who screamed and begged me to stop… but Beatrice? She risked biting her tongue off rather than betraying an ounce of pain. She was strong that way."

"A lot fucking stronger than you know."

"I don't get it." He sounds genuinely baffled. "What did you get out of that arrangement? Was it all for my empire, my legacy?"

I snort. "In your fucking dreams. I didn't need to take anything from you. Anything I decide I want, I *build* myself."

"So then, you and Beatrice, it was just—"

"It's called *friendship*, Zanetti," I hiss. "It's called *family*. Not that you'd know anything about either one."

"Friends," he scoffs. "Family. They're all just weaknesses that weigh you down. A strong don doesn't let petty concerns like that get in the way of a viable alliance. A *mutually* beneficial alliance."

"Why do I get the feeling you're going somewhere with this?"

"I'll be straight with you: I was angry after the wedding. You duped me. You sold me a pot of shit after promising me gold. I thought allying myself with the Irish would satiate my need for revenge."

"Let me guess: you got tired of the Irish dogs?"

His snort is all the confirmation I need. "They're fickle and superstitious and they're not half as capable as they pretend to be. I'm done with them. I'm ready to put this whole ordeal behind us."

"Are you now?" I ask with amusement. "And what makes you think *I'm* interested in putting this whole ordeal behind us?"

"Because you have a new family to think of," he simpers. "You have a pretty new wife and a precious little bundle of joy on the way, I hear. Do you really want to be looking over your shoulder every time you step out of that palatial penthouse you call home?"

I say nothing. If he wants to threaten me, he can do it without my help.

"Come meet me tonight at Soling House. Bring your men if you don't feel safe. We have much to discuss."

The line goes dead. I turn to find Aleks staring at me with his mouth open. "Do *not* tell me you just agreed to a fucking meeting with that psychotic asshole."

"He wants to renew our alliance."

"And you're going there just to… spit in his face?"

"I'm going there to make him think I'm agreeable. And just when he gets comfortable… *that's* when I blow his fucking brains out."

"Brother, this is a risky plan."

I nod. "It is. But I'm done playing it safe. My son is due any day now and I want this shit over soon. If I can cut the snake off at the head, it's over. The war will be won."

"Dmitri—"

"I know the risks, little brother, and I've decided they're worth taking." I walk up to him and tap his cheek gently a few times. He opens his mouth to counter, but I shut him up with a raised hand. "It's not up for discussion. I've made my decision. My son will be born into a world ready for him. I'll die if that's what it takes to make that happen."

38

DMITRI

Soling House.

Like a speakeasy fucked a country club and spat out this gaudy monstrosity. It's all polished bronze and cigar smoke, a shady place with shady corners for shady people to conduct shady business.

It's no surprise that Vittorio owns a stake in it.

It's no surprise that it's quiet when I drive up, either. This is not the sort of venue where men like to be seen. They slip in and out, slimy enough to leave ooze in their wake.

I don't plan to be here for a second longer than I have to be.

Aleks is the only one in the car with me, though two more vehicles full of Bratva men trail behind us. The streetlights are out—whether that's a coincidence or not, it's impossible to say, though I'm not the kind of man who believes in such things—which means the moon is the sole source of illumination.

"Something doesn't smell right," Aleks mutters as I cut the engine.

"It's Vittorio," I point out. "Nothing with him ever smells right."

"This is a trap."

"I'm aware."

Aleks twists in his seat to give me an incredulous look. "And you *still* insist on walking in there alone? You always call me the dumb one, but lately, man, I dunno…"

"At ease, soldier." I clap him on the shoulder. "I plan on striking fast."

"And if he happens to strike first?" he demands. "What then?"

"Then you will be the new *pakhan*," I say, squeezing where my hand still clasps him. "And I expect you to protect my family."

"Dmitri—"

"I'm serious, Aleks." He falls reluctantly silent. "You need to promise me that you'll take care of Wren. And my boy."

"For fuck's sake, man," he swears angrily, "you don't even have to ask. Of course I'll protect them. But *you* should be the one protecting them. You should be the one around for them. Let me go in. I'll—"

"It has to be me that goes in there, Aleks. Anyone else, Vittorio will simply kill on the spot. We can't leave any room for error here."

"Ironic, considering you're waltzing into enemy territory blind as a bat, with nothing but hope and a prayer. Some might call that 'an error.'" He tilts his head to the side and gives me his puppy dog eyes. "I'm not above begging if you make me, brother. Let me come in with you. Just me."

"No. If they take me down, you need to lead the Bratva. Someone will have to avenge my death."

"If Bee were here, she'd have smacked you over the back of the head. At least twice. Maybe more. I just think—"

"Enough," I say in my *pakhan* voice, the one that brooks no argument. "It's too late to turn back now. There's nothing worth discussing." I pull out the envelope that I prepared just minutes before I kissed Wren on the forehead as she slept and slipped out of our room. "If things go south, give this to Wren."

Then, without waiting for Aleks's answer, I climb out of the car and stride towards Soling House.

The door is nondescript in the way all speakeasy entrances are. You'd never be able to spot it if you didn't know where to look. When I knock, it's answered immediately by an old man whose tattoos have turned wrinkly along with his skin.

He swings the door open and steps aside to let me pass. When it slams shut, it feels like one chapter is ending and another is beginning.

"Down the corridor," he croaks in a smoker's rasp. "Make a left. Another left. A right at the staircase and then the fourth door on your right."

I nod and start walking down. I hear a click and, when I turn, the man is gone. No sign as to where he might've passed to. No sign of any other life, either.

With a grimace, I walk. The only sounds are my feet striking the marble floors and my breath coming in even, controlled exhales. I feel no fear. I show no weakness.

Enemies are watching.

And my son and wife are waiting.

I take the first left, as instructed. And the second. A right at the staircase. There's one door, a second, a third…

Then my destination.

This door is indistinguishable from the others. Simple wood, brass knob, though the frame is thick and sturdy. When I touch it, the handle is cold as the grave.

I twist and step through.

There's only one dim lamp lit in the corner. Enough to illuminate how old this room is. The air is musky, dense, like a crypt sealed for decades on end.

Something is wrong.

I turn on the spot. There are windows but the curtains are drawn tight. I walk over and pull them apart…

To discover that they've been bricked shut from the outside.

The fuck?

That's when I hear it. A firm and decisive *click* from the door. I make a run for it but it's too late. I'm locked in.

"You bastard, Vittorio!" I yell, punching at the door with my fists.

As if in answer, my phone starts to ring. Gritting my teeth, I pick up, making sure my voice is calm. "This is a new low, even for you."

He chuckles. "I'm surprised you came alone. It was brave—but stupid."

"Come out and face me like a man."

"As you so often like to remind me, I'm an *old* man. And old men have the luxury of falling back on their brains as opposed to their brawn. My days of strutting into enemy buildings to face my foes are done, boy," he hisses. "I want this war done."

I can hear rumbling in the foundations of the building. And that's when it hits me. The building is empty and lifeless…

Because it's about to come down.

"This doesn't win you the war, Vittorio," I growl. "My brother will take off your head even if I don't."

The foundation creaks like the old man Vittorio claims to be. Even the shutters have started to shake. That's when I spy the massive teak cabinet in the corner of the room. It looms like something out of a nightmare, huge and overwrought and twisted.

"I had hoped he and the rest of your idiot band of merry fools would accompany you into the building. One stone, many birds, as they say. But you decided to be *noble*. Disgusting."

"Even death won't protect you from me, Vittorio Zanetti," I warn as the starter explosions begins to pop off around the perimeters of the building. I rush towards the teak cabinet and throw the doors open. I have no idea if this will work, but it's my only shot. "My ghost will kill you, even if I don't."

He's cackling with laughter when I hang up on him. I have just enough time to shut the teak doors before an earth-shattering boom from the far side of the building splits the world into a million little pieces. The next one might very well be the last thing I ever hear.

I'm fumbling with my phone trying to send off a text to Wren. If these are my final few seconds on earth, I want to spend them writing to her. Leaving her with my last words, my last promises.

"C'mon, c'mon, c'mon," I mutter as my fingers fly over the keyboard.

I finish and hit **Send**, but I don't know if the message goes out before the closest explosion erupts. Even through the thick wardrobe, it's awe-inspiring. Death by fire. A fitting end, if it is indeed my end.

Heat and heaviness knock me in every direction at once as the teak cabinet topples on its side. It feels like I'm being crushed to death. No, I *am* being crushed to death.

If the weight on my chest doesn't kill me, the dust in my lungs will.

My phone lights up, and even though it's barely an inch from my fingers I can't reach it. I can't move.

The darkness, the heat, the fucking *weight...* It's swallowing me up between its black teeth. I desperately want to fight, but the jaws are too strong.

As consciousness starts to fade, I have only one thought. One feeling. One name on my lips.

Wren.

39

WREN

It's been a while since I've had a bad dream, but this one's a doozy.

I dream that I'm locked in a cage hanging over the ocean and Dmitri is lying on the beach, wrestling with a giant, black serpent with fangs almost as big as he is. I can see the serpent's moves before he makes them, but my voice is gone. Even when I try to speak, nothing comes out. Only my screams echo across the air towards the sandy wasteland where Dmitri is fighting for his life.

I feel helpless—able to see the future, but unable to make a difference in the outcome.

"Dmitri! He's coming for your feet! Feint to the left! The *left*!"

But it's like some invisible fingers have reached down my throat and ripped my voice clean out. The snake licks its fangs and I know somehow he's about to go for Dmitri's head next.

No! I groan on the inside. *I can't watch this. I can't...*

But it's too late. In a blur of black motion, the serpent has clamped its jaws over Dmitri. One powerful bite and my husband is gone. Where he once stood, there are now only bloody streaks of gore and a wisp of his cologne.

The serpent rears its black head and looks up at me. It rises, uncoiling itself higher and higher and higher until it can look me levelly in the eyes. Its irises are a stunning and terrifying blue.

"Please," I whisper because now, somehow, I've gotten my voice back, "not my baby."

"Your baby's already dead," the serpent hisses happily, smiling wide enough that I can see the remnants of my husband on its teeth.

I open my mouth and scream as the serpent lunges for me. It doesn't hurt like I expected. It just feels *inevitable.* I'm washed up in the heat of his mouth. Wet and sticky and lonely.

"No!" I scream. "No! No…"

My eyes fly open and I realize that I'm not suspended over the ocean in an iron cage. There is no snake and there is no beach and neither my husband nor I are dead.

I'm lying in my bed, surrounded by feathery cushions and a pregnancy pillow tucked under my legs. "Dmitri," I whimper, reaching for him the way I always do when I'm scared or uncertain.

But my hand meets only empty space. There's no sign of him anywhere. Not in the bed and not in this room. I had fallen asleep with him beside me, though, hadn't I?

The dream…

It felt so damn real. The damp death I felt just as the snake swallowed me... I can still feel it now. On my legs...

Throwing the sheet off me, I realize that my legs are in fact wet. *Not only was that the worst dream in the world, but also, I've gone and peed myself? When it rains, it pours, huh?*

Except... that's not urine.

I touch it, horror winding through my gut, and I brace myself to see blood on my fingertips.

But it's not that, either.

It's clear. It's thin. It's watery.

"Oh my God," I breathe as my unease turns to a cautious excitement. "It's time. The baby's coming."

I lurch out of bed so fast that I almost tip over. I throw on all the lights and then grab my phone and call Dmitri with trembling fingers.

"Come on, come on," I beg to my empty room. "Pick up!"

I cut the line and call him again. No answer.

Again. No answer.

Again...

I repeat the process until it becomes cripplingly obvious that he isn't going to pick up. Now what? Gripping my belly tightly as though it might fall off, I hobble to the next room, hoping that Dmitri's going to be there, so lost in his work that he hasn't noticed his phone vibrating.

I fling the door open to discover it... empty.

"*Dammit!*" I cry out. "Dmitri!"

I turn my back on his office and stumble my way towards the living room, clutching my phone and trying desperately to think of who I can call. *Why can't I remember anyone's names?!*

"Aleks!" I yell out loud, hastily dialing in his number. "Come on, come on… please pick up. *Please!*"

He doesn't.

And that's when the excitement starts to curdle in the pit of my stomach. Because there's no way Dmitri *and* Aleks would both be unavailable unless something big had happened. Unless something *serious* had happened. Unless…

The nightmare!

I wrack my brain, trying to remember the details of the nightmare. Was it just a throwaway dream or was it a prophecy? A warning? Was it trying to tell me that I'm on my own now?

"Calm down, Wren," I snap at myself. "Don't panic. Just breathe and stay calm."

I'm still working on my first breath when a flash of pain travels up my body. A scream rips its way from my throat and sends me keeling over from this new throbbing agony I've never experienced before.

"Shit, shit, shit, shit, shit…" I groan obsessively as I stare at my useless phone. When the pain finally releases its clamp on me, I shove myself back upright. "Fuck it! I'll get myself to the hospital."

I start to limp to the elevators and smash the button to summon a ride down.

Except…

Nothing happens. I pause at the access code pad, realizing with horror that I have no idea what code actually opens the steely silver doors. I start guessing. But again and again, the red light flashes and the beep scolds me for daring to try.

Access Denied.

Access Denied.

Access Denied.

I'm sweating now. Dripping under my arms, between my thighs, down my back. It's like the pain is melting me from the inside out. Another contraction scours through my body and I bite my tongue until it throbs, place my hands on the elevator, and try once again to breathe through it.

"What am I going to do?" I whisper feverishly to the empty penthouse. "What am I going to do…?"

I twist around and, with my back on those silver doors, I sink down onto the carpeted foyer floor. I can't even pull my feet up to my chest because my stomach's in the way. Instead, I sit there, legs sprawled on either side, my fingers clinging to the short-haired rug as I do my best to think of a way out of this.

But thinking is a joke. I'm useless right now in just about every way. I feel like I'm back in that carnival machine with Rose when we were little girls, trying to snatch dollar bills from the air as a wind tunnel blew a hurricane around us. I reach to seize something but it's gone before my fingers close.

Another contraction.

More pain.

More sweat.

Heaps more panic.

I close my eyes and pray.

"Rose... Bee... help me..."

An old memory flutters at the periphery of my mind. This one lingers long enough for me to grab hold of it.

"Rose!" I gasped when I saw her lying in her bathtub, submerged in bloody water. *"Oh my God, oh my—"*

"I'm okay."

I stopped short, terrified and unable to process. Rose turned her gaze on me and, true to her word, she *seemed* okay. Her eyes were alert; she looked to be in control of her faculties. But then—she was sitting in a tub of bloody water, so "okay" was a stretch at best.

She must've read my mind, because she raised her wrists to show me they were whole and unharmed. *"I didn't try to end it, if that's what you're guessing."*

"Then why the fuck is your bath water red?!*"* I demanded. *"Why does it smell like blood and death in here?"*

She closed her eyes and two huge tears squeezed out. *"Because I'm losing another one."*

I dropped to my knees beside the tub. Her bathroom was made up of dreary yellow tile and a clerestory window too narrow to let in more than a brief snatch of light.

"You're pregnant?"

"Not anymore. I'm losing the baby." She dragged her eyes up to mine. *"This is the furthest along I've ever gotten. Next week would have been three months."*

"Rose, why don't we get you out of—"

"No!" she'd shouted with so much force that I stumbled backwards and fell on my ass. *"No. I want to stay here with my baby for a little while longer."*

So I sat there with her for a long time. Neither of us said anything because what the hell do you say in a moment like that? For most of that hour, I didn't know.

And then it came to me.

I was speaking before I knew what I was saying. *"If you let me take you to the hospital now, I will help you become a mother,"* I swore to her. *"I will help you make a baby. Use me. Let me."*

The shudder on my spine turns to a shiver of pain as yet another contraction tears through my body. I bite down on my tongue and force myself back to my feet.

I promised Rose I'd bring her baby into this world.

I'll be damned if I back out on that now.

I locate my phone where I dropped it on the carpet and pick it up with some effort. I dial in Pavel's number, but wherever he is, there's no signal. "Who else?" I ponder out loud, pacing back and forth along the foyer. "Who else, who else, who—"

That's when her name jumps into my head. *Rogan!* Dmitri always relied on her in a bind. She was older, yes, but she was sharp as a whip and capable.

I find her number in my contact list and dial. She answers right away, and the sound of the line connecting is like manna from heaven. I sink to my knees and sob. "Hello, Mrs. Egorov. How can I help—"

The words come out in a rush without pauses for breath between them. "I'm in labor and Dmitri and Aleks aren't picking up and I can't get out of the penthouse because I don't have the access code and… and… I'm freaking out!"

"I see," she says, calm as a glacier. "Don't worry; I will call in reinforcements." *What does that mean?* "They will be there in the next five minutes."

Click.

I take the phone off my ear and stare down at the screen. "Did she just… hang up on me?"

I almost scream when a heavy mechanical *clunk* sounds behind me. Turning in equal parts horror and amazement, I see the elevator start to move.

But it doesn't open to my floor.

It goes up.

If some sweaty construction worker putting in overtime on the upstairs renovations comes down to deliver my baby, I swear to God I'll strangle Dmitri with the umbilical cord next time I see him.

The elevator reverses course. The cables whine. The car descends, closer and closer and closer toward me…

The light flashes green. The doors open.

Ding.

And when they part, there is one person standing there, wearing a soft cotton jumpsuit and a sheepish, apologetic smile.

"Hey, babe," Bee says to me, like everything is fine. Like she didn't die months ago. "Guess it's go time, huh?"

And since I can't comprehend who this person is standing in front of me, since I can't think of what to say in response, I do the only logical thing a person can do in my position: I let go.

Darkness makes more sense than life right now, anyway.

40

WREN

I wake up from the scorching pain reverberating in my stomach.

My first thought is, *Well, this is bullshit.*

I mean, it's bad enough that I died during childbirth. Why the hell am I *still* in pain? Shouldn't I be floating somewhere on a magical cloud? Or getting ready to meet my maker? Or being reunited with Rose and Bee?

To be fair, Bee *had* made an appearance. It was suitably dramatic, yet strangely underwhelming at the same time. As my memory serves, she came in on an elevator, not a chariot flown by unicorns, and she was wearing a blue cotton jumpsuit, whereas I would've expected ethereal white robes and a halo. Or at least—

Aaaarghhh!

More pain. Like I said, this is total bullshit. Death is supposed to free you from the tribulations of mortal suffering.

More to the point: if I died in childbirth, then why the hell does it feel like I'm *still* giving birth?

"Wren…"

Ooh, is that God? I always knew He was a She. Which would be so much more awesome a discovery if I didn't have to die to discover it.

"Wren!"

"Be patient with her. Her body's going through a lot. Just give her time."

Is that… Dr. Liza? Last I checked, she was still a member of the living world. Which means either she's dead, too…

Or I'm not as dead as I think I am.

"Wren, it's okay; I'm right here. Everything's gonna be okay."

That voice makes no damn sense to me. But I'm guessing solving the mystery is going to require some sight. So, with a groan, I blink my eyes open and promptly cringe against the blinding fluorescents.

Surely heaven has no room for fluorescent lighting. That shit belongs in the depths of hell.

"Hey, you. Good to see ya." Bee's face blocks out the lights on the ceiling, creating an eerie halo around her head.

"B-Bee?"

"I know it's a shock to see me here—"

"You're supposed to be *dead*?" I feel a squeeze on my arm. "Or… am I the one that's dead?"

"No one's dead!" Bee laughs. "You're alive. I'm alive. We're all alive up in this joint."

I pull my arm out from underneath hers. "But… but… *how?!*"

Her gaze flickers to Liza helplessly for a moment. "Do you wanna maybe do the whole explanation part *after* you have your baby?"

"*No!*" I bark at her. "Unless you wanna be kicked out of this room in five seconds, start talking."

She smirks and pats my hair. "I missed all that feistiness."

"Bee!"

She holds up her hands. "Okay, okay. Very long story turned very short: my funeral was a hoax, my death was faked, and I went into hiding in the upstairs penthouse." She grins down at me awkwardly, waves some even more awkward jazz hands, and adds, "Surprise!"

I blink.

I stare.

I blink.

I stare.

And then I say, "I swear to God, if I weren't in labor right now, I'd fucking *kill* you."

She titters uncomfortably. "Honestly, I wouldn't blame you."

"I just can't—" But another contraction swallows up my words before I can spit them at her.

Bee jumps back to my side and clutches my arm. "It's okay, hon. I'm here. We're gonna do this together."

"B-but Dmitri… H-he should be here for this…"

"I know. I'm sure he'll be here as soon as he can. Until then, consider me his representative."

"So he *knew* you were alive this whole time?" I gasp between breaths.

"Uh, maybe we should talk details after—"

"Bee!"

"Yes, he knew," she sighs reluctantly. "And honestly, I don't know why he decided to keep this from you. But I'm sure he had his reasons."

So it was *his* decision. Somehow, that hurts more than these fucking contractions do.

"Okay, Wren," Liza announces, coming into my line of vision with an enthusiastic clap. "I know you've got a lot going on right now, but this baby is ready to be born. So we're gonna have to table this conversation for later."

My protest disappears underneath a scream. Yup, the baby's definitely coming.

Bee squeezes my forearm and looks me in the eye. "Hold on as tight as you want. I can take it."

"Yeah," I grunt. "I've heard that about ghosts."

She chuckles. "Glad to see you haven't lost your sense of humor."

"*Aargh!*"

"Screaming's not gonna help, Wren," Liza informs me from between my legs, both of which are being held up by thick, ugly stirrups. "Just breathe and push. He's crowning."

Have I been given an epidural? Is it really time? Am I ready to be a mother?

Considering how impatient I've been the last few weeks of my pregnancy, it's ironic the questions stampeding through my head right now. But as the pressure builds deep inside me, I know there's no waiting any longer. Not even for my husband.

"He's coming!" Liza announces in a steady voice.

I give one final push that almost sucks the last bits of life out of me—and then suddenly, my ears are bursting with the sound of his cries. Loud and strong and *angry.* "Oh my God," I murmur over and over again. Or maybe that's Bee who's talking? I laugh through my tears at the sheer ludicrousness of having my baby with Bee at my side.

Life sure is a bitch. But sometimes, *sometimes,* she's a nice bitch.

"Where is he?" I cry out, trying to see through the blurry veil of my tears. I know he's around because he's still screaming bloody murder.

"Don't worry. He'll be with you in a second," Dr. Liza assures me. "Just getting him cleaned up here."

Then Bee steps to the side and a little blue bundle is placed into my arms. I stare down at the little creature swaddled in the warm blanket and I feel my chest expand in a new direction, one I didn't know existed until just now.

"Hi, sweetness," I whisper to him, grazing his cheek with my fingertips. "I recognize you."

"Wow," Bee breathes from my shoulder. "He looks just like his papa."

His papa. That word is heavy with emotion for me. I feel joy and relief, but I also feel sadness. And a deep-seated sense of betrayal.

Because despite all his promises, despite all his assurances, despite all his vows—he lied to me.

Again.

41

WREN

"*Ugh*, I could just eat him up!" Bee coos as she peers over my shoulder. "Seriously. I'm actually not joking. A little Nutella on that cheek and it's *bon appetit* for me."

"He's barely two hours old, Bee. Let's not terrify the baby."

She doesn't hear me over the gnashing sounds she's making with her teeth. I've spent the last two hours trying to work up the appropriate level of fury to throw her way. But infuriatingly enough, the relief of knowing she's actually alive beats my sense of betrayal.

For now.

"… gobble you up… yes, I will, yes, I will…"

My son starts to wail, so with a weary sigh, I scoop him up and position him to latch on for another feeding. The first one was a bit of a struggle, but we found our groove toward the end. And this second round gets off on much better footing. He quiets and gurgles as he drinks.

"You've got *great* boobs. Just saying."

I narrow my eyes at her. "No number of compliments can make me forget the fact that you made me believe you were *dead,* Bee. For freaking *months!*"

She sighs and sits down at the edge of my bed beside my feet. "I'm sorry, okay? I knew it was a mistake to keep it from you, but—"

"You let him call the shots?"

"He's the *pakhan.* You know this."

I click my tongue at her. "It's pathetic that you and Aleks continue to use that as an excuse. He's your best friend. This whole power dynamic thing that exists between you is fucking *weird.*"

She slaps my ankle lightly. "Watch your language—there's a baby in the room."

I don't laugh. "You were right above me the entire time?"

"Yeah." Bee's face falls flat. "Yeah, I was."

"Do you know how much easier the last couple of months would have been if I'd just known that you were alive?" I hiss at her. "That you were safe? Do you realize how badly I missed you?!"

"I missed you, too," she swears. "You have no idea how many times I thought of riding that elevator down and just revealing myself."

"But you didn't."

"No," she sighs, "I didn't."

"Because as usual, you chose him over me."

"That's not true—"

"It most certainly *is* true. You may not have agreed with his decision, but you went along with it, and that makes you complicit."

She opens her mouth but then snaps it shut again, biting down on her bottom lip. "You're right. There's nothing else I can say, but… I'm sorry. I really am, Wren. So deeply, deeply sorry."

Sighing, my gaze drifts to my beautiful little son. He's perfect. He's perfect and he's here and he's safe. And in light of that gratitude, I'm finding it hard to keep up the same level of indignation.

"Okay," I say at last.

"Okay?"

"I'm not totally over this yet," I warn her. "But I *am* over the moon that you're alive."

She grins from ear to ear. "I'll take it." Scooting up to my head, she leans down and pops a wet kiss on my cheek. "By the way, I *love* his name. I couldn't have picked a better one myself."

The door to my room shivers like someone's coming. I wait for Dmitri to rush through it, but nothing happens. No one enters.

"Where is he?" I whisper, unable to keep it in any longer.

Bee straightens up. I can sense the worry wafting off her, too. She's been doing a good job suppressing it so far, but I smell it coming off her pores. "I'm sure everything—"

"I'm done with lies, Bee. Even if you think they'll protect my feelings. I want the truth, no matter how hard it might be."

She swallows. "Dmitri was meeting Vittorio tonight. I'm thinking something didn't go according to plan."

"Dmitri was meeting Vittorio *tonight?*" I lean up and my eyes bulge out of their sockets. My son whines at my breast, so I grimace and settle back down, though my heart is now racing.

"Vittorio claimed to want to negotiate a new truce."

"And Dmitri actually *bought* that? He actually went?" I exclaim incredulously. "Is that where Aleks is? And Pavel and the rest of the men?"

"Most likely. I haven't heard from any of them in a few hours now." She checks her phone again and looks anxiously towards the door. "If their silence stretches on much longer… Well, fuck. If it goes much longer, we'll have to put the evacuation plan in motion."

"You're not serious."

Bee nods. "Dmitri told me he already briefed you about the contingency plans he made just in case things went south. Well, the same goes. I'll be your sherpa."

This is supposed to be a happy day. But all the joys of childbirth are quickly being replaced by the fear of the unknown.

"I don't want a sherpa!" I cry. "I want my husband."

"I know, babe. And trust me: if I could bring him—"

She breaks off at the sound of heavy running footsteps. The baby senses my nerves because he breaks off my breast and starts crying. A second later, the door bursts open…

And Dmitri is standing there, looking like he's literally been fighting the giant snake from my dream.

"Jesus Christ, Dmitri!" Bee cries. "What happened to you?"

"Later, Bee," he snarls, pushing past her to get to my bedside. "Wren, baby, I'm so fucking sorry I wasn't here." He looks truly repentant as he moves a little closer. I try to soothe the baby as he launches into a higher pitched wail, but I can't take my eyes off Dmitri.

He's bleeding from a thousand different cuts. Soot clings to every inch of him and the first signs of some heinous bruising are already beginning to show on his throat and face.

"My God," he whispers as he looks down at our son in my arms. "He's perfect."

"What happened?"

He meets my eyes. "It's a long story. But the important thing is I'm here now."

"The *important* thing is I need the truth!" I yell. "Because I've had enough lies to last a fucking lifetime."

He tosses Bee a glance over his shoulder and sighs. "You're right. And I'll tell you everything. But first, can I see my son?"

I don't have the heart to deny him. So I twist the baby to the side and peel off some of the blanket so Dmitri can see his face.

He just breathes, his expression smoothed free of fear and anger in a way I've never seen before. I could love a man who looked like that all the time. I can trust the angry Dmitri to keep us safe. I can trust the arrogant Dmitri to keep us fed and clothed and sheltered.

But a Dmitri who looks like that…

I could *love* him.

"His name is Mischa. I named him myself and I'm not changing his name now," I tell him firmly.

Dmitri smiles and nods like he's lost in a dream. "I wouldn't change it even if I could."

His appearance is going a long way in softening up my anger. "I'd hand him over to you, but…"

He looks down at himself and laughs incredulously. "I'll hold him later, when I'm fit to."

I switch Mischa onto my other breast and swallow the complicated knot of emotions threatening to rupture inside of me. "Is it over?" I ask quietly. I'm hoping beyond hope that he looks the way he looks for a good freaking reason.

His chest rises and falls and I sense immediately that it's not over. It's not even *close* to being over.

"Tell me," I insist. "I want to know everything."

Bee doesn't move from her spot in the corner of the room, but she chimes in, too. "She deserves to know, Dmitri."

Dmitri nods. "Very well. I'll tell you everything."

And he does. He tells me about Vittorio's call, about his plan, about the trap laid for him and lastly, about the entire building coming down on his head. The more he explains, the colder I get, the more terrified, the more panicked.

It's the knowledge that I came very, very close to losing Dmitri tonight that unsettles me to my core. My son could have lost his father before he had even taken his first breath.

"How the hell did you survive that?" Bee whispers, floating to the opposite side of my bed.

"Luck. And some quick thinking on my part. I took cover in the wardrobe in the room I was trapped in. The rest of the building collapsed around it, but it held strong by some miracle. Aleks led the men in and they literally dug me out. I had passed out when they found me, but they brought me back."

"Fuck me, that's insane," Bee says, shaking her head at him. "Only you. Luckiest bastard alive."

"You cheated death yourself," I remind her icily. "Birds of a freaking feather."

They both have at least enough decency to look guilty. But shame won't temper my anger for much longer. Now that I know they're here, that they're not going anywhere yet, that rage is rising up and boiling over.

"You had no right to take that kind of risk," I snarl at Dmitri. "You had me to think about. You had *Mischa* to think about."

"I *was* thinking about you and Mischa," he insists with a swallow. "Why do you think I risked it all? I wanted this over before he was born. I wanted to give us a fresh start."

"You went in blind! It was reckless, what you did tonight." Mischa unlatches and promptly starts to cry again. Silently, I pass him over to Bee, who walks him to the far end of the room, though probably just to get out of strangling range. "It was also short-sighted. Just like your lie about Bee."

He sighs in a way that suggests he knew this particular lie would come back to bite him in the ass. "I'm sorry. I should have told you about that."

"Then why *didn't* you?" I yell. "You had plenty of opportunities and you didn't. I asked you so many times about the noises I was hearing from the penthouse upstairs. 'Renovations,' you told me. *Reno*-fucking-*vations*! You lied to my face, Dmitri! Repeatedly. You promised to be honest, and even *as* you were making the promise, you were lying to me some more!"

I've worked myself up into full-on fury. Every cut on his face, every bruise on his skin is just another reminder of how careless he was with our lives.

"I thought I was doing the right thing—"

"For whom? For us? Or for *you?*"

The silence hurts in a way I don't know how to deal with. It stings and throbs and aches and burns all at once.

In the end, though, who do I have to blame but myself? Honestly, I'm not sure why I ever expected a different answer.

He rises and takes a few steps back before pausing at the foot of my bed. "I know I've hurt you, Wren. I'll give you the space you need. But we're gonna get through this. I promise you that."

For our son's sake, I hope he's right.

But I'm running low on hope tonight.

42

DMITRI

Not even one month into my marriage and we're already living in separate apartments.

I have to get an appointment any time I want to speak to my wife—and even then, she barely lingers in the room long enough to have a conversation.

She usually leaves me with three things—the baby, instructions, and blue balls.

Whenever I try to open up the conversation to something else, she gives me a weary expression and a sigh that warns me to give up before I've even begun. *"I told you already, Dmitri: I need space. I'm just here to make sure you know how to take care of Mischa for the next few hours."*

Then she disappears, usually with Bee at her back. It's infuriating: I'm relegated to glorified babysitter, while Bee gets to share the most intimate parts of Wren's life. Not that she hasn't been a useful mole during this emotional cold war, but still—I shouldn't need a mole in the first place.

In the absence of progress, I've decided to put all my energy into making amends in the hopes that one day, she'll forgive me. Not an easy thing to pull off when she refuses to be in the same room with me for more than a few minutes.

Which is why I find myself here, skulking around the kitchen in the lower penthouse at one in the morning, stocking up the cupboards with all of Wren's favorite snacks and foods. I make sure each room has a stainless steel bottle filled with ice-cold water, just the way Wren likes it.

And of course—the notes.

A few months ago, I would've recoiled in disgust at the thought of it. Now, I don't give a fuck. What's the point of dignity when you don't even have your wife to share it with?

So fuck it, I'll grovel. One handwritten note at a time.

I'm pinning up the last scrap of paper when Bee walks into the kitchen in a fluffy blue bathrobe with her hair piled up in a bun at the top of her head.

"Oi, Romeo—still littering the kitchen, are we?"

"It's not littering if she reads them," I growl as I finish taping it up and step back to check my handiwork. "She does read them, yes?"

"She reads them," Bee admits. "I just don't know what she does with them afterwards."

"You haven't seen them in the trash?"

Bee's jaw drops theatrically. "Do you really think I'm in the habit of rooting around in the trash like a raccoon?"

I roll my eyes. "Forget I asked."

"Consider it forgotten." She grins and claps her hands abruptly enough to startle me. "Guess what? The little master said his first word today!"

My expression flatlines. "Don't fuck with me."

"What?" she protests. "He *did!* He said my name. *Bee.* Amazing, huh?"

"He's a couple of days old. The only thing he was trying to convey was indigestion. For fuck's sake, the whole point of you being here is so you can give me *real* information."

She shrugs. "Just trying to lighten the mood. And I thought the whole point of me being here was to be a shoulder for Wren to lean on."

"That, too."

"You're too tightly wound about this, Dmitri," Bee advises with her stern tutor's expression on. "Seriously, she—"

Her lecture stops short as the baby monitor on the kitchen island hums to life. It activates any time Mischa moves, and he usually only moves just before he wakes up, so I leap into action. "Time for my son to eat."

Which has also become code for "papa time." Wren and I agreed that I would take the 1:00 A.M. feed so that she could get extra sleep during the night. I whisper to him the whole time as he suckles at the bottle. I promise him futures, tell him about the world, make my amends.

If only his mother would give me the same kind of chance to make amends with her.

"I'll go get the little tyke so you can finish your love notes." She winks at me and sashays out of the kitchen.

I finish my last note and place it on the kitchen island where I know Wren has her breakfast every morning. Then I grab a labeled package of Wren's milk from the freezer and heat it up before transferring it to Mischa's bottle.

Bee's already in the living room when I get there, Mischa mewling hungrily in her arms.

I whip off my shirt and take him expertly with one arm. Then I settle him against my naked chest and ease the bottle into his mouth. It takes some coaxing before he accepts it—not that I can blame him. I'd prefer Wren over this fake, plastic bullshit, too.

Bee lowers herself down to the floor at the foot of my chair and turns to take in the view of Chicago through the window. "It's weird, don't you think?" she muses to herself. "I wanted so much to avoid being a mother—and here I am, desperate to babysit that little guy whenever I can. Wonders never cease."

Smiling cryptically, she reaches up to stroke her fingertips through his downy hair. It's dark brown like mine, but he's got his mama's eyes. A deep, unbroken green. Bee says that Wren's convinced they'll turn brown eventually.

I hope they don't. I like that I can see her in him. I like that it's undeniable.

"How's she doing?" I rumble.

"You should ask her yourself."

"You don't think I've tried?" I snap. "She refuses to talk to me. Any question I ask is met with a one-word response or just straight-up silence. Then she makes like the wind and disappears as soon as she's handed over the baby."

"You've gotta get creative."

"I promised her space. I can't go back on that promise by invading her space every chance I get."

"She's hormonal and she's hurt. But she'll soften up the moment you make a grand gesture."

I feign enthusiasm. "Great suggestion. Why don't I make the grand gesture of giving her an apartment? Or maybe I should get her the job of her dreams? Or perhaps I should propose to her with a giant ring? Oh, wait…"

Bee throws up her hands sardonically. "Okay, okay, so you're running short on grand gestures. Maybe it doesn't have to be grand? Go the other route with it, you know? Maybe it has to be simple."

I gently free the bottle from Mischa's lips and hand it over to Bee while I burp him. He whines and fusses for a moment until it comes free and he can settle back into place, reunited with the bottle again. His eyelids are getting heavier and heavier with every passing second, though. Sleep isn't far away.

"You didn't answer my question," I point out as I lean back into the chair.

Bee sighs. "She's doing well, all things considered. The breastfeeding wears her out. She's already lost so much weight from it. But she never complains. And she's so hands-on with everything. If it were me, I'd have, like, three nannies on call around the clock."

"That's not Wren's way."

"No," Bee agrees, "it's not. I think she's also trying to keep herself distracted." She looks over her shoulder towards the

Tangled Decadence

rooms and lowers her voice. "She misses you."

"Did she—"

"Of course not. She'd never admit that out loud. But I can tell. I know her well enough to read those forlorn, lovesick sighs she does when she thinks I'm not paying attention. She misses you, Dmitri. Just because she's pissed at you doesn't mean she's stopped loving you."

I despise how eagerly my heart leaps at those simple, offhand words.

"She probably hates being cooped up in the apartment," I venture.

Bee chuckles. "That's a definite yes. No mind-reading required to confirm that one. She goes stir-crazy every now and again—but honestly? I don't think she wants to go out on her own. And she doesn't want to expose me, so she just kinda deals with it. And by that I mean, we eat a bunch of ice cream and gossip about who's who on *The Masked Singer*."

"Take her out," I blurt before I can think better of it. "A mother's class, maybe, if she needs an excuse. And lunch. Somewhere nice. You'd have to take care not to be recognized, of course, but I..." I sigh heavily. "I don't want her to feel like she's trapped. I think an outing might do her some good."

Bee's staring out at the view now and I'm pretty sure she's not listening to a word I'm saying. "We'll go to *Les Freres Halles* ... oh, their duck with the beurre blanc sauce... I've had dreams about it... and the lamb with the red wine jus... and the creamed lobster in those buttery vol-au-vent pastry shells... *God,* I'm horny just thinking about it." She twists to face me with an ear-to-ear grin. "We're gonna rack up a big bill, okay? Fair warning."

I suppress my own smile. "Order whatever you want. Sky's the limit."

"Music to my ears," she murmurs dreamily. "For the record, if I were Wren, I'd take you back."

"You're talking with your stomach now." I swap to a sterner expression. "Just make sure the security detail is strong. Subtle, but strong. I don't want either those Italian fucks or the Irish scum picking up on the fact that my wife and son are out and about without me."

"Got it, boss," Bee says, saluting me.

Mischa hiccups off the bottle and I put it aside. He's nearly finished his four ounces, which means he's got one good burp left in him before he sleeps for the next few hours.

I raise him upright and run my hand down his soft little back. It always amazes me just how small and breakable he feels. I want to cradle him in my arms so anyone who wants to hurt him would have to burrow through all of me first.

And his *smell*. He smells of powder, warm milk—and *her*.

After he gives me another satisfying burp, he starts mewling softly, tired but unable to sleep. "It's okay, little man," I say softly, cradling him against the crook of my arm. "I'm here. You'll be back with Mama in the morning."

When I look up, I catch Bee staring at the two of us with an awed glaze in her eyes.

"What?" I snap.

She smiles and shrugs. "It's just kinda trippy, seeing you like this. Fatherhood has really changed you. It's softened you. Made you feel less... *pakhan*. More human."

"And that's a good thing?"

"It's a very good thing. This whole family man thing suits you, Dmitri, in case you didn't know."

I scowl. "Except I don't really have a family at the moment, do I? My wife's barely speaking to me and I get to see my son in brief midnight shifts."

"I know, I know," she says, rising and adjusting the ties of her bathrobe. "All I can say is this: you two are madly in love with each other. It's gonna take more than a little lie to break the kind of connection you two have."

"It was more than a little lie."

"She forgave you for killing her sister, Dmitri!" Bee reminds me with a not-that-soft rap of her knuckles on my skull. "If she can forgive that, she can forgive this."

"It keeps adding up, though," I whisper, as much to myself as to Bee. "One lie, after another, after another…"

"So don't add anymore," she scolds. "Let this be the last lie, the last secret. You wanna be a family? Well, then—*be* one. The only person stopping it is you."

With that, she slips out of the room and disappears. Mischa is snoozing against my chest, so I sit in the dark with him for a long time. Not moving, barely breathing. Hell, I'm barely even *thinking*, really.

It's just one thought. One endlessly looped thought, burning a hole in my brain.

For them, I will fight until my last breath.

43

DMITRI

It's been almost two weeks and she's still freezing me out.

My wife is a ghost. I can smell her on my son, I can hear her in the next room—but she's never actually a presence in front of me for long enough to be real.

Our longest interactions happen when she comes to relieve me or vice versa. So it's no surprise that I've come to look forward to those precious few minutes whenever I can steal them.

I've had Mischa now for two hours. He's due for his next feed so I'm expecting Wren to come and get him any minute now. Of course, there are the unwelcome times she sends Bee in her place—but today, Bee is already with me.

Mischa opens his deep green eyes and gives me a quizzical look. *I'm not some football to be tossed back and forth, you know.*

"I hear you, little guy," I whisper softly. "But your mama can be stubborn."

"Oh, *she's* the stubborn one, is she?" Bee remarks without looking up from her computer.

"It's been two damn weeks and she still won't talk to me about anything apart from Mischa. I've *given* her the space she wanted."

Bee rolls her eyes as she slams the lid of her laptop closed. "Ugh, when are men gonna learn? Sometimes, we don't actually say what we mean!"

"Wren's not like that."

"Wren may not know what she wants right now. She's all over the place! She's tired and emotional and sick of staying in this penthouse all the time. Do you know that she burst into tears at her appointment with Liza last week?"

"No," I growl, "because you never told me. Why the fuck *didn't* you?"

"It felt personal and I didn't want to betray Wren's trust by telling you."

"You're telling me now."

"I know that," she snaps. "But only because I have a point to prove. Which is that she's vulnerable and she feels like she's doing this alone and she'd probably feel that way even if she were surrounded by a barrage of people every single day because none of them are *you*."

"What would you have me do?" I demand.

She arches one eyebrow. "Fight dirty."

Mischa coos in my arms and I give him a pained, tentative smile. "Do you agree with that plan?" I ask gently. "Do you think we need to try a different approach with Mama?" He tries to lift his little fist and then gets angry when he can't. I sigh and kiss the top of his head.

"Ahem."

I twist around to find Wren at the threshold to the living room. She's wearing soft white pants and a black tank top that proves that, in just a matter of weeks, she's got her figure back. But there's still a certain softness to her, a new dimension in her hips and breasts that doesn't do a damn thing to diminish my desire.

If anything, it only makes me want her more.

I stride toward her. As usual, she flinches anytime I get too close, but she stands her ground because I have her son.

Which is why I don't hand him off so easily. The longer it takes me to pass him to her, the longer she's forced to stay in my company.

"How are you?"

Her brows pinch together. "Fine." She lifts her arms. "He must be hungry—"

"You look beautiful."

"Are you mocking me?" she asks as her hands falter and drift back to her sides. "Because I've been living in this tank top for two days now and Mischa peed on me just before you came to get him. I meant to change, but I was so exhausted, I collapsed before I could. So when you say I look good—"

"I didn't say you *smelled* good."

For a brief, beautiful moment, I genuinely believe she's going to crack a smile. Then her mouth decides otherwise and turns down at the corners. "Dmitri, we have a doctor's appointment to get to and I still have to feed Mischa and take a shower myself. It's his two-week checkup and I don't want to be late."

So much for that.

"No, of course not. How about you feed Mischa here and I'll keep an eye on him while you shower and change? Then we can go to the appointment together."

Her frown just deepens. "No need. Bee is taking us."

"Actually, she's busy today," I lie smoothly, "so I'll be your chaperone."

Wren looks around me at Bee, who's typing frantically away on her laptop. She pauses only long enough to glance in our direction. "Yup—sorry, hon. Something popped up last minute and I gotta handle it. I'll be there next time, okay?"

She doesn't wait for Wren to reply. She goes right back to typing, giving Wren no way out. I'm pretty sure I can see her grinning like a hyena in the reflection of her computer screen.

"Fine," she sighs. "I guess you could take us just this one time."

"Excellent. Want to feed him by the window?"

She eyes the armchair suspiciously, as if I have the damn thing booby-trapped or something. "I'll feed him downstairs in the nursery. If you come get him in twenty minutes, I can have my shower and we'll leave."

Mission accomplished, I happily hand over Mischa to his stony-faced mother, who leaves without a goodbye. Once she's gone, Bee drops the *working too hard for conversation* act, leaps to her feet, and applauds wildly.

"Now, *that's* what I'm talking about!" she cheers. "It's about time you started getting creative."

"She'll be pissed at you for bailing on her."

Bee shrugs. "She can't be too pissed at me. I'm still recovering from my very recent death."

"How long do you think you can get away with milking that excuse?"

"I'll let you know when it runs out. Now, *go.* This is the first time you've got her all to yourself in weeks. Make the best of it. I can't put this family together single-handedly, you know. God knows I'm trying."

Snorting, I head to my room for a quick change, because as it happens, Wren's not the only one Mischa likes to pee on. Then I head down to the lower penthouse to wait with our son while Wren gets ready.

The flash of skin as she readjusts her nursing bra is enough all on its own to make me rock-hard. "I'll just be ten minutes or so," she says, a faint blush tainting her cheeks.

God, how I've missed that.

It takes the entirety of her shower before my erection deigns to come down. And then she walks out of her bedroom and I'm right back to where I started.

"My God," I breathe. "You look incredible."

She's wearing a soft floral dress that seems to move even when she's standing still, pink fabric fluttering in some invisible breeze. Her hair is a loose tumble over one bare shoulder, thick and luxurious enough that I'd pay dearly to wind my fingers through it.

"Oh. Thanks," she mumbles. It's a totally different reaction from her first one upstairs. And it makes me wonder... *Did she dress for me?*

"All set?"

Wren nods. "Just gotta grab Mischa's baby bag—"

She dips down to get it, but I beat her to the punch while balancing Mischa in the crook of my right arm. "I've got it."

She straightens up self-consciously and nods. "Okay, I guess we can leave then."

She makes a point of not looking my way at all as we make our way downstairs to the Rolls Royce purring on the curb. After I've strapped Mischa into his car seat, she gets into the back with him.

I look at her in the rearview mirror as we pull away. "Wren—"

"I don't want to talk, Dmitri," she announces firmly.

"You don't have to. I'm asking you to listen." I sigh and adjust my grip on the steering wheel. My free leg is pistoning up and down with unspent nerves. "I know I have no right to ask you for anything, but I'm a selfish, arrogant bastard, so I'm going to do it anyway. For the sake of our family."

Ripping her eyes from mine, she redirects them out of the window. Her silhouette alone is stunning. It occurs to me, not for the first time, that she is my wife and that that itself is a miracle I have yet to process.

"Fine," she grunts. "Be my guest."

I clear my throat. "I know this sounds like bullshit now, but I *was* going to tell you about Bee. I had every intention of doing it—and then I came to our room and your nose blew up and I had to rush you to the hospital."

"Not good enough, Dmitri." Her gaze veers slowly back to mine in the rearview. "You didn't *want* to tell me. You were looking for excuses not to."

"You're right. I didn't want to—"

"Why?" she blurts out. "Why the hell not?"

"Because, in my own way, I was genuinely trying to protect you. I was just doing it the same way I had always tried to protect Elena: by keeping you separate from the Bratva. By keeping you removed from the gore of it all. I figured, when I'd won the war and Bee could move around freely again, I would tell you."

She bites her bottom lip. "You didn't tell Elena *anything* that happened in the Bratva?"

"Nothing. And she preferred it that way. I guess I just took it for granted that you felt the same."

"You bet your ass I don't," she snaps, placing a protective hand over Mischa as we turn a corner. I wonder if she even realizes she's doing it or if that need to protect her loved ones just flows from her without a second thought. "The whole point in being married is that we share everything with each other, Dmitri."

"I know—"

"It's what you promised me when we got married."

"I *know*."

"Why promise something you had no intention of keeping?"

"Because I was going to tell you the truth eventually," I assure her. "I just didn't want to do it then, while you were so pregnant and dealing with so much."

She gnashes her teeth in frustration. "The 'so much' that I was dealing with also included mourning one of my best friends. A friend who was very much *alive* and living right on top of us."

"I know it doesn't make any sense now—"

"No, it doesn't. It sounds like you were just trying to keep me out of your life."

"*Moya devushka*, I married you because I wanted you in my life. Forever."

"Why?"

I blink, confused. "Why what?"

"Why did you even ask me to marry you?" she explains. "Was it some twisted attempt at controlling me? At making sure I could never leave you?"

I hate that she's even gone there. That she's questioning our marriage now, too. But I'm the one who's brought this on by lying to her in the first place. I have only myself to blame.

"No, it was not."

"Then why?" she presses softly. "You could have proposed, yes. But we didn't need to get married immediately. We could have waited until the baby was born. Until I knew about Bee. But you insisted it all happened right away."

At that, I stop the car in the middle of traffic. Horns blare as cars swerve around me, furious, but I don't give a fuck. This needs a moment.

I turn in my seat to face Wren in person.

"Yes, I did. Because that night in the hospital, for the first time in my adult life, I was fucking terrified. I didn't know what was going on and I was convinced that I was going to lose you." Wren's face is frozen, not certain yet which way to crack. I keep going. "That fear made everything clear to me. I realized that what I felt for you went so far beyond love. I realized that you were the most important person in the world to me, and I couldn't bear the thought of living my life without you. And I figured, if by some cruel twist of fate, life took you from me or me from you, I wanted you to be my wife first."

What I would give to reach out and touch her now. It feels like forever since I last held her in my arms. If space weren't what she needed, it would be intolerable.

"As I said before, Wren, I'll give you the time you're asking for. As much of it as you need. But I also need you to understand that I'm not giving up on us. Not now. Not ever. We are a family. You and Mischa, you're the only things in the world that matter to me."

"What about your Bratva?"

"I would give up my Bratva in an instant if that's what it takes for you to forgive me."

I hold her eyes. She holds mine. More cars honk in fury, but I still couldn't care less. This break in time is for my wife and me.

This is healing.

This is hoping.

This is forgiving.

At least, that's what I want it to be.

In the end, she blinks first, breaking our hypnotic eye contact. "We should go inside," she says quietly, reaching for the baby bag.

"Leave it. I'll get it."

She nods, allowing herself to give me a small smile that flutters at the corners of her mouth like a ghost and disappears too soon. "Okay. Thank you."

It's not progress. Not exactly.

But it's something.

44

WREN

The rattle falls out of my new friend Jessica's hand and clatters to the floor, rolling to a stop a few inches shy of Mischa's head.

"Shit!" Jessica exclaims, rushing to retrieve it. "I'm so sorry, Wren."

I pick it up and hand it back to her. "Don't worry about it."

"I'm so damn out of it today." She brushes her hair out of her face and passes the toy back to her little boy. "I barely got any sleep last night. Michael was supposed to take the night feed and he completely slept through it."

Lana and Faith make commiserating *tsk* sounds with their tongues. "At least Michael offers to take a night shift or two every once in a while," Lana says with a grimace. "Jordan claims that as the main breadwinner, he can't afford to miss even one night of sleep."

"Sounds like Adam." Faith nods miserably. "Except he forgets that the only reason I can't work right now is because I *literally shoved his child out of my vagina."*

"How quickly they forget."

All three women turn to me at the same time, with matching expressions that demand I share a "useless husband" story of my own.

"Uh, for sure," I mumble weakly. I'm painfully aware that I most definitely do not have the same kind of problem that these women do. But how do I chime in with the truth? What can I say?

My husband takes every single late night feed so that I have an uninterrupted stretch of sleep?

My husband changes every diaper he's around for uncomplainingly? He sings while he does it? He stocks the pantry with my favorite snacks and rubs my feet before bed?

They'll hate me. Hell, *I'd* hate me. And for some inexplicable reason, I do want to fit in with these mothers.

I love Bee, of course, but there are just some things she can't relate to. Like bleeding nipples and month-long periods. She listens—it's just that she's always got this pinched expression when I talk about childbirth stuff that suggests she'd rather be listening to anything else.

But Jessica, Lana, and Faith? None of them wrinkle their noses when I complain about stomach cramps and blood clots. None of them look disgusted or horrified. They nod sympathetically and tell me all the little home remedies that have worked for them. We may not be lifelong friends, but if we can support each other through *this* part of life, that'll be enough for me.

It's just another reason I have to be grateful to my husband. Bee told me that this Mommy & Me class was his idea.

I'd been over the moon—just not over the moon enough to, y'know, actually go to him and thank him. So instead, I'd taken a leaf from his book and wrote a little note that I had Bee stick up on his room door.

Thank you—Wren.

I'll be expecting my Pulitzer in the mail any day now, thank you very much.

I wanted to write more, but I also didn't want him to think that my note meant I forgave him. The next day, I received a reply.

You're welcome—Your husband.

I laughed, against my better instinct. Then I took the note and deposited it into the Prada shoebox where I kept all the rest of his patient scribbles.

Yes, I kept them all. Yes, I wish I could bring myself to burn them instead. Yes, I'm aware my resolve is right next to useless.

I tried to resist; I really did. I thought about throwing them out with a vengeance that first day I walked into the kitchen to find the cabinets covered with his blocky, all-caps handwriting.

But then I read one and started tearing up.

And then another.

And then another.

By the time I finished reading all the notes, the papers were soaked with pathetic tears and I was ninety-eight percent of the way ready to sprint up to the top penthouse and beg him to move back in with me.

But I stopped myself just in time. If I forgave him too fast, he'd just think he could get away with pulling this crap again next time we reached an impasse.

And this is a battle I can't afford to lose. I want a future with Dmitri Egorov so, so badly—but it can't be a future where I'm his doormat. I want *in*… no matter what that might mean.

So this is how it has to be. Notes hidden, if not burned. Smiles felt, if not shown. It's as much a punishment for me as it is for him.

But the notes help.

I read through them every night before bed. Sometimes, they make me cry more; sometimes, they make me laugh.

Mischa smiled at me today. It reminded me of you.

I miss sleeping next to you at night. It feels like I'm missing a part of my body.

Bee's driving me crazy up here. Can't wait to kick her out one day. Probably through the door—possibly through the window.

I heard you singing to our son in the nursery yesterday. It makes me prouder than you know to see you become his mother. I couldn't have chosen better if I'd tried.

Some of my favorite ones are the simplest, though.

I love you.

I miss you.

I dream of you at night.

Once the class is done, I say goodbye to the girls and settle Mischa into his blue baby Björn. I leave the class with a sense that maybe it's time to turn the page on this weird state of limbo I've been living with Dmitri.

WREN: *Hey Bee, class is done. You can bring the car around.*

BEE: *Be there in five. Just picking up a couple of pints of Häagen-Dazs for our movie date tonight.*

WREN: *You're a saint.*

Per protocol, I'm supposed to stand inside the building until I see Bee's car drive up, but I'm so inside my head today that I forget and wander out onto the pavement. It takes me a couple of seconds to register that the two black SUVs that usually accompany me to the class are no longer parked on the opposite side of the road.

The sidewalk is weirdly empty, too.

No pedestrians. No passing traffic.

Hell, the crows that normally hang out on the deli awning across the street aren't there, either.

Why does it feel like someone made it all go—

"Hello, my dear. It's been a while."

A shadow accompanies the voice. Both make my skin crawl.

I take a step back before I even see his face. "Vittorio," I hiss, wrapping my arms around the baby Björn protectively.

He's aged since I last saw him. New wrinkles like cracks in the earth of his skin, and cold sores peppering his lips. But that smile is as slimy as it ever was. "Your security detail won't be coming for you anytime soon, my dear," he croons. "I'm your ride today."

My body goes cold and I step back. "No—"

He moves forward and snatches my arm. He may be old and one strong breeze away from death's door, but his grip is like iron around my bicep. "Cooperating is in your best interests, darling, especially with that precious little bundle strapped to your chest." His tone is almost paternal, but the glint in his eyes is most definitely not.

Bee, where are you?

Vittorio twists me towards his flashy silver car. "Let's take a little drive, shall we?"

I try to conceal my phone as we head towards the car, but just after he pushes my head into the backseat like some second-rate criminal, he leans in and presents me with his open palm. "I'll take that, if you don't mind."

I scowl at him. "And if I do mind?"

"You can either hand over the phone or the baby. Your choice." I shudder and hand over the phone and he nods with satisfaction. "I thought so. Now, strap in, *tesoro*. I want you to be safe."

The moment he shuts my door, it locks with a thud, sending a shiver of dread down my spine. Right on cue, Mischa starts crying. I hold him as tight as I can and whisper into his ear, "It's gonna be alright, little one. I promise, I'll keep you safe."

God only knows how.

45

DMITRI

"What's this?" I ask as Rogan hands me a flat wooden box with my initials engraved on the front.

"Open it and see."

I can tell from her smile that she's pleased with herself. It makes me feel guilty for asking the woman to work at her age. She should be on some Caribbean beach somewhere, with her feet kicked up and a martini in hand, basking in the glow of an early retirement.

I decide that will be my Christmas gift to her this year. *Go and be free. You've earned it.*

I open the box to find six fat cigars, each nestled into their own little groove. "You didn't have to do this, Rogan," I murmur.

"Of course I did! You're a new father. My husband smoked a box each after both our children."

I snort. "Fyodor always knew how to celebrate properly. I miss the bastard."

"As do I," she agrees without a trace of self-pity for her loss. She pats my upper arm. "I'm expecting to see the little tyke in the flesh soon."

"You will. Very soon," I promise. "I'll set it up."

"I'll hold you to that, sir."

I give her a kiss on her cheek and she waves me off to my office. I've just stepped through when I get a whiff of a sickeningly familiar scent. Cigarette smoke and Hugo Boss cologne.

I glance to the side and find Cian standing there, with his back to me, perusing my bookshelves.

I slam the door shut and he spins slowly around. "You've got some fucking nerve," I snarl, pulling out my gun and aiming it at his head.

He raises his hands in surrender. "I come in peace."

"Like hell you do." I walk right up to him until the barrel of my gun is kissing his forehead. "Give me one good reason why I shouldn't blow your brains out right fucking here."

To his credit, he doesn't flinch. He stands his ground and gazes at me, his chest rising and falling with steady breaths. "I'm here as a friend."

"We're not friends, Cian."

"But Wren and I are," he insists. "And I don't want this escalating any more than it already has."

Gritting my teeth, I decide to wait a little longer. Hear him out. "You'd better talk fast. My finger is starting to slip."

"I've been working with Vittorio—"

"No shit, *mudak*. I already got the memo. If this is the information you're about to offer me like it's worth something, I've got news for you: it's worth absolutely fuck-all."

Cian sighs and leans forward, his skin rippling in divots around the mouth of my weapon. "The alliance with the Italians wasn't my doing, Dmitri. It was completely out of my hands."

"You're trying to blame this on Cathal?"

"Only because it's true! Vittorio approached Cathal *years* ago. Back when you were still married to… Elena." His voice dips when he says her name, like he's keenly aware of just how sensitive a trigger that is for me.

For a moment, I genuinely consider unloading my clip in his smug face.

But instead, I think about Wren. I remember that she's out in the world with our son—and suddenly, the timing of Cian's visit feels awfully coincidental.

I don't believe in coincidences.

"Why would Vittorio approach Cathal when he had already formed an alliance with me?"

"Because he wanted you to believe he was a friend so that you'd never suspect who he was really working for: *himself.* Vittorio Zanetti has only ever worked for himself, Dmitri." Cian clears his throat and I find my gun hand lowering. "The alliance he made with you only showed him how powerful you were. He didn't like playing second fiddle and he didn't like taking the smaller percentages, the scraps, the pity and disrespect. So he decided to take you down without risking the alliance he had brokered with you. He went to my brother, who was just the right combination of bloodthirsty and stupid to agree to the plan."

"A plan that involved murdering my wife, you mean."

Cian cringes; he's sweating from the temples now. His blue eyes are clouded and his voice trembles when he speaks. "It was obvious that she was your biggest weakness. Vittorio was trying to pave the way for a future match between you and Bee."

I swallow and turn around. It's not only what he's saying, which makes too much sense to be denied; it's also the way he says it. Cold and calm and unblinking.

He means it.

Every word of it.

I've been after the wrong man.

"Yes, he managed to get rid of Elena," continues Cian. "But you went after Cathal in revenge. You succeeded, and that left Vittorio's hands tied. He had to amend the plan—"

"Meaning what?" I snarl, whirling around to face the Irishman again. "He came to *you?*"

"A year ago," he confirms. "And I turned him down."

I raise my eyebrows skeptically. "You honestly expect me to believe that?"

"I can only hope you do, because it's the truth." His voice catches. "I'm… I'm not like my brother, Dmitri. I didn't inherit the bloodthirstiness that he did. My intention was to keep our businesses running and keep my men employed. Apart from that, I wanted a quiet life. A safe one."

I frown, recalling something that Wren said to me a long time ago. Something I had failed—no, something I had *refused* to listen to.

"... someone's pulling his strings, Dmitri. He's not the one calling the shots... I don't think he wants to do any of this..."

"Well, clearly, you changed your mind," I point out. "You agreed to work with Vittorio."

"Because he threatened my life, my men's lives," Cian says without shame. "And yeah, I caved because... well, call me a coward, but I actually do want to live." He squares his jaw and looks me in the eye. "But I've seen too many innocent people get caught in the crosshairs of cruel and ambitious men's games. I'm done standing on the sidelines and watching it happen."

My heart thuds in my chest. Every beat hurts worse than the last.

"If Vittorio finds out you've come to me, he'll kill you."

Cian nods. "Like I said, I'm not about to stand by and watch bad things happen to good people. And Wren is a good person."

That sends a shiver straight to my heart. "He's planning something," I guess. "Isn't he?"

I don't wait for an answer; I turn to my desk and snatch my phone, cursing a soft stream in Russian under my breath. I dial Bee and wait.

Cian is still talking—about the wedding, about Vittorio's plans for Bee, about his rage and his spite and all the things I have seen for far too long as nothing but petty, minor irritation—and the phone in my ear keeps ringing, and ringing, and ringing, and ringing, and ringing…

Then it clicks.

I look up into Cian's pale blue eyes as the other end of the call opens with a torrent of engines roaring and wind screaming and Bee crying out, "… He's got her, Dmitri, I'm so sorry, I lost them, they were speeding through traffic, I lost them, that bastard, my fucking father. I'm sorry, I'm sorry, I'm so, so sorry…"

The phone slips from my frozen hands and clatters on the desk. "You want me to trust you?" I croak to Cian. "Here's your chance."

46

WREN

Vittorio gives me a salacious smile as I try to soothe Mischa.

"Shhh, little one," I coo softly. "It's gonna be alright. You're safe. I'm here."

He chuckles. "We start lying to our children so young, don't we? And we don't even realize it."

"I will do whatever it takes to keep him safe," I spit with a vicious glare in his direction. "You're not hurting my son that easily."

"Don't you worry; I have my sights set on a much bigger Egorov than the little runt in your arms."

"Is that meant to be reassuring?"

"I can understand that you're angry, *tesoro,* but it's no use being angry at me. Dmitri's the one you should blame. It was careless of him to leave you out in the open for anyone to just… take. Plucked like a ripe strawberry right off the vine."

"I'm not some object to be taken as and when you please."

He chuckles again, a harsh, grating sound like hot oil poured over broken glass. "And yet here you are."

I bite my tongue. Hard as it is, I swallow my insults and focus again on trying to get Mischa to settle down. But no matter how much I murmur and rock and hum, his cries only get louder.

Eventually, I give into the one thing I know will calm him, as much as I don't want to partially undress in front of Bee's sick fuck of a father. I do my best to twist away as I ease Mischa into nursing position at my breast.

The whole time, I can feel Vittorio's eyes locked on us. He doesn't even pretend to look away.

"Do you mind?" I snap.

"Don't be shy. Your son needs to be fed. Do as nature intended."

Fucking pervert. I ignore him as Mischa latches. Instantly, he quiets down and I stroke his cheek gently, hoping to God that Bee saw what happened and that she has eyes on us.

"I can see why he chose you," Vittorio remarks as his lips curl up into more of that same unsettling smile. "A nice, normal woman without any unnatural proclivities."

"If you're talking about your daughter—"

"Shut your fucking mouth!" My lips seal immediately and he nods in violent approval. "See? A true woman knows when to be silent. A real woman knows how to obey."

I'm speechless with disgust, but Vittorio is off in his own world now. He strokes his chin as he continues musing. "She could have been useful. But she decided to be *different*. An aberration against nature and good taste. Naturally, I had to do something about it. I wasn't going to be made a laughingstock. I wasn't about to have her abnormalities splashed around for the underworld to mock. And clearly, your husband wasn't interested in reining her in. He had *you* to play with. What did he care if Beatrice chose to spend her nights sinning like a repulsive beast?"

Goosebumps race over my body. "You're disgusting."

He slaps the steering wheel and his face skews into a hideous grimace. "*She* was the disgusting one! Which is why, once I figured out the little ruse the two of them were planning on foisting on me, I had to act. She had to die."

My jaw drops. "*You*? I thought it was—"

"The Irish?" he interrupts with a *tsk*. "Ha! You really think that fucking lightweight, Cian, would have killed Beatrice so openly? No. He's nothing like his brother. At least Cathal had some spirit, some ambition, some *balls*. Cian is nothing more than a castrated pup trying not to get stepped on."

"How could you do that?" I whisper. "She may not have been who you wanted her to be, but she was your own daughter. Your flesh and blood."

He shrugs, utterly nonchalant. "I tell this to any young man who has potential: don't waste time forming emotional connections to anyone. Not even your own children. It blinds you. Limits you. It prevents you from doing what's necessary in order to preserve your legacy."

"Your children *are* your legacy."

"Not when they're a fucking disappointment."

I cringe back at the venom in his tone. How could a parent hate a life they helped make? I glance down at the babe in my arms and I'm baffled at the thought of ever doing anything but loving him with every fiber of my heart.

"She was a lot more than that," I say quietly. "She was a wonderful, kind, caring person. She was talented and funny and—"

"Ultimately useless," he spits. He turns his gaze towards the window and clears his throat. "I don't deny, she had positive traits. Traits that made me believe there was hope for her. Whenever I took the whip to her back, she took her lashes better than some of my own men."

I shake my head. "I saw what you did to her… I saw her back. I saw—" I stop short, my eyes going wide as something strikes me. A snippet of a conversation I had with Dmitri months ago.

I found Elena's body four days later… There were small cigarette burns all over her body. Whip lashes across her back that had cut her skin open…

"What is it, little lamb? Have I frightened you?"

"Elena," I whisper, gently plucking Mischa from my breast and holding him up to my chest. "They found her with…"

Vittorio's face breaks into a slow, sinister smile. "Took you a while to put that together."

I feel the very real urge to throw up all over his shoes. The only reason I don't is because I'm holding my son who still seems unsettled. And who can blame him? We might just be sitting in front of Satan himself.

"She was an innocent woman."

He snorts. "She was another useless obstacle—and besides, you should be thanking me."

"*Thanking* you?" I gawk at him.

"I'm the one who paved the way for you to swoop in with those pretty green eyes and steal away his heart." He laughs, as if there's one single thing about any of this shit that's even remotely funny.

"You weren't paving the way for *me*," I snap. "You were paving the way for *yourself*. You wanted to marry Bee off to Dmitri so that you could steal some of his limelight one way or another."

He doesn't bother replying to that. The car comes to a stop and he swings the door open. "Welcome to your new home."

I'm quaking with nerves as I step out of the car, making sure I keep a tight grip on Mischa. No matter what happens, I'm not letting anyone get near my son.

The house is surrounded by trees and grass. It has the illusion of being hidden away but I can hear the congestion of traffic from just beyond the trees, which means the highway is not so far from where we are.

Men mill around the property aimlessly, like they don't know what to do with their hands. I ignore all of them and keep my eyes on Vittorio.

"What do you plan on doing with us?"

"I plan on holding you as ransom." Vittorio gives me a triumphant wink. "If Dmitri wants his precious wife and son back, he's going to have to give me everything. Every inch of Egorov Bratva property, signed, sealed, and delivered. And then he'll have to bend those arrogant knees of his in front of me. I want to watch him beg for your lives. He'll kiss my feet and *plead*."

"He'll never do that!"

Vittorio shrugs. "It seems that I know your husband better than you do."

My heart sinks at those words. Hadn't Dmitri promised me just the other day that he'd do whatever I asked of him, including giving up his Bratva altogether? It wasn't a bluff; I could see it in his eyes how serious he was.

Which means Vittorio is right: if it comes down to Mischa's life or mine… Dmitri will do whatever he's asked.

His lips twist up into an awful grimace. "Having some doubts, little lamb?" He laughs openly at my distress before his face hardens and sours. "Take her up to her room."

As two men approach to carry out his orders, I back away with my teeth bared. "Don't fucking touch me."

"Don't be foolish, girl," Vittorio advises. "If you don't cooperate, I have no problem using the lash on you."

"Go ahead!" I cry out. "If Bee could take it, then I can, too!"

He sighs, a whistling sound like midnight breeze through a graveyard. "I know you think that sounds brave," he says, sauntering down off the first step. "But trust me: that whip burns like the fires of hell."

"Fuck you."

His saggy cheeks ripple with anger. "You're right. I do believe you can take the whip. But I wonder… do you think your little boy feels the same?"

He's close enough to try reaching out to touch Mischa's cheek. I beat him to the punch—literally, more or less—and crack Vittorio across the face as hard as I can.

The sound of skin meeting skin echoes out. His men all freeze.

So do I.

So does he.

I might've just made a very big mistake.

Eventually, Vittorio moves. His fingers rise up to graze where I just struck him. He inspects his fingertips like he expects to find blood there, though unfortunately, I didn't hit him hard enough for that.

His face roils and burns like some monstrous thing hidden beneath burlap. I don't know what's going to burst out: rage or curses or cold, furious death.

He sighs with disappointment. "So much for the quiet obedient archetype of a perfect woman. It seems you need to be taught a lesson, same as my useless daughter."

He raises his own hand to return the favor I just gave him. To be honest, I'm actually relieved—I can handle a slap or two. If he thinks that is what will break me, he is dead fucking wrong.

I just make sure to tighten my hold on Mischa so he's not hurt.

And then—

"You so much as touch my wife and I'll make you eat every finger on that hand before I cut your throat from ear to ear."

Vittorio's hand freezes in place as we all whirl towards the doorway where my husband stands. Tall and proud and undeniable, his expression black with fury.

I want to be relieved. I want to fall into his arms and cry tears of joy.

But I can't. Not yet.

Because every single man in this room is loyal to the Zanetti don.

Every single man in this room has a weapon in their hands.

Every single man in this room is ready to unleash death in every direction as soon as Vittorio gives the order.

And I'm standing in the center of it all with my infant son.

47

DMITRI

"I wouldn't be so quick to threaten the man who has your wife and child in hand."

"I'm not particularly frightened of your hands, Vittorio," I answer coolly. "And you're running out of additional help."

That gets his attention. His eyes flare wide as he glances around to realize that, while he was gawking at me in the front entryway, my men were infiltrating the house from every other side. The army he thought stood at his back is now gagged and bound on the floor, my troops standing tall over them.

"What—"

"Like I said, it's over, Vittorio. You've used up your last life. But if you let Wren walk over to me, I promise to take it quickly."

He glowers. "That's not as attractive an offer as you think it is, Egorov."

"Considering what I have planned for your death, I'd grab it now while it's on the table. Better to live as a coward than die a brave man."

"That's where you and I differ," he snarls, skin pale and eyes wild.

"We differ in many ways," I remark as I saunter toward him with my gun held loosely. "For example, I would move mountains to protect my child—whereas you would throw yours to the wolves in an instant if it meant saving your own skin."

Vittorio nods triumphantly. "And if I'm willing to do that with my own flesh and blood… think what I'm capable of doing with *yours.*"

He raises his hand and strokes back a lock of Wren's hair. She shudders silently but doesn't move. I want to reassure her, but I can't—not yet. Not until I've made the world safe for her and our son.

Stay strong, baby. I'm almost done.

"How did you find me?" Vittorio asks, as though he can't stop himself from asking.

"I had a little help."

Vittorio's eyes widen. "That Irish fucking scumbag! He'll pay for—"

"Seriously, Papa, this is getting pathetic now." Vittorio freezes as Bee's voice fills the room just before she joins me. She brandishes her own pistol and gives her father a greeting nod. "If I were you, I'd surrender and preserve what little dignity you have left."

"Y-y… *you*," he hisses.

Bee nods. "Me. The prodigal daughter returneth. Or whatever. I was never much of one for Bible stories."

He bares his teeth, gawking at her in disbelief. "I can't... How...?"

I throw her an annoyed glance. "You were supposed to stay in the car."

She gives me a look in return. "You really thought I was gonna pass up the chance to watch my father die?" Her gaze veers pointedly to him. "Fat fucking chance."

There's sweat beginning to form on Vittorio's brow. "Beatrice... Bee, *tesoro*... Would you really hurt your own father?"

She tosses her head back and guffaws as though he's just told the world's funniest joke. "Come on, Papa! It's only fair that I return the favor. Especially considering *you* were the one who arranged the hit on me."

"I... I took no pleasure in—"

"Oh, *bullshit!*" Bee barks. "Every time you took that whip to my back, you fucking *reveled* in it. You really expect me to believe that my death was any different?"

"Bee—"

"It's over, Papa," she says firmly. "You're surrounded. Your men are dead and gone. The only thing you can do now is give up with a little bit of—"

Before she can finish her sentence, Vittorio lunges at Wren.

All I can think is, *Bad move.*

The moment his arm moves up, Aleks calmly steps in from behind and breaks his elbow in one fell swoop.

Vittorio collapses to a moaning puddle on the ground. Aleks kicks his weapon out of the way and coaxes Wren back out of Vittorio's reach.

I advance on the Italian don's huddled form. He's stammering, muttering half-broken nonsense. "Y-you can't do this... you can't—"

"It's already done," I tell him coolly. "It's time to take your lashes like a man."

My men part and the sound of footsteps announce Cian's appearance. He's holding the whip in his hand. When Vittorio sees it, his cheeks turn deathly pale.

"What do you say, Papa?" Bee asks, stepping forward. "Let's see if you can get as good as you give."

Cian hands the whip over to her as Aleks leads Wren out of the house on my orders. She doesn't need to see this. The others clear out slowly in their wake, leaving behind Vittorio, who stares up at the loose circle that surrounds him.

"You would r-really do this to an old m-man?" he stutters, abandoning even the appearance of bravery now that there's no one around to watch.

"You're no man," Bee spits. She crouches down so that she's at eye level with him. "I want you to know something, dear father. I want you to know that if you'd been a *half*-decent person, a parent who simply accepted me for who I am, things could have been so different. Not only am I capable of running your empire, I'm capable of making it thrive. Look what I did to you in a few months from beyond the grave."

Vittorio's eyes bulge as he realizes the obvious connection. "*Locksmith*," he hisses. "You were... are..."

Bee smiles and curtsies. "Yeah, that's right. The one and only." Then the smile vanishes and she spits in his face. "You never had the power to control me. And now, you never will."

She gets back up to her feet and offers me the whip. I look at it with confusion. "I thought you wanted to do the honors?"

"I still do. But I'm giving you the first lash. For Elena."

For Elena.

I take the whip gratefully and give Cian a nod. He twists Vittorio around and drags him over to the staircase, where he and Bee tie him up and slice his shirt open so his back is bared. Once he's secured, they step out of the way.

The handle of the whip is thick in my hand. Solid. Cool to the touch. I give it an experimental crack through the air and Vittorio screams like a pig in a slaughterhouse before it's ever even touched him.

Then I raise it and flay open the man who killed my wife.

He screams again. It's nauseating, but I don't flinch. I give him three lashes. The blood on his skin sets my own blood alight with a strange kind of fire. It feels like the scales are being made even.

Balance. Repayment. Revenge.

A chapter closing, one lash at a time.

But when I'm done and my arm is heavy from the effort, I wouldn't say I feel *better*. Hurting him doesn't bring Elena back. It doesn't undo years of heartache and rage.

In the end, the chapter may be closed—but Vittorio isn't a monster or a villain or even an enemy. He's just an old man tied to the banister in an empty house, screaming as his life hurtles towards its end.

So it's easy to pass the whip along to Bee. "He's all yours," I tell her. "Make it count."

She nods, flexing her arms purposefully before she accepts it. "I'm not coming out until the job's done," she informs me in a hard voice.

"Understood."

I gesture to Cian to follow me and the two of us exit the building together to the echo of another desperate scream. Closing the door cuts the sound in half, but not nearly enough to completely drown out the sounds of Vittorio's wails or the crack of Bee's whip. That's probably why Wren is in the furthest jeep with the windows up.

"Dmitri."

I turn to Cian, who's looking broken and lost. "I came to you to make amends—" He barrels through before I can interrupt. "—and I know that bringing you here isn't enough. So—"

"You're going to make me an offer I can't refuse."

Cian sighs, his eyes darting past me for a moment. "I'm offering you... myself." I raise my eyebrows and he swallows. "I'm offering myself as a sacrifice for Elena's and Rose's deaths. Just as long as you leave my men and their families alone. Let my death be the end of this feud. End it. End me."

The night is hushed around us. Birds titter in the trees and distant highway traffic drones like an ocean we can't see.

Amazingly, I believe him. Even more amazing? The man has actually succeeded in impressing me. Perhaps Wren was right about him all along. I glance over my shoulder to the car she's sitting in. I already know what she would say in my place.

"My men won't take revenge for my death," he adds. "They won't move against you at all." He turns his gun around butt-first and offers it to me. "Go ahead." I accept the gun as Cian closes his eyes. "I know you'll think less of me for this, but I'm not interested in looking death in the eye."

His chin is thrust proudly in the air, his face smoothed of all concern. I switch the gun from hand to hand. Like the whip, it's heavy and cool in my palm.

I could do it; it'd be easy. Clean. Simple. Death for death.

But I'm finding that I'm not so interested in killing anymore.

So I open the clip and let the bullets clatter to the ground. Cian cracks open an eye at the noise and gawks down at our feet as the bullets scatter in every direction and find resting places amongst the dirt and gravel.

"Open your eyes," I tell him. "Today's not the day you die."

His jaw drops. "You're not going to kill me?"

"My wife thinks you might not be the villain I've always assumed you were. And... she may just be right. So you get another chance," I concede. "But one chance is all you get. Understood?"

Cian's face splits into a smile. "Understood."

"Now, get out of my sight before I change my mind."

Without bothering to see if or where he goes, I twist around and run straight to the jeep where my wife and son are cloistered. The moment the door springs open, Wren is on me, engulfing me in her warmth and her flurried touches.

"Wren!" I snarl. "I'm so fucking sorry. I was—"

She silences me with her lips and, as much as I want to say more, I find myself completely losing my train of thought. When we finally break away, new adrenaline is surging through my body.

"What happened to needing space?" I can't help but tease.

"Fuck space," she snaps in a tone that's far more Bee than Wren. Still, it suits her. "I almost lost you today. And it made me realize that I'd rather fight with you every single day for the rest of our lives than live a life without you in it."

My God, that feels good to hear. "So I can come home now?"

Tears shine brightly in her eyes. "Please."

I wrap my arms around her tight—and apparently, I squash my son in the process, because he cries out loudly. I take him from Wren and kiss his forehead. "You hear that, little man? Mama's ready for us to be a family again."

"We were *always* a family, Dmitri," Wren corrects with a contented sigh—just before her eyes turn bright and dangerous. "But I swear to God, if you ever keep secrets from me again—"

"I know, I know: you'll kick my ass."

"Ha! Your ass will be the least of your worries," she warns, seizing my balls in a tight grasp. Then, giggling, she releases them and kisses me hard again while our son coos between us. "Now, for the love of all that is holy: let's go home."

More beautiful words have never been spoken.

EPILOGUE I: DMITRI
SIX MONTHS LATER

This time around, there are no wedding planners.

No over-the-top fanfare.

And sure as hell no unwanted guests.

What we do have is a simple outdoor ceremony that Bee and Wren planned together. She wanted a sunset ceremony by the ocean, which is how we ended up in Tulum at one of the best hotels in Mexico's Riviera Maya. I bought out the entire hotel because, well, because I *can*.

Okay, so maybe *simple* is a little bit of an exaggeration.

Whatever I can do to spoil my beautiful wife, I will.

She gave me a lecture about extravagance after the fourth set of jewelry I had sent to her room. Told me that she didn't need all the excess. But fuck it—she's the queen of my world now.

And in my world, queens wear jewels.

As the first notes of the wedding march sound out, Bee strides up the aisle, right behind Madison Montgomery, who was called in to check on the bride half an hour ago for some last-minute bridal touch-ups.

We call her a friend as well as a client these days; she'd been so thrilled with the work that Wren did on her Chicago boutique store that she hired Egorov Industries to design two more flagship sites in London and Versailles. Of course, that meant more travel for Wren, but that was another reason for the private jet purchase. Much to her horror, I named it *The Wren*.

"The ceremony was supposed to start fifteen minutes ago," I remind Bee as she slips into place just behind me. "She's late."

She barely deigns to look at me as she adjusts the collar of her black Prada suit. "A queen is never late," Bee prattles in a fake English accent, quoting some movie or other I've never seen and never will. "Everyone else is simply early."

The rolling of my eyes is damn near audible.

Bee giggles and gives me a nudge. "Cool your jets, Romeo—she's coming. And even if she doesn't, what does it matter? You're already married."

"I—" The ready retort on my tongue dies the moment I catch sight of Wren exiting the hotel in the near distance. A shimmer of white, like a mirage in the desert. *"Ya na nebesakh,"* I murmur under my breath.

Am I in heaven?

Madison and Wren have educated me repeatedly on women's fashion in the last few months, so I know that her dress is a bespoke cream chiffon dress with subtle fuchsia accents traveling up the voluminous skirt. I know that the

Epilogue I: Dmitri

strapless corset is inlaid with hundreds of tiny pink seed pearls and I know that each one glitters wildly as she walks down the aisle under the setting sun.

I know that her heels are three inches tall because, when I told her she should wear comfortable flats instead, she gave me a double middle finger and then blue balls for daring to boss her around (though the blue balls didn't last long, because she's as thirsty for me as I am for her.)

Given the heels, I'm impressed that she can even balance Mischa, but she manages admirably, keeping our son hanging off her hip without breaking stride.

The little man looks grumpy. His huge green eyes rove from side to side, utterly unimpressed with everything and everyone he sees.

Luckily, Wren doesn't have to carry him for long, because Aleks walks up and takes the baby and her arm in one motion.

I'll admit, I actually get a little choked up watching him walk her down the aisle. I had no idea he was going to do it.

"Did you know about that?" I mutter to Bee.

"Yup. Fitting, don't you think?" She smiles. "And look at that baby! Isn't he just a little heartthrob in his tux?"

As Aleks and Wren approach the altar, Syrah comes forward to take her turn with Mischa. My brother kisses Wren's cheek and retreats to his place in line while the music crescendos and Wren takes the first of the steps up to where she belongs—right in front of me.

She fought the idea of this wedding initially. *"We're already married. Who needs another ceremony?"*

But I wore her down. I thought I'd never feel complete if I didn't get to see her like this one more time.

Pure. Perfect. Beautiful.

And the look in her eyes says it was the right choice. She dispensed with the veil and her face is clear. I've never loved anything more.

Aleks clears his throat as he takes the mic. He's pulling triple duty today: best man, bridal escort, and now, officiant. I'm sure he'll bitch about the workload for months to come.

"We are gathered here today to celebrate Wren and Dmitri. I was there at the beginning of their strange, non-traditional courtship and, lemme tell ya, it was a doozy." Wren bursts out laughing and his grin spreads as he continues. "They went through a lot those first few months. More than most people go through in a lifetime—and yet somehow, they found each other at the end of it. They found love and friendship; they found mutual respect and trust. I can't think of any two people more suited for one another. And to all the powers that brought them together—" Aleks makes a show of looking up at the sky with a wrinkled frown. "—nice job. But also... *twisted.*"

I shake my head at my brother, who gives me a little wink in return. He launches into a more traditional speech about life and love and I find myself tuning him out. Who could pay attention to anything like that when you're staring at a goddess?

Wren blushes prettily in front of me, then mouths shyly, *You look very handsome.*

I wink back at her and she flushes an even deeper shade of scarlet. Aleks wraps up his part and passes Wren the mic for her vows.

"Dmitri," Wren starts, holding both my hands tightly, "I had about five months to think about what I wanted to say to you today—unlike the first time, when I had, like, five hours. And when you have that much time to think about vows, you find yourself going back to the beginning. You find yourself thinking through every moment you've shared together." She takes a deep breath. "We have been through so, so much. We've overcome so, so much. There were times I didn't think we'd make it and days when I thought we were all wrong for one another. But time and time again, you proved me wrong. You fought for me. You cared for me. You protected me. And I've never had that in my life before I met you. So my vow to you today is this: I know marriage is hard and life is harder. So no matter what comes our way, I promise to keep forgiving you; I promise to keep loving you. For the rest of our lives."

Aleks chuckles as he hands me the microphone. "Good luck beating *that*, bro."

I lace my fingers through Wren's. "*Moya devushka*, you are my queen, my goddess, the music in my life. I wasn't aware my world was so dark until you stepped into it and brought the sun with you. I didn't know what I was missing until you gave me a son, a family. And for that, I will always be grateful. You are my equal in every way. I will always protect you and I will always love you. From this day until my dying day."

She sucks in a breath as I finish and a few stray tears slip from her kohl-rimmed eyes. We don't bother waiting for Aleks to give us the green light—I just yank her into my arms and kiss her like it's the first time all over again.

We come together, sealing our promises in the heat of that kiss. And when we break away, it's to the cacophony of the hollering crowd who've flown all this way to bear witness to our second wedding. Some faces, I'd always expected to be here: Rogan and her family, my vors. Others are more surprising, like the Italians who swore loyalty to Bee after Vittorio was dethroned. And Cian, of course.

It's an interesting group, a curious amalgam of what we've managed to create in the last six months. It's proof that peace is possible under the right circumstances, with the right people at the helm. It's a perfect metaphor for this life we've built.

Tangled and twisted and gnarled and fucked up beyond all recognition more often than not.

But beautiful.

So beautiful it hurts.

EPILOGUE II: WREN
TWO YEARS LATER

"... so I'd like you all to raise your glasses to our new Director of Design at Egorov Industries: Mrs. Wren Egorov!"

I hide my face behind my glass of apple juice as my colleagues start cheering loudly to Syrah's toast in honor of my promotion. I've been actively resisting any kind of celebration since the news broke. My first instinct was, of course, *I don't deserve it.*

My second thought was, *They can't promote me; I'm the boss's wife.*

But when I look past the unavoidable facts of my position in this company, I have to admit: I *do* deserve to be here.

I mean, yes, the CEO of Egorov Industries also happens to be my husband. And yes, maybe that teensy little detail factored into him giving me that initial design job in the first place.

But *I* worked hard to achieve the rest. *I* worked from the bottom rung up in the design team and it helped that my immediate superior, the one solely responsible for giving me the promotion, is *not* my husband.

Speaking of, I maneuver through the crowd until I reach Nancy Meyers. She lifts her glass as she turns to me, beaming ear to ear. "Congratulations, Wren. You deserve this."

I can spy Jackson Mitchell in the far corner of the room, bitching about something (me, no doubt) to a few other temps and assistants from the design department. "Apparently, not everyone thinks so," I mutter.

"You can't please them all," Nancy says with a dismissive shrug. "And you shouldn't bother trying. You got this promotion because you put in the time and the effort. The Davidson project and the Langdon Estate were all you. That kind of work ethic deserves recognition."

It's hard to keep myself from smiling big enough to match Nancy. "Thank you. I promise, I won't disappoint you."

She winks. "I know you won't." Then she leans in and lowers her voice. "There's always gonna be people—jealous, nasty people—who like to spin the story that you got this job because of who you're married to. Don't let them stop you from taking charge and being the boss, Wren. This is *your* job now. This is *your* team."

For the first time since Nancy told me what she had in mind, it hits me: *I'm* the boss. I call the shots. I'll have a team of two dozen working directly under me. For the first time in my life, I'll be the one with the P.A.

"Stranger than fiction" doesn't even begin to cover it.

She gives me a bracing pat on my shoulder and melts into the crowd to mingle. I hear a chorus of giggles and then the

Epilogue II: Wren

ranks part as a three-foot hooligan races right at my legs. He's wearing a pointy party hat and clutching a balloon that's bigger than he is.

"Whoa there, little man!" I exclaim, kneeling down to grab my son. He giggles and tries to wiggle out of my clutches. "Mischa Egorov! How much cake have you had?"

"By last count, it was three pieces," Bee offers, appearing in front of us in her red Louis Vuittons. "I tried to say no to the third piece, but honestly, he was too far gone already."

I roll my eyes and get to my feet while Mischa makes growling sounds, icing smeared across his cheeks like war paint. "I'm a bear, Mama! A big, scary bear!"

I kiss the top of his dark brown mop of hair. He smells like cake, too. Bathtime is going to be a knock-'em-down, drag-'em-out affair tonight, I can already tell. "Okay, you big, scary bear—off you go!"

I release him and he proceeds to jump back into the crowd, growling louder and louder as he goes. "This sugar high is *your* doing, so *you're* putting him to bed," I inform her icily before my face breaks into an irrepressible grin.

"Let the child live." Bee giggles fondly. "He's having a blast."

Yvonne appears at Bee's side and wraps an arm around her waist. According to Dmitri, this is the longest relationship Bee's been in since… well, ever. Next week will be their first anniversary and I can tell that Bee's both excited and freaked out by that milestone. Which is why I think Yvonne, a perpetually calm serial monogamist who's been in two other super serious relationships before Bee, is perfect for her. They balance each other out.

"You know we'd be happy to babysit if you need the night off," Yvonne offers generously.

"Jesus Christ, Yv, are you out of your mind?!" Bee screeches. "He's all hopped up on sugar! We'll take him tomorrow when he's docile."

"You slacker," I tease.

Bee laughs and looks around. "Speaking of slackers, where's your husband?"

"Um…" I bite down on my bottom lip guiltily.

"Uh-oh. What did you do?"

"I *might* have asked him not to come tonight—" Bee's face goes taut with shock, so I continue quickly. "—but he was totally fine with it! And I promised to make it up to him."

Yvonne pats Bee's arm gently. It's her way of calming down Bee whenever she gets worked up about something and it works like absolute magic every time. "Everyone already knows he's your husband, Wren. I'm sure it wouldn't matter if he were here."

"I know." I sigh and my shoulders slump forward. "I regret it now. I guess I just didn't want to remind people of the whole *thing* we've got going on here."

Bee rolls her eyes. "Fuck the doubters. You got this job because you're fucking awesome. Not 'cause you're fucking the boss!"

"Will you keep your voice down? And watch your language?" I yelp. "These are my colleagues."

Bee looks immensely unimpressed. "Nuh-uh. They're your *subordinates* now. You're the boss, remember?" She winks at

Epilogue II: Wren

me. "Own the title, baby. You deserve it. Besides... you don't even have to feel bad."

I frown. "What makes you say that?"

"Because Dmitri didn't listen." She gestures over my shoulder to the entryway with her glass of wine.

I twist around and catch sight of my husband, looking gorgeous as ever in the charcoal Hugo Boss suit I love and that broody frown that completely disappears the moment he lays eyes on me.

As soon as I see him, I forget that we're surrounded by my colleagues. I forget that I asked him not to be here. I only care that he *is* here, ready to support me as always.

I fly towards him, but Mischa beats me to the punch.

"Papa!" he cries. "I'm a bear!"

Laughing, Dmitri snatches Mischa by the underarms and tosses him into the air. "And what a fearsome bear you make! I like your hat, too."

"Rogan gave it to me," he explains, patting his hat proudly. He smiles widely when he sees me. "Guess what else, Papa? There's a cake with Mama's name on it!"

"There was," I acknowledge as I join them. "Except *someone's* already eaten so many pieces that Mama's name is pretty much gone now."

Mischa smiles sheepishly and ducks his face into Dmitri's shoulder. The moment Dmitri sets him down, he's gone, back to pretending to be a bear again.

Dmitri laughs as he wipes off the frosting smear that our son left behind. Then he turns to me and frowns again for a brief moment. "Before you say anything, I'll only stay for a minute."

I grab his hand and pull him into me. "Don't you dare. Stay with me."

"I thought—"

"I was being stupid and childish," I admit. "And insecure. You're my husband and I want you here. So will you forgive me and stay? Please?"

"Say no more, *moya zhena*. I'm with you 'til the end of time."

I make it up to him by giving him a full-on kiss, right on the lips, in view of every Egorov employee present. I'm usually pretty strict about stuff like that, but tonight, I decide to make an exception.

Mostly because I've got more than one thing to be happy about.

Which reminds me...

"Do you have a moment to spare or do you wanna get to the cake before your son finishes it all?"

"The only thing I want to eat tonight is you."

My cheeks flush instantly. "*Dmitri*!

"Don't blame me. You're the one who's a stickler for honesty."

Shaking my head at him, I grab his hand and lead him through the crowded room to one of the balconies that surround it. The moment we're outside, the Chicago wind hits us from all directions.

"It's cold as hell out here," Dmitri curses. "Let's go back in."

"No!" I stop him. "I want someplace quiet. Away from the crowd."

That seems to get his attention. "Okay? What's going on? If it's that little shit, Mitchell, giving you problems about—"

"It's not about Mitchell, or about this promotion—which, by the way, I'm over the moon about." I move into the circle of his arms and immediately feel warmer. "And I couldn't have done without you."

His voice is a soft rumble in his chest. "Nonsense. You did it all on your own. I was just smart enough to recognize your talent and get out of your way." He kisses the top of my head. "Anyway, I should be thanking you. You've doubled my profits for the Design division."

I can't help smiling proudly. But I didn't bring him out here to talk business. "How about we call it even? Because I've got a promotion for you, too."

I feel his confused frown. "You didn't get promoted *that* high just yet, Mrs. Egorov..."

Laughing, I put both of my frozen hands on either side of his face and look up at him. "I think I did, actually. Because I'm promoting you from father of one... to father of two."

It takes a moment for the news to process. When it does, his jaw falls open and this incredulous look of wonder takes over.

My *God*, how I love that look. It makes me want to bear Dmitri's babies again and again and again just so I can see it a million times.

"I—You—We—*Fucking hell*, how long have you known?" He doesn't wait for me to answer before he pulls me into his arms and lifts me off my feet to spin us both around in a circle. It's still cold out and Mitchell still resents me and my sister is gone and a million and one other problems await us in the future.

But for right now, right here, life is perfect.

Not a damn thing out of place.

EXTENDED EPILOGUE: WREN
SIXTEEN YEARS LATER

Click here to check out the exclusive Extended Epilogue to **TANGLED DECADENCE!**
https://dl.bookfunnel.com/b8zdcaa6qq

Made in the USA
Las Vegas, NV
25 July 2024